KARMA & MAYHEM

I0548998

❦ Excerpt ❦

Janay rose out of the fog of slumber so deep, so peaceful that she hated to surface, but the jostling and undulating of the mattress beneath her sent pain radiating from her rebuilt hip.

Was she on a troop carrier?

Opening her eyes, she beheld a black velvet canopy draped over the ebony wood posters of a medieval-sized bed.

Where was she?

Panting grunts were followed by hot breath on her lower belly.

The terror of rape lightninged through her, and she faintly whispered, "Poke!"

The dirk didn't come into her hand, but the jostling stopped.

"Trond!" a male voice uttered.

She lowered her gaze to find Poke's hilt protruding from a mass of long dark brown hair that veiled a man's face. Poke's blade tip held steady against the man's Adam's apple.

The man was on all fours, fully dressed in a midnight-blue turtleneck and matching knit pants, the uniform of a Guardian of the Law.

"It's okay," the irate man said. "I'm dressing you. Putting clothes on you, not off. Tell your screwy dagger to back off."

❦ Praise for Catherine E. McLean's

KARMA & MAYHEM

It's all the fun stuff between the Prologue and The End that keeps you turning the pages to the unexpected twist. I'm not much into the Romance genre, but I do enjoy a good SF/F book, and if there happens to be romance in it, that's alright, too. Archangels (yes, plural), samurai, veeds, warriors, sex, and mayhem. Lots of mayhem. For what more can a reader who loves a good escape ask? — Lenora G.

Well titled—the mayhem doesn't stop and the ending has a very nice twist. There are a lot of elements here that could easily extend into other stories and the world-building is exceptional. I hope to see more from this author soon. —Bex

Karma and Mayhem is delicious. Ms. McLean provides us with an extremely creative and intelligently written story about love, adventure, and self-determination in a dark world of witches and angels. I love the evolution of the book's heroes and their interaction with each other. I absolutely love the mystical veeds. If you want to be transported to an exciting realm full of exquisite mayhem, carefully and expertly written, this is a novel for you. — Kelly W.

I thought that this book was a wonderful work of fiction. The off-world setting and mysteries kept the story interesting. And the subplot of an Ancient Japanese Samurai warrior and weapons gave the book a totally new prospective from what I usually read. Ms. McLean has a smooth hand in weaving plots together and characters to make for an enjoyable book. I really enjoyed this book, and I am sure you would too if you read romance or paranormal books.— Night Owl Reviews

KARMA & MAYHEM

Book One of the Bonded Souls Series

By

Catherine E. McLean

http://www.CatherineEmclean.com

~ 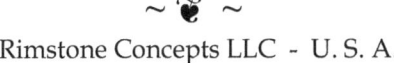 ~

Rimstone Concepts LLC - U. S. A.

Karma & Mayhem

First copyright 2012 by Catherine E. McLean
Originally published by Soul Mate Publishing
Re-issued © 2017 by Catherine E. McLean

All rights reserved, including the right to reproduce this book or portions thereof in any form whatsoever electronic or mechanical, including photocopying, recording, or by any information storage and retrieval system, without permission in writing from the copyright holder and the publisher. The only exception is a brief quotation in printed reviews. For information, address: Rimstone Concepts at www.rimstoneconceptsllc.com

Cover by Mark Saloff Designs

This book is a work of fiction. Names, characters, places, and incidents depicted in this book either are products of the author's imagination or are used fictitiously. Any resemblance to actual events or locales or persons, living or dead, is entirely coincidental and beyond the intent of the author or the publisher.

The scanning, uploading, and distribution of this book via the Internet or via any other means without the permission of the publisher is illegal and punishable by law.

Please purchase only an authorized edition and do not participate in or encourage piracy of any copyright materials. Your support of the author's right is appreciated.

● Thank you for reading *Karma & Mayhem.* If you enjoy it, please consider telling your friends or posting a short review. Word of mouth is an author's best friend and very much appreciated.

Catherine E. McLean website—
http://www.CatherineEmclean.com
Catherine@CatherineEmclean.com

ISBN 978-0-9885874-6-5
V 2.0

❦ Acknowledgments ❦

Thank you for believing in me and
for appreciating a good story—

R. M. M.
J. D. M
W. B. M.
T. M.
K. W.

Also, my sincere appreciation to those who
took the time to give this book reviews.

A portion of the sales for Karma & Mayhem will be donated to the Paralyzed Veterans of America whose programs help bring Paralyzed Veterans back to a useful and enjoyable life. Paralyzed Veterans of America promotes medical research to find cures for spinal cord dysfunction and related problems.

❦ PROLOGUE

On the celestial horizon of the star-spangled heavens, at the deserted entrance to the cloister of the Angels' Hall, the soul-spirit of Kiyoshi the Samurai stood and wondered once again why he had been summoned. He rang the tiny prayer bell, which tinkled as softly as glass chimes.

A moment later, the raven-haired Archangel Adrada appeared. His massive golden wings, heavily edged with mournful purple feathers, silently folded back.

In somber reverence, Kiyoshi held his eyes downcast. He bowed.

"Honored samurai." Adrada's deep voice intoned a cordial greeting. "The Infinite One, the All Merciful Lord God of Creation, has a task for you. If you succeed, peace and enlightenment will heal your spirit and you shall achieve nirvana."

Elation opened like a lotus blossom in Kiyoshi. Then he reined in his joy. He must not allow such feeling to override good judgment. Very likely redemption came at a high cost. "What must I do, Great Shogun, to attain ascension?"

"Return to the realm of the living and become an executioner of demons."

Men seeking power were often demons, but killing real demons, the ones who served Satanus? Was that possible? Kiyoshi stroked his short black beard, then slid his fingers down his Fu Manchu mustache to the tip that ended mid-chest. If redemption were at hand, forgiveness was attainable—*and a samurai was a samurai*. Kiyoshi nodded once. "Give me my daisho. Set me before the fiends."

"I cannot give you the two swords."

"I do not understand."

"You must first be reborn, reside in a new body."

"The body can be trained, the mind enlightened. I will hone

the body into a warrior and the vilest demons will quake before his swords."

Adrada slowly shook his head. "The body you shall dwell in will have a mind of its own, one with a heritage of darkon magic and power. You are forbidden to reveal yourself to anyone, including your host, until the wakinzashi weeps."

Until the short sword wept? Ahh, perhaps the Great Shogun meant *chiburui*, the shaking of blood off the blade. Did demons bleed? "What of the katana?"

"It, too, has a mind of its own."

Another riddle? Kiyoshi slowly wrapped the end of his mustache about his index finger. He was samurai. Honor bound by the Bushido, the code of the samurai. Only the code's precepts were like Zen *koans*, insoluble riddles subject to argumentation and, far too often, selective interpretation. Yet, discovering their answers lifted one to a new level of enlightenment.

He unwrapped his finger from his mustache. "In truth, Great Shogun, what you tell me is most perplexing."

Adrada nodded. "The situation is complex. The darkunskyve surges as Satanus readies an ancient text to change hands. He intends to awaken a wizard who will enslave mankind. You can prevent the exchange. Be patient, bide your time before you act. Honored samurai, you are clever, resourceful, *skilled and wise.*"

Ahh, yes, in life he had been such a man, such a samurai. But wise? No. He had been blind to a simple truth—that love ranked far above duty. Now he was offered a chance to fill the void left in his spirit by his past iniquity. Opportunities came rarely, so whatever the task, whatever the complications, he must prevail because—

Because a samurai was a samurai.

Eyes downcast, Kiyoshi put his hands together, bowed deeply, and let his words carry his conviction. "It is my honor to serve, Great Shogun. I gladly do the bidding of The Infinite One, The True Emperor, the Lord God of Creation."

❦ Chapter One

*I have no parents; I make the Heavens and
the Earth my parents.* — *The Samurai Creed*

*Empire of Triangulum Australe, Planet Civisyr,
Imperial City of Bhutar, Akran Bay Warehouse District*

Sleep was the illusion. Nightmares the reality. Or was it just
the insanity of a restless soul?

Questions without answers. Answers without questions.

Janay sighed. Such neurotic thoughts. It was foolish to stalk
the night seeking the intangible, nameless something that would
make her life worth living, but she would be damned before
taking any more of those little pink pills.

She turned into another alley between four-story warehouses.
With each step, the discomfort radiating from her rebuilt hip
reminded her that her hour's walk had only muted the deep,
aching-pain.

At the back of her mind, the voice of the Chief of Orthopedics
again gave his verdict that there was nothing more modern
medicine could do for her hip.

Skom the Fates for condemning her to the ranks of a civilian
of the Empire! No more wearing body armor. No more carrying a
disrupter-rifle. No more living out of a rucksack.

Come to think of it, living out of a rucksack wasn't all that
great.

Whoooooommmm. Whoooooommmm.

Terror seized Janay. She froze, immobile.

Skom! What had her neurotic thoughts awakened now?

In her right boot's sheath, Poke swiftly flew up, silently hitting the palm of her hand. Janay gripped the dirk, taking comfort in the blade's warmth and reassurance that it could do serious damage to any demon.

In her other boot sheath, Fox stirred, but the dirk did not rise.

Seeing the moon-made shadows near the end of the alley, Janay quieted her breathing and, with silent footfalls, sidled into the blackest of shade. She strained to hear, to identify, what kind of demon traveled the night.

The whooming became more distinct, closer, louder.

Yet, nothing descended toward her.

It was as if the thing winged down the adjacent avenue on the other side of the rooftops where she couldn't see. By the sound, the demon headed toward the main street.

She gazed across that street where perimeter lights illuminated the age-grayed siding of the Chapel of J'Hi Baldama. The old chapel marked the northern boulevard, the end of the Imperial City and the beginning of the Ozieron Colony—a Zantharian colony, one of witches and warlocks, the summoners of devils and demons.

Damn them all to the abyss.

A downdraft of sea-brined wind sent her ebony, collar-length curls tidal waving against the cloth band that kept the hair off her face. She fought the urge to reset the loosened headband, but it was more important to find the demon before it found her.

Her line of sight gave a good view of the wrought iron fence bordering the length of the sidewalk. At the back of the chapel, high atop a metal pole, the security light's orange rays glazed the dew-wet grass, the overgrown clumps of trees, and the top of the ironwork archway to the Labyrinth of Meditation.

The labyrinth was her objective. A place to walk, to soothe thoughts that pain had churned into a tangled, tormented loop and, for a little while, a chance to quell dementia.

Whoooooommmm.

Whoooooommmm.

Whoooooommmm.

For a moment, the riptide of fear grabbed her. She stepped closer to the warehouse, taking care not to touch the mossy slime on the siding. She gripped Poke tighter, and the blade pulsed that it was ready.

From the shadows near a cluster of palm-plumed trees at the rear of the chapel, a mummy-brown tormantrata, its webbed wings teetering to maintain balance, backed into the light and avoided the fisted claw swung by the smaller of his two demon cohorts.

Small? What was she thinking? By any measure the scrawny tormantratas topped out at two meters. Such spike-headed gargoyles had sent many of the survivors of the Valley of Rathe into the throes of insanity. Those demons screeched with joy when she and her comrades were put in straightjackets and locked in padded cells.

Memories flicked of the night she had regained her sanity to summon Poke and Fox. She'd disabled two dozen of the demons with her dirks, which enabled General Tarfooga, using his executioner's broadsword, to cut off those demons' heads.

But that was then, this was now.

She could easily maim the three tormantratas if she had to, but killing them? Not likely.

The whooming shifted three octaves lower.

Soon a tall, black-winged, darkon angel came into view and glided to the sidewalk near the demons. The moment his booted feet settled on the ground, he closed his wings, but the tips barely cleared the pavement. He flipped back the hood of his ebony cloak.

Evil often came packaged in beauty like this darkon with his shoulder length, white-blond hair. The sides of his hair were swept behind his ears, framing his face and accentuating the snakeskin band circling his forehead. The scales on that band shimmered like mother of pearl.

No mere angel he. No. The headband marked him as one of Satanus's archangels.

The darkon pulled the fronts of his cloak open, forcing the fabric back, over his hips.

Odd. Black long-sleeved shirt with buttoned cuffs. Baggy black pants. Not the usual tight fitting black battle leather? No sash? No sword belt? Which meant he wasn't out for the collection of a soul or intent on havoc of major proportions. So, what business did he have with tormantratas? Those demons did their best work alone, on drugged, inebriated, or neurotic people. There was no one on these streets except her — or was there?

She moved as close to the edge of the shadows as she dared before gazing up and down the street.

No one.

She turned her attention back to the demonic quartet.

One by one the tormantratas replied to something the darkon said, their words a soft, guttural gargle. Moments later the four abruptly turned, facing the street corner where a petite woman headed toward them. She extended her arms out the side slits of her ankle-length black cloak and folded back the wide front band of the voluminous hood so it rested on the top of her head. As she patted her straight, fiery-red bangs flat, moonlight glinted off the ring of her left hand. She halted in front of the angel and began rapidly speaking. Like demented bats, her hands punctuated her words. Each time she pointed at the tormantratas, they cringed and shuffled back a step.

All in all, it was a surreal image if one was insane. Only this was real. Seeing angels, demonic or angelic, was the curse of the peacekeepers who lost their guardian angels in the Valley of Rathe. Only she, because she possessed two twice-blessed dirks, had the added curse of seeing the likings of *otherlies* — the wretchedly deformed creatures that had been spawned from the darkest aspects of the universe — and hell.

The darkon angel nodded, said something to the tormantratas, then took flight, heading due east toward the spaceport island in the bay. The tormantratas winged away, northwest, up the high ridge that sheltered the bay.

The woman extended her left arm in front of her, as if aiming her palm for the bright moon. A ruby light momentarily flared about the ring on her little finger. With her other hand, she pulled her hood down to completely cover her face, then drew her hand back under her cloak. On the next breeze, a snatch of rhyming, foreign-sounding words feathered past Janay.

A chant.

Skom! The woman was a witch.

Fear roiled into a gagging lump in Janay's throat. She wanted to turn and run away, but her military training kicked in. She clutched Poke with a white-knuckled grip, and held her ground, remaining immobile, not giving her position away.

Should she summon Fox? Would two twice-blessed dirks be enough to match a witch?

As the witch continued chanting, white flecks of light split the air in front of her. Seconds later, she pulled her ring hand beneath her cloak. The flecks of light coagulated into an oval that whirled into a vortex. Still chanting, the witch stepped into the vortex and vanished. A moment later, the portal shrank into itself, disappearing.

Janay quietly panted with heartfelt relief. It was none of her business what witches or demons did as long as she was not their target. She whispered, "Poke, home" and opened her hand.

The dirk dropped to her boot and snuggled into its sheath.

A gust of night wind off the bay billowed the summer-weight fabric of her khaki slacks and shirt. These days her fatigues hung too loose on her once strong, muscular frame. That wind, saturated with moisture, was a breath away from becoming fog.

An unholy night.

Definitely another reason to seek comfort by walking the labyrinth.

Before taking another step, she listened for demon wings in flight, then glanced about, checking the area. All seemed quiet. Normal.

Ever vigilant, she crossed the street.

Passing under the archway behind the chapel, she hesitated. Seeing tormantratas and resurrecting memories of Rathe—which were best buried—perhaps seeking the comfort of a holy angel, even a bronze one, would offer more solace than the labyrinth?

Yes. It would.

She headed toward the tree shadowed Abbot's Garden and the two story tall statue of Adrada, the Archangel of Departing Souls.

The moonlight made it easy to weave through the stand of fragrant, flowering dwarf trees and spot the statue, which stood on a three tiered, pewter-gray stone dais. On the steps leading up to the dais, half a dozen bouquets, the customary farewells to recently departed souls, filled antique brass, cone-shaped receptacles. Passing under the shadow of a gnarly tree's twisted beige branches, Janay beheld the moon-blessed statue.

Adrada's booted feet were set apart, giving him a balanced stance to counter the curved-forward mass of his partly opened wings. Those immense wings rose high above his bowed head and the tips trailed to the edge of the dais. A skein of his waist-long hair draped over the right shoulder of his tunic and, with both hands, he held the crossbars of his Great Sword of Judgment, its tip touching the dais.

Moments later, she paused to study Adrada's face.

The artist who'd created the statue had captured the spitting image of the archangel, even to his long eyelashes and caret-shaped eyebrows that were not hair but tiny black feathers. A memory winked of her standing beside Adrada in the Valley of

Rathe and plunging her dirk deep into the neck of a karsk about to bite Adrada's arm in half.

The archangel's living image flared vividly in her mind. Adrada was a kind, loving, raven-haired, black-eyed Archangel of Departing Souls who sorted out, like the Saint Peter of Earth's lore, where souls of the dead went — to purgatory and reincarnation, to heaven, or to hell. As simple as that. J'Hians looked forward to commending their souls to the angel's judgment.

She was no longer a practicing J'Hian, but she had more than once commended her soul. Only she survived. Lived. Always lived.

The hairs at her nape prickled.

Instinct shoved thoughts aside, and she looked for the danger.

Night in a city was never truly quiet but, strangely enough, it seemed much too quiet.

At the base of Adrada's right boot, where the toe peeped out from under the drape of his wide-legged pants, a bulge shifted, receded, stilled. She strained to see what crouched in the darkest curve of Adrada's massive wing, where the granite slab of a contemplation bench set half hidden, sheltered, in ebony shadow.

In the depths of that shadow, a firefly spark of creamy-yellow light winked.

Dread surged through Janay.

Poke reacted, springing from Janay's boot to her hand.

Another movement within the shadow sent Janay's heart thudding against her ribs.

Fox leapt to her left hand.

She gripped both dirks. Adrenaline flowed. Her heart rate revved, tripling its beats. Muscles tensed, ready to throw, jab, or slice.

Wait a minute. Since when did demons trespass on holy ground?

A whimper came from deep in the shadow of Adrada's wing where the light had sparked, and Janay recognized the echo of fear in that mewling.

Well, well, well. Whatever was in there was afraid of her. As it should be. She was The Grave Digger, the digger of demon graves. She possessed two twice-blessed dirks. Double the maiming power, double the hurt.

She mounted the steps and headed for the interloper with quick, sure strides.

"No, no!" the whimperer's voice squeaked from the deep shadow. "Please, don't kill us."

Us? More than one demon hid there? Yet, how strange. No demon she had ever encountered annunciated words so clearly. Which begged the question— what was she about to go up against?

Janay cautiously stepped onto the dais.

A puff of wind hit her face, and she inhaled the scent of cloves. No, not cloves—esquivalum. A potent sedative. Her next inhaled breath brought other scents that mingled with the esquivalum—the painkiller hokusia's sweet pea fragrance and mickilstone's mind controlling bouquet of wine-rich ferment. The odors were unmistakably intense, unmistakably the concoction known as varnum. Few mortals could live with that reeking cocktail of drugs in their system. Perhaps he wasn't Australe.

What if he were Zantharian? Human hybrids they might be, but they embraced darkness and magic, potions and perversions.

In Adrada's shadowed wing, cloth shushed apart to reveal a soccer-sized glowing ball. Its light illuminated the unkempt, sandy-colored hair surrounding a young man's face. A face with a broad forehead, an aristocratic nose, and a trace of a darkening beard. Grime-smudged tear tracks streaked his cheeks. Panic flashed in the depths of his dilated eyes, and his trembling hands attempted to cover the light by closing his cloak about his bare chest and shivering body.

Janay took another look around the area.

Other than the high-in-the-sky drones of shuttlecraft making their way to and from the spaceport out in the bay, nothing seemed out of place. She stepped closer to the boy. Would he bolt and harm whatever it was he held?

Seeing him scoot back, she stopped beside Adrada's sword. She released her dirks, mouthing more than whispering, "Home. Home."

Both dirks went to their sheaths.

She lifted her hands with open palms toward the boy. "I mean you no harm."

"I don't believe you, witch!"

She'd been called many things but never a witch. "Do I look like a witch? Do I wear the black of Demon Dark's minions?"

The youth swallowed hard enough that his Adam's apple bobbed. He clutched the glowing ball closer to his chest.

Janay schooled her voice to the timbre as soft as a mother's. "What do you hold so dear in your arms?"

Almost reverently, he said, "Tal. My veed."

Veed? What in J'Hi's name was a veed?

"I'll die before I let you have him!" His determination to fight flared brightly in his eyes and was underscored by the jut of his uplifted chin.

Courage to challenge her, well, that warmed a jaded sergeant's heart. "If you die," she said evenly, "who will take care of Tal?"

His head nodded and nodded, the flickering light from the bundle dancing in his eyes. "Tal will die with me. We die together."

"Why do you condemn him?"

"So you won't have him!" The thunder in the boy's voice was part pain, part rage, part desperation.

Maybe asking a different question would sidetrack him, calm him enough so she could get closer, have a better look at him and his bundle. "What's a veed?"

"You know what it is, and you can't have Tal!"

"I'm sorry, but I truly have no idea. I'm not from this planet."

The boy hiccupped a breath. "You aren't?"

"No. I'm here for a few months. Look, if I'm to help you and Tal, don't you think it would be a good idea if I knew what a veed was?"

"Tal is . . ." He took a slow, calming breath. "I can't tell you. Must keep secret."

"I'm very good at keeping secrets."

"You are?"

She nodded. "Level One military security clearances. You can trust me. Truly you can. I promise-promise upon my honor and upon my soul never to tell." How childish that sounded to her own ears.

"Oh . . . Okay . . . Tal is qi. Energy. He's my symbiote." Then the boy wailed, *"They took him out of me!"* His tears trickled anew.

An energy symbiote?

And just who were *they*?

Janay covertly eyed the bundle's fading light.

Whatever was inside that bundle was too big to fit in a human body. Then again, if it had been removed from the boy, varnum could mask the pain. Only where was the wound?

"Are you bleeding?"

"They bled me, but I'm okay." His nodding was more a series of jerks.

"Bled, as in vampires feeding?" Now where had that weird

thought come from? Likely from being in this damn city.

"Vampires? No." With the back of his hand, he wiped aside a tear that had trickled to the edge of his lip. "I don't want to die. *I don't want to die!*" His whimpering sobs renewed, and his suffering touched her heart.

She didn't want him to die out here, huddled, cowering, drugged out of his mind, even if it were on hallowed ground or at the feet of Adrada.

"Tell me what I can do to help you both live."

He quieted, then sniffed back his tears. "You would help us?"

"Yes."

"Why?"

"Because I'm a soldier. A peacekeeper." For once she prevented herself from adding, *I am The Digger of Demon Graves.*

"They're looking for me. I have to hide. My blood's on fire. You're one of them. Witch! Witch!"

So much for his sanity. Now what?

A violent shudder wracked the boy hard enough that the glowing ball slipped out of his hands.

Janay lunged forward, catching the ball before it hit the dais. The ball was an egg-shaped bundle, one that weighed no more than an inflated balloon. The dry outer covering looked and felt like flesh-colored crepe paper. Only the whole thing was warm, like . . . Skin?

From inside the sphere came a soft-spoken, childlike voice speaking in Janay's mind. *I, Tal. Please, help us. We die if not rejoined before sun rises.*

Startled, Janay nearly dropped the bundle. She'd been traumatized by Rathe, lost her mind, gone comatose, but to be awake now and have a nightmare like this?

Please, not be frightened! There no hate in you. Calm my lord Rowen, please – him fights – the poisons torment him mind. I so afraid.

Janay muttered, "No shit." Her own fears aside, she knew about herbal drugs, had processed, mixed, and memorized hundreds of their scents and tastes when she was young. Had a knack for it. But in the aftermath of Rathe, she'd learned how such drugs felt, in quantity, in her body. Doctors administering sedatives and tranquilizers along with anti-psychotics but never treating the underlying cause of the continued terror— the tormantratas.

Please, lady peacekeeper, please, help. The thing inside the sphere broke into soft weeping. *We dying!*

Dying . . .

Images winked in Janay's mind of quelling street riots. Terrorist attacks. Police actions. Civil unrests. Many comrades had died at her side at Croatsia and Saeger's Ridge. Too many in the Valley of Rathe.

She gazed up at the bronze face above her, whispering, "Adrada, Great Archangel, I have need of an angel's guidance."

From behind her came a familiar male voice, a voice as deep as thunder echoing down a mountain valley. A voice owned by only one, the Archangel Adrada himself. "Any particular angel, or will I do?"

Janay turned with a smile of welcome on her lips.

Adrada glided to a standstill on the fourth step below her, making himself eye level to her. Across his forehead gleamed the narrow band of golden tattooed words of holy blessing and ancient scripture.

No matter how many times she beheld his chiseled-to-perfection face, he had seldom returned a smile of greeting.

His huge golden wings, their edges tinged with mournful purple feathers, closed and folded back.

There seemed to be more purpling than when last she'd talked to him. Yet, nothing existed that did justice to the dimensions of his great wings nor the contrast of them with his working white attire—his baggy pants and the billowing sleeves of his shirt, a shirt any buccaneer of sea-faring Old Earth would have proudly donned.

Laying diagonally across that shirt set a white shoulder sash. On it, over his heart, rested one blood-red teardrop, the top burning with a blue-white flame. That was the symbol of J'Hi's everlasting love. The sash also meant Adrada was empowered to grant just about anything he cared to.

Her gaze rose to meet his serene, dark-eyed gaze. "Thank you for answering, Adrada. I've found a young man and this—" She lifted the weakly glowing bundle up a few centimeters, then lowered it. "There's a thing inside, a veed, that the boy called Tal. The veed says it and the boy are dying."

"They are." Adrada's words were softly spoken truth that cut like cold steel on a winter's night and whispered that death had closed in on Rowen and Tal.

"I'm sorry," Janay said. "I did not mean to interfere."

"Humans have free will. Who is to say you are interfering in the business of the universe?"

"J'Hi, the Great Spirit, the Lord God of All. Your master and mine."

"He does not. And before you ask, He told me so when He sent me to assist you. *Janay, you are free to choose your path.*"

Free to choose? Ha! She'd had a path, a military career. She wanted it back and to perdition with being a citizen.

Rowen's moan alarmed her, and she twisted at the waist to look at him. He convulsed, went rigid, then collapsed backward, his head thudding against the statue's bronze wing.

Her heart skipped a beat. Was he dead?

Adrada stepped a pace sideways to peer at the boy. "Fear not, he has only passed out."

Tal wailed, the sound plunging dirk deep into her heart.

"Here, you take this." Janay shoved the veed-bundle toward Adrada.

He shook his head and crossed both arms over his chest.

She lowered the bundle. "Look, I'm tired of dealing with death."

"I know." Sympathy mirrored in his eyes. "Some moments, so am I."

J'Hians believed Adrada's wing feathers turned mournful purple because of the atrocities of war and evil, demented people. She knew it was more than that. It was a psychosomatic result of the accumulation of grief along with the depression from millenniums of service as the Sorter of Souls. Purple stood for his grief over the tragic loss of children and the innocent. Purple for remembrance . . . She knew too much about grief and remembrance.

"Janay?" Adrada's voice entreated.

"What?"

"Your thoughts have strayed."

"Right, sorry— Death forever waits." Feeling helpless, she gazed at the bundle she held. "No one should die alone, Adrada. Any objections if I stay with these two until their end?"

"The two do not have to die tonight."

"What do you mean?"

"To live, they must be rejoined. Unfortunately . . ." He shook his head sadly. Two feathers near his elbow deepened three shades to purple.

"Finish the sentence, Adrada. What's the catch?"

"You cannot do it by yourself." He raised his hand to stay her *Why not?* "The boy is Zantharian."

Janay's heart raced, then steadied. "He doesn't look old enough to be a goddamn warlock."

"J'Hi has not damned him."

"Evil is evil. I'll have no part of its spawns."

He frowned and spoke sternly, yet softly. "You are being too judgmental."

Guilt whipped like a cat-o-nine-tails. "Blame it on the Valley of Rathe, and answer the question. What's the catch?"

He unfolded his arms. "Rowen is as human as you are — begot of the same genetics — but with one exception. Zantharians have in them a measure of celestial energy, the qi of the universe. For Rowen, that energy is manifested as Tal, his veed."

"Meaning a veed is energy like you? A veed is an angel?"

"Think of it as a seventy-generation, little cousin, one thrice-thrice-thrice removed. It is a long story and I remind you that the boy and his veed do not have time for a lengthy explanation."

"Sorry."

"I will tell you this — and remember it — a veed is a Zantharian's soul and their conscience. Joined at birth, joined in death. Goodness, light, and love have been the boy and his veed's choice. They are the greatest of friends."

"Meaning Tal and Rowen are good enough to get to Heaven?"

He canted his head in thought.

"I take it something changed? That he's not good enough anymore?"

"Defiant teen angst. Temptations of the flesh. When the witches —"

"Spare me the details. Tal said they would be dead by sunrise — that's Tal and Rowen dead, not the witches. From the look of the sky, dawn is an hour away."

"Correct. Do you want to save the boy, or stay until he dies? Or, do you want to walk away?"

Figures the decision would be tossed back to her. She looked first at Rowen, then at the sphere she held. Whether one failed or triumphed, death was inevitable. So, why care about the boy and his veed?

Because life was precious. Because the boy and the veed were friends. Because — *a true friendship was as hallowed as it got.*

"Janay? Quickly. What is your decision?"

Damned if she did and damned if she didn't. "I want to reunite them."

She caught the ghost of a smile on Adrada's lips before he

turned. He pointed toward the chapel. "The street on the other side of the chapel is Realm Avenue. It dead-ends in a kilometer. Wolcott House stands on the western corner. It is a walled-in property, a split-level of gray stone and six chimneys. The boy's brother, Tienan, lives there."

"Is Tienan home?"

"He is."

"And he can rejoin the two?"

"No."

"Then how do I get Tal back inside Rowen?"

Adrada faced her. "Behind Tienan's house, beyond the pergola, is a circle of pavers engraved with a pentagram. It is a blessed place of Zantharian celebration and ceremonies."

"Tienan is a warlock priest?"

"Not a priest but an Eighth Power Hautonne Warlock, the highest rank, and *Tienan is a Guardian Of Occult Law.*"

"A GOOL!" Janay swore vehemently before stopping herself. She bore her gaze into Adrada's fathomless eyes. "I hate GOOLs."

"I know."

"So you're telling me that if I want to save the boy and his veed, I have to face his brother-the-GOOL?"

"More than that."

"How much more?"

"You must submit to Tienan."

"Submit? I'm supposed to have sex with him? Have you lost your mind?"

"Forgive me. Wrong choice of words."

"Then rephrase."

"Tienan's veed, Zad, is extremely powerful. Tienan's will and Zad's power must be channeled through a female, one capable of handling a great deal of qi power."

"You mean pain."

"No, power."

"You're saying I can handle the power? You crazy angel, maybe a Zantharian can do it but I'm plain human."

"You are consecrated, Templar Knighted. One with twice-blessed dirks. You only have to let the qi—the energy of life—flow through you to your dirks. Pokeweed and Foxglove will use Zad's energy to reunite the boy with his veed."

Adrada's wings swept back, and he squatted. Using a fingernail, he scratched a pentagram on the dais's polished surface. He X'd a spot. "Here, in the center, the boy must be naked, in a fetal position, facing the rising sun. He must cuddle the cocoon, that is, the sphere you hold, against his chest with Tal facing him. Your dirks go here and here." Adrada X'd two more spots. "Plant Pokeweed and Foxglove to the hilt. They must be as close as possible to the boy's body but not touch his flesh. You kneel here." Again he pointed. "Keep your hands tightly closed on your dirks. Under no circumstances let go. Tienan will be behind you, on top of you, he'll cup your breasts — "

"I thought you said no sex."

"Must you reduce everything to sex?"

"I'm human. Deal with it."

"The joining isn't about sex despite you being naked."

"I have to be naked!"

He nodded. *"To succeed, there must be a complete flesh-to-flesh joining.* You must give Tienan unrestricted contact with your body because Zad cannot send his energy straight to your dirks. Tienan and your body must filter the sun's energy as Zad synthesizes its qi, focuses it, and sends it to the dirks, otherwise, the boy and his veed die."

"And that's it?"

Adrada nodded.

From behind her, Janay heard Rowen's muffled groan.

Adrada waved a hand over the sketch and the marks vanished. Rising, his wings partially opened. "Let Zad's power flow into the dirks from when the sunlight first strikes the edge of the pentagram until the sun's rays light the entire circle of pavers. Pokeweed and Foxglove will break the circuit, then stop the energy within a moment or two after that. Zad will know what to do. Trust him."

It sounded simple enough, but maybe not. "What else?"

Adrada quirked a feathered eyebrow up a fraction. "What a cynic you have become.

She shrugged. "So what else should I know?"

"You may be injured or die from the power transfer. Your body is, after all, frail, not because you are human but because of your ordeal in the Valley of Rathe."

"No shit."

"Dawn is nearing, Janay."

"If all goes wrong, will you personally come for my soul?"

"It would be my honor to do so."

Janay gently bit her lower lip. Death no longer held her in fear. Life, however, well, these days it was more a living hell. Life was for the young. Life was for laughing and loving and— *To dance in the day.* "Adrada. I want them to live."

"Then waste no time." His great wings unfurled.

"Wait a sec, how do I get the drugged boy and his veed to Tienan's house?"

"I can walk," Rowan said.

Startled, Janay pivoted around.

Adrada leaned forward and whispered in her ear, "Wolcott House was the boy's destination. Remember Deepford Reach." He stepped back. In a sweep of wings and the glitter of iridescent angel light, he vanished.

Deepford Reach? Skom. That was endless marches to prepare for a battle that never happened.

Rowen came out of the shadows. When his knees threatened to buckle, he stumbled but found his balance. "The drugs, they work in fits. I should be fine for fifteen minutes, maybe longer."

"We need twenty. Let's go."

Dread surged with each beat of homicide detective Tienan De'Argossi's heart, but it did not drown out the images his imagination conjured of his brother on a morgue slab.

Tienan turned and again paced before the bay window of his study, ignoring the brilliant, luminous moonlight shafting through the panes. With his next pivoting turn, he glanced at the comlink on his ebony lacquered desk, silently urging it to buzz, for Rowen's voice to say, "Hi, Bro!" as if nothing were amiss. But everything was amiss.

Tienan put a hand to the turtleneck collar of his Guardian of the Law uniform and stretched the midnight-blue fabric as wide as it would go, only the stretching of the silken knit didn't lessen his choking anxiety.

The comlink softly buzzed.

Tienan spun on his heels, sending his heavy braid of earth-brown hair swinging across his back. Facing the fireplace at the corner of the room, he jabbed his left thumbnail to the underside of the heirloom warlock's ring on his little finger, triggering the signal and activating the house's computer system. In a voice hoarse with desperate hope, he said, "Answer. Main terminal."

Apprehension coiled like a python about his chest. Each

breath became more and more a labored effort. He couldn't move, couldn't stop staring at the two-meter wide picture of flowering vorvoolt vines above the mantel that became a pale-blue screen.

An image appeared.

It wasn't Rowen but Boots. Her grave expression had Tienan blurting out, "They found him?"

Boots shook her head, sending a wisp of her dyed mahogany hair onto her cheek. She tucked the wayward strand back into her unkempt topknot. Every wrinkle line on her face seemed to be etched half a century deeper. "Just checking in." Her voice held the gravel of worry. "I thought you'd want to know that twenty minutes ago we traced Rowen to Ricco's."

Tienan inwardly cringed. Ricco's was a strip club at the southern end of Akran Bay. A club notorious for booze, sex, and drugs.

Boots cleared her throat. "Surveillance at the club shows your brother left at 0145, alone. Drunk. Very drunk. Look, Tienan, he's probably sleeping it off in an alley."

Drunk was preferable to a dead brother with his veed cut out of him, wasn't it?

Boots tucked another wayward strand of her hair into her topknot. "And before you ask, yes, the commander authorized drones to search the alleys in a five kilometer radius."

"That'll take time." Tienan felt like raking his fingers through his hair, but he would be damned before he would mimic his partner's irritating habit.

A buzz sounded from somewhere near Boots. She glanced left, then looked at him. "Have to go. We'll find him. *We will find him.*" The screen went blank.

"End call." Tienan touched his thumbnail to the backside of his warlock's ring, signaling the computer to standby mode. The screen reverted to the vorvoolt picture.

In Tienan's mind's eye, his veed Zad's marble-sized, swirling ball of energy brightened, revealing a rainbow of colors. The veed's cultured voice intoned in Tienan's mind, *Easy, my good lord.* Zad's energy ball shimmered whiter before morphing into his three-finger tall, noncorporeal form — a white lion with a black, nappy mane. Zad sat on his muscular haunches and brought his long tail forward. He flicked the tip, fanning its mop of black dreadlocks across his front paw.

Tienan looked inward, into Zad's eyes, which were forever dramatically framed in black, as if kohl had been applied with an extra heavy hand. The black enhanced the veed's wise, but somber, demeanor.

Dawn is near, my lord, Zad said. *Light will reveal truth.*

Another one of Zad's blasted Confucianistic phrases. Tienan spoke in his mind-voice. *What is the truth, Zad? Is Rowen dead or alive?*

I am not a seer, my lord, nor are you. If you factor in the circumstances, the odds are likely fifty-fifty.

"I'd prefer they be one hundred percent!" Damn the powers, he hadn't meant to snap at Zad. Nor at Rowen.

Why had he lost his temper with his brother, sending him storming out of the house? It was a stupid argument over — ? Confound the powers, he couldn't remember what they'd argued about.

Again the image of Rowen on an autopsy table flared to life in Tienan's mind. In the past three months, four other males, both twenty, both with cocooned veeds about to madl — to hatch — had been found dead. Autopsies revealed the victims had been drugged with varnum and raped. Each had a remnant of their veed's cocoon bonded to their chests. Each throat had been slit in an attempt to hide the pricks of vampire fangs. Each had been drained of half their blood.

Why half their blood? once again slithered to the fore.

It was documented fact that vampires didn't drug their victims and, when they drank, they tended to drain every drop. So, who was the psycho killing young Zantharians?

Speculation abounded at HQ. Was it a Zantharian killing to feed his mediocre veed so it became more powerful? Veeds did feast on veeds. Or was it as Granger believed? That the killer was a true, veeded Zantharian vampire who belonged to the Elders of the Circle of Draqoolq. Those ancient vampires were nearly impossible to find, let alone destroy. Their appetites and darkon ways knew no bounds. How many more young men had to die before the task force would know what they were up against?

Tienan ratcheted in a noisy breath through his nostrils. He began to pace, praying that his brother hadn't become victim number five.

❦ Chapter Two

I have no home; I make the Tan Tien my home.
— The Samurai Creed

Akran Bay, the Old Warehouse District

A light flashed behind Annelisa Quorn, startling her. She swung around, the quick movement sending her long, seal-brown hair swishing like the silk of her many tiered peasant skirt. Seeing the dazzling blue-violet shafts of light forming an oval near the immense fireplace across the room, she relaxed. The light heralded a portal forming, its duvara, its center, yawned ever wider.

A moment later, the cloaked Celinae stepped out of the duvara. Her booted feet thudded softly on the blood-red bricks of the Druid's Circle framing the pentagram on the floor. When the portal vanished, Celinae flipped the hood of her siddirelling cloak back and pulled her braid of fiery-red hair free of the cloak's massive hood. She patted down her long bangs insuring every hair hung perfectly straight before she faced the pentagram's center. There, the coal-black marble pedestal seemed to flow up, out of the floor, into an oval black marble altar with a white pentagram inlay at the center.

Panic assailed Annelisa. Was Celinae looking for a spatter of candle wax? A drop of blood? She had been so very careful to clean and polish every surface.

"They didn't find him." Celinae's voice resonated with viperish frustration.

A deeper, colder panic chilled Annelisa. "If Rowen gets to his brother—"

"He won't. I made sure of that."

"How?"

Celinae faced Annelisa. A gleam of self-satisfaction shimmered in the depths of her chestnut-brown eyes. "I summoned Shelzat. He dispatched three more tormantratas to Wolcott House. Should Rowen make it there, he'll be greeted by five tormantratas." She held up her hand, splaying her five fingers for emphasis. "Shelzat's explicit orders are for the demons to destroy the cocoon and carry the boy's corpse off, out into the bay, and drop him into the briny waters. It'll be weeks before his body is found, if at all." She ran a slender finger across her lips and tapped them twice. "You know, we can't be sure he was headed for Wolcott House. Drugged as he was, he might have passed out somewhere." She fluttered her hand out in an arc, emphasizing the direction of the warehouse complex behind the building.

"But Sweets said—"

Celinae scowled. "Yes, yes, I know. Sweets is infallible." Her words didn't hide her contempt. "I assure you, Annelisa, either by sunrise or by the tormantratas, Rowen and his veed will be dead, and dead men— correction— dead boys tell no tales."

"I hate to say I told you so, but I told you not to pick Rowen for our next victim. There are—"

"Get it through that thick skull of yours that *Rowen represents the last of the second house of Hautonne Zanthara!*" She wagged a scolding finger at Annelisa. "That bloodline produces men with Behringgreat Veeds of the eighth power. We partake of that maturing power, coupled with the other veed energies we've already ingested, and no one—no high society, Hautonne-bred witch or warlock—will be our equals!" She stilled, her facial muscles relaxed. She calmly said, "One Behringgreat of the De'Argossi vintage is worth six of any other house."

Annelisa knew that, but she couldn't dispel the idea that Rowen could be found alive and identify the three of them. Her stomach swirled like a spell gone wrong.

"Are things tidied up here?" Celinae looked about the renovated warehouse starting where she usually did, with the corner behind the pentagram. There, the shiny stainless steel, walk-in freezer doors proclaimed the unit's newness. Her gaze swept past the tool storage cage, the plain paneling of the communications-cum-computer kiosk, and the cupboards of ceremonial vessels. Only for a second did her gaze linger on the base where the *Fourth Book of Xenobia* was secreted away.

Celinae turned, glimpsing the sidewall of white lattice panels where a row of copper caldrons contained bloodwood vines in various stages of growth. Yet, for some reason, Celinae's attention paused on the longest vine. The mother-vine's thick, gnarled stem draped over a dozen wrought iron hooks on the lattice. Sweets had planted the thing from the last tuber produced by an eighty-year-old vine that had once grown in a biodome. Annelisa's stomach contracted in distaste, and in remembrance of how Sweets, like a mother to a child, lovingly spoke to that disgusting old vine.

Slowly Celinae's gaze traveled along the vine's twining stalk to the arch, where the vine's profusion of elephantine, forest-green leaves obscured the aisle leading to the shipping dock door. Celinae turned again, ignoring the proliferation of herbs, bushy shrubs, and dwarf trees growing in containers on top of neatly gridded aisles of gravel drainage. All the plants were rare. Poisonous. Toxic.

Celinae nodded. "Good. No sign of what went on here." She faced the soot-blackened fireplace. A few embers glowed among the ashes of what was left of the alabaster wood kindling. Celinae sniffed. "Well, well, I don't smell any varnum. You've finally learned how to clean it away." She swung about, sending the hem of her cloak fluttering, and gave Annelisa a wide smile. "Join me for breakfast."

Food? How could Celinae think of food? "With all that's happened, I couldn't eat a thing."

"Best you do. Can't afford to have you faint and lose a day at work, now can we?" She headed to the left of the fireplace, toward the wood-paneled, double front doors. "Come along, or must you be at work first thing this morning?"

Annelisa followed her. "I'm not due at the manor until noon. Her Grace went to her monthly card party last night. She'll have played kumdak 'til dawn. Probably won a small fortune." Why was she blathering?

"Ah, so, you have plenty of time. You know, I'm of a mind to cook us a brunchy-breakfast feast!"

Annelisa's stomach lurched. What she needed was a soothing cup of tea.

Janay passed under yet another street light and into dimness beneath another ancient daoka tree that lined the avenue of stately homes with their manicured lawns and terraced gardens. A wisp of fog slithered across a low spot along a flagstone wall draped with crimson flowers.

She again eyed Rowen's purposeful strides. She had to give the boy credit for his single-minded determination and his ability to endure the drugs rattling his mind. She would have given her eye teeth for such an uncomplaining recruit like Rowen during Deepford Reach's endless marches.

In her arms, Tal's glow flickered weakly.

Was that good or bad? Tal hadn't emitted a sound or a wink of light since they had begun this trek.

Best not dwell on it.

A moment later, she spotted the open gates of Wolcott House. Correction. Mansion. She'd seen the gloomy-gray stone edifice when they'd made it halfway up the hill. The split-level set nestled into the crest of the hill, sprawled out longer than wider. Three-quarters of the end of the house was taken up by a gigantic fieldstone, double chimney that towered above the roof and all the other chimney tops.

Hearing the wind rustle through the broad, moon-silvered leaves of the tall old daoka trees surrounding the house, Janay glanced at the tree nearest the driveway's gate.

The tree had a few late white blooms on it. As a petal fell from one of the flowers, something dark swayed at the junction of a branch and the tree's trunk. Janay soon spied the spikes on the back of a tormantrata.

Leave it for one of those gargoyles to smell the drugged boy and come to torment him until he was raving mad. Time was running out. Dawn brightened the horizon. She didn't need a schizophrenic episode to delay them.

Rowen turned for the driveway where stone greyhounds perched on top of the fieldstone pillars supporting the black-barred gates that stood open.

Janay whispered to Rowen's back, "Halt!"

The boy obeyed, but gazed over his shoulder at her. Puzzlement and pain wrinkled his sweat-dampened brow.

She put a finger to her lips to silence him, then whispered,

"We've got company. A tormantrata."

"A what?" he whispered back.

"*A demon.* They don't have the best of hearing, but they can be vicious. One has scented the drugs in your system and has come to harass you."

Rowen eyed the driveway, the walk, the house, the nearest trees.

"Trust me, Rowen. It's there. Now, listen up. You will walk on the left side of the drive. You will turn onto the brick path and go straight into that house. No matter how much commotion or screaming you hear, *you will not stop.* You will not look back. Got that?"

He nodded. "But —"

"If you don't do exactly as I say, you're dead. So is Tal. Just put that formidable will of yours to the task. Concentrate on getting inside the house. Nothing else."

He nodded. With trembling hands, he took Tal from her.

She crisscrossed his cloak fronts so they covered the veed's cocoon. No sense taking a chance Tal's light would wink on and alert the tormantrata. "Ready?"

"What are you going to do?"

"What The Grave Digger does best."

At her command, Poke and Fox rose into her hands.

The doorbell rang, shrilling through the silence of Wolcott House, echoing about Tienan's study.

"Bless the night, let that be Rowen!" Heart racing, he triggered his warlock's ring and shouted to the house computer, "First floor, all lights on." He jogged out of the room, across the few meters of the foyer, and to the front door. He flashed his ring to the control panel at the base of a wall sconce and the front door opened inward.

Tienan glimpsed something whiz away from the doorbell. Then, through the graying dawn, he spied Rowen approaching.

Praise the powers, his brother was home!

A burst of wind flipped the front of Rowen's cloak open, revealing the veed cocoon he held to his bare chest.

Tienan's joy died. His mind went silent.

Rowen walked with purposeful strides forward, his labored breaths resonating like wheezy bellows. Sweat and tear tracks streaked his cheeks.

Zad shouted in Tienan's mind, *Move! Help your brother.* Tienan jogged out the door and across the portico.

My lord! Look — Behind Rowen.

Tienan spied a woman with a riot of ebony curls crowning her head. In each hand she held a knife and slashed into the air as if fighting something.

Zad, Tienan ordered, *keen.*

In a pulse-beat, Tienan's muscles tingled with energy and his sensory perceptions heightened. Zad transitioned Tienan's vision to veed wavelengths. Tienan now saw the thing the woman slashed at — a spiny-headed gargoyle's wing.

The beast banked sharply.

The woman's blade sliced air.

Behind that gargoyle, near the right driveway pillar, a small gargoyle flopped on the ground, its wings tattered, one foot cut off.

High overhead, wings beat the air. Three gargoyles darted around the broad spread of the towering daoka trees. One swooped in from behind the woman, heading for Rowen.

The woman threw her right blade. The knife whacked into and sliced across the swooping beast's shoulder, snapping the tendons to the wing. The gargoyle screamed and tumbled, crashing into a hedge. The knife then hacked itself free, spewing white petals and red twigs about. Seconds later, the blade flew back into the woman's hand.

Amazing weapon, Zad muttered. In his noncorporeal form in Tienan's mind's eye, Zad rose onto his cat feet. He unsheathed his long black claws. *Shall I assist the lady and tear the demons to pieces?*

No! Rowen comes first.

Rowen tripped and the cocoon flew out of his hands.

The fourth gargoyle dove between daoka branches for the cocoon.

Veed-enhanced leg muscles sped Tienan forward. Veed-enhanced coordination aided Tienan in ducking the incoming taloned feet. Veed-enhanced reflexes enabled Tienan to catch the cocoon, tuck it under one arm, ram his shoulder into his brother's stomach, and lift Rowen into a fireman's carry. As Tienan took in his next breath, he spotted the woman.

"Fox. Chop!" She flung the blade in her left hand straight for him.

Why was she attacking him?

The blade angled upward.

Gargoyle wings flapped from high above his head.

Trond! He had to get out of here. He pivoted for the safety of the house. A stride later, the gargoyle overhead screeched. Its dismembered foot thumped onto the sidewalk and bounced onto the grass near Tienan.

The woman's voice boomed, "Get Rowen inside! Hurry!"

Taking a firmer hold on the cocoon under his arm, Tienan scurried for the front door. *Zad! Cover us.*

Veed energy flowed out of Zad, encasing Tienan's body in a blue-gray aura in the shape of the ghostly lion. The aura expanded to envelop Rowen and the cocoon.

The whooshing air from a gargoyle closing in had Tienan sensing its gnarly hands reaching for the cocoon. Tienan sent his feet pounding for longer, faster strides. Out of the corner of his eye, he glimpsed the gargoyle's claw-tipped hands meet Zad's energy-aurora, heard the sizzle of the contact, then saw the gargoyle's flesh ignite and flame.

The gargoyle shrieked and reared sideways. Its wings labored, backstroking, taking it away. The flames raced with increased speed up the demon's arms. Its blackened slime-skin dripped off like candle wax, falling, flaming out on the boxwood hedge in front of the study's bay window.

Tienan made it under the portico, over the threshold. He turned to kick the door closed but, seeing the woman knocked to the ground by the last gargoyle, he hesitated.

The gargoyle banked sharply before diving for the woman with its talons extended.

She threw both her blades, which spun in flight and sliced off the creature's talons.

Squealing in pain, the gargoyle veered, its wings straining to avoid crashing into a tree. The injured beast labored for altitude to get away from the oncoming slashing blades intent on chopping off chunks of its feet.

The woman rolled over, grunted, then staggered to her feet. She hobbled at a run for the house.

Once she made it inside, past him, he kicked the door shut. Her blades came through the doorway a second before the door closed with a resounding click of the latch.

"House, defend!" Tienan yelled. Tiny green lights flickered on the control panel beneath the sconce indicating the energy shield had gone up around the house.

Would the shielding meant to keep roaming veeds out keep gargoyles at bay?

A screech echoed through the door. Another scream came from outside the bay window of his study.

Evidently the shielding worked.

Tienan breathed a sigh of relief. *Zad, end aura, but keep me powered.*

The veed withdrew its protective aura, contracted its energy into its noncorporeal self, and once again appeared inside Tienan's mind as the docile, sitting lion.

The woman's breath rasped from exertion and pain. She swayed and grabbed the newel post of the stairs that led down to the lower level of the house. Momentarily steadied, she took in her surroundings of an open living area, of the great room and its butter-cream colored walls, a contrast for the dark brown and light green decor. Her gaze flitted to the open kitchen and alighted on the French doors to the backyard.

"We're safe," Tienan said, hoping to reassure her. "The house is spell protected."

"Your brother — he isn't safe." She took deep, ragged gasps for air, but her labored breathing barely eased.

"What do you mean?"

"We have to join him — and his veed — by sunrise — or both die. Hurry. Pentagram." She grabbed the cocoon from Tienan and jogged for the French doors.

His brother mustn't die! Tienan squelched the urge to question her and followed. Thanks to his still heightened sight, he got a better look at the two dirks that leapfrogged behind her. Both blades were intricately sculpted with vines and flowers flowing in an art-nouveau pattern.

My lord Tienan, she is not witch. Zad's voice held awe. *I hear no veed song. Sense no p'si. Not even an embryo. And yet, she registers a most unusual aura.*

Darkunskyve?

No, my lord. A rainbow. See.

An image flared in Tienan's mind of what Zad saw — two dainty, interlinked, rainbow-glittering tiaras sitting on the crown of the woman's head.

Hurrying after the woman, the weight of his brother taxed

Tienan's strength. With the next labored inhale of air, the odor reeking from his brother registered. *Varnum!*

Yes, indeed, my good lord. It is varnum, and a heavy dose. Yet, I think, not one strong enough to kill him.

The woman stopped, frantically checking the wall for a control.

She wanted out? "The gargoyles — "

"They're gone. They roam the night. It's dawn." She paused, panting. "We need to get to the pentagram."

My lord, she brought Rowen home. Let us trust her.

"Si'anee!" Tienan gave the ancient word for the house's computer to yield to his override. "Open patio doors."

The doors opened and the woman rushed out.

Tienan shifted his brother for better balance, grunted, and followed her.

The woman stopped at the edge of the pentagram. "Where's the sun rise from?"

"To your right."

"Set Rowen in the center of the pentagram."

Tienan soon lowered his brother and, free of the weight, staggered back a step.

The woman commanded, "Get rid of his cloak."

Tienan nodded.

"Rowen," the woman said, "assume a fetal position."

Pulling the cloak free of his brother, Tienan noticed Rowen's pasty cheeks and closed eyes. "I think he's passed out."

"Skom! It's all up to us."

"To do what?"

"Rejoin Tal and Rowen."

"You can do that?"

"No. You and your veed can. I'm the conduit." She placed the cocoon against Rowen's chest. "Tal, face Rowen."

Rowen moaned and drew up his knees, his arms hugging the cocoon. Rising, the woman winced in pain and put a hand to her right hip.

"Are you injured?" Why had he voiced the obvious?

She ignored him and eyed the rays of the sun winking across the rooftop. "The sun's coming!" She jerked her sweat-soaked shirt out from her pants. "Poke, Fox. Boots. Undo. Then strip the boy. Dispatch everything onto the grass." She shed her shirt, tossing it aside.

Tienan could only stare, watching her blades work the catches of her well-worn military-issue boots. She soon kicked her feet out of the boots, sending them tumbling into a flower bed, then she pulled off her socks.

Her two blades slashed away at Rowen's clothes, wound themselves about the edges of his pants and underwear, and yanked the cloth free. The material was swiftly deposited on the grass. The blades slit and tugged away Rowen's dress boots and socks.

Rowen shivered. His eyes seemed glazed, unfocused. "Hurry . . . please . . ."

Tienan, my lord, Zad's voice held astonishment, *we are to perform a ceremony!*

"My lady, do we need anything? Candles? Oil?"

"Skom! He didn't say." She shed her slacks.

"He?"

"Adrada. Never mind." She grabbed her hairband and flung it aside.

In her seamless sports bra and boxer panties, he saw the seared gash across her rib below her breast. How much pain was she in?

She took a ragged, fortifying breath. "To make this work, I'm supposed to submit to you — and we're not talking about sex. *I'd sooner slit your GOOL throat than have you ride me.*"

GOOL? How did she know he was a GOOL? No, wait, she probably meant ghoul. The Australes often called Zantharian's ghouls.

She scowled at him. "You're to get behind me, straddle me, cup my breasts, and channel your veed's power into my dirks."

My lord, she's talking about the Ritus Uniten, a ritual of unity.

Details, Zad. Details — now.

A very ancient rite. Zad paused. *I read of it in the old book, last year's required reading . . . Yes. Yes! The Rite of Reunification could save Rowen and Tal.*

Could? You mean it might fail?

Success depends on this woman withstanding the channeling of considerable qi energy.

The woman stepped closer to the center of the pentagram.

Did she grimace from the coldness of the pavers, or pain? Did it matter? No, because — "My lady, can you handle the channeling of my veed's power?"

"I'm not your lady, and I have no idea, but what choice do we have? If we don't do this channeling thing, Rowen and Tal die. I didn't come here to let them die." She glared at him. "Why are you still dressed? You have to be naked."

In the interest of speed, my lord, I shall undress you.

In a flash of veed light, Zad vanished Tienan's clothes as well as the cloth threaded through his braid. His long hair unwound. A twisting hank flopped forward, over his shoulder.

The woman stilled, her eyes widened to gaze first at his hair then downward, to his chest of hair, then lower, to his groin. Her jaw slackened and her lips minutely parted.

Any other time he would have enjoyed a woman taken aback by his genitals and the dark hair crowning them.

Her gaze suddenly shifted to the jagged scar on his left thigh. A faint smile lifted the right corner of her lips.

She smiled? Most women found that scar repulsive.

My lord, allow me to expedite the undressing of the lady. Zad sent out a thread of azure-blue light that touched the woman's panties. The garment vanished.

The woman gasped, swore, pivoted, and faced Rowen's back.

Zad's energy alighted on her bra. It vanished.

She jerked with surprise, shook her head as if to clear her thoughts, then knelt. "Rowen, tuck yourself as tight as you can and hold on to Tal."

He moaned but obeyed.

"To hand. To hand."

Her blades flew to her waiting palms. She gripped the weapons and raised her arms. Her muscles flexed. In swift downward strokes, she pounded the left blade at Rowen's feet, the right one near his head. Both blades went into the polished stone up to their hilts. Neither the blades nor the granite shattered. She shot a glance over her shoulder at him. "Your turn, GOOL. Get aboard."

"Stop calling me a ghoul. I'm not a demon. My name is Tienan."

"I know your name, and you are a GOOL—as in Guardian of Occult Law—a ghoul to be sure, but it doesn't matter how you spell it, you're one in the same to me, and we have no time left. Get your ass over here and do your thing."

She knew he was a GOOL? How?

"Skom, man, the sun's coming!"

Tienan glanced up and found the sun cresting the top of the woods, the rays glistening the dew on the grass only a meter from the edge of the pentagram.

"Look, GOOL, do you or do you not want to save your brother?"

He did. Nothing else mattered. He dismissed his questions and his uncertainty.

As he went to position himself, he noticed the ripening red welts on the woman's right shoulder. Those gargoyle welts were framed between old, jagged scars that tapered to nothing by mid-spine. How many demons had she fought in her lifetime?

As he lowered himself to his knees, the silken glide of his stomach and the brushing of his genital hairs against the woman's sweat-cooled buttocks set off a frisson deep in his groin. His knees buckled.

Overpowered by the sensations of his nakedness melded against her, he didn't feel the pain of his knees hitting the pavers. *By the powers, Zad, her body aligns — as if I belong between her legs.*

Zad growled. *My lord, do pay attention. We need a flesh-to-flesh joining for this rite, not a mating.*

Yes, of course. Leaning forward, Tienan's next breath brought with it the fruit-peachy odor of the woman's fog-dampened hair.

Such a feminine scent. One at odds with a warrior woman.

Rowen moaned.

"Be still, Rowen." The woman's voice had been soft-spoken, but the tone made it an order.

Tienan eased his hands around and gently cupped the woman's breasts. Her aureoles shriveled hard beside his thumbs. He heard her sharp intake of breath.

My lord, the lady does not like this.

Do you think I do?

No, my good lord. However, there is the matter of her magical blades. If they can slice gargoyles, I fear they can kill us if we should offend her.

Which was Zad's not-so-subtle way of reminding him to be careful what he touched.

The woman's body went rigid.

"No, don't tense." Tienan strove to keep his voice gentle, soothing. "Relax so Zad's power flows through us."

"Right. Sorry. This isn't about us, it's about Rowen and Tal. Right . . ."

Her body relaxed, and Tienan settled his cheek to her cheek, his chin on her collarbone. Again, he smelled her peachy scent, felt the pleasure of her cool skin on his heated flesh.

My lord, Zad's voice reprimanded, *change your thoughts.*

Trond! He needed to concentrate. "Start the mantra."

"What mantra?" the woman replied.

He grabbed the first one that came to mind. "*Esiojer en eth, senwen ov, eith dae.* It translates to something on the order of *rejoice in the newness of the day.*"

She haltingly repeated the phrase and, by the third repetition, she said it smoothly.

Now Zad, Tienan commanded.

The veed's blue-gray aura mushroomed over Tienan and began to envelop the woman. Zad's HOMMMMMM knelled for a minute before Zad began the ancient words of the reuniting spell.

❦ Chapter Three

I have no divine power; I make honesty my
Divine Power. — The Samurai Creed

Janay tried to concentrate on the mantra but there was the god-awful tingling of Tienan's warm skin against her cold, sweat-sheened flesh that had nothing to do with a veeded power surge but a hormonal surge—hers.

The image of Tienan's nakedness flashed in her mind. The last time she'd seen such a physique, such a muscular chest, or such a cannon of a penis was on her ex-lover, Lieutenant Samuel Creamer, armorer at the Jian-Qun Fortress. Only Sam didn't pulsate with regal masculinity the way this GOOL did.

A skittering sensation slid over her upper arm. She glanced at it. Some of the GOOL's dark brown hair, that glistened with mahogany highlights, had fallen forward. *Such silken hair . . .*

Zad's blue-gray aura slipped over that hair and down both her arms to her hands which gripped Poke and Fox. Surprised by the sight, she inhaled sharply, triggering a burning pain from where the tormantrata's talon had sliced her rib. The demon had come up behind her while she'd been whacking off the foot of the first tormantrata that had attacked.

She shifted, spreading her knees to balance the weight on top of her and ease the strain of her burning side. The movement set off a jaw-tightening ache from her rebuilt hip. Skom, how much damage had she done to her hip?

Match-fire heat struck her toes. She jerked, arching her spine into Tienan's hard-as-a-rock chest.

"Easy," Tienan whispered. "Nothing to panic about."

"I don't panic. Something's frying my toes."

That would be the sun resonated in her mind from a deeper, somber voice.

Although momentarily rattled by the voice, she managed a civil, "Who's inside my head?"

"Zad, my veed." The whisker stubble of Tienan's jaw grazed her cheek. "He's engulfed us with his energy. You'll hear him when he speaks."

"Right. Sorry."

"Mantra, woman. Concentrate on the mantra, not on your body — or mine — or any voice in your head."

"Easy for you to say," she muttered. Veeds talking inside her head give a whole new meaning to the phrase 'being possessed.' Enough. The mantra. *I am The Grave Digger. I dig demon graves.* No. Not that mantra. "Esiojer en eth senwen . . ." With the fourth repetition, warmth cascaded up her calves. Then came the unmistakable silken touch of Tienan's hardening erection.

"Pay no heed," Tienan whispered. "It's a natural reaction, just like your wetness."

Wetness? Skom! Her vagina was pouring out fluid like a ferine in heat.

"Mantra, woman, mantra," Tienan whispered. "Clear your mind."

She swung her mind to the task. "Esiojer en eth . . ." Only her concentration was not so great that she didn't feel Tienan's thumbs settle beside her teats, or smell his daoka-spiced aftershave, or feel the vibrations from Zad's aura that became a scalding wave flowing over and through her. Yet, that heat felt soothing. Welcome.

When the molten gold sunlight edged up and over her hips, it quenched the pain in her bad joint. Prickling energy soon skittered down her arms to engulf her dirks. Poke and Fox superheated in her hands. Seconds later they emitted one, then two, then a cat's cradle of thread-thin connections of red, green, yellow, azure, and purple light between them.

HOMMMM. Zad's voice reverberated in her mind. Then came an electrifyingly potent sensation like roiling flames searing down her arms, into her hands, and into her dirks. She wanted to scream, but no sound came forth.

The red line between the dirks flashed blue, then all the lines became a diamond-white, glittering brilliance which held her enthralled. She no longer felt the scalding energy throbbing through her body. Only words whispered in her mind. Zad's voice. Tienan's lighter timbre. Both reciting not the mantra but words that blended, in sync, but at different pitches. She matched her inner voice to theirs, joining the chant. Time seemed to slow, then nearly stop. The chant resonated as one ancient voice, one heartfelt prayer.

Tal's cocoon expanded until it tore from top to bottom. Inside the cocoon, a white baby panther stirred, then rose on wobbly, oversized paws. The cocoon shriveled into a single, narrow, rag-like strip. The white kitten lifted its scrawny tail, which had a tuft of rabbit fluffy, charcoal-black hair at the end. Tal curled his tail up and over his back, revealing the cocoon strip being sucked into a small hole under his tail. The end of the rag vanished with a *snipht*. The hole sealed shut, leaving a tiny, black diamond-shaped mark.

Janay had seen enough cats and kittens, including ferines, to know that this cat had no genitals. It didn't even have a rectum.

The kitten purred while it stepped forward, shrinking as it entered Rowen's abdomen. The boy convulsed, then stilled.

Time advanced, faster and faster. The line of the sun slipped off the edge of the pentagram to turn the grass a glossy blue-green.

In her hands, Poke and Fox felt hotter than the end of a branding iron. Janay held on with a crushing determination to maintain her hold on the blades. Yet, coursing through her mind came the voice of reality reminding her that she was burning alive and Death awaited.

The ancientness of the combined voices chanting in her mind modulated. Tienan stopped speaking and so did she. A heartbeat later, Zad's voice silenced. The light-threads winked out between Poke and Fox. A whirlwind updraft set her curls flapping about her cheeks and Tienan's long hair whipping against his hands, which still held her breasts. Although she couldn't see Zad's aura recede, she gloried in the coolness that came in its wake.

Poke, then Fox, squirmed in her hands.

She released her grip. When she let go, the weight of Tienan on her, and nothing to hold onto, sent her pitching forward. She had enough presence of mind to drop her left shoulder, twisting sideways, hitting the paver near Rowen's knees.

Tienan wasn't quick enough to break his fall. His head hit the stone near Rowen's feet. Tienan jerked his leg free from under her and scooted clear.

Janay's heartbeat thundered erratically in her ears. Strained muscles ached. Pain flared from her injuries. Her gaze drifted to Rowen.

He sat up, grinned, and hugged his knees. Tears of joy trickled down his face.

The boy was alive! She wanted to hug Rowen, but she couldn't move. She'd reached her limit. Ah, well, it was a good morning for Rowen to dance in the day. *Adrada, I commend my care and soul to thee.* She closed her eyes, welcoming the darkness settling over her.

It took Tienan two attempts to sit. He wasn't sure how much time passed before the backyard stopped spinning and his eyes clearly focused on his brother, who sat hugging his knees. Tienan crawled to Rowen, holding back tears of relief until he embraced Rowen in a bear hug.

Trembling, Rowen hugged Tienan, then abruptly stilled. "By the powers!" Rowen pushed Tienan aside.

Dread lanced through Tienan. He blinked back his tears, clearing his vision, and looked where his brother stared.

The woman, eyes closed, face deathly pale, didn't stir. Her lungs barely rose and fell.

"Fear not," a male voice as deep as eternity said from behind Tienan.

Startled, but not afraid, Tienan gazed over his shoulder at a male angel with massive gold wings edged in various shades of purple feathers. Across the angel's forehead ran a band of gold symbols that glistened without the aid of the sun's light. The angel's waist-long, unbound black hair lay in stark contrast to his white, seemingly casual shirt and baggy pants. But what intrigued Tienan most was the angel's shoulder sash where a flickering flame danced brightly over the top of a blood-red teardrop.

Was he hallucinating? Could the drugs in Rowen's body have migrated into him from Zad's aura-meld? Why else would he be imagining such a bizarre looking angel?

"Tienan," the angel said, "you are not hallucinating."

"How did you know—"

"It was obvious from your expression. I have seen it countless times and, before you ask, it is by special dispensation that you are permitted to see me."

My lord Tienan, Zad said, *the angel is qi, unbelievably pure qi.*

"Hello, Adrada," Rowen said.

One of the angel's brows quirked upward. "You know my name?"

"Tal, he told me. Have you come for the lady's soul?" Rowen's voice held bitter sorrow.

"It is not yet her time. She has passed out and requires care."

"I'll go call an ambulance." Tienan struggled to get to his feet, but his legs didn't cooperate.

"Rest a bit, Tienan De'Argossi, and listen to me." A smile nestled in one corner of Adrada's lips. "It is not necessary to summon an ambulance and, knowing her as I do, she would kill herself before allowing you to take her to any hospital for treatment by a physician."

"Then we'll take her to one of our healers."

"An excellent idea, but not now. Take her to your bedroom. Keep her in the darkness for six hours."

"Why?"

"Once you have her in bed, you must lay beside her so Zad can siphon away the residual energy coursing through her and you. Zad must retrieve his power, put himself in balance."

"What about Rowen?"

"There is no residual energy in him or Tal. Go now, I will see Rowen to his bed where he, too, may rest. He has had a rather arduous night."

The angel's tone said his brother had been through one hell of an ordeal. Tienan got up, his bare soles warmed by the sun-glossed pavers beneath his feet. That sun also felt hot on Tienan's naked flesh. He eyed the woman. *Zad, give me a hand. Increase muscle strength so I can pick her up.*

Zad didn't reply.

Zad?

My lord, I don't seem to have energy to give you.

"Allow me." Adrada opened both his hands, palms up. A golden aura formed at this fingertips. In the next instant, the woman's limbs moved, arms crossing her chest, knees tucking up. Her body then rose and floated into Tienan's waiting arms. The weight of the woman nearly sent his knees buckling. She might be slender, but she was solid.

"Wait a moment," Adrada said and went to the woman. His index fingertip glowed, emitting a beam of azure light over the welts on the woman's shoulder and the gargoyle-seared rib. When he doused the light, there was barely a trace of the wounds.

"Amazing," Tienan muttered. A part of him felt awed but another part of him knew he should be afraid of the power this angel had.

"Tormantratas talons are pure darkunskyve," Adrada said. "Like acid, its icy-burn would have doubled every day until she died of the pain." Something gleamed in the angel's ages-old black eyes. "Know, Tienan De'Argossi, that your prayer is answered."

"My prayer? Zantharians don't worship a god or pray to angels."

"You pray to The Power of the Swords, sometimes to The Pure Ones who gave those swords to humankind, do you not?"

Tienan nodded.

"The Great Spirit of Light and Love has a billion-billion names — and forms. Now, go, take her to your bedroom."

As Tienan entered the house and padded across the cold kitchen tiles, he puzzled over the angel's words. His prayer had been answered? What prayer? Ah, yes, of course. He'd prayed Rowen would come home alive.

Only steps from the camouflaged lift in the corner of the kitchen, Tienan realized his warlock's ring didn't pulse to indicate the lift system had activated. He paused, damning the failsafe that prevented children and non-Zantharians access to a house's MS, its Magical Systems.

Trond, he would have to manually override it. No, better not. What if the woman woke? Outsiders were not to know the secrets of Zantharian magic. Gritting his teeth, he strode to the foyer, and took the stairs. With each step down to the bottom floor, the weight in his arms became heavier. Every breath became an effort.

What a burden. *No, this woman was not a burden.* She'd saved Rowen. She was a blessing. He owed her. He would take care of her even if the effort killed him.

Reaching the bottom of the stairs, he turned left. "Open," he commanded. His bedroom door shushed aside. His arm muscles began to cramp, and he hastened to his four-poster bed. After setting the woman on the bed, he grabbed the nearest bedpost to steady himself, to catch his breath, and to let the ache in his arms recede. While he recovered, his gaze alighted on the Templar cross over the woman's heart. It took him two breaths before he became aware that what he stared at was not a tattoo but scar tissue. Who had branded her with that cross? And why?

His gaze rested on the miniatures of her dirks, which stood centered below the cross. They were not scar tissue like the cross but summer-tanned skin.

In his mind's eye, Zad lay, head on his paws, seeing what Tienan saw. The veed whispered, *My lord, do you think the brand and tattoos are the mark of a cult or a coven?*

Hard to say. Unbidden, Tienan glanced at the woman's breasts. He recalled holding those heavy delights during the reunification rite, the areolas puckering, the teats hardening. He felt an erection stir.

A natural reaction. Nothing more.

He studied her pale face. Who was she? What was her name?

Tienan woke to the soft shushing of his bedroom door opening and closing. Rowen walked toward him, a candle-orb in his hand. The orb gave off a soft glow to light his way.

Tienan breathed in the powdery, fruity scent of the woman spooned beside him. That peachy odor, along with remembering she was naked, awakened his penis, which began to swell to attention.

When Rowan got to the bedside, he whispered, "Great, you're awake. How're you doing?"

Tienan's replied in a like whisper, "What time is it?"

"Late afternoon. How's Zad?"

Looking inward, Tienan found Zad, in his noncorporeal lion's form, lying with the tip of his tail curled around to the side of his left front paw. Zad's head rested on both paws, and his eyes were half open.

Zad muttered, *These old bones are fine, my lord.*

You don't have bones.

True enough, my good lord. I am tired, that is all.

"Tienan?" Rowen's brows pinched with worry.

"Zad is fine. He's grumbling he's tired."

Rowen's gaze shifted to the woman. He smiled at Tienan. "The lady fits you well."

Tienan glanced at the woman's naked shoulder peeping out from the black satin quilt. Her words flitted to mind, *I'd sooner slit your GOOL throat than have you ride me.* Followed by *you are a GOOL, as in Guardian of Occult Law.* How had she known he was a GOOL? No one knew, particularly not Rowen—or did he?

"Rowen, what did she tell you about me?"

"Nothing. Why?"

How did he phrase it without giving himself away? "She seems to have a dislike of me."

"Don't think it's personal. She hates GOOLs. Probably with cause."

Had Rowen meant GOOLs or ghouls?

The woman jerked from a muscle spasm in her leg.

Alarmed, Rowen stepped back, whispering, "Is she awake?"

Zad spoke to Tienan and Tienan whispered to Rowen, "Zad assures me she's in a deep sleep, but we might wake her, so let's go outside." Tienan untangled himself from the woman, taking care not to wake her or expose her nakedness to his brother. Tienan padded across the carpet to the closet, donned his velvet robe, then headed through the doorway into his private lounge.

Behind him, Rowen snickered.

Tienan glanced at his brother. "What's so funny?"

"You wearing pajama bottoms."

"I'm a gentleman."

"Yeah, right."

Tienan couldn't keep the exasperation out of his voice. "If you must know, I figured if the woman woke in a strange bed beside a naked man, she would use her dirks first and ask for an explanation later." Actually, he had thought of putting a pair of his pajamas on her but realized that much jostling would wake her and net the same result.

Almost to the fireplace at the far end of the lounge, a wave of nausea hit Tienan. He lunged for the wingback chair and sat down.

"Are you okay?" Rowen turned off the candle-orb and set it on the mantel next to the antique ceramic clock. He took the chair opposite Tienan's.

"I'm a little queasy. Nothing to worry about."

"There's plenty to worry about." Rowen's tone warned that he held pent up anger at bay. When Rowen rested his forearms on the chair's armrests, his fingers took a purchase along the front edge. "How long have you been a Guardian of Occult Law, and when were you going to tell me?"

Confound the powers! Rowen knew. He knew!

Why be evasive, my lord? Zad said. *Rowen obviously resents you keeping your GOOL status a secret from him. Brothers should trust brothers.*

Tienan ignored Zad, but he couldn't ignore the look on Rowen's face. "I take it," Tienan said coldly, "your rescuer told you I was a GOOL?"

"No. I might have been drugged, but I had some sane moments. Tal and I overheard Adrada tell her you were a GOOL. How long have you been a GOOL?"

Before he could censure himself, Tienan replied the standard, "Secrecy is the hallmark of a GOOL." Then he added, "If it had ever become absolutely necessary, I would have told you."

"Which amounts to never." Rowen's lips pursed, confirming his escalating anger.

Guilt put a vise grip on Tienan, reminding him that such anger had sent Rowen out of the house and into the night to become a victim. That must not happen again. He met Rowen's gaze head on. "I joined the year after mother was murdered."

"To avenge her death?"

"Initially. But after a while, it became a matter of seeking closure."

Rowen's anger faded and he relaxed. "Thanks for telling me. And—" His voice mellowed. "I want to apologize for the things I said to you last night. I was wrong."

Rowen apologizing? Zad said. *The universe must be imploding.*

Hush, Zad. "Apology accepted, and I apologize for bellowing at you. I know I'm overprotective—"

Rowen snorted. "That's putting it mildly."

"Rowen, you can't imagine the hell I went through when you didn't come home. You and I are all that's left."

"I know . . . I promise to be more careful."

"So what happened? How did you get kidnapped? How was Tal taken out of you?"

Rowen looked away, to a spot at the back of the fireplace. He frowned in concentration. "Everything's a blur. I hear snatches of witches—lots of them, maybe half a dozen?"

"A coven."

Rowen shrugged. "Don't know. It's all jumbled. I was blindfolded, didn't see faces, just heard voices, the wild chanting."

"Could you recognize any of the voices if you heard them again?"

"I honestly don't think so. I don't know." Frustration flitted over his face, then he frowned. "One thing I do remember. It seems as strange to me now as it did when I realized it."

"What's that?"

"They didn't tie me up."

Tienan recalled the autopsy reports of the other victims. The summaries stated there was no bruising, no evidence of restraints being used, and likely none were needed because of the amount of drugs in the boys' bodies. "Perhaps they figured you were too drugged to go anywhere."

"But I wasn't. The potion faded for some minutes. When I figured that out, come the next reprieve, I pulled off the blindfold. No one was around. I saw the cocoon, heard Tal wail for me, wrapped him in my cloak, which I was lying on, and I headed through some sort of maze of bushes. A door opened. I went down a tunnel." He rubbed his forehead. "I'm getting a headache trying to remember."

"Don't force it. Your memories will come back when the drugs wear off. I'm sure the lady will fill us in, help ID the perps."

Rowen shook his head. "She never saw them. I didn't meet her until she came to that angel statue at the bottom of the hill. Don't recall how I got there, but I was hiding under the statue's wing—" He cleared his throat. "I need to change the subject."

"All right."

"We three have to stay together until the new moon."

"We three?"

"You, me, and the lady."

"Why?"

"Tal is a premature veed birth, and, well—" His face flushed embarrassment red. He stammered, "Tal is, right now, a female."

"What!"

Rowen blurted out, "When Adrada took me to my room, he told me a veed's sex is set in the last hour before coming out of its cocoon. When a veed first enters the cocoon, it reverts to the primal female form so it can transition to adulthood. Gawd, Tienan, who ever heard of a Zantharian male with a female veed? How am I to troth or bond, have kids, or have my veed genate to give my offspring veeds?"

"Don't panic."

"Listen to me! Adrada said Tal can become male when—" Rowen clasped his hands together, as if praying for calm and understanding. "When you and the lady do the unification rite again, but under the darkness of a new moon."

"Again? What do you mean? What went wrong?"

"It wasn't a totally flesh-to-flesh union."

"It was!"

Rowen shook his head. "Adrada said your penis wasn't inside her vagina."

Shock silenced Tienan's mind.

Zad's eyes opened so wide with astonishment that the whites showed.

"She—" Tienan cleared his throat. "She was emphatic that there was to be no sex."

"That's right, no sex, just the insertion of your penis into her. That would have completed the flesh-to-flesh circuit. Since it didn't, instead of the cocoon going inside me, it burst. Tal had to step into me. I'm sort of his cocoon now. Tal needs a proper birthing to be whole."

"Would you like to explain that to the lady? And by the way, *what is her name?*"

Rowen's brow crunched down in concentration. "I don't know."

"What do you mean you don't know? She brought you home."

"I was in and out of my mind because of the drugs. I don't think she ever formally introduced herself." His frown vanished. "Oh, wait. I remember. She said she was a peacekeeper. That makes her Australe." Rowen frowned anew. "She . . . She said she was The Digger of Demon Graves, The Grave Digger."

"What does that mean?"

"I have no idea, but another really weird thing about her is that she summoned the archangel. They talked a lot."

"About what?"

"Not sure. Tal was fading in and out of consciousness like I was. We picked up snatches of what they said. Like everything else, it's more or less a blur."

A long moment passed in silence.

"Tienan. I slept, even had a bowl of soup, but I have to tell you, I'm feeling sick. Sicker by the hour. Tal is barely responsive. I'm worried about him. I want a healer to check us over. You've been in bed more than six hours. If Zad is okay, can we—"

"See a healer?"

Rowen nodded.

"Good idea. Go sit with the lady. If she wakes, reassure her everything is fine. I'll call headquarters, fill them in." He smacked the base of his palm to his forehead. "Confound the powers! I have to call off the search for you."

"You had Guardians searching for me?"

"You were on the list."

"What list?"

My good lord, Zad said, *if you are to have Rowen's trust, tell him the truth. After all, your brother should know if he truly is to appreciate the danger he was in.*

He wanted Rowen's trust. So be it. "The list contained the names of fifteen young warlocks with cocooned veeds due to madl in the next month."

"You GOOLs keep such a list? Why?"

Tienan got to his feet, relieved the room didn't revolve, but his stomach gave a half-lurch. "I've already said too much."

"Stop treating me like a baby! I have a right to know."

Zad muttered, *He has a point, my lord.*

"All right. If you insist, Rowen." Tienan held Rowen's gaze. "Four boys your age are dead. They were kidnapped, raped, their throats slit, their veeds taken. Obviously, you were next."

Rowen paled. "There's a killer out there and you didn't warn me?"

"Couldn't. Headquarters wants this kept quiet to avoid unrest in the Imperial City. We are a colony here. You know our presence at times doesn't set well with the Australes. Think of what would happen if they got wind of a serial killer."

"But no one is killing Australes. They're killing Zantharians. How many more will die before the Guardians alert our people?"

"That's not my call. Look, you got away. With your help, we can stop these perps."

Rowen slumped in his chair, color draining from his cheeks. "I could have been the fifth victim."

Now it registers. "But you weren't, Rowen. You're alive."

"Only because of her." He pointed to the bedroom door. A moment later, he rose from his chair, swayed, and slumped back down. "I think you better have headquarters send someone to come get us."

"Why?"

"I doubt either of us is in shape to drive in rush-hour traffic all the way to the spaceport."

His brother was right. Once upstairs in his study, at his private comlink terminal, the queasiness in Tienan's stomach set off dry retching.

You need a healer, Zad said. *I keep calming your stomach, but it doesn't last.*

I know. Thanks for trying.

You are welcome. My lord?

Yes, Zad?

Although I believed I was fine, I must now admit I am not feeling well. I need a healer too.

❦ Chapter Four

I have no means; I make Docility my means.
— The Samurai Creed

Janay rose out of the fog of slumber so deep, so peaceful that she hated to surface, but the jostling and undulating of the mattress beneath her sent pain radiating from her rebuilt hip.

Was she on a troop carrier?

Opening her eyes, she beheld a black velvet canopy draped over the ebony wood posters of a medieval-sized bed.

Where was she?

Panting grunts were followed by hot breath on her lower belly.

The terror of rape lightninged through her, and she faintly whispered, "Poke!" The dirk didn't come into her hand, but the jostling stopped.

"Trond!" a male voice uttered.

She lowered her gaze to find Poke's hilt protruding from a mass of long dark brown hair that veiled a man's face. Poke's blade tip held steady against the man's Adam's apple.

The man was on all fours, fully dressed in a midnight-blue turtleneck and matching knit pants, the uniform of a Guardian of the Law.

"It's okay," the irate man said. "I'm dressing you. Putting clothes on you, not off. Tell your screwy dagger to back off."

There was something familiar about the voice. "Why are you dressing me?"

"We're going to the hospital. Thought you'd prefer wearing

something instead of being nude."

Hospital! She elbow-ratcheted herself up. "No hospital. Poke!"

The blade was instantly in her palm. She grasped the dirk, twisted her wrist and arm, then rapped Poke's hilt to the side of the man's head.

"Ow!" He reared back from the blow and rocked onto his heels. He swore unintelligible words and rubbed his injury. "Put that thing away."

She held Poke tighter and scooted backward, wincing from the pain of her protesting hip and feeling a twitch where the tormantrata had clawed her back and shoulder. She soon came up against the solid, carved dragon relief on the headboard. Sitting up, she felt the coolness of fabric against her skin. She wore black silk pajamas. Men's pajamas. And skom, the man glaring at her looked familiar. Such dark features . . . the shadow of a beard . . . Tienan? Yes. His name was Tienan and he was—he was— *The GOOL!*

She quickly panned the room from right to left. Black walls. Ebony enameled furniture, Japanese styling. Lighting fixtures hidden behind crown molding. Short black velvet curtains covering high windows above a desk-computer terminal. In the corner, an upholstered black velvet, wingback chair. Everything deathly dark. *Demon warlock dark.*

Poke wiggled out of her hand and vanished.

Why had the blade abandoned her? She glanced about the room again. Quiet. *As restful as night* . . . Maybe Poke thought she wasn't in danger anymore? "This place could use some color." Had she just said that?

Tienan stared at her. In his stony-gray eyes, patience warred with uncertainty. "I rest better in the heart of darkness."

Rowen popped his head around the corner of the open bedroom door. "Boots just called. She's turned the corner by the chapel. I told her to come to the side door—" He glanced at Janay, then back to Tienan. "I see the lady's awake. Better hurry."

With the hardness of steel in her voice, Janay enunciated each of her words. "I am not going to any hospital."

A momentary spark of anger flashed in Tienan's eyes making her aware of how formidable, how determined, a man he was. *A man used to giving orders, not taking them.*

Rowen came to her bedside and spoke in a tone as quiet as the silence found in the eye of a hurricane. "Did you not pledge your soul and care to Adrada's keeping?"

A memory winked of the aftermath of putting Tal back into Rowen. She'd glimpsed Adrada, thought she was as good as dead, and had said *Adrada, I commend my care and soul to thee.* "I thought I was dying."

"You're not dying. At least we don't think so. Can't be sure without someone examining you." Rowen swayed, then sat on the edge of the bed. "Adrada was adamant—Tienan had the care of you."

Who was she to question the archangel? Only— "Why the GOOL's care and not yours?"

"I've no idea. Never thought to ask, but it might have something to do with the three of us staying together for the next few weeks."

"What are you talking about?" She had no intention of remaining in the company of these warlocks for a minute longer than necessary.

Tienan's exasperation crackled in his voice. "Look, lady, we are linked because of the unity ceremony, and we all are sick!" He crawled to the edge of the bed, got to his feet, and clutched the bedpost. "My brother's veed is unresponsive. You've been mangled by gargoyles. Who knows what internal injuries you've got."

"Been busted up worse than this in barrooms. I'm fine. You go to the hospital with Rowen."

Tienan's lips pursed so tight they went white. "Woman, the healers are at Guardian Central, *at the spaceport in Bhutar!*"

Rowen put his fever-warm hand over hers.

Funny, he didn't look feverish. She studied his hand on hers. Maybe it was her hand that was ice cold. That couldn't be good.

"Look at me," Rowen commanded with gentle force.

She obeyed.

"Tal wants to know why you don't like doctors."

"They use drugs. Drugs create madness . . ." Her voice faded. "They'll strap me down, lock the door."

Rowen removed his hand. The ensuing silence was as dark as the room, a room that seemed to be closing in on her.

Tienan shook his head minutely.

Was he having a conversation with his veed?

Suddenly he nailed her with his gaze. "What's your name?"

"I am The Grave Digger. I dig demons' graves."

"Stop that!" Rowen's sharp tone made her wonder if she'd lapsed into being irrational or illogical—or maybe both. Not good.

Was she about to lose control over reality again?

"According to Adrada," Rowen said evenly, "you dig the demon graves, but you can't dig them unless the executioner is with you."

The only executioner of demons she knew was General Tarfooga, and she no longer soldiered for him. "That makes no sense."

Rowen shrugged. "Adrada didn't take time to give details. He only said to tell you *all would be revealed at the proper time.*"

Leave it to Adrada to be cryptic.

Tienan swayed. "We need medical help."

Janay half-shrieked, "I'm not going to a hospital!"

"Yes, you are!" Tienan's voice matched her outburst octave for octave.

"Quit shouting!" Rowen yelled. "This is getting us nowhere."

"Obviously," said the slender, middle-aged woman with dyed mahogany hair who stood with her hip resting against the doorjamb. She wore a midnight-blue, long-sleeved turtleneck top and knit slacks along with a jacket bearing the insignia patch of the Guardians of the Law. The pips on her collar meant she had rank. As she entwined her arms across her chest, a wisp of hair floated down from her topknot.

In turning to face the woman, Tienan swayed and clutched the bedpost with both hands. "When'd you get here?"

"A minute ago. Well, long enough to hear the lady is adamant she won't go to a hospital." The woman's keen hazel-brown eyes studied Janay. "Forgive Tienan his bad manners. My name is Lieutenant Valenteena McMurdy, but everyone calls me Boots." She pointed to her black patent leather half boots which had suede tipped toes. "I'm Tienan's partner."

Janay gritted her teeth. "Another damn GOOL."

Boots leveled a questioning gaze at Tienan.

"She knows who and what we are, but she's been evasive about giving us her name." Tienan glared at Janay, his voice hard-edged. "And we are not the damned!"

"Meaning I am?"

"Ah, ah, ha. Be nice children." Boots came into the room. "People who are sick often snap at one another, so everyone take a long, slow breath. Now, I, by rank of seniority, hereby order you, Tienan, and you, Rowen, to the van. Get going."

"I'm all for that." Rowen stood up, took a moment to steady himself, regained his equilibrium, and left.

The room began to spin and a second before the darkness overtook her, Janay heard Tienan say, "Bless the powers, she's finally passed out."

Janay woke with a headache thumping at her temples interspersed with razor-sharp flashes whizzing across her brow. She quickly took in her surroundings. She lay on the carpeted floor in the back of a van, a van that reeked with the faint orange-oil scent of air freshener. Her shoulders rested against the back seat. Despite being bundled in the black quilt that she remembered had been on the four-poster bed, she felt as cold as when on arctic maneuvers.

By the commotion behind her, the voices, and the rocking of the van, Rowen and Tienan were disembarking with the help of medical personnel.

Skom, they had taken her to a hospital! She sat up, tucking herself in a corner, shivering, feeling bile rise along with flashbacks of the asylum.

The back doors of the van opened, and the parking garage lights shed a gray pallor across Boots' face. Beside her, an emaciated-faced man held a medical diagnostic wand in one hand and a hyposprayer in the other.

No doctor was going to tranquilize her! She tossed the blanket back and sat straighter. "To hand, to hand." Both Poke and Fox instantly obeyed.

Seeing the dirks, the doctor backed a step.

"Curse the powers," Boots muttered, then more loudly she said to Janay, "It's all right. He's a healer."

"Bullshit." Janay loosed Poke at the hand holding the hyposprayer.

When the blade sliced the hyposprayer in half, the drugs it contained splattered over the man's flesh and onto his medical jacket. Wide-eyed, he gaped at Poke. The dirk slid up his sleeve, twirling, wiping the drugs off itself, did a back flip, and returned to Janay's hand.

The terrified man dropped what was left of the hyposprayer, and it clattered to the cement. Guardians in uniform rushed forward. Two of them grabbed the man and bustled him behind the van.

Boots turned, facing a Guardian-uniformed man who held a rodgun. "Put that away and back off."

The man reluctantly nodded and retreated out of Janay's line of sight.

Boots turned to Janay, but her focus was on the dirks.

"If you're trying to figure out how to get these away from me," Janay said, "forget it. No one touches a twice-blessed dirk that doesn't want to be touched."

Boots nodded ever so slightly. "You're ill. Getting sicker by the minute. But, have it your way. I'll wait until you pass out."

"I might pass out, but the blades will stand guard and you'll never touch me."

"Boots!" came a woman's sharp command. "Stand aside."

"Neejera. Bless the powers, it's you." Boots stepped aside.

Into Janay's view came a slim, gray-haired woman whose short cropped hair lay close about her oval face. She wore a witch-black pantsuit and around her neck dangled a modest silver medallion along with two gray-silver chains. She walked with a cane that had a small, beribboned bouquet of silk daisies tied just below the curve of the handle.

"You're just the person we need," Boots said.

"No doubt, you ruffian. So much for my going home at a descent hour. Now, be off with you and do keep the boys and girls back. I want no fracas or distractions."

Boots backed out of sight. Voices soon whispered like buzzing bees before feet shuffled away. Silence ensued, except for the patter of Neejera's rubber-tipped cane that marked her progress toward the van's bumper. When she stopped, she placed both hands on the top of her cane. Her entire body glowed with a milky whiteness. "I am Neejera Nagva. I am a Zantharian Witch, a Priestess Healer of the Eight Power. Even from here I feel your turmoil and the pain pounding in your head."

"Bully for you."

Something flashed deep behind the witch's pale blue eyes. A second later, she nodded, and a comma-curl of a smile settled in the corners of her wrinkled lips. "I have no hyposprayer or medical wand, nor anything medicinal on my old person. My ring —" She lifted her hand and flashed the large silver ring where an onyx cabochon was surrounded by a circle of tiny gold leaves. "The golden rune in the center is called nyd, for endurance, survival, destiny — the hallmark of an Eighth Power Zantharian

Witch. The ring is solid, no hidden reservoir of powder or potion. Make no mistake, I intend to touch your left wrist, and my veed will not permit you to slice my hand off nor puncture any part of me."

"And just why should I let you touch me?"

"To pull away your pain so you can think rationally."

"I think your touch will knock me out."

"I am a healer. I heal. Wouldn't you like that headache to vanish?" There was utter sincerity in her voice.

But a witch was a witch.

Never trust a witch.

With each passing second, Janay's headache intensified toward a blackout migraine. She would likely wake drugged and restrained. So, logically, the witch's offer was the lesser evil. Still, no sense in giving in too easily. "If you lie, you die."

"Fair enough." Neejera set her cane at the corner of the door. "By the way, what shall I call you?"

The Digger of Demon Graves. No, not that. "Janay. My name is Janay Cholyn."

Neejera leaned into the van. Her left hand settled on the carpeting for balance before she reached for Janay's wrist with her other hand.

Although fear skittered along every nerve, Janay didn't shrink back. Instead, she tightened her grip on Poke and Fox.

The woman's gentle, warm fingers slipped under the thin pajama sleeve cuff. A second later, heat raced into Janay's veins. Her headache eased and faded away. When Neejera removed her hand, she sat on the carpeted floor, her back to Janay, and gazed into the garage area. "You, there." She pointed to someone on the left. "Yes, you. Come here."

A long-haired blond beauty, dressed in maroon slacks and a ribbed knit sweater, came forward. She clutched a maroon leather satchel-purse in one hand.

"What's your name, dear?" Neejera said, her voice gentle yet commanding.

"Adesko." The woman cleared her throat. "Ioni Adesko, ma'am, second assistant to the senior advocate."

"Ioni, dear, do you know who I am?"

"Oh, yes. You're the greatest healer in the quadrant."

"Tsk, tsk, such flattery."

Ioni looked flabbergasted. "I didn't mean to—"

"It's all right. I do not consider myself the greatest. Good, definitely. Perhaps a little great, but not the greatest. Now, I know you were probably on your way home, but could you spare a few minutes? I need a quick favor."

"Yes, ma'am. Just ask."

"Go to the cafeteria and fetch me a glass, no make it a carafe, of maleet juice and a jigger of sugar."

"Yes, ma'am." She hurried off.

Neejera turned to Janay. "Your blood sugar is quite low. I'll mix the sugar into the maleet juice, and you will drink as much as you can."

"Any chance of getting a jigger of DeLupian whiskey into it?"

Her old eyes danced with mirth. "Definitely not today."

"And how much tranquilizer are you going to sneak into the maleet?"

"Not a drop. You don't need a tranquilizer. The only thing wrong with you is exhaustion, muscular exertion, and residual pain from some old injury to your right hip. You are more in need of food and rest than anything else."

"You deduced all that from a touch?"

She leaned toward Janay and, in a conspiratorial whisper, said, "I am the greatest healer in the quadrant."

Janay struggled not to smile, but she would err on the side of caution. She would wait and see what happened with the maleet juice.

❦ Chapter Five

I have no magic power; I make personality
my Magic Power. — *The Samurai Creed*

Two days later, Janay woke in Tienan's bedroom, lying in his black four-poster bed, spooned next to him, wearing another pair of his black pajamas, but they were of a loose mesh weave.

In his corporeal form, Zad faced her. His black eyelids were closed, his energy-heat wafting warmth that surrounded her. He softly purred.

No, not purring. The sound reminded her of a puttering little motor. A pleasant sound. Relaxing. Reassuring.

Tienan sputtered a gurgling-snore into her right ear. One of his arms pillowed her head, the other rested across her belly.

Oddly enough, each time she laid beside this man, this warlock, this GOOL, she felt uncommonly safe. *Protected.*

Which was downright ridiculous.

But considering the past few days, what harm was there in enjoying a few minutes of respite from the world? Enjoying a bit of solitude? Peace of heart?

She placed her hand over Tienan's and closed her eyes, sighing and savoring the spooning, including the warm scent of the man. Only her thoughts didn't silence. They drifted back to her being at Guardian Headquarters.

Fifteen minutes after she drank the sugary maleet juice, she'd felt well enough to get in an antigrav-chair and follow Neejera to a very private corner cubical in the hospital wing. Another blond with long hair, but packing many more pounds, brought in a tray of stew and thick slices of heavily buttered toast.

Janay remembered wolfing down the food while she watched the goings on in the exam room across from hers. Neejera said Rowen would likely never remember what happened to him because of the high dose of drugs that he'd been given. Then she'd promptly diagnosed Rowen as suffering morning sickness. He puked on that revelation. As to Tienan, the healer diagnosed him with frazzled nerves. She pronounced his veed exhausted, and ordered Zad to something called a "sun chamber" to reenergize.

Janay then watched a ball of swirling light pop out of Tienan's forehead and morph into a huge, snow-white lion with ebony kohl markings rimming his eyes and a black, nappy mane. In his corporeal form, Zad's muscles rippled with regal pride, and he soon exited the room. It was one of those moments when reality seemed stranger than fiction. She'd been too surprised to question or comment.

Another image flared—of Neejera eyeing test results on a monitor, shaking her head, then ordering the three of them to go immediately to The Black Room. That didn't set well with Tienan's commander—one Uzanna Dag, a slight woman with a general's commanding presence. Dag demanded statements from the three. Neejera invoked her authority as Chief Medical Officer. Dag argued but, in the end, conceded.

Another image surfaced—The Black Room. Black walls, black ceiling, black everything, including the bedding on the row of black cots. A room much like a cheap version of Tienan's bedroom. When the doors shut, the lights went out. Strangely enough, the silent blackness brought with it a tranquility she'd never experienced before and a deep, restorative sleep.

By noon the next day, the endless questioning ended, they signed their statements, and the three left. It was a silent return to Wolcott House because none of them wanted to talk about the ramifications of the unity spell. According to Neejera, and the experts she'd consulted, no precedence existed for a veed surviving outside its cocoon nor for one cocooning inside a host's abdomen. Tests indicated Rowen was going through an accelerated natural pregnancy. Rowen almost fainted at that pronouncement. Speculation had, of course, ensued about the ways Rowen might give birth to Tal.

Recalling Tienan's horrified expressions at each revolting scenario, Janay softly giggled.

"Hush, Janay," Zad whispered. "Sleep."

She let the grin fade and listened to Zad's purr become a deep, lullaby-like rhythm plucked as if on the strings of a bull-fiddle. She recognized the tune. It was the one that had calmed her in The Black Room after her dirks had gone berserk. Other memories flitted of that room . . .

Rowen had taken the single cot closest to the bathroom in case he had to puke. Tienan had gone to the middle of the row of cots. She'd headed for the far end, the farthest from the guys as she could get. That's when her dirks appeared in front of her. They pointed their blade ends at her. Although she ignored them, they frantically struck each other's tips, setting off tiny sparks, and advancing toward her. They'd never done that before.

Tienan folded the blanket back on his cot and then glanced at the dirks. "What are they doing?"

"Beats me." She backed a step. "Poke, Fox, scoot. Go play somewhere else." She was about to take a step forward when the two broke apart and came at her, tips first.

Alarmed, she backed and backed until she bumped into Tienan who wrapped his arms around her, pinning her arms to her sides and ordered, "Zad, meld."

Zad's aura covered Tienan and her.

Always before she'd done the protecting. Now she was the one being shielded, protected. It was a strange sensation physically and a puzzling one mentally, but Zad's aura-shield stopped the dirks.

She turned her attention to the dirks. "Poke, explain."

Poke turned to Fox. Using the flat of her blade against the flat of Fox's, she tapped out a message. NEED. VEED. SLEEP.

Janay's voice held the hard edge of her frustration. "What kind of message is that?"

Poke repeated the message.

"What are they saying?" Tienan eased his hold on her.

"*Need. Veed. Sleep.* They just keep repeating those three words."

"Do they need to sleep with Zad?"

"Poke, Fox, is that what you want? To sleep with Zad?"

Tapping.

"Make sense. I don't understand."

More tapping. J SLEEP WITH Z HOST.

"J? Do you mean Janay is to sleep with Zad's host?"

"What?" Tienan blurted out.

"Don't interrupt, GOOL!"

Tienan growled deep in his throat but remained silent.

"Poke, Fox, do you mean for me to sleep with Tienan?"

YES.

"I am not sleeping with him."

YOU DIE.

A chill ran through her.

"Janay, what's the matter?" Concern resonated in Tienan's whisper.

Janay ignored Tienan. "Poke, repeat."

The blade clicked away.

Skom, she hadn't misunderstood.

"Janay," Tienan whispered, "what's the problem?"

"It seems I will die if I don't sleep with you."

"Is this their idea of a joke?"

She again ignored him. "Poke, I don't want to sleep with Tienan."

MUST OR DIE. MUST OR DIE. MUST OR DIE.

"How will I die?"

The dirks floated apart and were silent.

"Answer me." Janay fought her rising ire with the dirks.

The dirks did an about face, putting their backsides to her.

"Great. Now you won't speak to me?"

Zad's energy began to fade. When it was gone, she felt bereft.

The dirks did an about face.

"Janay." Tienan's voice held uncertainty. "Maybe your dirks are just tired and cranky."

"Kids get cranky, dirks don't."

More emphatically he said, "Whatever it is, it's likely temporary. We're all tired. Why don't we push two of the cots together and worry about this later?"

And that's what they did. Only she ended up snuggled against Tienan on his bed. The craziest thing was, she had slept without stirring, without waking to the fear that the tormantratas were about, which she did far too many nights after being stressed. And, as silly as it struck her now, she'd felt as safe as if Adrada himself held her.

No, it was more than that.

Other memories winked to life. When they'd gotten back to Wolcott House, Rowen had gone to his suite. It was when Tienan decided he would take a nap in the easy chair in his study that her dirks had once again done the hack-slash routine and tapped out

T SLEEP WITH J. Tienan had scowled at the idea.

"Fine," she'd told the dirks, "but first I have to make a call. Let Tienan go to bed. I'll join him. Word of honor."

Tienan began to protest, but she silenced him with, "GOOL, do you really want to argue with my dirks?"

"No, but this sleeping together has got to stop."

"Agreed. And, as much as you're the last man in the empire I'd choose to have under my covers, the dirks are intelligent life forms. Let me make my call and maybe get an idea of how to deal with them."

Tienan relented, and she called General Tarfooga. He was out in the field on maneuvers and wouldn't be back for days. She left a message for him to contact her ASAP and then had taken a nap with Tienan. They'd laid back to back in his enormous bed, yet she'd found herself longing to be held in the warmth of his arms. Which was ridiculous.

Then, last night, when she figured to sleep in the guestroom, the dirks had again gone berserk. Now it was another day. Another day of being in Tienan's bed and again questioning a need to be held. But what also struck her as crazy-odd was enjoying Zad's nearness.

With Tienan's next snore, she found herself wide awake.

Zad's eyes opened.

She put a finger to her lips. "Shhh." After slipping over the veed and out of the bed, she made her way into the adjoining lounge. The plush black carpet muffled her footsteps.

Zad belly-crawled off the bed and followed her on silent paws.

Automatically, the wall sconces turned on, illuminating the lounge with a soft light. Although she'd only glimpsed the room yesterday, she padded slowly forward, taking a better look around. The lustrous parquet floor was cool beneath her bare feet.

Light mirrored on the mantel and framing around the fireplace that was coal-black stone. Variegated gray marble bricks radiated around the hearth. A fluffy white bearskin pelt lay between two satin-striped, wingback chairs. Except for the plush burnt-orange upholstery on the chairs, everything in the room was decorated in Japanese style—heavy on the black lacquer, resplendent splashes of gold, silver, and red dragons along with cherry trees and cherry blossoms.

Turning, she spotted a display of five katanas on the far wall near the doorway to the game room. Curiosity had her going to the display. Above the swords set a large, framed parchment. On the left side were Japanese kanji and, obviously, on the right, in Earth Standard, was the translation. The title, *The Samurai Creed*, had been done in glossy black, brush-script letters.

Janay lowered her gaze to the swords, which were arranged from top to bottom, smallest to largest. Each had a brass plate engraved with the sword's name and historic data. The bottom one, the oldest katana, beckoned her touch.

After examining the exquisite detail of the dark stingray skin on the grip and the hilt guard's decorative oval plate, she ran a fingertip down the length of the wooden scabbard. A moment later, she pulled the weapon out, the sound a soft kiss when the blade slipped from its sheath.

The *nakago*, the metal piece that attached the sword blade to the handle, held the Japanese sword tester's results. An image flared of that sword tester taking the blade and cutting through the bodies of corpses—or soon-to-be corpses—starting with the small bones of the body and moving on to the larger ones. This blade was marked as a three-body blade, one perfectly balanced, deceptively powerful.

Gripping the katana with both hands, she swung the weapon slowly, reverently.

Cut . . .

Down . . .

Upward . . .

Tienan woke to a draft across his chest and the feeling that Zad was out of his body. Janay wasn't in his bed, and the door stood open to the lounge, the light on.

He spotted Zad perched on the black lacquered chest, the one with red dragons slithering about the edges. Ears pricked, tail laid straight along his side, the tail's dreadlock tips dripping over the chest's side, Zad stared enthralled by something in the direction of the fireplace.

What was going on out there?

Tienan quit his bed and stopped on the threshold of the lounge doorway. What held Zad's attention was Janay prancing in the open area on the other side of the white bearskin rug. Holding a katana in both hands, she performed a kata. He knew the second she dropped into *zenshin,* being one with the sword.

When she made a graceful pirouette, she saw him and stopped so abruptly that she twisted her hip. She swore, hobbled back to the rack, and sheathed the sword. "Sorry. I couldn't resist. It's a fine weapon."

It took him a moment to get his wits organized. "You handle that katana like a pro."

"I know basics. I'm better with a dirk." She looked about the room, glancing at the various cabinets. "Having all these Japanese samurai weapons and stuff, are you any good with the swords?"

He shook his head. "I only collect them." He went to the tall lacquered cabinet, unobtrusively passed his warlock ring before the locking sensor, and opened the doors. A light winked on, spotlighting a complete set of samurai warrior armor encased by glass. "This is my most prized acquisition."

Janay came over, her limp barely noticeable. "Impressive. Is it real or a reproduction?"

"Real. Dates to around 1855." Unbidden he added, "I've always been fascinated by the samurai's honor, their code of dignity, their unflinching ability to face death."

"Accept your death and there is nothing more to fear."

He nodded. "Do you fear your own death?" Why had he asked that?

She hugged herself. "Not since Rathe."

"Rathe?"

"A peacekeeper action. I understood it was the leading news story for months. Surely you heard about it?"

Snatches of news headlines whispered to him. "Hallucinogens—airborne hallucinogens made a brigade of peacekeepers think they were fighting demons."

Bitterness sharpened her voice. "That's what you and your GOOL buddies want the public to think." She blinked as if hellish memories flickered, then whispered, "Demon beasts the karsks, but not as vile as Qtalq, the white bull. *The Eater of Souls.*" Her expression shifted, unreadable. Then she eyed him with a frown between her dark brows. "Do you see yourself as a samurai warrior?"

He would take the hint for a change of subject. "When I was a child, it beat being a knight." Now why had he revealed that? "What did you want to be when you grew up?" Why had he asked that?

"I wanted to be an ice skater. Hey, don't look so shocked." An impish smile crossed her lips. "I spent three years applying myself to the sport only to discover I hated freezing my ass every morning. My saving grace was being introduced to karate. I was a natural at it."

"And the dojo was warm?"

She chuckled. "Oh, definitely! Stinky too."

Zad hopped off his perch, morphed into his white ball of energy, shrank to the size of a marble, and leapt. His arc took him into Tienan's forehead.

Janay almost gasped. "Holy Mother of Mercies! Does that hurt?"

"No. It's the usual way veeds move in and out of their hosts." At headquarters, he'd discussed her exposure to veeds with Commander Dag. It had been agreed that since Janay held such a high military security clearance, she could be trusted with knowledge of Zantharians. After all, they couldn't afford to have her deceived by warlocks or witches, and she had to remain in protective custody until Tal birthed. "Janay, I assure you Zad's transfer is normal and painless."

"But, Zad's so— Huge."

"He's about average for his type."

"Average? A meter tall is average?"

Tienan nodded. "Actually, Zad is over a meter tall when in his corporal form outside my body. When he's in his noncorporeal form, the form he takes in my mind, he's only three finger's tall, if that."

She stared at him in disbelief. "And the marble-sized ball thing?"

"His condensed energy form. Zad can appear in my mind's eye in that ball form, but it's pea-sized."

"Does he take other forms?"

"Veeds are limited to only the ball, the noncorporeal, and the corporeal forms."

"Weird." She shook her head and walked back to the katanas. "Really, really, weird."

He closed the armor cabinet, locking the doors with a reverse pass of his ring.

"Jeez, Rowen!" Janay said. "Don't sneak up on a person like that."

Tienan turned.

A pale-faced Rowen stood in front of where the lift was

hidden. Rowen held a plate with two meat-stuffed sandwiches and three individual sized jugs of milk. Fear mirrored in Rowen's eyes. "Tienan, we're in deep shit. Silence called. She's on her way over. She'll be here in ten minutes, maybe less."

Tienan felt his heart skip a beat. "She mustn't see you in your condition."

"I know. I'll be in my room with the door locked." Rowen exited by way of the game room door.

"Hey, guys," Janay said. "Who's Silence?"

Tienan ignored her and headed for his bedroom, relieved and thankful that his brother hadn't used the secret, connecting passage from the lounge to his own suite of rooms.

After quickly donning a clean uniform, he came out of his walk-in closet and found Janay standing with her shoulder against the doorjamb, a scowl on her face.

"Who's Silence," she said, "and why the panic?"

"Silence is our grandmother, our mother's mother. Silence makes it her business to keep an eye on me and Rowen. She never approved of my becoming a Guardian — and she must never know I've become a GOOL or find out Rowen is pregnant. I'll get rid of her, you just — "

"Keep mum, stay put, and be quiet?"

"Exactly." Tienan left and took the stairs two at a time to get upstairs. He couldn't risk revealing the lift or any of the other hidden features in his house to Janay.

As he stepped into the foyer, the door's chime softly pealed.

His grandmother had arrived.

❦ Chapter Six

*I have neither life nor death; I make A Um
my Life and Death.* — *The Samurai Creed*

When Tienan opened the front door, Sabrina 'Silence'
Tomosukovia stepped into the grand foyer with a smile on her
glossed lips and the usual, "Good afternoon, Tienan, dear boy."

"Welcome, Grandmother." He eyed the tooled leather
portfolio tucked under her arm and instantly recalled the reason
for her visit. They were to go over her plans for re-landscaping
Wolcott Manor.

Confound the powers! He'd put off this meeting with her
twice. What excuse could he give to send her away now?

Silence paused and proffered her cheek.

As he whisper-kissed that cheek, he caught the musky scent
of her makeup and the citric blend of her cologne. "New perfume,
Grandmother?"

"No, dear boy, it's one I haven't worn for awhile. It's *Flowers
Of Heaven* by Dashaar."

Dashaar. Had to be him. He blended fragrances for society's
elite, and Silence considered herself the elitist of the elite.

Silence headed for Tienan's study with her usual, queenly
grace.

Always impeccably dressed. Today in a tailored burgundy
pantsuit. Demure diamond earrings glimmered beneath the
feathered tips of her short, platinum-gray hair. Diamond chips
also twinkled around the wide wrist-com bracelet she wore.

Elegance and manners, beauty and passion were her forte, but the elegance was cold steel. The passion always directed to wielding power. Commanding. Demanding. And this year relentlessly insisting Wolcott Manor's landscape be updated.

He followed her to his study, where she set her portfolio on his desktop. "How soon before Rowen joins us?"

Tienan blurted out, "He's not coming."

"Oh? Why not?"

He grabbed the first idea that came to mind. "He's recovering from a hangover." Which wasn't far from the truth. Maybe he could make this quick and simple. "Grandmother, I have a busy schedule, so let's get to those drawings, shall we?"

She canted her head, her sharp hazel-going-on-brown gaze studying him. "As you wish." She took a seat.

He pulled his chair over beside hers.

Half an hour later, Tienan had to rein in his irritation. Five large drawings of possible landscape designs littered his desk.

Silence pulled out design number six.

How was he to send her on her way?

"Dear boy, this is the last one. You may find it a very pleasing color scheme." There was a hint of pleasure in her voice.

She placed the drawing in front of him, fussing a little to get the edges straight.

Was this the one she favored? He focused on the rendering to make it look as if he carefully scrutinized the design. Any of the proposals would do, but to Silence? No. Only the best would do. Which meant, this likely was the most costly, the one most likely to bankrupt the De'Argossi fortunes and turn the place into a Hautonne showplace.

A screeching scream caterwauled throughout the house, setting the hairs prickling over Tienan's entire body. He bounded to his feet. Without having to ask, Zad keened his senses to hyper-awareness. A second scream rent the air, and mingled with it came Janay's "Demon!"

Had a gargoyle made it into the house? Was it after Rowen or Janay?

Silence seemed frozen to the spot, her face deathly pale, eyes widening with shock. She faintly whispered, "Liss?"

Zad morphed into his noncorporeal form inside Tienan's mind's eye. *My lord Tienan, Liss is not in Silence. If Janay has seen Liss – *

She wouldn't know the difference between a veed and a demon. With dread clutching his heart, he sprinted for the study's camouflaged lift. Hand raised, his warlock ring triggered the sensor and, a stride later, he stepped into the tube. He punched control tiles, one to get him to the lounge, another for emergency speed, and one to turn on every light downstairs.

The lift door revolved closed and he felt the drop. When the door opened, he entered an empty lounge.

Thrashing and thumps came from his bedroom. Another scream. This one nearly split his eardrums. *Zad, end keen before I lose my hearing!*

Zad obeyed, and Tienan's hearing returned to normal.

Tienan raced for his bedroom and slid to a halt a step inside the room.

Janay was on the floor at the foot of the bed, tangled in the bed clothes, growling and swearing, trying to free herself.

Hearing scratching and grating noises by his closet, he found Liss, his grandmother's Dragryphon Veed, crucified to the wall. At the joint where the veed's feathered wings attached to her body, Janay's dirks had gone hilt deep. Liss struggled to balance on her hind lion's feet. The golden talons of her front bird legs swatted at the dirks but her reach was too short to claw them. Her lion's tail lay tight between her hind legs, the silver-gray tip flattened to her golden-haired chest just below her neck feathers. Terror blackened Liss's eyes, making her beaked face look demonic.

"I'll dig your grave, demon!" Janay crawled away from the covers, heading for Liss.

"No!" Tienan grabbed Janay around the waist. He hoisted her to her feet, turning her until she faced him. Not easy to do with her intent on getting to the veed.

Liss silenced and stopped struggling. "Help me, Lord Tienan. Please! Help me."

"Demon!" Janay raked both hands through her curly hair, a futile attempt to clear the curls dangling before her eyes.

"Wake up!" Tienan commanded. "It's not a demon. It's a veed."

"I'm awake. It's ugly. Demon."

"No, Janay—VEED!"

"That demon-veed was under my blanket."

"What?"

Her words came out in spastic breaths. "That ugly thing—put its face—between my legs. It poked my vagina."

"Confound the powers . . ." He drew her close to him in a hug. "It's okay. I'm here. You're safe. Hush, sweet Janay, hush. Calm down."

She put her forehead against his chest. To either side of his waist, her hands grabbed fistfuls of his knit shirt and held them tightly. He couldn't be sure she was crying, but he was sure she was shaking.

She filled her lungs with air and slowly let the breath out, which ended her shakes.

Her head came up, her hands let go of his shirt, and she stepped back. Her wet lashes rose and her dark brown eyes held a plea for understanding. "I dozed off."

She swallowed as if to down the last of her fright. "Got woke by a draft on my feet. Then came this cold feathery sensation at my ankles. I saw this huge blob under the covers. Thought I was dreaming. I summoned Poke and hit the blob with the hilt." She pushed a wayward curl off her brow. "One minute I was in the bed, next, the sheet under me was jerked, and I was pulled over the footboard. I—I cracked my head on the damn footboard." She touched the lump on her head and scowled. "The demon threw the bedclothes off and dumped them on me, but I saw it—an ugly, ugly thing. I ordered the dirks to get it away from me."

Out of the corner of his eye, Tienan caught movement. Silence stood by the lounge-bedroom doorway, clutching the doorjamb with both hands, staring incredulously at Liss splayed against the closet wall.

He asked the question that popped into his mind. "Grandmother, what is your veed doing in my bedroom?"

Her gaze flitted from dirk to dirk, but she didn't look at him. "I don't know."

He demanded. "*Why is Liss out of you?*"

"We were behind schedule this morning. Liss didn't have time to energize properly. When I arrived here, I freed her to use your pentagram and sate her need. I didn't require Liss to discuss the landscaping plans with you. It was safe to let her reenergize. After all, *we are family.*"

Janay faced Silence. "She lies."

It was an unemotional statement, but Silence's body language shifted. She let go of the doorjamb and stood like a queen on a throne, facing Janay with imperial audacity.

He'd seen that posture too many times in his life. The Dowan of Hautonne Tomosukovia was about to deliver a stinging putdown.

Tienan stepped to Janay's side. For a second, he wondered who he was trying to shield—Janay or himself—from his grandmother's coming wrath.

"What did you just say?" The tone of Silence's voice seemed to drop the room's temperature thirty degrees.

Janay didn't flinch. "I said you lie. And stop with the hiss and spit. You might think yourself the lioness, but I assure you, I've stood before ferines and those guard-cats are the only ones worth fearing when they have a hissy fit."

By the powers! How could Janay be so oblivious to the fury escalating in Silence's eyes?

Silence squared her shoulders.

My lord, Zad said, *how does Janay know Silence is lying?*

Janay chuckled derisively, but never took her gaze off Silence. "Ah, so, you ask yourself, old woman, how do I know you lie?" The military timbre in Janay's voice was unmistakable. "Because the pentagram is at the opposite end of the house from the study—*on high ground.* To get to this bedroom, *which is below ground,* your demon-veed had to go around the house to the side, where the hill drops away, and use the lounge entrance. That entrance faces north, between the trees, below the bank, in shadows. There isn't diddly in the way of sunshine to reenergize anything out there."

Silence didn't waiver. "Don't be ridiculous. Release my veed at once!"

Janay stepped away from Tienan and faced Liss.

Fear and uncertainty mirrored in the veed's black eyes. Its trembling lower jaw suddenly clamped shut.

Waiting in fear are you beast? Janay took two steps forward. "Those dirks are mine to command, demon-veed."

"Stop calling my veed a demon!" Silence ordered. "Liss is a noble Behringgreat and deserves respect."

"Demon is as demon does," Janay replied, not looking at the woman but noting she turned her glare on Tienan.

"Grandmother . . ." Tienan's tone cautioned.

"I will have your witch-whore banned from every coven in the land if she does not immediately release Liss!"

Janay chuckled, not knowing which was funnier, her being thought a true witch or her being called Tienan's witch-whore.

"Blasphemous bitch, no one laughs at the Dowan Mazen Magestrata of Coven Ozieron!"

Ah, the intimidation tactic of invoking her illustrious title. Well, it wouldn't work. Not to someone who had stood before the fury of generals, even the ill temper of Fadis Riboji, Emperor of all

Triangulum Australe. But desperation made people do rash things, say rash things, didn't it? "I laugh at your words, not you, old woman."

"Old?" Silence's temper flash-fired her words. "*Tienan!* Order her to release my veed this instant!"

"Tienan has no power over me nor my blades and, if you do not immediately shut up, I will dig the blades deeper into your demon-veed and sever its wings."

Silence's cheeks went rose-red with fury. "You wouldn't dare!"

"Grandmother." Tienan's voice pulsed with conviction edged with indignation. "Don't provoke Janay into doing something we all will regret."

Silence silenced.

Now it was time for truth or dare. "Demon-veed," Janay said, "if you lie to me, my dirks will know, and they will slice off your wings." She had no idea if Poke or Fox could determine truth or lies in veeds, but it was worth the bluff if it worked. "What were you doing in Tienan's quarters?"

The veed did not look at its host but kept its gaze on Janay. Something like pain flashed momentarily in its eyes.

"The truth . . ." Liss's voice quivered with fear — or maybe pain. "The truth is that I did not require more energy. I was doing Her Grace's bidding, as I always do when visiting Wolcott House."

"And what exactly does your host always bid you do when you're here?"

"Search Tienan's suite."

Tienan sucked in a breath but said nothing.

"What were you looking for?" Janay caught the slight twist of both Fox and Poke.

Liss's reaction to the pain was to minutely shudder and briefly close her eyes. Her words rushed out. "First I was looking for any items in his collection or furnishing which would allow ladies to flatter his ego and make themselves look desirable as a mate."

"What ladies?" Janay did not regret giving in to her curiosity.

"The daughters of the Ladies of the Inner Circle of Ozieron, ones who will attend the Sahhar Ball."

Tienan swore but abruptly stopped. "Grandmother, did your snooping result in half a dozen women at last year's ball dressing in Japanese gowns, the sides slit up to their waists?"

"Tienan, dear boy—"

"Don't *dear boy* me. I'm a full grown man capable of finding my own women!"

Anger belched out of Silence. "You're thirty-five and you haven't trothed or even bonded. You haven't begot a child to carry on the De'Argossi line." She took a deep breath, puffing up her chest, standing as regally as an empress, and used her Olympian voice. "It is your duty to the family to see that there is another generation."

"I know my duty."

"Oh, yes, to the Guardians! Since you became a lieutenant, you do not take tea with me anymore, you do not circulate in society, you do not attend coven. You have become a stranger." She took in another deep breath. "Do not scowl at me, Tienan. Yes, I took the initiative to find suitable females so you might fall in love with one and troth, but you have not!"

"So you have Liss burglarize my home to justify that end?"

"I'll do whatever it takes to insure the line."

"Ah, folks," Janay said, "airing the family laundry is lamentable, but I'm a tad curious what the demon-veed was looking for on today's recon mission in Tienan's bedroom."

Liss quickly replied, "To see if Tienan had been entertaining guests — male or female. Hopefully female. We, that is Her Grace and I, we feared Tienan to be homosexual."

Tienan swore words Janay had never heard before.

He glared at his grandmother. "I am not gay."

Silence seemed relieved.

Liss then said, "When I heard snoring, I came to see who was in Tienan's bed. First I was delighted to find you, a female. Pretty of face. A bit slight. You wore Tienan's pajamas. The room held your feminine scent mingled with his."

"And you just had to put your snout between my legs to sniff me and be sure we'd had sex?" That idea set Janay's temper to a quick roil.

"Yes."

"And you got yourself a good whiff, did you?"

"No! You hit me on the head. I panicked. I tried to get away. The daggers, they slammed into me, pinned me to the wall. Please, dear lady, I did you no harm. Please, let me go."

"No harm?" She could still feel the demon-veed's touch on the insides of both her thighs, the feathery sensation skittering clear down to her knees. And there was a prickling on her vaginal mound and a tingling deeper between the labia folds. Maybe those sensations were psychosomatic, a way for her mind to emphasize how violated she felt.

Tienan came over to Janay. "Release Liss. I want her and my grandmother out of my house."

Silence stepped forward, but the scowl Tienan sent her made her halt.

"You forget your place, Tienan."

"On the contrary, Grandmother, it is you who have forgotten your place and who I am." His voice turned glacier cold. "I am Archdruid of the Second House Hautonne, the Suzerain of De'Argossi. My title is Lord and you will address me as such from now on."

In scathing tones, Silence replied, "Who is this scrawny witch that has inveigled herself into your bed and into doing her bidding?"

Like a katana being slowly unsheathed, a smile appeared on Tienan's lips. "She is Janay Cholyn. She is—" His pause filled the room with the silence of a blade raised for the kill. "My familiaris."

Both of Silence's hands went to her chest. Her face blanched as platinum as her hair. Her breaths choked. Yet she managed a softly spoken, "You can't mean that. You wouldn't. You couldn't."

"Janay. Is. My. Familiaris." Each word was like the katana blade slicing deep into the old woman, but Tienan ignored his grandmother's anguish. He addressed Janay with no hostility or demand. "Please, Janay, release Liss."

He was right. This family disagreement had to end, but it would end with a bit of personal satisfaction. "I quite agree your grandmother is unwelcome here, but I've been assaulted, which, Guardian, I believe is a criminal act."

Shock registered for a second in Tienan's eyes. "You want me to arrest my grandmother for assaulting you?"

Janay faced Liss. "For a veed, which is more lasting, being blind or being mute? I have a mind to slice the demon-veed's tongue off or at least carve out an eye."

Silence whimpered.

"No!" Liss pleaded. "I give you my word, magestrella, good lady, I shall never again pry into Tienan or your affairs or prowl about Wolcott House."

"Janay," Tienan said, "either retribution is too severe. You were not physically hurt, were you?"

She shrugged. He didn't have to endure the tingling between her legs, which seemed to have worsened. Still, she felt violated. No, dirty. In need of a bath. "You may be right, Tienan." An idea occurred, one likely to scare the demon-veed but save face. One that would certainly provide a bit of entertainment and get her mind off the tingling. "Tienan, would you like your grandmother out of this house as fast as possible?"

"Yes."

"How long do you think it will take her to exit the lounge door?"

A frown lightly creased his brow. "Twenty seconds if her veed enhances her muscles."

"Very well then." She faced Liss. "Listen up, veed. On the count of three, I will summon my blades back into my hands and you will be free. However, on the count of twenty-five, I will throw my blades. You have that long to get yourself back into your host and get yourselves out of this house. Understood?"

"Yes, magestrella. Yes!"

Tienan put his hand on Janay's arm, staying her count. He looked at his grandmother. "Two things, grandmother. One, don't tarry once you're outside. As soon as you're clear of the gates, I will reset every spell so you cannot enter the property. Secondly, if you interfere with my life — or Rowen's — or attempt to match-make again, I will begin proceedings to have you evicted from Wolcott Manor. Do you understand?"

Her eyes mirrored her astonishment, but she nodded. "Yes. Yes — I understand."

Janay pulled her arm free of Tienan's grip. "Right then. Poke, Fox, on the count of three, to hand. One. Two. Three." The blades twisted and came out of Liss.

The veed screamed, but as soon as the dirks' tips cleared, Liss morphed into a ball of energy and sped into her host, who uttered, "Keen max!"

Janay had reached a count of fifteen when the door in the lounge, the one that led to the outside of the house, snicked shut behind Silence.

Tienan went to the desk on the other side of the bed and flashed the back of his hand before the ornate work on the center drawer.

On the wall above the nightstand, a screen appeared along with a holographic keypad. He tabbed keys. Views of the lounge's outside exit door flicked to a view of the side of the house.

Janay waited beside the bedpost, watching Silence jog to the driveway and get into her vehicle. When she drove her town car away, Tienan tabbed more keys. The black, wrought iron gates closed and latched. He spent several more minutes at the keypad before he turned the unit off. He stood and faced her. "My grandmother no longer has access to the property." He headed into the lounge.

She followed.

He opened a corner cabinet, one built into the bookcase catercorner from the fireplace, and took out a bottle of liquor and a glass. He poured himself a three-finger deep drink of dark liquid and chugged it down. He raised the bottle, offering to pour her a drink.

"No, thanks." She stood beside the curio cabinet that held figurines of geishas, dragons, fighting samurai.

He refilled his glass and put the bottle away.

"Tienan," Janay said, "will you regret banishing your grandmother?"

He heaved a sigh. "No. After last year's ball, I knew she was matchmaking. I guess I didn't want to believe how desperate she was for me to bond and produce an heir. I should have put a stop to her machinations then."

"Hindsight is such an awesome thing."

A smile quirked one side of his lips before he took a sip of liquor.

Between Janay's legs, the tingling intensified, but she shoved the sensations away. She had one more thing to resolve before she could hit the shower. "Okay, GOOL, about me being your familiaris. Think again. I am not your pet, never will be."

He chuckled. "I realize that."

"Ah, so. You told your grandmother I was your familiaris in order to put her in her place, right?"

"Not quite."

"Meaning?"

"For the duration that you stay with Rowen and me, you will be my familiaris, *my companion*. One who is under contract and paid for specific services which have been mutually agreed on."

"No sex involved," Rowen said from behind her.

Janay reeled to face him. When had he arrived? She hadn't heard any door opening or closing—then again this house had the quietest doors she'd ever encountered.

Rowen took a seat in the wingback chair by the fireplace. "Curiosity got the better of me, brother. I listened—*at the door*. Heard you kick Grandmother out." He looked about the room before grinning at Janay. "Considering my brother's fondness for all things Japanese, I think the better description, and a more apt one, Janay, is that a familiaris is a geisha."

Tienan chugged down his drink, depositing the glass in a recycler unit next to the liquor cabinet.

"Look you two, I'm no geisha." The tingling on her legs upped to needle-like stings. She rubbed the worst area of her inner thigh.

"Janay?" Tienan headed for her. "What's wrong?"

"Nothing."

He stopped before her and grabbed the hand scratching her leg in earnest.

Looking down, she found she'd clawed through the thin pajama fabric. "It's nothing. It just tingles. No. It prickles. No. Wherever that demon-veed touched me between my legs itches."

Rowen fairly leapt out of his chair.

A knowing look passed between brothers.

❦ Chapter Seven

I have no body; I make Stoicism my Body.
— The Samurai Creed

"**I** take it," Janay said, using her free hand to scratch the other side of her inner leg, "that this tingling is not psychosomatic?"

Tienan seemed transfixed on her scratching hand. "Do you get phantom symptoms after being terror-stricken?"

"No. Well, the only time I did have a twitch, it was after I killed a juvenile tormantrata in a nightmare, which turned out not to be a nightmare." She stopped scratching. "Am I dreaming?"

"No." Tienan seized her wrist. "Stop scratching."

The fleeting thought whispered that she should protest him holding both of her wrists, only that thought was interrupted by his stern, "Janay, look at me. LOOK AT ME."

She gazed into his concern-darkening gray eyes where, in the depths of his irises, firecracker sparks ignited.

"The glimmer you see in my eyes is Zad looking back at you, and for the love of the powers, Janay, take slower breaths or you'll hyperventilate."

Skom! *She was panting.* Gathering her will, she began slowly inflating and deflating her lungs.

"Janay, I need to look at your legs. I'm going to let go of your hands and pull your pajama bottoms down. Do you understand?"

She curtly nodded.

In one swift jerk, Tienan had the pajama bottoms pooled at her ankles. He squatted and studied her inner thighs. With every second, furrows plowed deeper and deeper across his brow.

Her own warm, feminine scent came with her next breath, along with her inner voice reminding her that she was female, that Tienan was male — all male — and that she had no panties on. She peered down and found a rash erupting red speckles. The rash crept upward, onto her groin.

Tienan stood up. "You've got a gredle rash."

"What's that?"

"The rash is caused by low-grade veed energy that's propelled out through a veed's mouth and nose. That energy goes through fabric and, when the spittle comes in contact with flesh, it short circuits the skin's nerve endings. It starts as tingling, then intensifies to burning."

"You mean your grandmother's demon-veed spit on me?"

Tienan nodded. "Likely it happened when you hit Liss on the head. You frightened her."

"I frightened it! This rash is my fault?" An image winked of her in the bed, of lifting and bending her knees, of spreading her legs to dig her heels in and push herself back, away from the thing under the covers. Another image flared. When she hit the veed on the head, her legs had been wide apart. "Oh, skom, skom, skom!"

"You couldn't have known."

"But you obviously do."

"It's part of growing up with a veed. Veeded children sometimes . . ."

Rowen smirked. "Often."

Tienan gave his brother a quelling glance. "Children being children, it's natural for them and their veeds to get into spitting matches."

Rowen chuckled. "Mother was furious when you came home covered in rashes from scuffling with Benny."

Before Janay could ask who Benny was, Rowen met her gaze and said, "Benny was the neighborhood bully. From when we summered at Ubrey Falls. That's the family camp north of here."

The tingling itch escalated, creeping over Janay's groin. "So, what's the cure for this gredle rash?"

Rowen smirked again. "You're not going to like it."

"What else is new?" She caught the tight set of Tienan's lips. "Well, how bad is the cure going to hurt?"

"It shouldn't hurt. The rash is spreading rapidly. You'll have to trust me, Janay, and not question anything I do to neutralize it."

The prickling suddenly became needle sharp. The areas she'd scratched were now tiny embers burning deep into her flesh. She fisted both hands. "It's getting worse. Much worse. Do what you have to do."

"Rowen, fetch the imolorn." Tienan scooped Janay into his arms so fast she had to wrap her arms around his neck for balance. Yet, in the reflection from the glass on a curio case, she glimpsed Rowen stride into the bookshelf wall and vanish.

Damn veeded warlocks and their magic.

Tienan moved so fast that she had to hold on tightly. Once in his bedroom, he set her on her feet by the nightstand. Zad's glow coated his hands, and he stripped the bed to the bare mattress. "No sense taking chances." He stuffed the bedclothes down the laundry chute which was part of the closet wall.

"Are you saying the bedding's contaminated with the spittle?"

"More than likely. It dissipates, but slowly." The glow on his hands winked out. He entered the walk-in closet and returned with a black comforter that he shook out so it settled onto the mattress. "Lie down."

With a shrug, she complied and laid down, pulling the pajama top's tails until they covered her naked, scarred hip. A second later, Rowen came through the door carrying an opaque, lavender bottle. Both his robe pockets bulged. As he handed the bottle to Tienan, Rowen's gaze alighted on the dark hair of her pubic mound.

Janay ordered in her sergeant's voice, "Avert those eyes, mister!"

Rowen's face flushed, his cheeks going crimson. "Yes, ma'am." He fumbled to pull out a potato-sized amber pod from his robe pocket. "Vorvoolt." Eyes downcast, he set the pod on the nightstand. "It's a moisturizer. For afterwards." From his other pocket, he drew out a glass bottle. The bottle contained three layers, equal amounts of black and white granules with a centimeter topping of pink. Before setting the bottle on the nightstand, he shook it, blending the ingredients into a dull pink color. Rowen looked at Tienan. "Anything else you need?"

"Towels."

When Rowen returned with the towels, he set them on the bed, near Janay's feet.

Tienan unscrewed the cap on the lavender bottle he held. Lowering his voice, he said to Rowen, "We don't need an audience."

"Oh, right." Rowen headed for the door. "Holler if you need anything."

Once the door snicked shut behind him, Janay eyed Tienan, who pushed his right sleeve up to the elbow before squirting a blob of the purplish goo onto the palm of his hand.

Though he was a meter away, the gel gave off a beeswax odor.

He showed her the glob. "Imolorn Sap is not real sap, but it has a sap-like consistency. It's a metallic powder that's held in suspension, somewhat like an electroplating solution."

"You're going to plate my rash?"

"Not exactly. The sap will penetrate the layers of your skin, then Zad will send a current into the sap to draw Liss's energy to my hand and into himself."

"And you're protected by the aura?"

He nodded. "This won't hurt, or at least I don't remember it hurting when my mother treated me." He paused, as if remembering an incident, a smile flickered at the corners of his mouth. "I had spittle on parts of my anatomy that—never mind."

Images of his balls turning a rashy, raw-red flickered into her mind, but she ruthlessly quelled them. She had problems of her own, with her own genitals, her hymen strumming with tingles. "Enough chatter. Get on with it."

"Right." Zad's aura flowed down from Tienan's elbow, covering his forearm and hand like a long-sleeved, translucent-white glove. The purple sap shimmered and floated on top of the aura.

Janay clamped her jaws together. Prepared for the worst, she spread her legs.

Seconds after Tienan applied the sap to the burning area on her inner thigh, the one she'd scratched raw, the fiery sensations vanished. The area became cold but not icy. She kept silent, first because she'd promised not to question what he did and, secondly, because she caught sight of the intense look of concentration on Tienan's face. Once in a while, he looked up at her, but said nothing. Yet, each time he looked at her, she glimpsed a silver flame in the recesses of his irises. Were he and Zad melded as one? Or just melded to their task?

The gentle treatment soon had her both pain and itch free except for what festered on her vulva and hymen.

Tienan grabbed a towel and gently wiped the excess gel off her skin. When done, he stood, and wiped his own hand. "How do the legs feel?"

"Fine. All right. No problem . . ."

He titled his head left, then right, blinked, then focused on her vaginal area. "Janay, were your legs spread very far apart when you hit Liss's head?"

"I don't know. Maybe, sort of—" Her voice whined. "Oh, skom, Tienan, there's tingling on my hymen."

He grabbed the bottle and squirted the sap onto his index finger, which immediately became encased in Zad's aura along with his hand. "Just relax. Spread your legs."

As she moved her hips apart, the soreness in her right hip escalated. She clutched handfuls of the comforter she laid on, gritted her teeth against the discomfort, and widened her hips.

When Tienan slid his finger between her labia lips, she felt the pressure glide over her clitoris. The tip of his finger soon stopped at her hymen. In the wake of his touch, the horrid prickling sensations ceased. He withdrew his hand.

She let out the breath she'd been holding and relaxed her hips.

Tienan's cheeks seemed to pale, and his worried gaze met hers. His voice sounded grave. "Zad thinks that in your panic, your muscles contracted and you sucked Liss's energy inside you. Possibly farther than my finger can reach. We need to get you to a hospital before there's permanent damage."

Permanent damage? Panic revved her heart rate. "I hate hospitals. I hate doctors. Isn't there some other way?"

"Perhaps a healer, like Neejera. She can put her hand directly into you—"

"Ewe—NO WAY. Are you sure some got inside me?"

"No, but why take the chance? Do you want your guts fried?" He suddenly cocked his head to the left, as if conversing with his veed. When he again looked at her, it was with uncertainty. "Since we may not be able to get to a healer or a hospital in time, Zad and I have come up with an alternative but—"

"I'm not going to like it?"

He nodded.

"Just tell me what it is."

"Zad will give me an erection and extend his aura over it. I'll coat my penis with imolorn. We enter you, neutralize the spittle." His voice lowered, hardening with resolve. "No sex, Janay. I'll not give nor take pleasure. It's this or a trip to hospital or Neejera and, by the time we get to either, you may have internal damage."

Considering her options, what choice did she have? "So bite the blade and do it. Now!"

A waft of azure veed-light dispensed his pants to the nearest chair, then his black briefs.

Tienan's penis quivered to life.

Definitely a cannon rising to duty's call.

Better not be caught looking.

She closed her eyes.

"Janay? Are you all right?"

"Yes. Why?"

"Your eyes are closed rather tightly."

"You want me to watch your penis do its thing? Pervert."

"Sorry. Yes, by all means, keep your eyes closed."

She heard a glob of imolorn noisily squirt out, and imagined Tienan's fingers slathering it on his hard erection.

No, no, she mustn't indulge in such thoughts. She took a new purchase on her handfuls of blanket.

As Tienan knelt between her knees, his hair-dusted legs touched hers.

A moment later, he was over her, the tip of his penis slipping through her hymen and into her.

No pain. No tightness. Skom — she was so wet. Would the sap still work or be diluted by her vaginal fluids?

The whoosh of Tienan's warm breath fanned across her pajama top.

Had he been holding his breath? Why? What had he been so unsure of?

He lowered himself.

Pajama silk met knit cloth.

What would it be like without the clothing?

Skom. Why were her thoughts taking that direction? *Because she was female and he was male.*

Tienan rebalanced on his elbows.

She silently thanked him for keeping his weight off her hips.

As he eased deeper into her, his head lowered. His ear touched her cheek, his breath skimmed along her neck. The warmth of his body odor held a musky, potent mix of testosterone, pheromones, and daoka.

A blissful euphoria nuzzled into her mind, and she let go of the covers.

Velvet silence muffled out the sounds of Tienan's breaths.

Her own heartbeat relaxed, slowed, faded. In the deepening silence of her mind, she drifted toward the siren's call of her deepest, primal femininity. She heard, and felt, Zad's rhythmic, yet somber, bull-fiddle purring which soon faded to the background as a skittering of harp strings began. The simple harp melody soon accompanied the sound of a twangy, metallic, stringed instrument she could not readily identify. The tune seemed ancient, yet somehow, familiar. A ballad. One of desire, adoration—a love divine.

"Janay." Tienan's thready voice seemed far away.

She stifled the urge to tell him to shut up but managed, "I'm fine." She sighed and luxuriated in the sensual euphoria the ballad evoked. Then came the booming demand of the bull-fiddle, pulsating with a primordial beat and urgency to mate.

"Janay, stop tightening around me."

Tightening about him?

She shifted focus to the sensations coming from her vagina.

She was gushing honey-smooth warmth.

Tienan's silken penis vibrated with tension and continued to mushroom.

"Janay, please," he murmured, as if fighting his own male urges. "Stop."

She opened her eyes and met his gaze. "It isn't me doing the tightening. You're the one that's swelling."

His eyes went wide with disbelief. Deep in his irises flared an eruption of sizzling, rainbow sparks.

"Tienan? What's going on? Your eyes—"

"Zad. Damn the powers! He wants me to breed you."

The word bestiality boomed through her mind with the impact of a disputer rifle's recoil. "*Poke!*" The dirk smacked into her palm. She gripped the dirk and raised her arm to stab Tienan.

"No, Janay!" Horror reflected in Tienan's eyes. In the depths of those eyes, Zad's sparks solidified into a red-gold ember. "Zad's stopping. He apologizes. He doesn't know what came over him."

She stayed her hand. Should she believe him?

Zad's ember-fire flickered deep in Tienan's eyes and Tienan's brows crunched together in puzzlement. "*You're beautiful music?*"

"What? What did you say?"

Tienan's jaw dropped, then closed with a snap of teeth. He glared at her.

"Tienan? What's going on?"

"You—you have a veed song."

"I what?" She lowered her dirk.

He withdrew his penis from her and scrambled off the bed. As soon as he pulled down his shirt, covering his deflating erection, he snatched his clothes off the chair. "I'm going to take a cold shower—in the guestroom. You bathe. Use the LDM." He grabbed the bottle off the nightstand and tossed it onto the bed. "Shake it. It's soap. It'll break down any remaining imolorn. If your skin feels dry, use the vorvoolt oil." He pointed to the pod on the nightstand and left.

Janay released Poke, who vanished before she could utter, "Home." Like an obedient zombie, she headed for the master bath to take a shower. All the while, the ballad looped in the back of her mind, fading only when the warm water cascaded over her.

As soon as she activated the soap dispenser on the bottle, the musky odor of daoka flowers wafted into her nostrils, followed by the remembrance of Tienan's scent.

Other images flitted in and out of her mind of what had just happened in Tienan's bed. *She'd almost had sex with a warlock and his lion of a veed.* That was pretty kinky sex, especially for someone as reserved as she tended to be. So, why didn't that disgust her?

Okay, so maybe her senses had initially been overwhelmed by the gredle rash. That may have allowed her to succumb to Zad's bull-fiddle purring, which, in turn, lulled her into giving in to her own need for sex. That had to be it. No big deal.

Half an hour later, she donned the black velour toweling robe that hung on the bathroom's wall. The robe smelled of sunshine and fresh air, not a trace of Tienan's scent.

And just why should she want to wear something with his scent on it? Silly woman— no, stupid soldier. She needed clothes. Which meant borrowing something of Tienan's—but without his scent on it. Right. To the closet. No scent.

About to enter the walk-in closet, she heard Tienan's angry voice, "You have disgraced me and all that is veed!"

She detoured to the lounge doorway and peeked around the jamb.

Fully dressed in a long-sleeved black turtleneck shirt and black slacks, hair pulled back into a tight damp braid, Tienan stood with his hands braced on the fireplace mantelpiece.

Zad, head bowed low, sat on the bearskin rug wearing a massive black collar. A chain linked the collar to his four shackled feet.

Janay headed for the wingback chair catercorner from Tienan. She sat, tucking her legs beneath her, covering herself with the robe. "Why is Zad hogtied?"

Startled, Tienan turned. How had the woman snuck up on him? Barely able to keep his self-loathing and anger at bay, he stretched himself to his full Hautonne height. "It's none of your business."

"Sorry, I'm making it my business. Zad shouldn't be made a scapegoat because things between us — our coupling — got a tad out of hand."

Tienan scowled at her. "A *tad* out of hand?"

Things had gotten way out of hand. Zad had done the unspeakable. His worst nightmare had been confirmed. Zad had crossed the line and partaken of the dark side of the qi.

"Okay, Tienan, enlighten me. What did Zad do to warrant him being shackled?"

Tienan glimpsed movement, the curling of Janay's toes that peeped out from under his old robe. Those toes were prune-shriveled from her shower. Was she naked under his robe? No. He would not indulge in such thinking. He was Zantharian. She was human. She didn't understand. "I am Zantharian, Janay. A warlock of the Eighth Power. I am Royal Hautonne peerage. You are nothing more than a *jossierj* — an outsider, a citizen of the empire." He took a deep breath and vanquished his turmoil. "It's complicated."

"Human I might be, but I'm not dumb or blind." She eyed Zad, who looked at her with puppy-sad eyes. "Zad, what's Tienan's real problem?"

Zad quietly said, "I have done the unthinkable. I manipulated my lord Tienan's body, his penis, when it was inside you."

You've done more than that! blared through Tienan's mind. "That will be enough, Zad, or do you want to wear a muzzle?"

Zad hung his head and studied the floor. "Forgive me, my good lord, for speaking without permission."

"Tienan!" Janay's voice was military sharp. "Why should Zad be punished for biological urges, your biological erection?"

Tienan rammed his hands into his pants pockets. "It was not biological. Zad enhanced my erection. He took control of it and my body *without my permission*."

"So you chained him up like a rabid dog? No, I don't believe you. What's really going on between you and Zad?"

Should he lie to smooth things over, silence her? No. She was too smart, too intelligent, too astute. She would recognize a lie. He was sure of that. So it had to be the truth. He took his hands out of his pockets and crossed his arms over his chest, taking a defensive, feet-apart, stance. "Zad has been — has become — beguiled by the darkunskyve."

She didn't flinch. "What's darkunskyve?"

"Dark qi." He looked away from her, to Zad, but he didn't

really focus his sight on his veed.

"Tienan, are we talking about the dark qi that spawns demons? Are you saying Zad's become some kind of monster?"

"Yes. No. I'm not positive." The fear that Zad had turned evil slithered about his stomach. "The first signs of a veed embracing the darkunskyve is them taking over their host's body in unobtrusive ways, then forcibly, often torturing their host into obedience. When a veed gets control, they become vile creatures." He glared at Janay. "I've seen it happen." Ghostly images of Granger rose in Tienan's mind. "Host and veed are bound in birth, bound in death. To destroy a darkunskyve veed, you have to kill its host."

"If your so-called proof of Zad's dive for the darkness is one erection, you're paranoid and jumping to conclusions."

"I am not!"

"Ah, so, this has happened before, has it?"

He looked away, at the nearest curio cabinet's display of geisha figurines.

"Tienan, talk to me. Explain!" She underscored her exasperation by thumping her fisted hand on the chair's arms.

"All right, if you insist on knowing, I stopped having sex with women because of Zad." He pointed toward the bedroom door. "I didn't make the connection until now, in bed with you."

"Good god, Tienan, you are such a control freak. Intercourse is a natural bodily function and, sure, at some point in the process, it becomes nigh on to impossible for a man — or a woman — to stop an orgasm but that's not what happened between us."

Blood thundered in his arteries and pumped anger into his voice. "Confound the powers, Janay! When it comes to Zantharians mating there are four parties involved. The man, the woman, and their two veeds. The last three women I bedded became agitated when I neared my climax, and not in a good way. When Zad went to genate, their veeds panicked!"

"Genate?"

Some of his anger dissipated because he realized she didn't understand. "Genate is a term for when veeds create baby veeds."

Janay eyed Zad, who didn't look at her.

Tienan turned. Once again he put his palms on the mantel, striving to control his anguish.

A moment later, Janay asked quietly, "By any chance, does veed singing go on in a Zantharian mating ritual?"

Veed singing? Tienan looked over his shoulder at her. "Veeds have a harmonic string-song of energy, but I doubt a human, like yourself, could hear such a subatomic noise."

"Well, I heard something. Three somethings actually. There was the initial sound of Zad's mellow bull-fiddle, like his purring when I sleep beside him. Then there was a pleasant harp-song. The third was a twangy tune from some metal-stringed instrument, not a guitar or a banjo— oriental, I think. Maybe a shamisen? Not sure."

"Three songs? That's impossible!" Tienan turned and met Zad's confused gaze. "One song angelic, one song demonic, and one pure darkunskyve, eh, Zad?"

Janay half yelled. "*Wrong*. All were angelic."

Tienan glared at Janay and spoke sternly. "That's impossible."

"Impossible or not, all I know is that I heard three distinct melodies and all blended nicely together."

Darkunskyve was said to be a siren's song that brought out the negative aspects of a person. Did Janay have darkunskyve in her? "Did any one of those tunes reverberate in you?"

"No, they seemed to beckon me like the dirks. Ohmygod." She sat back, the shock of comprehension causing her lips to remain parted.

"Janay? What is it? Janay!"

She swallowed hard. "The connection—*it's soul singing to soul*." She stared at Zad. "I'd forgotten. My dirks once told me I have a harp soul-song that they liked."

Her gaze nailed him. "Skom, Tienan, you and your soul sang to my soul."

Tienan wanted to shake Janay. "Veeds are souls, Janay. A person cannot have two souls. That's ridiculous. Insane."

Her cheeks flamed with two red spots. "*I am not insane*. Think man, think. What if another veed hears Zad's soul song and then yours? Wouldn't they be as confused? As scared? Wouldn't they react like you have? And wouldn't they jump to the same conclusion you have? That your veed has gone to the dark side of the qi? Wouldn't that freak them out?"

By the powers . . . Could she be right? Did he have a soul? No, Zad was his soul.

In the blink of his eyes, Tienan realized the disastrous sexual encounters he'd had could easily be explained by the additional soul-song rising during a mating. "Maybe," he whispered. "Maybe."

She smiled. "Well, aren't you glad I cleared that up for you?"

He didn't feel relieved. "You're guessing. I need proof."

"If proof is what you want, proof is what you get."

"Meaning?"

"Poke. Attention!" She held out her hand.

The dirk appeared, tip hovering above her open palm.

"Beloved Infanatas that you are Pokeweed, kindly seek out the dark qi in this room."

The blade tilted forward, bowing, before flitting to Tienan. It circled him twice before whizzing over to Zad. The dirk spiraled about Zad from nose to tail tip before returning to Janay where it hovered, its blade tip pointed at her injured hip. The dirk bowed and vanished.

Janay sent him a scalding look. "Mr. Warlock, the only dark qi here is what's left in my hip from the Valley of Rathe."

The shock staggered him. He went to the other wingback chair and sank into its cushions. He studied Zad.

At headquarters, he'd learned that Janay's dirks were purest qi, capable of fighting and destroying the darkest qi. And now, her dirk had found no dark qi in Zad—or him. None. Damn the powers, he'd let fear overrule his judgment.

Reaching into the depths of his mind, Tienan conjured the ancient words, chanting them in his mind-voice, then directed the telepathic power toward Zad. In a flash of psychic energy, Zad's chains and shackles vanished.

"Thank you, my good, good lord." Trembling with relief, Zad laid down. He rested his chin on his paws.

Tienan eyed Zad. "How can I and my veed each have a soul?" It was more a question he asked himself than Zad.

"Beats me," Janay replied. "You're the guy with a veed."

"My good lord," Zad said, "I recall a conversation of long ago, your cousin with the one blue eye and one brown. He had a veed with two string songs. The second soul—"

"Was his dead twin's." Could it be possible that he was a twin? That his twin died in utero and since he wasn't born, that veed's soul attached to him? But who was there to ask? His mother and father were dead. So were his De'Argossi grandparents.

A loud chime resounded and Boots' voice bellowed, "Tienan, why am I locked out? Open the gates."

Trond! In changing the security codes to keep his grandmother out, he'd forgotten to notify Boots. She was going to be royally pissed if she had to wait to gain entry.

❦ Chapter Eight

I have no eyes; I make The Flash of Lightning
my eyes. — *The Samurai Creed*

The Warehouse

With each sentence Annelisa spoke, the heightened pitch of her voice screeched down Celinae's spine.

"I tell you, Celinae, I've never seen Her Grace so furious." Annelisa took her watering can to the next clump of hokusia at the back of the warehouse. She poured out the water as fast as she poured out her frustrations.

Celinae took in a fortifying breath. Ten minutes was more than she normally allotted to Annelisa's rants. Only, today, the benefit of listening longer had been learning Tienan De'Argossi had kicked his grandmother, Her Grace, Silence Tomosukovia, out of Wolcott House. Oh, such immensely delighting news!

Celinae took out a mobcap from the ceremonial cupboard drawer and placed it over her long hair. She tucked every hair under the cap, then gritted her teeth to the dreadful sensations of bending back her bangs to be sure no stray hair fell into the planter and came into contact with the bloodwood tuber, else she would be the victim along with the chosen one. She put on her brown service robe, double checking to be sure it fully covered her short-sleeved blouse and navy slacks. Planting the tuber was such filthy business.

One wave of her ruby witch's ring before the wall sensor triggered back a section of the floor tiles. A stainless steel table rose up and clanked into place. After putting a large glazed pot on the table, Celinae fetched her slat-handled basket. She grouped the basket's contents on the table in the order in which she would use the items. Setting the basket aside, she felt the stab of a sliver. She eyed the offending fragment imbedded in the pad of her index finger. A large sliver. Deep.

Using the fingernail of her other index finger, she pushed the sliver deeper into her flesh, welcoming the sharp, piercing pain.

Voz, now.

The veed reacted to her mind-voice, sending energy gushing down her arm, into her finger, to push the sliver up. The pain of the exiting sliver shivered through her. Celinae grabbed the bloody shard and pulled it out. Pain shot up her arm. Glossy red blood spurted. She pinched the skin to either side of the wound, forcing it to bleed more. Before blood spilled over the edge of her finger, she licked the blood off, savoring the copper warmth. *Voz, heal it.*

Her veed cauterized and healed the injury with a sizzling prick of energy.

Oh, how she loved the taste of blood, the sizzle of such pains. One day she would be immortal, a veeded vampire, the consort to Shelzat, and pain would be her ecstasy.

Annelisa approached, heading once again for the water spigot on the wall at the end of the workbench. "By the blessed darkness, Celinae, when I left for the day, Her Grace was still enraged — and pacing. She never paces. Since the moment she got back from Wolcott House, she yelled at me, at the housekeeper, the cook, the butler. I don't know what I'm going to do." From her apron pocket, Annelisa took out two fertilizer tablets, dropped them into the watering can, and turned on the spigot. "I should quit."

My lady, she cannot quit! Voz stood inside Celinae's mind in her cobalt blue peacock form. She flicked and flicked her long tail feathers that dragged behind her, an indicator of how agitated she had become. *We have gone to a great deal of trouble to place Annelisa in Her Grace's employ. Do not let her quit.*

Memories flitted of Sweets bragging of her cunning cow-towing that had gotten Lady Bohem, Silence Tomosukovia's best friend, to convince Silence to interview Annelisa for her personal assistant. As soon as Her Grace contacted Protectors, Inc. for a background check, Celinae saw to it that Annelisa topped Silence's list as the most suitable candidate. After all, they had to keep an eye on the De'Argossi family.

Voz stopped flicking her tail. *My lady? Did you hear me?*

Yes, I did. To Annelisa, Celinae said firmly, "You will go back to work tomorrow as usual, Annelisa. *You must not quit.*"

With a sigh of resignation, Annelisa replied, "Yes, yes. I know." With a full water can in hand, the weight had Annelisa making a lopsided trek to the lattice wall. "I rather think it's odd that Tienan chose to take a familiaris, don't you?"

Ah, that curious, yet interesting, revelation. "I wonder what he could possibly want from such a female, a soldier."

"An ex-soldier. Ex-peacekeeper."

"Semantics, Annelisa, mere semantics."

"I suppose, and yet, it does make me wonder if there's more to Janay Cholyn than Sweets says."

So, Annelisa thought that too, did she? Celinae put on her gardening gloves. *Voz, your assistance. I'll tolerate no mistakes.*

Yes, my lady. Voz sent her veed energy throughout Celinae's body, concentrating power on the micro-movements of Celinae's finger and hand muscles.

Celinae picked up the fertilizer jug. Carefully balancing the jug above the pot, she poured the stinky, clumped mixture of veed-spell enhanced vampire bat manure and bog-slurry into the pot. After setting the jug aside, she unwrapped the black cloth protecting the bloodwood tuber. She lowered the pear-shaped root onto the pot until it was half sunk, then let go of it. The tuber slowly settled until all that remained above the slurry was the wide, navel-looking topknot.

"Well?" Annelisa demanded.

"Well, what?"

"Weren't you listening to me?"

"I was seating this tuber."

"Oh, sorry. You should have said something and I would have waited."

"So, what were you saying, Annelisa?" It wasn't that she was curious or that she enjoyed Annelisa's ramblings one iota. No. Listening to her was a way of deluding the girl into thinking they were friends, allies. When Annelisa's usefulness ended, her life and her veed's power would be taken. Not quickly, but slowly to savor the pulsing of the girl's blood. Celinae faced the girl. "Well, I'm listening. What did you say?"

"I said that I was jumping to conclusions. Sweets probably doesn't have much information on Janay Cholyn. Other than the woman is paranoid about hospitals, which is interesting, maybe useful. Anyway, it'll take days before the military releases her records to Guardian command. Then it'll take a couple days before Sweets gets a look at them."

Annelisa was as clueless as Sweets. Neither woman realized that she, Celinae Yvonne Sykes, who worked for the premier of private security companies, had resources neither of her two partners had. Yet, she wasn't about to tell them what her discreet inquiries had netted. Janay was the daughter of Alexander Cholyn, CEO of Greitz Bank in the city of Haylil on the colony world of Chytano, in the Omega Australe Solar System. He was rich. Old money. Five times divorced. A consummate womanizer. As to Janay's mother? The dark-haired Sheena Yetvetski was the reigning GNR News Broadcasting evening anchor. She resided in Weston Falls, a city half a planet away from her ex-husband.

In studying Sheena's datafile, it became obvious that the woman's youthful beauty depended on cosmetic surgeries. Yet, the most fascinating news about Sheena had come from the tabloids. Sheena companioned men of wealth and political power. She had romantic flings but never remarried. Which made Celinae again ponder why Janay, born into money and elite society, had chosen a military life. Sure, Australes were required to serve the empire, but rich people didn't. Legal loopholes allowed them to avoid conscription. So why had Janay volunteered for not one but three tours of duty?

Celinae picked up the ceremonial knife. Handling the white ceramic blade triggered snatches of her conversation earlier with Sweets about Janay's dirks being unique, that both tested positive for pure qi energy and that Janay manipulated them with speed and accuracy.

Where had Janay gotten such blades? What explained the telekinetic ability Janay used to control them? She was human, pure human. Or so Sweets had insisted. Adamantly insisted. Mayhaps too adamantly. Yet, pure qi power was what she, Annelisa, and Sweets were after. Or was Sweets intent on having more than her share of qi power?

Celinae turned the ceremonial knife over in her hand. Was it possible to assimilate the qi from Janay's dirks?

The bloodwood bulb burped.

First objectives first. She used the ceremonial knife to mince a packet of dried sea-moss. Yet, with each chop of the knife, her thoughts drifted back to the need for qi energy. Her primary objective was to enhance Voz's power. That meant working with

Annelisa and Sweets to get the De'Argossi veeds — and to punish Silence. Only right now, the two men were estranged from their grandmother. What could be done to repair the rift between them? As Celinae sprinkled bits of moss around the tuber to soak up the liquid in the pot, a scheme congealed in her mind.

Celinae turned and spotted Annelisa watering the last row of plants. Celinae spoke loud enough to be heard across the distance. "Silence and Tienan must make amends."

Annelisa stopped pouring water onto the ceramic caldron that held the mother bloodwood vine. "Why would you want Her Grace back in the good graces of her grandson? Seems to me it's better word get out of how she forced him to take a familiaris. Let Hautonne gossip shame her for a change."

Yes, Her Grace deserved shaming for the humiliations she'd dispensed to so many families, including hers and Annelisa's. But Silence had absolutely devastated Sweets' life, and for that the De'Argossi family would bleed.

Do not let your thoughts stray, my lady, Voz whispered. *Annelisa needs persuasion.*

Right. "Annelisa, surely you wouldn't pass up an opportunity to earn a bonus for giving Her Grace the key to saving face with her grandsons, would you?"

"A bonus? Her Grace never parts with her money unless she gets double value for her drails. She's more likely to think my pittance of a salary includes the idea you've obviously hatched."

Why did Annelisa have to be so thickheaded? "You're a bright girl, Annelisa. It's a simple plan. You only have to get Silence to welcome Tienan's familiaris into the Inner Circle of Ozieron society."

Annelisa turned so quickly that water sprinkled out of her can and onto the floor. She set the can down with a loud clunk. "You can't be serious!"

"Think about it. Who is most likely to get Tienan out of his house, leaving his brother alone and unprotected for several hours at a time. Time we could use to kidnap him?"

"His commander?"

"Don't be facetious."

"All right, I'll concede, his grandmother."

The girl could be so dense. "Not the grandmother, Annelisa — *Tienan's familiaris.*"

"Oh! You're thinking Tienan will want everyone to see the woman he's keeping just to spite his grandmother." Annelisa's lips puckered in thought. She picked up her watering can and stepped over to the pale-yellow poppies. "Tienan doesn't strike me as a man who would flaunt any woman before the Hautonne. He'll keep her to himself."

"Which is likely if she stays in his house, in his bed. But what if the familiaris can be enticed to enjoy society's many gaieties? Won't Tienan accompany her to prevent other men luring her away from him? Which means we'll know every event they attend because you, dear Annelisa, control the Ozieron Coven's, and the Inner Circle's, invitation lists. This is, after all, the Solstice Season, is it not? Balls. Teas. Dinners. Parties."

"Yes, but exactly what will that accomplish?"

"Getting our hands on Rowen, which would be much, much easier if Tienan were out with his familiaris."

"Maybe. I'm not sure."

Celinae fought the scream of frustration welling in her throat. "*Annelisa!* If we attack Tienan in his home, we will have to deal with his soldier-whore, who has telekinetic abilities and is deadly accurate with her dirks. Despite our veeds' new enhancements, we'll be slaughtered. We'll never get our hands on Rowen, we'll never become the witches we are destined to be."

Annelisa said nothing. She returned to the spigot. More minutes passed to the sounds of water splashing into the watering can. Annelisa's gaze drifted to the pot and items on the workbench. Her eyes widened. "Are you planting a bloodwood tuber?"

Now she notices. Celinae made a show of her hand going under her service robe. She took out the small case from her slack's back pocket. She opened the case and revealed the vial of blood to Annelisa. "Sweets obtained this."

"From which of the boys on our list?" She turned off the water.

"Not a boy, Annelisa. This is Janay Cholyn's blood."

She looked momentarily bewildered, then frowned. "Why would we need bloodwood for her?"

"Have you forgotten what bloodwood does?"

"No. It binds or shields, depending on how we weave the fibers. Are we going to use it to shield ourselves from Janay?"

Idiot! "Not her. Her dirks. Not shield but bind the dirks. Remember Sweets saying the dirks were pure qi, pure veed energy?"

"Yes, but— By the darkness! You're saying that makes them as dangerous as veeds?"

She shrugged. "We are being cautious. We'll use the fibers from this vine to trap Janay's dirks. Without her dirks, the woman becomes an ordinary Australe, an ordinary human." Celinae hardened her voice. "Do you want to take the chance Janay will prevent us from getting Rowen's and Tienan's veeds?"

"You've got a detailed plan worked out, don't you?"

Now and then the girl could be brighter than a candle-orb. Celinae took off her gloves. She opened and carefully tilted the vial so Janay's blood dribbled out and fell onto the top of the bloodwood tuber.

Drop.

Drop.

Drop.

Celinae ignored Annelisa watering the last of the plants and the clattering of the watering can being put away. When Annelisa came over and stood at the end of the work table, watching and waiting, the last drop of blood fell. Celinae capped the vial and discarded it into the recycler unit on the wall.

"So," Annelisa said, "what do you have in mind for mending the rift between Her Grace and Tienan? Do I get to tell Her Grace that Rowen is pregnant with his own veed so she feels compelled to go to him and care for him?"

"Don't be ridiculous, that won't help." What did help was knowing Rowen was pregnant. That revelation of Sweets' had been a shock but such a pregnancy meant Rowen's veed would be easy to remove, just cut it out of the boy's abdomen. If they acted at the time of the next new moon, the veed's immense power was theirs.

She smiled at Annelisa. "Pay attention. This is what you'll need to do . . ."

Wolcott Manor

The next morning, Annelisa entered the sitting room adjacent to Silence's bedchamber. Her Grace sat by the small round table near the picture window, where the royal blue tapestry curtains were drawn back but the pale blue sheers remained closed, muting the morning light. Her Grace's unkempt hair, her disheveled robe, and the deep worry lines on her face added fifty years to her age.

Annelisa silently thanked the cook who had, moments ago, warned her that Her Grace hadn't slept well. Oh, how satisfying it felt to witness the Matriarch of Tomosukovia and the Mazen of Coven Ozieron suffer such woe.

Data pad in hand, Annelisa strode through the room and took the seat across from Her Grace.

Silence didn't look up from pouring herself a cup of weak-brewed, green tea.

Annelisa stared at the full-length portrait of Silence's mother that hung on the wall directly behind Her Grace. *C'mon, c'mon, notice me staring.*

A minute ticked by before Silence glanced at the portrait. "Is it crooked again?"

Annelisa tacked a surprised expression to her face. "Oh, no, Your Grace. The painting is quite straight."

"Then why were you staring at it?"

"Well—because, that is . . . I . . ."

"Speak up, girl!"

"It's just, well, you've told me that your lady-mother was all that was good and kind, true Hautonne. And I was, forgive me, just pondering how she might have borne your father's three familiarises."

"The fact that she did shows the quality of her character."

"Yes, it does, but, well, I was also wondering if there was something she might have said or done that might work for dealing with your grandson and his familiaris."

Silence's brows collided in deep-furrowed thought. "My lady mother . . ." whispered from her lips. A moment later, she set the teapot down hard enough to rattle the teaspoons on the tray. "Bless the powers. That's it. The answer."

"What answer, Your Grace?"

"Quick. Fetch my finest personal stationary, my best pen, the finest gold—no, the raven-black wax!"

An hour later, with inner satisfaction, Annelisa proofread both of Her Grace's notes, one for Tienan and one for Janay Cholyn. "They're error free, Your Grace, and if I might add, excellently worded." She handed them back.

Silence signed them with a flourish. As she clicked the wax-pen, drops of melted black wax fell and pooled on the center of the flap for Tienan's note. She turned her witch's ring palm-side down and pushed, forcing the cabochon's stylized nyd rune deep into the wax.

Annelisa waited until Silence reached for the note to Janay. "Your Grace, do you want me to issue an invitation to Janay to the coven tea? You know, as proof of good will?"

Silence smiled. "A most excellent idea. Do so at once."

"Yes, Your Grace and, as soon as you're done, I'll post the lot. Shall I tell the courier service to get a signature upon delivery?"

"Yes— No! These notes are too personal for them to go astray or have people wonder what they contain." After a moment's thought, she said, "You will hand deliver them."

"Me!" Annelisa clasped her hands together on her lap. That wasn't in any of Celinae's scenarios. What if she went to Wolcott House and Rowen saw her, remembered her as one of the witches that kidnapped him?

No, no, wait. What could Rowen recall about her involvement with his kidnapping? She had not spoken, Celinae and Sweets had done the chants. Her task had been to augment their veed energy with hers and to pull the veed cocoon out of Rowen's body. Still, why take a chance on being identified?

She cleared her throat and spoke hesitantly. "Your Grace, I don't think Tienan will welcome me into his house. He knows I work for you, and if I call to make an appointment to see him, he'll surely cut me off."

"Nonsense. You are friends with Rowen."

"Friends with Rowen? Oh, no, Your Grace, it's more like acquaintances. He was a school classmate, one of three hundred and forty—"

"The point, Annelisa, is that you are well enough acquainted. He, being the considerate boy that he is, will hear you out. You contact Rowen, not Tienan. You will tell Rowen you are ascertaining if delivering my messages would be seen by Tienan as interference, which would get me ousted from the manor. As simple as that."

More than likely Rowen would tell her to go to Sh'olv.

"While you're at Wolcott House, Annelisa, you surreptitiously discern from Rowen if Tienan can be swayed to relent or find out what I must do to end this strife between us. It is, after all, a ridiculous misunderstanding on his part."

Annelisa assumed her meekest persona, head bowed, eyes focused on her lap, and clasped her hands. "I—I don't know if I can lie that well."

"It is not precisely lying. You tell whatever truths are necessary but give no extemporaneous explanations." Her Grace's cool index finger tip touched Annelisa's jaw and lifted, forcing Annelisa to look Her Grace in the eye. "Dear girl," Silence said, "do this and I shall give you an extra week's pay." She withdrew her touch.

Two weeks' pay would be better, but she would take what was offered. Only she mustn't seem too eager. "I could use the extra cash . . ." She focused on the portrait and counted seven breaths before saying, "Yes, Your Grace. Leave it to me."

❦ Chapter Nine

I have no ears; I make Sensibility my Ears.
— The Samurai Creed

Long after supper ended, Tienan entered the lounge's camouflaged lift. *Go to your study,* Boots had told him minutes ago. *Use that fancy com-terminal of yours and access the colony's Hall of Records for familiaris contracts.* Then she'd exited through the lounge's back door to place a dozen new sensors. Those units, updating of the house's door and window sensors, and increasing the energy shielding would help protect Rowen should his kidnappers try to get in.

Another precaution was Boots. She would be sleeping in the guestroom, staying in the house, making sure someone was with Rowen at all times.

Why was everyone so sure the perps would want Rowen back? Wouldn't it be better to kill Rowen so he could never identify them? And just why was Rowen's veed so valuable? Or the veeds of the other boys? Or their blood? None of the boys were related, none had the same type of veed, none had the same blood type.

The lift flashed it was about to stop. The warning light blinked, indicating someone was in the study. He tabbed tiles, and the monitor screen showed a view of his study where Janay sat behind his desk, facing the screen over the fireplace.

She said to the shaved-bald soldier on the screen, "Tell the general that I need to talk to him. *Need,* not want. Do you understand, Gunny?"

"Yes, ma'am. The moment the general checks in tomorrow, I'll tell him again."

"Out." Janay looked down at the desk. "Computer, end call."

Tienan heard the faint bleep of the disconnect and ignored the fireplace screen winking back to the vorvoolt picture.

After tabbing the computer controls on the desk, Janay propped her elbows to either side of the desktop screen. She rested her chin on her hands. Her two dirks flitted by the bay window so fast that the sheer curtains fluttered. They zoomed over her head, chasing one another.

Janay tilted her chair back until it hit the backstop.

The dirks tackled each other like kittens at play. Now and then their tips would click against the dark cherry tongue-and-grove ceiling.

He should go. No, she only came to make the call to her general. She was bound to leave in a minute. He would wait. His gaze alighted on her gypsy-black mass of curls held back by a tan headband. She wore her own clothes. The faded khaki pants, and an equally faded khaki tee-shirt, were ones Boots had brought back from the spaceport.

Boots' voice echoed in his mind. *Janay's been living out of a traveler's sleep booth . . . She's broke, Tienan. She likely spent every drail she has to get here to consult the experts at the teaching hospital . . . You make sure when you fill out the familiaris contract that you are extremely generous – and you better take her shopping. Get her a new wardrobe. It's the least you can do.*

What Boots hadn't taken into consideration was Janay's pride. She wouldn't appreciate a blatant handout.

Zad padded into the study in his corporeal lion's form. He paused when he spotted Janay. "Are you all right?"

She tilted the chair forward so fast she jarred herself. "I'm fine." She turned off the computer screen.

What was on the screen she didn't want Zad to see?

"What's up, Zad?" She gave him her full attention.

"I want to thank you for reasoning with My Good Lord Tienan after the fiasco in the bedroom today."

"Your good lord? Good, my ass. He shackled you."

"He is my host. I violated the Codes of Obedience. The punishment was within regulations."

She stared wide-eyed at him. "Codes of Obedience?"

"When a veed matures and comes out of their cocoon, the first thing they do is give an oath to their host to obey the Codes set forth by our society." Zad went around to the side of the desk and sat, his back to the lift.

Janay swiveled her chair around, facing Zad. He put a paw on her knee.

Tienan had to strain to hear Zad say, "Please do not dislike Tienan."

"I don't dislike him."

Zad removed his paw. "Then you like him?" There was hope and eagerness in his voice.

"Tienan aside, get to the point. Why are you here?"

"I was striving to be tactful."

"No need."

"I see . . . Very well. The reason I sought you out was to encourage you to become Tienan's familiaris."

"Ah, so you've come to enumerate his finer qualities and virtues?"

Zad chuckled. "Something like that."

"Don't bother."

"But, Janay—"

She held up her hand, silencing him. "Rowen has already done so. With every turn of the cards."

"If I may be so bold as to ask, what grand virtues of Tienan's did Rowen expound on as you played kumdak?"

"I wouldn't call them exactly virtues. More like Tienan is honorable, stubborn, generous, stubborn, kind, stubborn."

She and Zad chuckled.

Zad sobered. "Rowen looks up to his brother."

"That's obvious. *A man who is loved by his brother is truly blessed.*"

Zad cocked his head to the left, as if trying to recall the quote.

"If you must know, you curious veed, my husband used to quote that line, and many others."

The lift could have dropped Tienan to the planet's core. *Husband?* Janay had a husband?

Zad stammered, "You are bonded?"

"Bonded?"

"That is what Zantharians call a legal marriage."

"Well, I was legally married, but I'm a widow."

Again the floor seemed to open under Tienan and drop him a thousand meters in two seconds. *Janay was a widow?*

The tolling of the vesper bells of the Chapel of J'Hi Baldama knelled softly through the room. Her gaze drifted to the window.

"Otto was my husband's name. He was a J'Hian monk."

A monk? Tienan's knees threatened to buckle. She married a monk?

"I hear the sorrow in your voice," Zad said. "You must have loved your husband very much."

"Not the true way a husband and wife love each other."

"I do not understand."

She leaned back in the chair and stared at a spot on the ceiling. "I was eighteen, Otto was forty. He was the priest-instructor at my parish school. A true brother of the spirit." Her voice lowered. "He had a brain tumor. Inoperable. He didn't want to spend his remaining months enduring parishioners or his fellow clergy visiting, looking sorrowful." She heaved a weary sigh.

A moment later, she eyed Zad. "Otto and I made a pact. I desperately needed to be free of my grandmother. I wanted a life of my own choosing. In return for marrying and caring for Otto, he took me away from Weston Falls—that's part of the colony where I lived. We went to the islands . . ." She smiled, but tears glossed her brown eyes. "He died in his hoverchair, at dawn, as the gulls squabbled over bread I tossed out to them." Her voice choked. She wiped a tear from her eye.

Zad sniffed. He used a claw and triggered the top desk drawer to open.

Janay pulled out a tissue and blew her nose. "Eleven years he's been gone and I still get maudlin."

"To be expected when a loved one dies."

"Otto would not have wanted me to weep for him. He made me promise to dance in the day. To rejoice in life, help others. Only it has gotten a lot harder to find reasons to dance at all."

"And so it is with My Good Lord Tienan."

She dabbed moisture from her eyes and cleared her tear-clogged throat. "Zad, your host strikes me as a man who marches through life banging his own kettle drum."

"Sadly, no. He is a product of the Hautonne."

"What's that?"

"The elite, the thirteen founding families of our Zantharian culture and homeworld. He is Lord Tienan Haveloch Mordecai Wardell De'Argossi, Archdruid of the Second House Hautonne, and the Suzerain De'Argossi."

"King and emperor all rolled into one?"

"Not quite, but close. Since the First House Hautonne is no more— or we pray that it is no more — the second house possesses a wealth and power like no other."

"Meaning House De'Argossi has a history of wielding that wealth and power over the lesser houses?"

"Once perhaps, but societies evolve, populations grow. There are now a thousand of the Golva, the lesser houses. A republic prevails."

"And you tell me this because — ?"

"I wish you to understand that Tienan wants a loving wife, children, a family as much as I do, but — "

"How will he know a woman loves him for himself and not for his wealth or position?"

"Exactly!"

Tienan barely heard Janay's whispered, "Been there, hated it."

Zad's ears laid back, and he tilted his head as if puzzled. "Your husband was a wealthy monk?"

"Definitely not!" She half chuckled. "He took vows of poverty. We lived modestly. What I was referring to was my father. Just so you know, my mother married him for his money so she could enjoy privileged society. She said it often enough after the divorce."

The phrasing, the tone of her words, said the divorce had been hell.

"Sad to say," Janay said, "but my mother and father were extreme opposites and, damn the fates, opposites do attract."

Like she, the warrior, and her monk-husband?

"Yes," Zad muttered. "Opposites do seem to attract."

"What was worse was that my parents had big, ambitious agendas. Both were aggressively goal-oriented."

"You were traumatized by their divorce?"

"Don't be ridiculous. Mother got herself pregnant just so my father, who wanted an heir, would wed her and provide her the kind of accessories she felt were her due. I was a means to that end, raised by an old nanny and by the best of neighbors." Her smile held some happy recollection. "I was also very smart. At age fourteen, I got an advocate and petitioned the courts to let me choose my legal guardians."

"So your parents disinherited you." Zad shook his head sadly. "Cast you out to be a common soldier."

Janay laughed. "No, silly. The divorce settlement included trust funds for me — the lawyers insisted. I also invested Otto's life insurance policy. They're my reserves, which I don't tap into if I can help it."

"Boots said you were broke. She told Tienan to be generous with the familiaris contract payment."

"Ah, back to that familiaris thing, are we?"

Zad nodded.

She put her hands on Zad's cheeks, and her voice held sincerity of purpose. "Why would you, and only you, yourself, want me to be Tienan's familiaris?"

Zad did not readily answer.

She maintained eye contact with him.

After a very long moment, she withdrew her hands, and leaned back, waiting. Patiently waiting.

Zad finally spoke. "Because you are truly worth loving." He turned and, head down in defeat, left.

Tienan blinked back the wetness glossing his vision and swallowed the tears welling in his throat. Why was he being so emotional? He should be glad. Yes, glad. He'd found out more about Janay in the last few minutes than in the days since he'd met her. Yes, she was self-sufficient, bright, intuitive, but her secrets and her life, well, they were like a lake of still water, the depths unfathomable. One thing was for sure, neither Rowen or Zad had convinced her to become his familiaris.

He wanted her to be his familiaris.

That revelation sucker-punched him in the gut. It was followed by a second punch — the realization that she would never be any man's mistress.

Her two dirks whizzed by her head, shoving her headband into her face.

She swore at them and reset the band.

The dirks kept circling her and each other. The dirk with the darker veining on its leaf patterns suddenly spun and halted at the edge of the desk. It began tapping its tip on the desktop.

She shifted her gaze to the wall where the holograph camouflaged the door to the lift.

The tapping stopped.

"Okay, Tienan," Janay said, "come on out."

The blades knew he was here? For how long? Trond. He hit the key and the lift door opened. He stepped through the holographic projection.

Janay looked momentarily dismayed. "How much of my conversation with Zad did you listen in on?"

Only one way to answer that. "All of it."

She swore softly, then began to rise.

"No, please, Janay, wait. I need to say something."

She reseated herself. "Well, go ahead, I suppose I ought to hear your spiel as to why I should be your familiaris."

"I'm not here to argue, plead, or even beg. The truth is, in my anger at my grandmother, I made an irrational, impulsive, declaration that has put you in a bind. What I did, what I said, was not fair to you." He took a breath for courage and to infuse sincerity into his words. "I apologize. I withdraw my suit that you become my familiaris."

She stared at him as if she were seeing him in a new light. Which both pleased and disturbed him.

"Janay, I owe you for saving Rowen's life, but paying you back by causing you anxiety, mental anguish, whatever they call it these days, or forcing you to do what you don't want to do— Confound the powers, it's not right. I am sorry, Janay, truly sorry. Please forgive me."

"I'll be damned . . ." She grinned, reached forward, and turned on the computer screen. She hit the button, flipping the screen so he could read the centered header's FAMILIARIS CONTRACT.

Stunned, he grabbed the nearest chair and sat down.

"I filled this one out," she said. "It wasn't as complex as the other choices. I can live with this one."

It took him a moment to get control of the immense pleasure radiating inside his heart. Then he realized that Janay was, as Zad had said, worth loving. Only loving her was not in any equation for him. Paying her back for Rowen's life was. But what had persuaded her to be his familiaris? "Janay, I have to know, what made you decide?"

"Neejera. She told me that what prevented my hip from healing was me. I needed to take it easy, look after my body. Rest, eat, sleep. Have nonstrenuous exercise and fun—emphasis on fun. If I could do that for six months, my body was likely to repair my hip all by itself."

He would have to thank Neejera.

"In case it hasn't sunk in, *I am a peacekeeper* — in mind and soul and heart. It's a life I love—well, most of the time. I want a chance to get that life back."

"What if you don't make duty status? What then?"

"Neejera pointed out that if I wasn't peacekeeper sound, I should be sound enough to become a Guardian or apply to Protectors Incorporated to be a private guard or work spaceport security. I'm not sure either appeals, but the alternative is being a cripple for life."

She got up from the chair. At the bay window, she stopped and gazed out at a moon brightening the deepening twilight. "Most of the time, I'm a realist, Tienan. Right now, I have no idea what I'll do if my hip doesn't heal, but I won't give up the desire to wear a peacekeeper uniform until it becomes an impossibility. Staying with you, being your houseguest cum companion, is a wiser choice for the time being." She hugged herself.

He went and stood behind her. The thought that something else had made her decide being a familiaris was in her best interest suddenly assailed him. "Janay, if we're to have a relationship, we need to be honest with each other. Are there any other reasons that made you decide to become my familiaris?"

"Ah, a man who likes to be sure." She looked over her shoulder at him with a twinkle of admiration in her eyes that was quickly replaced by uncertainty. "How's this for honesty—I'm terrified of losing my sanity if I don't have a keeper." She turned her attention back to the moon.

"Your sanity?"

"Yeah. I'm terrified the tormantratas will sense a weakness in me, that they'll whisper their dark thoughts when I'm asleep, trigger nightmares of Rathe. But when I'm sleeping beside you, and Zad purrs, I feel uncommonly safe."

The two dirks came to rest, hovering, one over each of his shoulder blades, tips at slight angles. "Is that why your dirks want you to sleep with me?"

"Idiot blades! Who knows? They still won't answer that question."

The blades jabbed him. "Janay, your dirks are poking me in the back."

She glanced over her shoulder. "They do that to me when they want me to hug someone."

The dirks wanted him to hug Janay? "No problem." He put his arms about her waist.

The dirks retreated.

Janay leaned back against him. She cupped her hands over his forearms and stared out the window. Her voice came out low, ladened with remorse. "Can you forgive me?"

"For what?"

"For trying to kill your grandmother's veed. Truly, Tienan, I didn't know a veed could look demonic. What am I going to do if I see other veeds on the loose?" Her voice trembled. "How am I to tell the difference between veeds and demons?"

Resting his cheek against hers, he sensed the pounding pulse in her jugular. He smelled the powder-sweet odor of the soap she bathed with, and beyond that, to her distinctly feminine scent, the peachy one he found he couldn't get out of his mind.

There was pleasure in holding her but also arousal, as evidenced by the bulge developing in his pants. *He better distract himself.* "First of all, Janay, veeds are not usually out of their hosts. Certainly not in public. If they are, they become fair game, that is prey, for other veeds. A home is considered sacred ground, a safe place to turn a veed loose. Outside a house is safe only if it's walled in and spell-shielded to keep neighboring or marauding veeds out. It's hard to live with another personality, share a mind, so home is where host and veed can be apart, have some private time."

He felt her smile bloom. "Ah, so Zad sometimes drives you nuts?"

"Every once in a while. As to your question about recognizing veeds, maybe the question is, how do you recognize a demon when you see one?"

"Easy. They're downright ugly. Always dark colors, slate to coal blacks, mud-greens, puke-browns. Colors that blend with dirt, trees — the night shadows in hospital rooms, padded cells . . ."

He wondered about the padded cells but decided not to pry. "Are demons always dark colors?"

"I saw a blue one once, but it was dirty-gray blue, if that counts? Why?"

He kissed the pulse on her neck and grinned. "Veeds only come in six colors. Black, white, gold, silver, amber, and cobalt blue."

"Why only six?"

"Because they were created from the colors of the Swords of Power. Let me restate that. Although there are only six colors, they appear in combinations or an obvious mix of the colors. Some colors may seem not to be present, but they will be in tiny amounts, like one tooth or one claw or a tuft of hair inside an ear."

"Are you hinting that not all veeds are as big as Zad or your grandmother's?"

"No need to hint. Veeds can be as small as a house cat up to elephantine. Zad is average for a Behringgreat. Speaking of which, the veeds that walk on all fours are called Behringgreats. The ones that crawl, slither, or walk on two legs are considered

Behringlessers." Perhaps he shouldn't have told her so much? His society flourished only because outworlders didn't know about veed power. Yet, telling her about them would ease her concerns about living with him, being his familiaris, wouldn't it?

"I take it, Tienan, that veeds have a caste system?"

"Ahh, typical female, always curious."

"Ahh, typical male, endlessly evasive. So, are you saying this veed stuff is classified intel?"

"Yes." He wished he hadn't spoken so quickly. Janay needed information so she wouldn't kill a veed and take the host's life. *She needed information to save her sanity.* "Janay, will you promise to keep what I tell you a secret?"

She nodded. "My word of honor."

"There's a caste system with four distinct levels of veeds. The least powerful is the veed embryo. It's like a tiny veed-egg that never hatches. Having the egg gives the host psychic ability. They sense things before they happen. The next level is p'si-zaveed energy. No manifestation of a veed-egg or a noncorporeal entity. Such people possess one ability, one power. Like Boots. She has telekinetic p'si. She can cuff a perp from thirty feet away."

He gazed out the window at the serene night, the shadows, the moon-silvered daoka trees. "The third level is a veed, a true symbiote, like Zad and Liss and Tal. The fourth type, the vitari-p'si, is the epitome of veed power, where the energy is one with the person. Very rare. Exceptionally powerful."

"What causes the difference between levels?"

"Love."

"Come again?"

He softened his voice. "If I fell in love with a veeded woman, and she loved me, and our veeds were happy in our love, then our veeds would genate. That is, as we consummated our loving relationship—"

"Meaning copulation?"

"Don't interrupt. As I was saying, if we Zantharians are in love and want a child, and make love to conceive a child, our veeds commingle their energy. They then bestow veed power on the conceived child." He chuckled. "In the De'Argossi family, we have managed to marry for passionate love. Each generation has produced male children with Behringgreat Veeds manifested as wisdom white and judgment black. Always great cats. Lions, tigers, jaguars, even a couple of leopards." A part of him was relieved to tell her about veeds and, in his contentment, he held her, savoring the serenity of the moment.

He inhaled the fruity scent of her and the warmth of her femininity.

When he let the breath out, he no longer objected to those odors lingering in his nostrils or the scent drifting about his mind, tugging at him, setting his penis rising upward.

She turned and peered deep into his eyes. Thankful. Pleased. Becalmed.

Ah, my gypsy imp . . . He dipped his head and kissed her with a whispering, feathery softness of flesh on flesh.

She sighed.

He settled his lips over hers, taking his time to savor the silken edges of each lip, then, tentatively, he ran the tip of his tongue along her bottom lip.

She splayed one hand over his heart, the other dropped, palm against his building erection, touching, holding his penis almost reverently.

His erection burst to full height, the tip grating against cloth. The discomfort cleared the euphoric haze from his senses. *A De'Argossi did not fornicate with a* jossierj. He pulled back, ending the kiss.

She moved her hand away from his groin and placed it on his chest, opposite the hand she held over his pulsing heart. She pushed with both hands, taking a half-step back.

He let her go. "Janay . . ." he whispered, his voice more pleading than apologetic.

Her voice was hoarse with arousal, and regret. "Humans have conquered space and time, colonized new worlds, but our biology still undermines us." She put a finger on his lips, keeping him from speaking. "I know it started as a kiss of comfort, and I'll readily admit I needed comfort, so don't you dare apologize for doing what came naturally unless you want a right cross to your solar plexus."

Leave it to her to state the facts.

She headed for the door. "Bottom line, Tienan, you need me to save face. I figure to be your familiaris. Better look over that contract so we can finalize it."

❦ Chapter Ten

I have no limbs; I make Promptitude my Limbs.
— The Samurai Creed

It was after lunch the next day when Janay returned from town with Tienan. He drove his sporty red tekcar with ease and speed. Seconds after turning into the driveway to Wolcott House, Tienan swore.

Janay followed his line of sight to a large black Baronni, a classic town car on a sleek skateboard chassis, parked under the arched portico attached to the house and garage.

"That," he said between gritted teeth, "is Grandmother's car." He touched the console controls and the tekcar slowed.

"Look on the bright side," Janay offered with a smile, "maybe your grandmother has come to apologize."

"I don't want an apology. I meant what I said. She's not welcome in my home." When the vehicle stopped, the seagull-winged doors opened and Tienan exited. He strode for the side door of the house.

When she caught up to him in the kitchen, he stood to Rowen's right, at the round table in the corner near the fireplace. Tienan glared at the young woman on the other side of the table. She was impeccably dressed in a multi-colored turquoise top and dark, solid-colored, turquoise slacks. Her suit jacket lay draped on the back of her chair. The woman's face increasingly lost color.

"Where is she?" Tienan demanded of the woman.

Rowen cranked his head back to address his brother. "Who are you referring to?"

"Grandmother!"

Rowen replied,"She's not here."

"Her car is in the drive and that—" He pointed to the young woman. "—is her personal assistant."

"Tienan—" Rowen pushed himself away from the table, jarring the half full mug of his deep green saguenay coffee. His voice cautioned, "Annelisa is my guest."

Annelisa cowered. "Her Grace lent me the car . . ."

As he eyed his brother, Tienan's voice lowered to an icy depth. "This is my home, Rowen. Are you undermining my authority in it?"

"No. Sit down before I get a crick in my neck, and stop frightening Annelisa. Please?"

Tienan muttered something, grabbed the chair to his right, spun it about, and sat, straddling the seat. He looked like a Guardian about to interrogate a serial killer.

Annelisa's eyes went wide with fear.

"Janay," Rowen said, "allow me to introduce my friend, Annelisa Quorn." His voice took on a reassuring timbre. "Annelisa, this is Janay Cholyn, my brother's familiaris, of whom Grandmother has expounded on in volumes and who has made your life hellish."

Janay nodded to Annelisa.

"Pleased to meet you." Annelisa's reply was socially practiced politeness, but her eyes brimmed with veed sparking curiosity.

Janay seated herself in the only vacant chair, which put her opposite Tienan.

Seeing where Annelisa's gaze alighted, Janay had the urge to slip her hand under the table, but she didn't. She had become Tienan's familiaris and, by Adrada's darkest purple feathers, she would play the part.

Janay tilted her hand ever so slightly, giving Annelisa a better look at the rings. The compeer's ring matched Tienan's warlock ring, except that the nyd rune arched over an inlaid mother-of-pearl rosebud. That ring proclaimed she was Tienan's companion, or so Tienan had said. The ring made her feel—enslaved.

But it was the familiaris's gold ring next to the compeer's ring that eclipsed reality. That ring now held Annelisa transfixed. The bottom of the five carat, fiery red-orange, oval Padparadscha sapphire set cradled by an upper and lower arched band of tiny, flawless diamonds.

Rowen whistled softly. "That's some ring."

"Antique." Pride rang in Tienan voice. He met Annelisa's gaze.

"Be sure to tell Grandmother."

Annelisa nodded slowly. "Certainly, Lord Tienan."

Was Tienan bragging, or intent on proving to his grandmother that his familiaris was worth the outrageous cost of the ring?

Janay inwardly sighed. Probably both.

Rowen touched his brother's arm, and Tienan looked at him. "Please, Tienan, try to understand. Annelisa and I are caught in the middle between you and grandmother. Neither of us likes it."

Tienan seemed to calm. When he spoke, his voice was free of antagonism. "My apologies, Annelisa."

"Thank you, Lord Tienan." Her voice trembled, but her hands did not. She pulled her shoulders back, sat straighter. "It's understandable, my lord, that you have misgivings about my being here. I want you to know that Her Grace is sincerely distressed over the situation between you and her. I—I am too." She took a replenishing, fortifying breath, then fetched two small envelopes from the inner pocket of her jacket. She handed the top one to Tienan. Then she held the other one out to Janay. "This one is for you, magestrella."

Magestrella. That's what the store clerks had called her when she and Tienan were shopping for the familiaris's ring. Magestrella, Tienan said, meant mistress. But mistress had many connotations, mostly derogative ones.

"Look," Janay said, "I'm not one for titles. Just call me Janay." She took the missive from Annelisa's cold fingers. Poor girl. Rowen had the right of it, Annelisa was trapped between the rock—her employer—and, not a hard place but a hard man—Tienan.

Turning the envelope over, Janay noted the glob of shimmering blue-black wax and the deeply embedded rune. She broke the seal. On opening the note, a matte silver card slipped out. She caught it. The title lines said, *You are Cordially Invited to the Ozieron Coven's Annual Solstice High Tea*. After reading the note of apology, she looked at Tienan. "Swap." Once finished reading his note, she exchanged it for hers.

"Despite what's written, Janay," Tienan said, his tone sharp enough that Annelisa couldn't miss the message, "I don't believe Grandmother is repentant."

"How about we go outside where we can discuss this in private?"

Tienan curtly nodded and rose.

Once outside, under the pergola-covered terrace, where a

breeze surged the cool dampness of the nearby woods against the house like a refreshing incoming tide, Janay faced Tienan.

He stopped and kept his voice low. "I don't see what we have to discuss. I'm not relenting."

"Didn't ask you to, now did I? Square those big shoulders of yours, straighten that spine, and turn ever so slightly so Annelisa sees only your back and your lordliness in full glory of Hautonne ire."

A smile creased the corner of his lips. "My lordliness? My Hautonne ire?"

Keeping a blank face, she replied, "Whatever. We are stalling so Annelisa gets the impression that I have control over you. Not that I truly do mind you, but she is your grandmother's gofer and, maybe Rowen considers her a friend, but he doesn't issue her paychecks now, does he?"

"Ah, so you agree, Annelisa's loyalty is to my grandmother?"

"Exactly. Now, let's look at the situation. Rowen told me over breakfast that you and he are the last of the De'Argossies. Rowen wants a wife and family. Zad has told me you do too."

"That's right, but we want to choose our mates." The edge went back in his voice. "I won't permit Grandmother to interfere."

"Granted, but look, to me this situation is one of family strife, which is like civil strife only on a smaller scale, but which we don't want to erupt into civil war. So, how about we don't rile the populace and create anarchy?"

The wisp of a smile twitched the corners of his mouth. "So, peacekeeper, what's your diplomatic solution?"

"Actions speak louder than starship cannons."

"Are you equating my grandmother to a battle cruiser?"

She stifled a chuckle. "More like an old, ready-for-drydock destroyer."

He gaped at her, then laughter, both his and his veed's, bubbled up, brightening his gray eyes to diamond brilliance. He put his hands on his hips.

"Oh, good gesture."

"What?"

"You've put your hands on your hips. Annelisa will think you're really pissed."

He crossed his arms over his chest. "Okay, Janay, what's your solution to drydocking my grandmother?"

"According to the contract we filed, I am your familiaris for the next six months, which means I have to fit into your lifestyle.

As Rowen said this morning, that means fitting in with Zantharian society in general and, more specifically, with Hautonne royalty."

His face blanched.

"Oh good grief, now it occurs to you that I have to coexist in your society?"

He nodded. "And that's treasonous. We are Zantharians who take oaths to protect our wizardry."

"Idiot! If I can keep military secrets, Zhayoda secrets, and one of the Emperor's secrets, what are a few wizardly ones?"

He blinked. "You had that kind of military clearance?"

"Yes. I earned that status while serving General Tarfooga. Now, about your wizard stuff. I know your race is veeded. I know you have secret passages in the house so you can appear and disappear at will. Don't you think people, *particularly your grandmother*, will be suspicious as to why I'm clueless about what a familiaris should know?"

What she said made perfect sense. He'd reacted, blurted out she was his familiaris and now he was suffering the consequences. For better or worse, he had to play this familiaris thing out. He owed Janay for Rowen's life. Janay had to fit in. "You're right. Even if I initiate you into our way of life, Grandmother is a perfectionist. Anything you do wrong, she'll use as ammunition to — *to sink you*."

"You cannot sink a peacekeeper. We're army, not sailors."

He felt his grin crunch his cheeks back.

"Can the hilarity, mister."

He sobered. "What do you have in mind, Janay?"

"Right now? Well, we do something for an hour or so. Make Annelisa angst over getting an answer to take back to her boss."

"And what will that answer be, my little peacekeeper?"

"That we agree to a temporary truce. Maybe say we are willing to socialize but only at public events."

He didn't want to socialize with his grandmother. Then Zad spoke to him, and he reiterated his veed's words. "Where there are people gathered, Grandmother will be forced to mind her manners?"

"Exactly. Which means you need to make sure I don't embarrass us both. So, why don't we use our hour for you to tell me what I need to know about the basics of your Zantharian wizardry? That way I can't make a fool of myself."

My good lord, Zad said, *charge her ring.*

And baptize her with the blood of ages.

Yes, my good lord! An excellent idea.

"Come on, Janay." He took her hand, led her around to the side of the house, down the bricked steps, and back into the house through the lounge door. He stopped before the camouflaged lift. "I want your word, Janay, that you will never reveal, now or after the familiaris contract ends, what you learn, see, hear, or witness during the time you are my familiaris and in Zantharian society."

"Fox, Poke, bear witness." The dirks shot out of the tops of her boots and hovered in front of her. "Tienan De'Argossi, Zantharian Warlock of the Eight Power, and to Zad, your Behringgreat Veed, upon my honor and upon my life, upon the sacred cross on my heart and upon my sacred blades, I vow to keep all that is revealed to me about being veed, being witch or warlock, and to keep these secrets all the days of my life, unto my very death."

Well said! Zad preened with satisfaction.

Tienan reiterated, "Well said, Janay."

"A little corny, but the dirks treasure formality."

"So do veeds . . ."

She looked at the dirks. "Poke, Fox, I charge you with nudging me should I waiver in this vow, and I order you to take my life if I betray this oath."

The blades bowed.

"Dismissed."

The blades vanished into her boots.

Her ordering the dirks to kill her echoed in his mind until he realized that at the end of six months, he would give her the potion that would make her forget everything Zantharian—and forget she had ever met him.

A cold chill swept through him. Did he want her to forget him?

"So, what now, Tienan? Why did you bring me here?"

He made a show of raising his warlock ring. "A witch's or warlock's ring is the key to operating all the MS, the Majikal Systems, in our homes. Coven Halls also have entrance-exits and lifts that can only be accessed by authorization codes embedded in a Zantharian's ring. The idea is not to look like you're triggering a signal but rather you're invoking magic." He demonstrated. "We raise or turn our hand so the ring faces the sensors. They're mounted above the doors and lifts. We mouth, whisper, or say, *akmok* and, in the case of secret passages, we listen for the shushing of the door opening. I doubt if you'll hear the door. Our veeds usually enhance our hearing. Anyway, the door opens, and the holographic projection camouflaging the secret passage remains in place. We merely step forward." He walked into the wall of books and vanished.

Janay put her hand out in front of her and followed. Her hand hit something solid.

A second later, the holographic projection evaporated. Tienan stood in an aqua-blue, four-person, tube of a lift.

"I take it your MS system has a force barrier to keep non-Zantharians, out?" She entered the lift.

"And children. This tile deactivates it." He pointed to the bottom one of a vertical row of diamond shapes. "The tiles on the other side of the door are decorations, as are those on the back wall. To go up, hit the top one, to go down, the bottom. One tap per floor up or down." He hit the tile and the door closed. "If you're in a hurry, tap the bar twice for full speed." He pointed to the diamond shape, part of a black scrolled design in the door's center. "For emergency stops or to call for help, push the center."

When the lift door opened, she followed him into a basement. To her left machinery hummed. All were familiar heating units and electrical power cores that winked their bio and plasmic, yellowish-green colored operations' lights. Ahead, and to her right, stood a fieldstone wall.

He tugged her sleeve and she went left, following him. After flashing his ring again, a door opened and she found herself in the house's mainframe computer center.

"Give me your compeer ring."

As soon as she took the ring off and handed it to him, he went to a wall unit where he flashed his ring under a small, lion's-head knob.

Out popped a narrow drawer.

He set the compeer ring in the bottom of the drawer, on a center-mounted pedestal, and prongs clamped onto the ring. The drawer closed. Moments later, the drawer opened.

He gave her back the ring. "You now have access to the house and all its comlinks. Every room has at least one comlink, the larger rooms have multiples. To trigger a link on or off, briefly tap your thumbnail into the groove on the underside of your ring, then verbally state what you want."

She put the ring on and practiced getting her thumbnail into the groove.

"Let's test your ring." He took her back to the lift but faced the fieldstone wall instead. "Open this door."

Door? She eyed the upper rows of stone but didn't detect any sensor strip. Faith preserve her. She turned her hand, palm down, and commanded, "Akmok," then stepped forward, her heart racing with the certainty that she would strike solid wall.

Only she stepped through the holographic rocks into cool air that held the tang of fruit and musky herbs. Relief washed over her. She'd entered a room with rows of shelving interspersed by various sized bins.

On the far wall, glass doors protected labeled bottles in a myriad of colors, shapes, and sizes.

Tienan stepped to her side. "We store herbs and potions here."

She saw a bin marked POTATOES. "Fresh veggies too, I see."

He nodded, then strode to the other side of the room, facing another wall.

She followed and repeated the ring gesture but this time only mouthed the magic word. Once through the wall, the lights came on and goose bumps erupted on her arms. She wasn't sure if the gooseflesh was from the chill of the room, the years of incense that permeated the air, or the spooky black stone fireplace so large six men Tienan's size could stand side-by-side inside it.

Adding to her unease was a shiny black altar that balanced on a swirl of a pedestal. The silver outline of a pentagram had been deeply embedded into the room's black pavers. White marble bricks circled the pentagram.

Tienan went to the altar. "This room is known as The Sorcery, often called the ceremonial chamber, but sometimes it's called the Druid Chamber because of the Druid's Circle—that's the white brick circle on the floor. Now, Janay, come. Stand on the other side of the altar. I'll be right back."

He went to the back of the room and opened the largest of the oak-paneled cupboards that lined the entire wall. He took out and donned a monk's black robe.

Curiosity had her eyeing the side wall where the upper cupboards had stained-glass doors depicting ravens in flight. The lower cupboards had solid wood doors and black granite counter tops. Everything bespoke quality craftsmanship, age, money, and magic. Black magic.

From an upper cupboard, he took out a small parcel, unwrapped the cloth, and set a silver dragon chalice onto the counter. The dragon's mouth, which was wide open, supported a ruby-red glass bowl.

Tienan opened another cupboard and removed a black decanter. He unscrewed the cap and poured a small amount of dark liquid into the goblet. After putting the decanter back, he took the goblet and went to the other side of the room. From a base cupboard drawer, he removed a squat black box. Once back at the altar, he set the goblet down in the center of the altar's pentagram. He quickly pulled the two halves of the box apart. Centered in the base of the box was a U-shaped silver channel.

The gizmo reminded her of a cigar cutter.

"Put your finger, the one with your compeer's ring in the slot. I need to bless it."

"Bless it?"

"Please, Janay, do as I ask. It won't hurt. Trust me."

Trust him? She took a deep breath for courage and put her finger in the slot. The tips of the U clamped down on the ring and another set of bands clamped tightly over her finger. An image winked of her finger being severed, and she fought to rationalize that was not going to happen. She had to trust him.

"Janay, the unit must make a complete seal about the ring and the skin the ring comes in contact with. Now I'm going to chant and drop into a meditative state. Zad's energy will touch your ring and that energy will bond the ring to you. The ring will work only for you. No one else." He flipped the hood of his robe forward, covering his head and most of his face. After twisting his warlock's ring around until it was on the palm side of his hand, he set the ring down, over the band imprisoning her ring and finger.

A cold shiver of dread triggered an icy cascade down her spine.

He began to chant, his voice low, deep. Mesmerizing.

Soon Zad's energy aura flowed over his hand, circled his warlock ring, spiraling downward into her ring. She felt the vibrations from that energy intensify, needling the skin under the band of the ring. Suddenly Zad's energy dissipated. But not the tingling. Tienan raised his hand and stopped chanting.

The mechanism released her finger.

She jerked her hand away. When she pulled the ring up to her knuckle to check her tingling skin, she found white flesh where the band had been.

With somber formality, Tienan said, "You now bear the mark of a witch bonded to House De'Argossi."

She brought her finger closer to her eyes, the better to examine it. Her skin, no longer tingling, was covered with tiny designs.

"Those runes match the ones inside your ring. Zad copied them onto your finger."

"I'm branded for life?"

"No. They're more like tattoos. Zad can remove them when the time comes. And now, my dear familiaris, you know the real secret of Zantharian magic."

"Forgive my ignorance, but what secret?"

"That our magic is nothing more than clever technology coupled with hekatriaa, the power of mind and body enhanced by a veed."

"Why? Why go to such lengths?"

"To stay alive as a race. There are those who equate our veeds to monsters. Far too many Zantharians have died with stakes through their hearts, their heads and hands severed. Atrocities are committed by people who think only the devil's entity—or an alien abomination— can live inside a humanoid being." He took the goblet, raised it over the inlaid pentagram on the altar, closed his eyes, and muttered words. When he ended the incantation, he opened his eyes and looked at her. "I will baptize you now with the blood of ages."

She stepped back.

"It's not what you think."

"And what do you think I'm thinking?"

"That this is real blood or a wicked potion I've put a spell on that will enthrall you to me." Mirth whizzed merrily in his eyes.

"Granted, it could be either—or colored water. So, just what are you going to do with that concoction?"

"First, I'm going to sip it like this." He placed his bottom lip against the inside of the glass before tilting the goblet so the bloody liquid coated both his upper and lower lips. "Now, I'm going to kiss you."

She almost stepped back. "Is this another tattooing kind of thing?"

He shook his head and circled the altar toward her, obviously having a hard time suppressing his glee.

She stood her ground, heart pumping like she was locking and loading a MPAR, about to shoot the multi-use personal assault rifle.

What had she gotten herself into? She was his familiaris. And a deal was a deal. "Skom. In for a dyne in for a drail."

He handed the goblet to her. "Put both hands on the stem and drink it all."

She took the goblet, refusing to look at the contents or listen to her inner voice warn she was about to drink a bitter, poisonous brew. Heart accelerating and blood pounding in her ears, she chugged the odorless liquid down.

Sweet.

Smooth as syrup.

Realization dawned.

Her smile threatened to become laughter.

With a deadpan expression, Tienan said, "This is serious, Janay. No laughing at the altar."

She fought for control.

He took the goblet from her and set it on the altar. "Put your right hand to my heart. My hand goes over yours."

She obeyed.

His hand settled lightly over her heart, his warm palm resting on her breast.

"Now your other hand on top of mine." He placed his free hand over hers. Feeling Zad's energy glimmering, he knew his eyes must be sparking with his veed's energy. She didn't seem to notice. "*Voth egen ym worrelt ym anda familiarso*—welcome to my world and my family." He lowered his head.

The moment his lips touched hers, Zad fired a tendril of energy that skittered across his lips to hers, igniting the effervescence that exploded in the liquid.

Janay shuddered and opened her mouth in surprise.

His tongue plunged deep into her sweet cherry, candy-coated mouth.

Zad fired another energy burst.

The granules in the liquid exploded.

Janay squealed deep in her throat but did not pull away.

Like a man who had not eaten in a century, Tienan kissed and licked the liquid off her lips, deepening the kisses until Zad sent a sizzle of pain to his groin, making him aware of his erection.

My lord, do not go so far.

Tienan backed off, hating that this simple pleasure had to end. He feathered one last lick across her lower lip.

When he looked into Janay's eyes, he saw the depth of the desire he'd awakened in her. He hadn't meant to arouse her, and yet . . . He was aroused.

Both of them needed time to recover.

Seeing the goblet, he cleaned it and put it away. When he finished, he turned to Janay.

She seemed her normal self.

She grinned. "Wizardly ways, my eye teeth, Tienan. That was

the best choberimiz I've ever had."

"You've had it before?"

"It's used in J'Hian rituals, like when a child takes their first pledge of allegiance to the church, and in wedding ceremonies. Only, I have to admit, the J'Hian version is wine-dark. It never fizzes like your brew."

Confound the powers, someone else used the same kind of liqueur?

"Hey, Tienan, it's late. If there's nothing more, how about we go upstairs? I think Annelisa has waited long enough for a reply, don't you?"

He nodded and Janay was glad to follow him, to have a few minutes more to gain control of her emotions.

Choberimiz, or no choberimiz, never had her body reacted to a kiss like Tienan's. A kiss that had her curling her toes and heating her blood with a need to melt into him. Which likely meant she was, for some reason, craving sex. Lusting for the man.

No, not exactly lust. Been there, done that with Sam Cramer. Not going there again. Ever.

To mind came her husband Otto's words, *The soul seeks true friendship, the heart seeks true love. Having both in one soul is the miracle of bonded souls.*

Now why had that thought come to mind?

❦ Chapter Eleven

I have no laws; I make Self-Protection my Laws.
— The Samurai Creed

Annelisa silently congratulated her veed on having the foresight to remind her to wear loafers for the trek down the dimly lit alley between warehouses.

With her next breath, she silently cursed Sweets' paranoia and insistence she park along the street by Fred's Bar and Grill, then walk the two blocks to the warehouse.

Which was the lesser evil? Having drunkards and street walkers note her comings and goings or driving past security sensors that might record a glimpse of the boys they kidnapped? Likely the latter. Why did Sweets have to always be so right?

Ahead, near the end of the alley, stood the warehouse's back delivery door. The small night light above the door barely lit half the doorway.

Her gaze shifted upward, to where orange-gold night lights reflected off the peaks of taller warehouses and cast midnight shadows across the lower roofs.

Celinae had leased this particular warehouse because it set over one of the planet's natural magnetic spots. A powerful one. It also helped that the warehouse had been extremely insulated, soundproofed, and it was tucked among rows of warehouses where one building looked like another.

Annelisa eyed the building's corner where an ivy vine wound around a light pole. That vine reminded her of the plants inside the warehouse. From them Sweets and Celinae distilled bloodwood sap, mixed bloodwood poisons and aphrodisiacs and read incantations from a millennium-old text, *The Fourth Book of Xenobia.*

An image crystallized in Annelisa's mind of Sweets' smiling face, the delightful sheen of her brown eyes when she presented the book the first time. Sweets bragged how, after Shelzat told her about the book's contents, she'd figured out how to steal the book from the vault at Guardian headquarters.

A whiff of putrid air coming off a dumpster brought a distasteful memory of that book. Despite Sweets' assurances that the book's cover was animal hide, the leather reeked like decaying human flesh. Some of the pages smelled like raw sewage, others of coppery blood. Yet, the book intrigued her as much as its smells repulsed her.

And speaking of repulsive, it seemed strange that she, like Celinae and Sweets, felt no guilt for killing four boys. Nor for their veeds devouring those boys' veed energies.

She looked inward, at her own dainty, goose of a veed. Ahl had gorged herself on that veed energy and had been invigorated by the ensuing power surge. So invigorated that her tail blossomed into a fan of blue, silver, and amber feathers. Ahl's rounded beak had turned hawk-like and sported razor-sharp edges.

And Ahl could hardly wait to feast on the next veed.

Tonight it was her and Ahl's duty to prime their next victim to come to them. Doing such things should have given a normal person, a normal Zantharian, nightmares or at least second thoughts. Or was it like Sweets insisted? The three of them were special, ordained to become a triad, destined to reap all of the rewards bound in the pages of the *Fourth Book of Xenobia*?

Annelisa heaved a sigh. In truth, she was too inquisitive for her own good. And why did she always question every motive, every good thing, that happened to her?

Ahl suddenly flickered brightly inside her mind's eye, morphed into her marble-sized ball of energy, and hovered in place. Thread-thin dots of gold, amber, and blue appeared. Those colors entwined to swirl within the opaque whiteness of her energy. The ball was proper form for being in the company of other veeds.

Like soft laughter, a breath of chilling wind swept by her left ear.

She caught a whiff of an odor and inhaled more deeply the scent of ancient, primal pheromones smothered in myrrh.

Annelisa stopped short.

Apprehension settled like lead in her guts.

The scent belonged to Shelzat, the Darkon Archangel, the Obtainer of Souls, to whom she, Celinae, and Sweets—and their veeds—had signed blood bargains with.

All three bore Shelzat's tiny snake-squiggled S brand in the center of their triad-bonding tattoos. She fought the urge to touch the underside of her left breast where the tattoo resided.

"Good evening, Annelisa." Shelzat's voice came from behind her, masculine, not deep, yet forever seductive.

She turned, a practiced smile in place and avoided gazing at the snakeskin band across his forehead. Seeing that band always made her tremble with doom.

She clutched the fabric at the top of her cape and felt her cold knuckles graze her chin.

The archangel stood on the asphalt, his black-feathered wings tucked so the tips crossed and wouldn't drag on the ground.

In the dimness of the alley, his white-blond hair and icy-clear eyes stood at odds with his attire. A black, finely tailored Nehru jacket set over pants that tapered into matte black boots.

Shelzat wore no weapons belt, no sword, no shoulder sash of duty. Which meant she was not in any physical danger from him.

"My, my, my. How lovely you look, Annelisa. Dressed for a night of fun and laughter, desire and dancing?" His voice purred like a Tom cat on the prowl. "But what puzzles me, dearest Annelisa, is why are you here and not at a party?"

"I'm on my way to see Celinae." Thankfully her voice didn't give away her apprehension of being alone with him.

"Then go on in. Make your report."

She started forward, but paused. "Maybe you should go first?"

His face remained handsomely bland, like a Hautonne gentleman who suffered ennui.

Shelzat looked down his nose at her. His cold gaze sliced through her mind to Ahl, whose energy momentarily stopped swirling. "Dearest, you know how jealous Celinae becomes when any beautiful woman looks at me like you're doing now."

Oh, the darkon was outside of enough! "You know full well how charismatic you are—and doubly proud of it." Why had she said that?

Her heart fluttered in her chest.

Would he take offense?

A smug smile scrolled across his lips. "Charismatic? No, no, no. I am — *salacious*. Which makes it hard to keep Celinae's attention on business when other beauties are about." His voice didn't chastise, which meant his business wasn't urgent-urgent.

Only why had he sought her out?

"Surely your business with Celinae takes precedence over mine. I can wait."

"True enough." He walked a circle around her before standing by her side to stare at the warehouse door. He whispered, "You do know that she's made a personal bargain with me."

"So what? I've made one with you, and I'll bet Sweets has too."

He chuckled. "Are you not curious to know what her bargain with me is?"

"Yes." Damn her tongue, she'd spoken much too quickly. Then again, why had he brought up the subject of bargains?

He crossed his arms over his chest and gazed out into the darkness, as if thinking something through. When he focused on her, his eyes had gone stone-cold, devoid of emotion. "Do you trust Celinae?"

"I want to. Know I should, but . . . She can be vindictive, and she ferrets out secrets better than Her Grace."

"Does Celinae make you fear for your life?"

"Only when she's enraged with me."

He grinned. "Even I dread Celinae's wrathful tantrums." He abruptly stopped grinning. "Always remember that Sweets is a match for Celinae."

A match. Not superior? How interesting.

"And, dearest Annelisa, you do know Celinae considers you expendable, don't you?"

That tidbit of information confirmed what she'd realized herself when Celinae first proposed she become the third in the triad so they could access the *Fourth Book of Xenobia* and enhance their veeds' powers. "I know that, Shelzat. I also figure Celinae has convinced Sweets I'm expendable when the time comes."

"If you know they will turn on you, why serve them?"

"Because I have a deal with you, remember? Protection from all warlocks and witches more powerful than me. Which includes Sweets and Celinae." That had been her answer to insuring power for Ahl and herself.

Shelzat nodded. "Quite right, and I have your blood oath that you will deliver the *Fourth Book of Xenobia* to your cousin."

She nodded. Though it baffled her how he expected her to get the book away from Sweets.

"Now, best you report to Celinae before she checks the security sensors and sees you conversing with an invisible friend."

"Yes. Yes, of course." Heart racing, she hurried toward the dock's door, then took command of herself. She slowed to a normal pace.

With each step, she pondered what Shelzat said and wondered why and what business he had this night with Celinae.

Mounting the steps, she berated herself. She was too curious, just too curious — and suspicious. Only it was one thing to act naive and quite another to be naive.

Nearing the door, she hesitated. If she triggered the door open this late at night, the loud noise would catch the attention of the warehouse security robots that patrolled the warehouses two rows over. Those bots would come to investigate any night noise. She didn't need that.

She went back down the steps, entering the dark corner where the building abutted with a storage shed. She lifted her left hand, mouthed the code word, and her witch-ring triggered the secret door to open.

After stepping into the warehouse, the door soundlessly closed behind her.

She raised her hand to activate the lights, but hearing Celinae's angry voice, Annelisa stilled her hand. She couldn't make out Sweets' reply, but the tone reminded Annelisa of the last time she'd entered when the two were squabbling. Both women had promptly turned their tempers on her. She wasn't going to be their scapegoat tonight.

Maybe that's what Shelzat had been doing outside — delaying her entry, protecting her from their witchly wrath?

Ahl, keen hearing and sight.

The veed enhanced her sensory perceptions.

Annelisa quietly made her way along the path between the tallest vegetation.

Overhead lights mimicked pallid moonlight and ominous shadows veiled the herbs, shrubs, and dwarf trees. Reaching the archway, she stopped at the lattice side support where the bloodwood mother-vine's lacy, wine and green leaves draped everywhere, forming the blackest shade.

The molasses scent oozed off the vine's bark, causing Annelisa to recall Shelzat's words, *The mother-vine must be treated reverently, fondled gently. When cut improperly, its poisonous sap will spray into the air and kill everything it touches.*

When the time came, that bloodwood vine would be her weapon of choice against Celinae and Sweets.

Peering through the leaves, she spotted Sweets on her knees beside a caldron-pot where a bloodwood's three meters of vining had been laid straight on the floor. Sweets plunged her ceramic blade downward and, without a whisper of effort, the blade sliced across the wrist-thick vine, severing it from its tuber-root.

The vine began twisting. The soft twist traveled up the length of the vine, first slowly, then gaining speed. When the twisting reached the spear-pointed pod at the top, the pod snapped into four quarters, and the pieces shot away.

Celinae caught one piece in her black-gloved hand, then rounded up the rest, which were jiggling about on the floor's pavers. Luckily, none of the pods landed on the pentagram.

The first time they'd killed a bloodwood vine, one of the pod pieces had fallen on the pentagram and exploded, barbed seeds disbursing like shotgun pellets. Sweets later found out the seeds were sensitive to magnetic energy. The pentagram had plenty of that channeling up from the planet's core.

A moment later, Celinae placed the pods in a white bag and walked into the freezer.

Once frozen, the seeds would be crushed to extract their deadly, but fragrant, oil. By the time Celinae returned to Sweets, the reversed wringing of the vine had come halfway back down toward the cut end.

That descending twist became so hard it squeezed bloody-red sap out of the cut end and into a narrow-mouthed crock.

Only Sweets paid no attention to the sap. She remained busy slicing off the last clusters of the vine's leaves and flower buds, which she added to the pile she'd made on a fishing net.

Celinae flopped one end, then the other, of the net over the leaves, bundling them. She toted the bundle to the fireplace and heaved the debris into the fire. The leaves burned like tissue paper and gave off a crimson mist of smoke. The faint smell of burned acorns soon tainted the air.

Out of the corner of her eye, Annelisa saw the mother-vine's leaves quiver. The first time the mother-vine had quivered like that was when Sweets killed the first vine. Sweets said it was nothing more than the vine reacting to the acorn odor of burnt bloodwood.

Annelisa wasn't so sure. Maybe the mother-vine knew they'd killed one of its seedlings.

Celinae and Sweets donned clean, white gloves from the workbench. Using a white handled, ceramic-bladed knife, Sweets slit the vine's bark casing, then Celinae pealed the bark away. The bark went into the fire, shriveling before it caught and burned with a sickly yellow flame.

"Just don't stand there," Sweets ordered, exasperation in her voice. "We have to work quickly."

"I'm aware of that!" Celinae joined Sweets in lifting the woody strands across a copper rail. The two women fastened chains to the rail ends. Sweets triggered the hoist and the rail rose, lifting the vine off the floor.

Seconds later, she maneuvered the hanger in front of the fireplace and passed her witch's ring across the access panel on the fireplace mantel.

Two pavers moved aside, revealing fans that soon whirred warm air over the vine.

Annelisa stepped back. Time for her to make an appearance before Shelzat came striding in and chastised her for wasting his time. *Ahl, end keen.*

While Celinae tossed kindling onto the fire, Sweets pulled a long-toothed white comb out of her coverall's pocket. Her veed's aura coated her hand and she began combing, separating the fibers. As they quickly dried, the fibers turned a light gold color. She said, almost reverently, "Amber."

Annelisa spoke loud enough for her voice to carry above the fans. "Ambling Amber. A good omen, is it not?"

Sweets pivoted and faced Annelisa. Her gaze raked Annelisa from her seal-brown hair cascading in soft waves down to her waist to the A-line skirt of her raspberry pink, slinky knit evening gown that flowed out from under a deeper hued, knee-length cloak.

"About time you showed up." Celinae spoke without animosity.

"I know I'm late, but I couldn't help it. Her Grace had an emergency meeting with the committee handling the solstice tea."

"I thought the plans were set in stone a week ago." Sweets' voice held an I-think-you're-lying-to-me tone.

"Yes, the plans were, but two minutes before I was to leave for the day, Her Grace had me set up a conference call with her committee chairs. And before you ask the reason, it's because Margo Riboji is coming to the tea."

Celinae removed a comb from her robe pocket. "What's the big deal about that? Riboji often comes to colony events when it's an election year, and we all know the Emperor wants to be reelected. Hardly a reason to call a special meeting, is it?"

"Margo's appearance adds to the real problem." Annelisa beamed a smile at Celinae and enjoyed the feeling of pride she felt. *"Janay Cholyn accepted Her Grace's invitation to the tea."*

Sweets gasped.

Only one side of Celinae's lips curved into a smile. "I knew my plan would work. Nicely done, Annelisa."

"Thank you."

The heat in the room began to make Annelisa fear she would sweat and ruin her dress. She untied her cloak's frog closures and welcomed the cool air cascade over the skin exposed by her dress's plunging V neckline, and where faux-diamonds surrounded by tiny rubies nestled between breasts made for smothering a man.

Sweets glared at Celinae. "So, tell me, Annelisa, how did you get Tienan's woman to go to the tea?"

"Simple. I pleaded for compromise."

"Meaning?"

"Tienan's willing to socialize with his grandmother *only in public*." Annelisa chuckled. "Oh, how I wish you could have seen Her Grace. I thought she would faint when I told her Tienan expected her to prove she could be a kind and noninterfering grandmother!"

Celinae's eyes flashed with glee. "Tienan picked himself a gold digger, and I had the right of it, didn't I?"

Annelisa hated to admit it. "Yes. The proof of that astounded me."

Celinae demanded,"What proof?"

"Remember a month ago, while we shopped down on Lorado Boulevard and we drooled over a Lotus Blossom sapphire—the one that cost ninety-thousand drails?"

Celinae nodded. "Are you saying Tienan bought that ring for his whore?"

"Yes! Janay flashes it proudly, along with Tienan's compeer ring. Words fail to describe Her Grace's face when I told her about the rings."

A tune chimed and Annelisa opened the tiny panel cover on her faux-diamond encrusted bracelet and read the data. She snapped the cover down. "I have to go or I'll be late meeting Dominic." She eyed the vine's golden threads, the dried ends now wafting in the fans' breeze. "Is that Dominic's?"

"Yes." Sweets combed the fibers. "We should make a good start on weaving the cocoon-net tonight."

Annelisa turned to go but Sweets' voice penetrated her back like a dagger. "Is your ring full?"

Annelisa paused, but did not turn around. She lifted her hand to show her witch's ring. "Clean, filled, tested, refilled." She headed toward the rear exit.

"Make sure no one is privy to you hypnotizing Dominic."

"Yes, I know. I've done this before." As Annelisa passed under the archway, she fastened her cloak shut. About to trigger the secret door open, she heard the disgust in Sweets' lowered voice. "She dresses like a whore."

Who dressed like a whore? Tienan's familiaris, or — ?

On tiptoes, Annelisa returned to her original hiding spot by the bloodwood mother-vine. *Ahl, keen senses.*

Her veed obeyed.

"Oh, come now, Sweets, you don't mean that." Celinae forced her comb through the golden fibers hard enough to sway the hanger. "Okay, so Annelisa looks like a fifteen-year-old, and she can be dense about dressing like an adult — or even a lady — but her job is to seduce. She looked very seductive in that clingy dress."

"Yes, of course, she did but there is class and then there is class. Dominic is Hautonne. His preference is for sensual women, not vain little girls playing dress up and who make bargains with the devil for eternal youth."

That was said vehemently.

Celinae stopped combing. "How do you know she asked Shelzat for eternal youth?"

"I don't, but you can bet it was for something frivolous. Look how he treats her. He dotes on her like she was a favorite child."

"Ah, now I get it."

"Get what?"

"You're fuming. You only do that when Annelisa has done something to set your temper aflame."

Anger sizzled out with Sweets' softly spoken words. "She's the reason Rowen got away from us!"

"What do you mean?"

"I took a sample of the varnum we used on Rowen to the office and analyzed it. Annelisa put in half as much mickilstone as she was supposed to."

Shock waves of horror engulfed Annelisa. No, no, that wasn't possible. She'd followed the instructions to the letter.

"And you, Celinae, you were supposed to oversee her. Why didn't you catch her mistake?"

"Don't blame me. You're the one who said Annelisa could make the varnum. I believe you said it was her turn — your effort to make her feel like she was part of our team. All I did was get the ingredients. She followed the recipe off *your datapad*."

"That formula was the same one we used before. Annelisa is so simpleminded. She is not to be allowed to brew any more varnum." Under her breath, she added, "I shall be glad when we are rid of her."

"I agree, but not until our veeds become orgiak-pashaks."

Both combed the golden ropes with such vigor that the vine separated quickly into threads.

She knew they would kill her when they didn't need her. Shelzat had reiterated that. Only, hearing it from Sweets was like a knife cutting deep into her heart.

"Time to go, dearest Annelisa," Shelzat whispered into her ear.

For a moment, she froze, unable to muster a breath.

The darkon flashed her a smile and stepped into the walkway, heading for Sweets and Celinae.

Annelisa forced her lungs to inflate. Oh, how she hated him sneaking up on her like that! And yes, she should go, *but should she?*

Celinae abruptly turned. "Hello, handsome." Her greeting brimmed with her pleasure at seeing the virile male.

"Hello, my beauties." Shelzat's voice lacked the flattery he usually bestowed.

"By the look on your face," Sweets said, "I doubt this is a good evening. What's wrong? Did Annelisa — "

"Do not jump to erroneous conclusions. Annelisa is obedient and dares not question."

"Ah, but we do? Is that what you're saying?" Anger sizzled behind Sweets' words.

Shelzat immediately shook his head. "No, you two are insightful witches who are carrying out your agreements with me. Nothing is precisely wrong, but I must insist you speed up your timetable with Granger."

"Why?" Curiosity replaced Sweets' pique.

"An hour past dark tonight, he killed one of my most promising young vampires. I need Granger off the streets."

Celinae did not flinch and spoke with cold calm. "Our agreement was to turn Granger to the dark qi, not kill him. Wasn't it you who insisted that once he turned, he would sire a thousand vampires to ravage the human race?"

The fury smoldering deep in his voice was enough to rob the air of oxygen. "*I want Granger dead!*"

"It seems to me that your problem with Granger is more than him killing vampires. If we're to aid you in turning him to the dark qi, it would help to know exactly what plans of yours you think he'll disrupt or foil."

As Shelzat brought himself up to his full height, his wings tucked back more tightly.

In the silence, only the fans whispered.

Celinae stepped over to the mantel. She flashed her witch's ring.

The fans stopped whirling, and when the blades stilled, the fans lowered. The pavers snicked shut, once again hiding the fans.

No one spoke or moved.

The tension went out of Shelzat's wings and he seemed to relax. "You're right." He began to walk the Druid's Circle around the pentagram. "Between Granger killing my vampires almost nightly and that Cholyn woman and her dirks butchering my tormantratas, I am a feather away from suffering my Dark King's wrath! I cannot allow anything to taint the Yafranval of the Blood Moon."

"What's that?" Celinae's tone was one of entreaty and curiosity.

He paused and slowed his pace. "It is the celebration of the birth of vampires. It's only held once every ten thousand years, on planets where the occasion coincides with a moon the color of blood. If Granger discovers the Yafranval is being celebrated here, on this planet, I will pay dearly. And I assure you, if you fail me, so will you. Put more seed oil in Granger's blood and poison him. Kill him!"

"No can do," Sweets said with emphasis. "He has a very sensitive pallet when it comes to the blood he drinks. Too much bloodwood and he'll recognize something's been added."

"Then let him suspect someone is trying to kill him. That alone should divert his attentions and prevent him from killing my vamps."

"Oh, my sweet Shelzat," Celinae's voice cooed. "Do not despair. Give us time to work this problem out. Come back tomorrow evening and we'll present you with a plan."

Another round of silence. "Very well. I'll be here. At dusk." He walked forward, onto the pentagram. His form morphed into a dark whirlwind which rapidly vanished down into the heart of the pentagram.

On tiptoes, Annelisa retreated and left the warehouse. On the one hand she was pleased to know what Sweets and Celinae had bargained for with Shelzat — turning a Guardian of Occult Law's vampire to the dark side. On the other hand, they thought her vain, incompetent, worthless, expendable.

Well, she would show them.

🍎 Chapter Twelve

I have no strategy; I make the Right to Kill
and the Right to Restore Life my Strategy.
—The Samurai Creed

It was thirty minutes after midnight when Celinae siddirelled into the tiny clearing in the woods behind Wolcott House. Although heavily moon-shadowed by the towering trees, she spotted Shelzat and strode for him.

"Your plan had better work." Shelzat's quiet tone promised retribution if the plan failed.

"It will work. Have no doubts, my dearest darkon." She tossed back her siddirelling cape's massive hood and took pride in Shelzat's reaction—first surprise then revulsion. With a blink of his eyelids, his face took on its normal, passive mien.

She opened her black, wax-glossed lips and grinned, revealing her fake vampire fangs. "Will I pass for a century's old vampire?"

"More like sixteen centuries. What spell did you use?"

"No spell. It's makeup. It took Sweets hours to do my face." An entire hour to lengthen her nose. Another hour to wrinkle her forehead and add the three hairs to the wart.

Shelzat studied her anew. "The wart looks authentic. *Sweets is amazingly talented.*"

She should be. She'd worked as a makeup artist at the best theaters in town, earning money to attended college. Sweets had to. Scholarships only went so far. All that practice on others made it possible for Sweets to become a master of disguise. A talent that suited so nicely.

Disguised, Sweets had obtained the vial of Janay Cholyn's blood. Disguise as a scholar, Sweets had stolen the *Fourth Book of Xenobia* out of the Guardian's vault.

Shelzat studied her hair. "I like the hair."

"I certainly don't. The wig is heavy and the dreadlocks are a disgustingly carrot-red color no witch would dare call her own. Just to see where I was going, I had to tie the front back."

"The scarf gives you a risqué look."

"Sweets said the same." Celinae tossed the tail of the silk scarf back over her shoulder.

Shelzat gazed at her from the toes of her oldest, scruffiest half boots to her black bombazine dress, to a padded, high-necked bodice. He smiled. "I must say, you look very much like an overweight, middle-aged witch who's spent too much time in darkness enjoying depravities."

"That is the point, isn't it?"

Shelzat turned toward the house. "Half an hour ago, two of my gargan-tormantratas locked onto Rowen's dreaming. By now the boy should be having quite a nightmare."

"What about Boots?"

"I sent a young tormantrata to her mother. The fright resulted in multiple strokes, and she was rushed to the hospital. Boots remains at the hospital, but she called Tienan. He knows he's on his own tonight."

"Which means the only people in Wolcott House are Tienan, Janay, and Rowen. Wonderful!"

"Not so wonderful if Janay summons an archangel. Or had you forgotten she can do that?"

"No, I did not. Rest assured, my dear Shelzat, I came prepared. She won't get the chance." Celinae ignored Shelzat's snort of disbelief and eyed her gloved hands. It was hard to believe gloves could look and feel like crinkle-veined, crone's hands, complete with point-tipped, black fingernails, the kind ancient vampires were known to have.

The moon slipped out from behind a wispy cloud, burnishing the large black cabochon of an Eighth Power Witch's Ring that Shelzat held out to her on the palm of his hand. "Any Occult Guardian worth his shield will recognizes this ring belongs to a member of the Circle of Draqoolq."

"Marvelous!" She took it from him and wiggled it down her gloved finger. Someday, she would wear such a ring.

"Celinae, the true owner of that ring is a witch frozen in ice for a transgression against The Dark King."

She felt the threat skitter down to curl her toes. "Yes, yes, I know it's your duty to warn me that, if I fail, you have a worse fate in store for me, but I will remind you that last night, while Sweets and I stripped leaves off a Lacy Coin plant, you were delighted with our plan to give Granger a new quest."

Shelzat pointed to the triple bursts of light flashing out of Rowen's window. "There's the signal."

Celinae pulled the small black bag of Lacy Coin leaves from her skirt pocket. She then patted her sleeve cuffs, reassuring herself that the bags of Sweet Death were accessible should she need them.

She brought her cloak hood up, folding the front edge so it revealed her vampirik face.

The darkon stepped behind her, held her about the waist with his strong arms, opened his wings, and took off.

I am ready, mistress," Voz said. "Command and I obey.

Looking into her mind's eye, Celinae watched her noncorporeal blue peacock fan her massive tail. The eyes on her tail glowed with energy. A second later came the tingle of veed power heightening her sensory perceptions.

Voz cooed softly in anticipation of flexing her power, and the new abilities she'd gained. After consuming her share of four veeds, Voz's healing ability worked almost instantly.

But the greatest ability was slide-siddirelling. Her veed could now slide half a dozen meters through time and space without the need of a portal. Voz could also do it with minimum powering up preparations and minimum energy drain.

Only two things kept Voz from siddirelling into Wolcott House. One was that a veed could not siddirel to a place it had never been and, two, the distance from the trees to the house was too far to slide, so Shelzat had agreed to provide transportation.

Shelzat set her down outside Rowen's bedroom window and, because Sweets had accessed the installation blueprints, she was out of the line of sight of the newly installed security sensors.

Shelzat kissed her cheek, then flew back to the tree line, to watch and wait.

Now, Voz, put me inside Rowen's room. Celinae whispered the first line of the slide-siddirelling chant and surrendered herself to Voz's surging power.

Wolcott House

Janay opened her eyes to the darkness of Tienan's bedroom. Tienan snored softly on the other side of the bed where Zad had pledged to keep him while he slept.

She reached over to the nightstand and flashed her witch's ring. The clock mounted on the side of the lamp stand showed 1241.

Her stomach growled.

Well, that explained why she'd had a grand dream about chowing down the best food ever at Needle Notch Flats' mess hall — she was hungry.

As she swung her legs around to get up, she glimpsed the nightstand and the square gold and black box that held the Lotus Blossom ring.

As beautiful as the ring was, it was safer in the box than on her hand. Thankfully Tienan had understood her concerns about accidentally smashing it, like when slugging a tormantrata. He said she needn't wear the ring except for visitors and when they went out in public. Sometimes he could be downright accommodating.

She slipped out of bed and, barefoot, padded toward the lounge's doorway.

Cool though the air was, she was not cold because she wore one of her new, pure silk nightshirts. The emerald-green shirt had plain, three-quarter sleeves. Plenty of pin-tucks and tiny buttons but no lace or ruffles. She also wore the matching pants and silk panties. The fabrics made her feel . . . feminine.

Memories of her grandmother insisting she wear prissy underwear and prissy dresses flared to life. Then came the memories of that afternoon. Of sitting at the other end of Tienan's bedroom, at the small desk-cum-computer terminal, watching a holographic projection flick to a model's buttocks and her ruby-red, satin thong. Janay's disgust at the pictures of that thong style, in forty-two colors, had primed her temper like a grenade with its safety removed. She remembered yelling, "Tienan, this is whore-wear!"

Instead of him replying, she had heard Boots', "Your wrath is wasted."

Janay swiveled her chair around and gaped at Boots, who

used her witch's ring to close the bedroom door. Janay's frustrations and anger vanished. "I thought you were at headquarters for the day?"

"Was. Won't be staying long. Have to get back." Over her midnight-blue Guardian uniform, a turtleneck top over slacks, Boots wore an unbuttoned, black sweater-vest with a small bulge in the right pocket.

As she came closer, Boots finger-combed several long wispy strands of her hair back. She stopped and peered at the holograms. Her eyebrows quirked when the flickering screen presented a model wearing an off-the-shoulder, black lace body stocking with an open crotch. "Tienan is in the sitting room, pouring himself a stiff drink. He mumbled something about you having repressed sexuality."

"Did he send you in to convince me to strip and walk around buck naked?"

Boots chuckled. "Oh, you are so good for him."

"What does that mean?"

"Until you came along, no woman refused to wear what Tienan bought them."

"He hasn't bought me anything—yet. Look, I may have contracted to be his familiaris, but I am no way, no how, his mistress. Definitely not his whore, and I am certainly not going to wear pornographic underwear!"

Boots stifled a chuckle. "To the best of my knowledge, Tienan's never had a mistress or slept with a whore. Doesn't have to. Too many fine ladies offer themselves all too readily."

"And I suppose every one of those fine ladies likes this stuff?" Janay tapped her index fingernail to the screen.

Boots flashed a grin. "You bet. I had one of those in champagne-gold. It really spiced up my marriage bed."

Janay growled in her throat.

Boots crossed her arms over her chest. "So, what's with you and Tienan and the sexy underwear?"

"Tienan hates my militia underwear. Says I need women's attire like this—" She pointed to the holographic model now displaying a pink lace teddy.

"Janay, you're looking at the top of the line, exclusive, haute couture. Tienan buys from that site all the time."

"Just how many women has he bought stuff for?"

Boots chuckled. "Goodness, Janay, he's thirty-five. A virile man. He has had a few women between his sheets."

Janay felt her cheeks flush. "Okay, yes, I realize he's no virgin, but I'm not ever going to become one of his women. By contract, I'm his familiaris. I'm Australe. I cannot wear—"

A blond model strutted and gyrated her hips to show off a stretch satin halter dress with a handkerchief flounce that ended at mid-thigh. It required no underwear and the only thing keeping the bellybutton-plunging V neckline from letting the model's full breasts pop out was one short, horizontal strand of glittering crystal beads. Those beads seemed strained to the max.

Janay saw herself in that dress. Saw what it would reveal—a ferine scar. Rodgun pockmarks. A branch of the cross branded over her heart.

Boots spoke with sincerity. "With your dark features, pink's a good color for you. You'd look good in that."

"No way!"

"I would not have taken you for a prude, Janay, so what's the real point of contention between you and Tienan on the underwear?"

Maybe Boots could make Tienan understand.

Janay turned the monitor off with a flick of her witch's ring. "Look, Boots, I can't seem to make Tienan understand that I'm not the kind of woman who wears g-strings and thongs. I'm a practical person. I'm a peacekeeper, a soldier—correction—ex-soldier. "

"Oh, now I get it. You've got a few scars?"

Janay nodded. "More like a dozen, front and back. Besides, thongs would slice into the new tissue of my hip."

"But you're sleeping with Tienan. Surely he's seen—"

"Zad sleeps between us and keeps Tienan on his side of the bed. I wear my tee-shirt and briefs. Brown. Militia issue. Comfy-wear." She shoved aside that little voice in her head saying she had been naked for the reunification rite and naked from the waist down because of the gredle rash.

"I suppose you have a couple of tattoos?"

"One. Tarfooga's Own. The Templar's Cross over my heart—which you know about—is not a tattoo."

"So you need high necklines, long sleeves, long skirts and pants?"

Janay nodded. "I haven't had a beautiful body since I was twenty-two, or was it nineteen?"

Boots patted her shoulder. "Do not despair. There's sexy and then there's sensual. Sounds to me like you need sensual, and I know just the place." She used her ring to turn the computer back on and tabbed in an address. A catalogue page appeared. "You can browse whenever you like, but not now."

"Why not?"

"Because I'm on official Guardian business. Neejera needs a vial of your blood."

"She already got one. Said she only needed one."

Boots' face scrunched up as if she'd bitten into bitter lemon. "I believe you military types call it a snafu. Thanks to a new hire in the lab, your sample wasn't sent for testing for nanobots but ended up in the incinerator."

"I have to give more blood?"

"I can't leave without it." She pulled out the extraction kit from her vest pocket and took Janay's blood.

Then the two browsed through the catalogue pages where Janay spotted the emerald green nightshirt she now wore.

She ran her hand down the smooth fabric.

Definitely sensual.

A second later, her stomach growled.

By the next growl, Janay reached the mini-kitchen tucked into the corner of the lounge. As she raised her ring to activate the food dispenser's menu, a bright light flashed.

That light came from behind the coarsely woven fabric of the Japanese garden wall hanging. The one decorating the wall beside the display of five katanas.

Today she'd learned the house's secret passages. That panel covered the mesh screen on a narrow door that connected to Rowen's quarters. The panel allowed Rowen to see who was in the lounge before deciding to walk in.

She shrugged. Likely Rowen had made a middle-of-the-night raid on the kitchen. He was eating for two and Tal demanded calories to convert to energy. Rowen's stomach now bulged like a woman five month's pregnant.

Another flash of light.

That was strange.

Then came groaning, thrashings, a soft "Please," followed by an anguished, "No. No!" and a soft, but high-pitched, chanting. A thud. Then the sound of fabric ripping.

Poor kid. Best wake him before he shreds his sheets or goes sleepwalking. Did pregnant people sleepwalk?

She headed for the panel-door, flashed her witch's ring, and the door slid aside. Two strides into Rowen's room and she stopped short.

The high windows let in moonlight that silvered Rowen sitting with his back tight to his bed's oaken headboard. Eyes wide with terror, he stared at the cloaked witch at the foot of his bed. His blankets had been thrown, along with his pillows, to the floor near the windows. His pajama top had been ripped open, exposing his chest, and his pants had been pulled down to reveal his belly but not his genitals.

One gargantuan, wingless tormantrata sat on Rowen's right hand, holding his arm out from his side. A second tormantrata sat on his left hand.

Rowen didn't struggle.

The witch chanted, the crescendo rising. From a small bag, she pulled out tiny coins and tossed them at Rowen. They fluttered onto his exposed flesh, his face, his hair, and mingled with the other coins about him. The coins twinkled, one side silver, the other bloody-green.

The coins looked familiar. Where had she seen them before?

Tiny hisses issued from the coins on Rowen's chest, and the scent of quarry dust mixed with snow tickled Janay's nostrils. *Lacy Coins!*

"Your blood and veed are mine," the witch whispered.

"The hell they are!" Janay put her thumbnail to the underside of her witch's ring. "Code six, six, one."

Lights flashed on, illuminating the room brightly, causing the tormantratas to shriek and jump off the bed. Throughout the house high-pitched alarms echoed and resounded.

"Poke, Fox, to hand, to hand!"

As the witch turned, hissing her fury, the hood of her cloak slipped back, exposing her contorted face. Her black lips parted in anger, showing yellowed teeth — and fangs.

Skom! Not a witch-witch but a vampire-witch.

Seeing the vampire-witch lob something the size of a plum at her, Janay dodged sideways. Her shoulder hit the corner of the closet wall, stopping her, which allowed the projectile to thud against the bare flesh exposed at her neck. She damned herself for going to bed with the first two buttons of her nightshirt undone.

The projectile burst, spewing a cloud of dust in her face.

Involuntarily, Janay gasped, inhaling the putrid scent of Orach Poppies coupled with a hint of quarry dust and snow. *Poison — Sweet Death!*

She held her breath, grabbed the shoulders of her nightshirt and jerked the neckline up, putting fabric between her face and the dust cloud.

Backing, she ducked out from under the shirt and sent it to the floor. The dust wafted about in a roiling cloud sinking toward the floor.

Feeling her dirks hit her palms, she clutched them. While she lived, she would fight. She threw the blades at the vampire-witch.

Seeing the oncoming dirks, the witch flicked her cloak's hood over her head and face, muttered words, then vanished. Poke and Fox sailed through empty space, banked, and circled back to Janay.

Growling, and with claws and talons extended, both of the huge tormantratas headed for Janay.

She raised her dirks to defend herself. Readying for the attack, she took a breath, inhaling dust deeper into her airways.

The bedroom door opened.

Tienan stepped in, a blue rodgun in hand. He fired the gun.

A pip of brilliant white light flashed, the energy hitting the docked tail of one tormantrata. That energy flared into a burst of yellow-white fire.

The demon howled in pain.

That was no ordinary rodgun.

Tienan shot again.

The demon screamed from the blast, jumped his cohort, and rammed Janay, slugging her hard against the wall. With a burst of speed, the two tormantratas raced through the lounge and clawed their way up the fireplace chimney.

Tienan headed for Rowen.

Blood pounded in Janay's ears, her heart sledge hammered against her ribs. Her lungs demanded air, but she couldn't risk inhaling just yet. She released her dirks, who float-sat, and then she rounded the corner into the bathroom.

She grabbed the first towel she spotted, wet it, and wiped as much poppy dust off her face and skin as she could. She blew what air she had been holding out her nose, tasting the poison at the back of her throat.

How much had she inhaled? How far into her airways had the dust gone? How long did she have before paralysis set in?

Five, maybe ten minutes?

Maybe enough time. It had to be enough time. If she held her breath for as long as possible between breaths, she might be able to treat herself, then Rowen. Yes, she had time to do that. Lacy coins might be a cousin to Orach Poppies, but the coins worked a helluva lot slower. Unfortunately, both killed by paralysis.

She headed out of the bathroom and made it to Rowen's bedpost before taking a breath. Two breaths. She clutched the bedpost to steady herself.

Tienan looked at her, his voice quivering with fear. "He's paralyzed."

She nodded.

"Do you know what these are?" He pointed the tip of his rodgun at a pair of shriveled coin-leaves near Rowen's knee.

She nodded.

"By the powers! Your hair's covered with blue dust." He went to her, pulling off his pajama top en route. "What did you get hit with?"

She pointed to her naked chest that bore a faint robin's-egg blue splotch. "Dust cousin to coins." She took a breath. "Need zazzergum. Basement. Come. Help." She headed for the concealed lift in Rowen's room.

In the lift, Tienan helped her into his shirt.

Once in the basement, she began searching the root cellar for the lime-green tuber she needed.

What if he didn't have any? Terror sent her heart beating double time.

Tienan went to a panel, flashed his ring, and a screen lit. "Zazzergum!" Pause. "Come on, come on." A longer pause. "Okay, Janay. Got it. Bin four, row two. Ash Lily Root. It removes rust, mitigates curare poisoning, all Orach Poppy and *Cloisenis Laceum* — Lacy Coin Plant paralysis . . ." After reading more, he swore vehemently.

Likely he'd read how the coins killed.

She took a breath when she pulled the bin open and held her breath as tightly as she held the lime-green tuber. She made it to The Sorcery door before breathing again. Her heart thundered like a warhorse's at full gallop. With an iron will, she forced her lungs to override their involuntary urge to inflate.

She laid the tuber on the altar and took a breath. "Poke, Fox — mince."

The two blades slashed into the tuber reducing it to lime-green mush.

"Now what?" Tienan demanded.

"Bowl."

"Ceramic, glass, metal?"

She held up two fingers praying he would understand she

meant glass. She could feel the frostiness in her toes, cold rising toward her ankles. The paralysis hit the extremities first . . . Fingertips frosted . . .

"Now what?" Tienan demanded.

She exhaled "Strainer." She took in a deep breath.

Tienan fetched three strainers from a base cupboard.

She took the one with the finest mesh. Her chilled fingers had not yet gone numb, but gripping Poke proved harder than she figured.

Did she dare risk a breath to command the blade to shove the mash into the sieve?

Tienan snatched the sieve from her, held it under the lip of the altar, grabbed Fox, who was floating nearby, and used the dirk's blade to bulldoze the mash into the sieve. He set the sieve over the bowl.

Janay's lungs burned for air like they had when Mount Jadra blew off its peak. In the wake of that super-volcano, the air had been blizzard-thick with ash that clogged suit respirators, making the rescue of people and farm animals hell.

"Janay!" Tienan yelled, "What next?"

Another breath. "White wine. Driest."

He rushed back into the basement, returning with a bottle of wine. "Please tell me you don't need ceremonial wine."

She shook her head, scanned the bottle's label, grabbed the bottle, and smashed the top off. She poured the wine over the mash, the mixture erupting, foaming like carbonated soda, then green liquid gushed down into the bowl. She set the bottle down and took another breath. "Boil. Need steam."

Tienan set the sieve aside, then placed his palms on either side of the bowl, cradling it below the liquid level, and began a chant. His gaze focused on the center of the liquid.

Zad's energy flowed down his arms and cast a bright aura onto his skin that reflected in the bowl.

A few seconds later, tiny bubbles appeared at the bottom of the liquid.

Another breath.

Snowy-coldness numbed Janay's legs as high as her knees. Glacial coldness numbed her arms up to the elbows.

The liquid in the bowl steamed.

She let out a breath and bent forward, taking a huge intake of the minty-bitter steam.

Exhale.

Long slow inhale of steam . . .

Her heartbeat stopped thundering and warmth began to push the cold back in her arms and legs.

One more deep breath of steam.

Tienan looked at her, watched her breathe the vapor, but kept chanting, kept the heat slow-boiling the liquid.

One last breath.

"Go. Make Rowen. Breathe steam."

"Are you all right?"

"Yes. Go. When Rowen's mobile, keep him warm."

Tienan left the room with bowl in hand. Hearing the lift engage, Janay lowered herself to the floor and sat with her back to the altar.

Strange, the warmth in her legs seemed to be dissipating.

Skom.

She should have taken a few more breaths of the zazzergum mist.

❦ Chapter Thirteen

I have no designs; I make Seizing the Opportunity by the Forelock my Designs. —The Samurai Creed

From the depths of Janay's memories rose the numbing cold of taking her squad through Zearing Pass through hip-deep drifts with blizzard gusts of wind that whipped and swirled the snow at them. Frosted eyelashes. Toes numb. Fingers numb. Cold . . .

A wispy dirge looped in her mind —*We are the peacekeepers that march to hell and back, to hell and back, to hell and back—*

"I don't know how many breaths of the stuff she took, I wasn't counting!"

That was Tienan's anxious voice. He sounded far away. Skom, she was dreaming about him. No, maybe she was dreaming about Zearing Pass. She forced her eyes open. She was in The Sorcery. Tienan knelt beside her.

He sat back on his heels, facing her. "Bless the powers." More loudly, he said, "Neejera, she opened her eyes, and she's stopped humming that infernal tune."

Over the room's comlink came Neejera's, "Ask her if the paralysis is abating."

Paralysis? Janay took inventory of her body. She whispered, but she couldn't hear her own words.

Tienan said to the comlink, "She says it's on hold."

"That's not good, Tienan," Neejera replied. "You've got to scare her or make her angry or do anything you can think of that will send adrenaline flowing into her system. Our ETA is twenty minutes and that will be too late. Out."

Worried, granite-gray eyes studied her.

Was he contemplating what would scare her? She chuckled, but the sound stuck in her throat. She mouthed, "I'm scare proof."

Zad's power flickered deep in Tienan's eyes before he said, "Are you sure?"

"Bombs. Bullets. Been to too many hells. What don't kill you makes you a devil dog . . ."

Suddenly a smile wrinkled the corners of his lips. "What about paradise? Have you ever been to paradise?"

What was he talking about? "You're silly." Her eyelids felt ice-ladened, heavy.

"That's right, Janay, shut your lovely eyes. Feel the ecstasy."

What she felt was cool air waft up, under her pajama top. What she felt was warm fingertips on her rib cage making their way slowly, delicately up to her breasts. What she felt was his hands lifting, cradling her cold breasts in his warm palms.

She heard herself sigh.

He leaned closer to her, placing feathery little kisses behind her ear lobe.

She giggled.

He whispered into her ear, "I'm going to take all your clothes off, Janay. We are going to indulge in erotic foreplay. Then I'm going to have sex with you and — *you can't stop me.*" His thumbs fondled her nipples.

His touch felt so good, so right.

She leaned forward, pressing her breasts into his hands.

When his lips took hers, the kiss was exquisitely gentle. His tongue nudged, then pushed, parting her lips and teeth, deepening the kiss that soon warmed, no, fried her soul.

She shuddered with the delight.

He slowly pulled his tongue back, retreating, feathering little kisses on her lips. When he lifted his head, she felt bereft. He spoke in a deep, desire-husky whisper, "Pleasure me, Janay. Pleasure me." He kissed her, and she sighed again.

"Ah, Janay, you are my familiaris. *Bought and paid for. My mistress. MY WHORE.*"

Whore?

She was no man's whore!

Certainly not his.

She opened her eyes and beheld Tienan's triumphant smirk. Damn him. He thought he'd bought his way into her pants.

"You want me, badly, don't you, Janay?"

Fury at falling for his kisses, his touch, his seductive voice made her intake a lung full of air and realize how weak she was from the poppy dust, how powerless she was to stop him from raping her.

Fear stoked her heartbeat. She shoved both hands against his chest, but he didn't budge. Instead, he chuckled.

"That's my girl. Go ahead. Fight me. You haven't got the strength." He said the words with loverly ease, bent forward, and suckled her ear lobe. "I like a women in her place — under me."

Terror at her helplessness surged, forcing her lungs to process more oxygen, her heart to pump muscles awake, and this time, she brought her fisted hands down on his arms, forcing his hands to release her breasts. She shoved her fist into his gut.

He grunted and backed away. "Zad!"

In an instant, Zad's aura shielded Tienan's body. He scrambled to his feet and scooped her up, over his shoulder. "Now, *to bed we go!*" He carried her to the lift.

She wriggled and squirmed and pummeled his back, his shoulders, the side of his head. Even she knew her blows were not hard enough to hurt, but with each punch, her strength increased and her movements became more coordinated.

With the next blow, she realized how winded he was and that he had arrived in his bedroom. He tossed her onto his bed.

"Enough, Janay!" The tone of his voice rang through her. He would tolerate no fight from her. "For the record, and you can ask Neejera to confirm it, I was supposed to get your adrenaline flowing. That's all I did. I didn't mean anything I said. Everything I did was to provoke you. Your legs and arms are moving, and I'll bet my best tabard you feel warm, right?"

She took stock of herself. Her toes and fingers were warm. She swore under her breath. "I hate you." It came out as a statement not the shriek she intended.

"Bless the powers, at least you sound coherent."

A chime sounded and the comlink blared, "Lieutenant De'Argossi, this is Guardian Unit Four-Four-Eight-Six. We have turned onto Realm Avenue."

"Saved," Tienan whispered, then more loudly, "Unit Four-Four-Eight-Six, this is De'Argossi. The gates will be open. Park under the portico by the garage. I'll meet you at the side door. Out." He started to leave, then paused and looked at her. "Stay put. The CSI crew will want samples from your clothes, and Neejera will want to look you over."

Janay watched him go out the door and heard his footfalls taking the stairs two at a time.

She roused herself to sit on the edge of the bed. She had to wait for the crime scene investigators? And Neejera? Skom.

She pulled her shirt down. In doing so, she saw her stiff nipples and heavy, firm breasts outlined by the thin black fabric of Tienan's pajama top. Her senses were again assailed by the memories of his caressing hands, his nibbling kisses. Memories flickered of his choberimiz kisses and the kiss of comfort.

Her body reacted to the man, desired him. Oh, skom! *She was falling in love with him.*

No. No. No. Hadn't she had such an ah-ha moment with Otto? Sure, she'd found solace and support in Otto's arms, and they each needed the other. So, theirs had been a needful love.

And the second time she'd had that same I-love-him moment was with Sam Cramer. That Adonis had a sexual charisma her body lusted for, and so theirs had been a fantastic, erotic romp. Only when she blurted out 'I love you' during a climax, Sam had stilled, become aloof. On returning from a three-week assignment with General Tarfooga, she discovered Sam was seeing someone else, and she'd been the brunt of countless jibes. So much for lustful love.

Well, the past was the past. Lessons learned. If she were in love with Tienan, it wasn't likely going to be the everlasting kind.

It would be unrequited.

It would be totally inappropriate.

It would be . . . *Trouble in all capital letters.*

Otto's words flitted through her mind, *Since when did reason have anything to do with falling in love?*

A house-shaking rumble of thunder woke Tienan. He had dozed in the chair beside his bed. Outside the bedroom's high windows, where the center curtains were partly opened, flashes of lightning lit the morning, thunder boomed and rumbled.

He turned his attention to the bed and Janay tucked under the black coverlet, wearing a pale yellow nightshirt. One of her new ones. No frills, just pansies embroidered about the curved yoke.

It had taken Boots' reprimanding to make him realize the

obvious, that Janay's body was battle scarred. Not that he minded, but Janay obviously did. So, he'd agreed to let Janay wear what she pleased as long as it was feminine.

Her sleep-shirt hid most of her body, but the left sleeve was bunched up and the tattoo of Tarfooga's Own rode high on her upper left arm. The peacekeeper's tattoo. A simple, outlined T with laurel leaves. One blue tear and one blood tear dripped off the left bar of the T. Someday he would have to ask her what the two tears represented.

Zad's noncorporeal form stood inside Tienan's mind, staring at Janay. *She is pretty when she sleeps.*

I suppose, but I'm afraid we are looking at the calm before the storm.

I do not understand, my lord.

When she wakes, she'll be outraged at what I said and did to her in The Sorcery.

She will understand, my lord. It was necessary to save her life. After all, what choice did you have?

At the time? None. But it did not set well with him. He'd come to like the termagant in his bed, and out.

Mostly she was easy-going. Wise and weird. Smart. Unpredictable. Intriguing. And, oddly enough, somewhat virginal-minded. Insistent on avoiding sex — particularly with him — even after he'd been naked with her during the reunification rite, even after he'd been inside her for the spittle rash. Which made him wonder how she would handle letting him slide his penis into her for Rowen's forthcoming reunification rite.

Another rumble of thunder. This one was followed by a deluge of rain pounding the windows.

He closed his eyes and listened to the rain. Memories flitted of being in The Sorcery, of fondling Janay's heavy breasts, kissing her blue, frozen lips, and his erection blasting stiffer than he'd known possible. Even Zad had been caught unawares by it.

My lord, change the way of your thoughts because your penis is rising.

He swore to himself. *Stifle the erection, Zad.*

As you wish, my lord.

The brief sizzle of pain was not exactly what he had in mind, but the pressure in his groin ended.

The bedcovers rustled.

He eyed Janay, who had rolled onto her back. Her face no longer looked like that of a pasty-pale cadaver. Nor did she look like the determined, topless waif she'd been in Rowen's room after the attack of the tormantratas.

He recalled gazing into her eyes then, when she clung to Rowen's bedpost, and he'd seen Sergeant Cholyn eyes, soldier eyes. The determination, the single-mindedness of purpose that ruled her actions—to fight against all odds.

Images flashed like a whirlwind in his mind. Janay in The Sorcery, him boiling the Ash Lily, Janay breathing in the steam, Janay ordering him to take the brew to Rowen— He'd obeyed her like he was a grunt.

Then he became the soldier, one half out of his mind with fear, who ordered his brother, "Breathe, damn you, BREATHE!"

How many minutes passed while he sat beside his brother, holding the steaming bowl beneath Rowen's chin? The steam billowed upward into Rowen's face, some visibly inhaled, but not enough to make a difference.

The moment of utter despair came when Rowen stopped breathing, then, a second later, Rowen whooshed in a huge breath of the steam.

Throughout his brother's slow but increasing recovery, Zad maintained a simmer on the bowl. As the liquid boiled and evaporated, less and less remained in the bowl. Tienan silently prayed there would be enough.

It wasn't until he tucked the blankets around his brother that he realized Janay had not returned. When Zad ventured the thought that she misjudged how much steam she needed to counter the poison she'd ingested, he panicked. If she sacrificed herself to save Rowen, by the powers, she had failed! Rowen needed her for the repeat of the reunification rite.

He raced back to The Sorcery, found her slumped on the floor by the altar's base. Her hands frigid to the touch, body stiff, ice-cold toes and feet. Yet, she hummed a tune. A dirge.

The bed squeaked, and he returned his attention to Janay. She stretched and yawned, then opened her eyes. She eyed him from beneath the riotous curls dripping across her forehead. Her lips pursed.

Was she remembering?

"Good morning," he said as cheerily as he could.

No response.

"Janay, say something. Do you need Neejera?"

Her face relaxed and her expression became unreadable. "She still here?"

"She's with Rowen. Something about massaging his elbow joints and wrists every couple hours. They'd almost been dislocated by the giant tormantratas."

"What time is it?"

He swung his chair around to the small desk and tabbed the button on the edge. A screen on the desktop blinked on, then off. "Not quite 1000 hours. You should eat if you're up to it."

"Actually, I'm famished." She began to get out of bed.

"No, stay put. I'll fetch a tray."

Why didn't she make eye contact with him? Maybe she was embarrassed about last night. "Janay, about what I said to you in The Sorcery. It was the only way to get your heart pumping."

"I know. Don't worry about it." Her words rang false.

"Are you angry with me for what I said?"

"No."

"Janay?

"I need the bathroom. We can hash out your guilt later."

Defeated, he left the room to get her something to eat.

An hour later, the rain had not abated and, in the guestroom, Janay, dressed in her own clothes, knelt before her open footlocker, rummaging at the bottom until she found the purple Balakajaran wood box. She pulled it out and opened the lid. Six rilm rings ranging from ten to forty drails filled the top slots inside the lid. She put half of them in the top pocket of her field-duty, desert-camouflaged fatigues.

About to close the lid, her gaze drifted to the little prayer book nestled in the box's bottom. The ivory note card had slipped half out from under the book's leather cover. She lifted the cover, centered the card, and paused. She read the handwritten lines, words she knew by heart.

Beloved Janay, friend and companion,

I had a vision last night. An angel told me my time has come. I shall die and stand washed in the light of J'Hi's great love. Although love isn't love until you give it away and it comes back again, know that I have loved you dearly. Do not weep for me nor expect my reincarnation. Instead, rejoice, and promise me you will dance in the newness of each and every day.

Otto

Like the boom of the thunder renewing the storm outside the house, a tempest of loss and remembrance boomed through Janay.

A soul returned . . . Reincarnation.

The words echoed and touched another recollection, the metal twanging of the second soul — the soul that had sung to her soul during the gredle rash fiasco. Had Otto been wrong? Did Tienan bear Otto's soul? No, not possible. Stupid thought. Idiotic idea. After all, Zad and Tienan had been born before Otto died.

But what if it were someone else's reincarnated soul?

A boom of thunder shook the windowpanes.

"Janay." Neejera's voice held no reprimand. "Why are you not resting?"

Startled, Janay snapped the prayer book shut and closed the wooden box. She scooted around to face the healer, who stood just inside the doorway.

"I didn't mean to give you a start." Neejera rested both hands on her cane.

"Then don't sneak up on folks."

Neejera's attention seemed to focus on Janay's fatigues and then her militia boots. "Feeling better and dressed, I see."

"I'm sick of being treated like an invalid, sick of pajamas, and sick of soup and toast."

"Is that what Tienan brought you?"

Janay nodded.

"That's what I ordered for Rowen. You should have had a hearty meal."

"How is Rowen?"

"He'll be fine, physically, in a day or so."

"And mentally?"

"He's shaken. I've recommended counseling. He had quite the fright. He's afraid to go to sleep for fear he'll dream and those dreams will be reality."

"So you figure to drug him to sleep?"

"No. I've instructed Tienan to keep lights on, doors open, and to play recordings of surf and sea, or soft music. I have also recommended aromatic oils be used and placed on the nightstand when he goes to bed."

"I doubt any of that will stop the tormantratas if Rowen lapses into a nightmare."

"Spoken from personal experience?"

"Yes, but you know that, don't you?"

"Indeed. A copy of your medical file arrived early this

morning as well as I called in a favor and got the scoop on the aftermath of Rathe."

She didn't want to regurgitate Rathe or its aftermath. "Are you staying the day?"

"Likely until supper. Rowen's joints are swollen from the abuse of those tormantratas." Neejera eyed the box in Janay's hands. "Medals?"

"No, a keepsake from a friend." She put the box into the footlocker, grabbed her rainproof, hooded sweatshirt from the clothes pile, and closed the lid. She heard the lock click into place.

Neejera's eyeballed the sweatshirt. "Going somewhere?"

"Outside for some fresh air. Any objections?"

"It's storming."

"I'll be under the portico."

"Hiding from Tienan?"

"Why would you think that?"

"Because the man feels guilty about tricking you with sexual intimacies to get your heart pumping."

Sexual intimacies? "Look, I told him I understood why he did it, and I truly understand. What's with you people? Why won't you believe me?"

"Ah, that's the way of it, is it?"

"What are you talking about?"

Neejera smiled. "You're having a problem reconciling your feelings for Tienan."

Skom, was she that transparent? "Exactly what do you think those feelings are?"

"Frustration, loathing, love, fear, desire. Usual female responses to a desirable, virile man."

"You have an overactive imagination. Now if you'll excuse me, I need some real food and some fresh air." Janay strode out and through the empty game room, then through Tienan's suite to the lounge. She donned her pullover and instead of going to the mini-kitchen for food or taking the lift to the kitchen upstairs, she headed for the back door.

Poke and Fox appeared in front of her, tips aimed to stop her. She never broke stride. "I'm going out that door. If you intend to stop me, you better slit my throat."

One dirk went right, the other left. Both dived into their boot sheaths when she passed.

She flashed her witch's ring to the door sensor. The door opened and she stepped out, into a pelting, warm deluge of rain.

But it was the pelting of emotions about Tienan that cascaded over her. She needed time alone. Time to figure out how to extricate herself from Wolcott House because she had no business falling in love with Tienan.

Heaven help her, she couldn't be in love with a man who would never disgrace his heritage or his race by taking a mistress as his wife.

And, by all she held holy and dear, she would not settle for less than a man who truly loved her and a legal, binding marriage. Otherwise, she would be no better than her mother, the manipulative gold digger.

Janay's father's angry voice pealed, *you're just like your mother, the promiscuous, wanton whore.*

She would never be like her mother.

Never. Never. Never.

🍎 Chapter Fourteen

I have no miracles; I make Righteous Laws
my Miracle. — The Samurai Creed

Fred's Bar and Grill

Boots slid onto the seat opposite Janay. Her Guardian-blue poncho dripped rain onto the booth's seat and table.

Inwardly, Janay bristled. So much for her afternoon of freedom and wandering about like a regular citizen. And so much for picking the obscurity of this little bar.

She broke her hot biscuit in two, savoring its warm fragrance, then set the bottom half on the serving plate.

How had Boots found her?

Was there a homing device in the witch's ring Tienan had given her? Soon after she left Wolcott House, she set that ring onto Fox's blade. Despite Fox saying the ring didn't give off any signals, she ordered Fox to her boot with the ring. "So, Boots, how'd you find me?"

Boots wiped a hand through her hair, sliding back wet strands and shoving them into her unkempt topknot. "Sheer luck. I came in to get out of the weather and spotted you. You're soaked."

Of course she was. She'd been lost in thought, slogging through the grassy paths of the labyrinth behind the Chapel of J'Hi Baldama twice before she noticed the wetness and realized her aged sweatshirt was no longer rainproof. She had been wet before and would be again, so what did it matter?

Hearing laughing children stomp through every puddle

around Adrada's bronze statue in the Abbot's Garden, she followed suit and, with each splash, damned herself for being a fool to think she loved Tienan.

It was only when Otto's words, that love wasn't love until you gave it away and it came back again, looped in her mind, that she realized what drew her to Tienan.

The man had a compassionate strength, like that of a general, a warrior, a samurai. Tienan possessed a keen sense of duty and honor—to his brother, to justice, to righteousness. But especially, Tienan cared enough about her to take her in as his familiaris, to want her to live by calling her a whore to get her blood pumping to undo the Sweet Death poison.

Oh, yeah, she'd fallen in love with the man.

But he would never love her.

With that realization, she had shed copious tears and came to an irreconcilable conclusion—she could endure being around Tienan without being loved back, and do so until the new moon and Rowen's reunification rite. Then, and only then, would she leave Wolcott House.

It was the right course of action.

The right thing to do.

"This rain is something else." Boots tabbed the menu panel on the wall and ordered a mug of saguenay, forest green, the strongest brew. She glanced at Janay's nearly empty bowl and the empty mug of beer. "Tienan's out of his mind worrying about you."

If only he were. That would prove he loved her, not just cared about her well-being. Only to save her heart, she had to hang tough. No one need know how much she cared about him. "That's doubtful."

Boots' eyes momentarily widened as if shocked, then she frowned.

"Look, Boots, the man has a two-item agenda. One is his brother and—" She lowered her voice. "The other is being a GOOL." Janay picked up a pat of butter with her soup spoon and concentrated on smashing the butter down on the warm biscuit she held in her hand. "Tienan considers me a means to an end."

"I beg to differ."

Janay set her spoon in her bowl. "You don't strike me as the begging type."

"Janay! What's gotten into you?"

"I've had time to work through things. I fully realize my

obligation to Rowen since, by my own free will, I wanted him to live. By my own misunderstanding, it's my fault things went wrong with the ritual, so I'm honor-bound to repeat said rite. What is not of my own free will is being imprisoned at Wolcott House."

"You're technically under protective custody."

"Call it what you like, it's still a prison."

The bartender delivered Boots' steaming green coffee, along with Janay's second mug of dark beer.

When the bartender was out of earshot, Janay said, "I am also shackled by my dirks' machinations, which force me to sleep with Tienan. Lastly, I dislike being Tienan's familiaris."

"You agreed to the deal."

"I wholeheartedly regret there was no alternative." Janay finished her biscuit and bean soup. Swigging down her beer, she felt physically satisfied.

Boots lowered her voice and leaned forward. "Tienan can be high-handed but he's fair. Come back. Talk to him."

"I don't have anything to say to him."

Boots took a hefty sip of her coffee. "Janay, you have to understand the man is in an impossible position. He's head of his family, that is, what's left of it. He was only twenty-four when his father and grandfather died in a storm out on Lake Ubrey. Then his mother was murdered."

That revelation stunned.

"She was murdered?"

Boots nodded. "Tienan came home later than expected and found her dead. He feels that if he'd come home on time, she would still be alive but, more than likely, he would have been killed too. I've never been able to convince him of that." She sipped her coffee and remained silent for a little while. "Janay, he's afraid — really afraid — to love and lose."

That hit too close to home.

Janay diverted her gaze to the window.

Rain now fell as a misty-fog under the dark of a late afternoon sky.

A moment later, Boots spoke in a low voice. "I'm curious, Janay. Mind telling me how you managed to elude the new sensor system on the house?"

Changing the subject was she? Truth was, a heavy downpour had flooded the eaves and sheets of water had cascaded over one sensor, blinding it to her departure. That glitch might come in handy again for her, so why reveal it? "I'm a soldier, Boots, trained in recon and infiltration."

Boots nodded. "Granger said as much." There was an odd resonance to her voice when she spoke Granger's name.

"Who's Granger?"

"A fellow Guardian." The softness in her voice betrayed her love for the man. Boots turned and ordered a refill of her coffee by flagging the bartender's attention and pointing to her cup.

When the bartender came and refilled the cup, Janay put her hand over her beer mug so he knew not to ask about a refill.

After the bartender left, Janay's curiosity got the best of her. "Are you and Granger trothed or whatever you call it?"

"No. I'm still trying to convince him we should." Her voice reflected her efforts had met with disappointment. After a few sips of her coffee, Boots said, "Suffice it to say, Janay, if things were different, Granger and I would make one helluva team. Maybe even a better team than my first husband and I were."

"Guardians marry Guardians?"

She leaned forward, almost whispering, "For us GOOLs, it's a long-standing tradition." She then spoke in her normal voice. "Wife watches husband's back, husband watches wife's back."

"What about having kids?"

"Assignments become boring and have minimal risk or it's desk duty." The last words were said with distaste.

A group of people bustled through the door, all wearing kelly-green coveralls with white logos. The bartender scurried to serve the spaceport dock workers.

Boots checked the time and then took out a credit stick, inserted it in the slot at the end of the table, and paid for her coffee. She met Janay's gaze. "Wolcott House is a safe house."

"How can you say that after last night?"

"We have a better idea of what we're up against, and new measures are in place." She slid to the end of the booth. "I'm heading back. I'm not going to ask you to come with me because I think you're right. You need time to yourself, but I would encourage you to return before dark."

She was almost to her feet when Janay remembered to ask, "How's your mother?"

Sadness drained Boots' face. "Still in a coma. My brother and his wife are keeping vigil. They'll let me know if there's any change."

Through the window, Janay watched Boots make her way down the street to a cab stop and flag a taxi.

From the back of the bar came, "Twenty drails says nobody can beat four darts dead center!"

Two hours later, with eighty drails in her pocket from beating all comers at darts and, with more beers in her than she would have liked, she left the bar.

The rain had stopped and the air had been washed of the bay's briny bouquet. She circumvented a puddle and crossed the street, turning north, up Warehouse Row Boulevard.

A short, heavily muscled young man, dressed in a black leather jacket and pants with chains dangling from belt loops and pocket grommets, passed her and walked unerringly down the middle of the sidewalk. His hair, stiffened with gel into Mohawk spikes, had been dyed deepest black and the rest of his head shaved bald.

She found herself fascinated by his narrow-hipped gliding swagger and followed him at a distance until he turned down a narrow alley and met a dark-haired woman in a bright pink skirt so short his hand slipped between her legs without touching the hem.

The streetwalker grabbed and stayed his hand. She laughed softly, a teasing laugh, then tossed her long tresses over her shoulders. Raising her arms as she did showcased her large breasts.

A street lamp winked on, its glow reminding Janay that night was slithering in like the fog off Akron Bay and three kilometers lay between her and Wolcott House. She strode onward at a brisk pace.

Because of the rain, dusk came early and darkened Tienan's study where he sat in front of the small fireplace. The only light came from two half-burnt logs.

Boots sat in the other chair, filling him in on finding Janay.

"So," Boots said, "when I left the bar, I got a taxi, went around the block, found a spot to watch the bar from, and contacted headquarters. They dispatched a plainclothesman. When he showed up, I left. He's got orders to let HQ know when she leaves, but he's not to follow her."

"Not follow her? Boots—"

"I will remind you that Janay can take care of herself. Besides, how long do you think it'll take her to figure out someone's tailing her? And, who do you think she'll be furious with and blame for the watchdog?"

"Us?"

"No. You. Now, I'm going to go, call my brother, see if there's any improvement with my mother. Then I'm going to while away the time with Granger until Janay gets back."

"Granger is supposed to patrol the grounds."

"Do you want Granger dead? Oh, right, I forgot. You'd like that. Let Janay walk up to the house, sense a vampire, and slit his throat with her dirks." Every word was spoken with rising anger. "Granger was exonerated. He did not kill your mother!"

But the questions remained. Did Granger know who killed his mother? Was Granger covering up for the killer because headquarters ordered him to, or because he had a blood tie, either a family or a vampirik one, to the murderer?

Getting up to leave, she said, "Trond, Tienan, but you can be exasperating!"

The moment she was out the door, Zad came out from under the desk and settled himself beside Tienan's chair, his tail tight to his side.

Tienan stared at the crackling fire until the vesper bells of the church down at the bottom of the hill knelled through the study. "Zad, is it so wrong to want to protect the ones you love?"

Zad's eyes flickered with delight. "You love Janay?"

"No, not her. Rowen."

Zad's delight vanished. He laid his chin on Tienan's lap.

Tienan scratched the crown of Zad's nappy head. "Janay is *jossierj*. It would be wrong to fall in love with her."

"I know, my lord, but I think the question is, have you kindled the fire of love in Janay and now wish to douse it?"

"You think I've made Janay believe I love her? I never meant to. Everything I've done is to repay her for saving Rowen or to save her life."

"Yes, quite. I see . . ."

Did he? Tienan watched a red-hot ember burst and breathed in its wood-smoke vapor. "The question, Zad, is how do we fix this? Janay and I must be seen in public as a happy man with a happy familiaris, a couple of lovers in love, not quarreling."

"I am sure you will think of something, my lord. Now if you will excuse me, I must go below stairs and keep an eye on our vampire guest." He jogged toward the lift.

"Zad, do you think Boots loves Granger?"

"Is it love that blinds or love that binds? Difficult to tell the difference, is it not?"

Tienan shrugged. In truth, love could be downright confusing.

❦ Chapter Fifteen

I have no principles; I make Adaptability to all
circumstances my Principle.
— The Samurai Creed

To keep from imagining the worst that could happen to Janay out in the rain, Tienan sat at his desk doing a complete diagnostic of every security system, including the new ones he, Boots, and Granger had installed.

One of the new sensors half-bleeped, then bleeped strongly.

He triggered his warlock ring. "Display sensor W17 on the main terminal."

Across the room, the fireplace's picture morphed, and the image of Janay walking toward the back of the house appeared.

A tsunami of relief hit Tienan, but he took a moment to study her and reassure himself she was all right.

Moonlight radiated from between parting clouds and glittered on her rain-wet curls and on the tendrils of fog plowed aside by her boots. She paused. One of her dirks came up. She plucked something off the blade.

He tabbed touch screens on his desk's control panel, enlarging the view of her hand and her putting on her witch's ring.

She continued up the grade, onto the stone pavers of the patio, and stepped up to the lounge door. She smiled at the crescent moon as if to say hello to it, faced the door, and raised her ring.

"Link to com one one view," Tienan commanded. The images morphed to a panoramic display of the lounge where Zad lay on the white pelt, head on paws, staring at the empty fire pit.

"Rear door view," Tienan commanded.

The view switched to the back door opening and Janay walking in.

Zad's head went up. He spun around so fast and with such force that the pelt sailed into the wingback chair, scrunching into accordion folds. In three bounds, Zad reached Janay, reared up, and placed his front paws around her in a hug.

She staggered from the impact. "Jeez, Zad, you weigh a ton. Steady man, steady."

"You are back!"

"Yes, I am." She rebalanced, then looked about the empty room.

Was she expecting him to be downstairs with his veed? Or dreading it? And what was he doing watching her when he should be downstairs making amends?

He switched the comlink transmission to lift one. In the lift and on his way, he watched the small view screen showing Janay and Zad. He turned the volume up to listen.

"Zad, easy man—" Janay touched Zad's cheek. "Are you crying?"

Zad never cried.

"Hey, Zad, talk to me."

"I am sorry, magestrella." Zad's voice choked with tears. "I did not mean to distress you." He released her and backed away enough to lower his front paws to the floor. He then shifted his haunches and sat, head downcast, tail curling behind his front paws.

She knelt on one knee in front of him. "Are your tears of relief, joy, or something else?"

"Truly, relief. I imagined all manner of horrors that would befall you should you not return by dark."

"Silly, veed. The dark and the night have never frightened me." She wiped his tears away with her thumbs. "Now, suck it up and tell me why your host is not in sight."

"Tienan is in the study, checking the new security systems. Oh, I should tell you we have a guest."

"Neejera?"

"No. Granger."

"Ah, the infamous Granger."

"You know him?"

"Never met him, but Boots sort of silently sang his praises."

The lift set down, the door opened, and Tienan stepped out.

Janay spotted him. Like a soldier about to face a court-marshal-minded general, she drew in a lung full of air through her nose, squared her shoulders, patted Zad on the head, and stood.

Only her attention shifted to the connecting door to Rowen's suite.

Granger, then Boots, entered.

Janay's face went ashen and her dirks flew into her hands.

She threw, and the dirks whizzed toward Granger, who instantly transformed into his vampire self, baring his fangs. His skin shimmered with Enz, his veed, who enveloped him with its scrawny, ghostly blue-black lizard form, its bat wings beat the air, moving Granger to the left, out of the path of the dirks.

The dirks sailed through empty space — and toward Boots.

Horrified, Boots backed into the closed door.

With a hard thud, the dirks hit — one to the right, near her ear, the other to the left of her shoulder.

As Granger flew toward Janay, Tienan knew the vampire was beyond reasoning and would kill her, calling it self-defense.

Tienan bellowed, "No!"

Zad morphed into his energy ball, entered Tienan, and heightened Tienan's reflexes and sensory perceptions.

Tienan lunged, tackling Granger a few meters before he reached Janay.

Granger's body cushioned Tienan's and thumped onto the parquet floor. Granger used his vampire strength, coupled with his veed's power, to shove Tienan off, but Tienan hung on. The two wrestled, rolling into a curio cabinet whose glass shelves rattled from the impact.

In turning to slug Granger, Tienan glimpsed Janay racing across the room.

Granger kneed Tienan, who grunted and doubled over. The vampire got to his feet, but Tienan reached out and snagged Granger's ankle, tripping Granger, who fell chest first onto the floor. Granger's veed-powered fist whacked into Tienan's jaw, snapping his head back, but Zad compensated, absorbing the impact.

Tienan kicked Granger in the groin.

Granger roared from the pain and rolled away.

Tienan scrambled to his feet. In going after the retreating Granger, who was now on his feet, Tienan again glimpsed Janay.

She pulled the oldest katana from its scabbard and now pivoted around. She raised the katana and ran toward Granger.

By the powers! Heart thundering in his chest, Tienan changed directions and raced for Janay, stopping in front of her, arms out, blocking her path. "No, Janay! He's a Guardian. A GOOL."

She stopped, but her gaze remained fixed on Granger, who stood near the fireplace, suddenly looking unsure of what was going on.

"He's a hell demon!" Janay yelled with a voice born of hate and suffering. "He must die for what he did. He fed on mine at Blanoxx!"

Astonishment rang in Granger's voice. "You?"

Janay's grip on the katana became knuckle white. She shrieked at Granger, "I am The Grave Digger!"

"JANAY!" Tienan yelled with such force that Janay backed a step. *"You are not the executioner."*

Was that uncertainty mingling with logic that flashed in her eyes?

The katana swayed, as if her arms tired of holding the weapon high enough for a strike.

"Granger," Tienan ordered without looking at him, but watching Janay, "go to my study and wait."

"No!" Janay twisted and spun the katana, aiming the hilt cap to punch Tienan in the gut.

Zad shimmered his ghostly form over Tienan and sent power surging into a shielding aura.

The force of the katana colliding with the shield jarred Janay, but Tienan didn't feel the blow. He grabbed Janay's hands at the wrists and clenched them so tightly that she let go of the sword and it clattered to the floor.

She shifted her weight to lift her right knee to ram his groin but stopped. Whether it was pain from the hip or something else, he didn't care.

Janay stilled and the fury banked in her eyes. She glared at Granger, who was barely in Tienan's peripheral vision.

"Janay," Tienan said, hating the desperation in his winded voice. "Look at me."

Janay bore a steel-edged gaze into him. "I saw that hell-demon bleed my best friend." Her voice trembled with rage. "Two days later, she hung herself. He bled Jeff, who was so petrified that he was comatose for months. I heard the screams of my helpless comrades —" Her next words came out in an eerie whisper. "Six went forever insane."

"Yes, Sergeant Cholyn," Granger said, his voice solemn with

remorse. "I remember. You must understand, it was necessary."

"Necessary!" Janay kicked Tienan in the shin and struggled to get her wrists free.

Zad absorbed the kick. Tienan didn't let go of her wrists.

"Sergeant," Granger said, "let me explain. I had an artifact, a book, to deliver to Guardian command. I was being hunted because I had that book. There was no safe place, no one to trust. I and my veed desperately needed replenishment. Yes, I fed multiple times on the insane at Blanoxx. Who would believe a lunatic raving about a vampire? But upon my sacred honor, *I killed no one*. I took only what nourishment I needed."

"You dined on peacekeepers. You added to the nightmare of Rathe! Your witch created the beasts that tore our division to shreds and made us all question our sanity."

Granger stepped beside Tienan, no more the vampire, his veed withdrawn to a slight aura shimmering like a second skin. "I reported my actions to my commanders. I also reported I thought something strange was going on at Blanoxx because every mouthful of blood I drank was tainted with drugs, combinations of drugs which made me sick to my stomach. I even reported the dirks that danced outside your doorway, threatening me, and you, kneeling, your hands moving as if digging a hole. Your vacant eyes . . ."

"I was digging a grave for the demons." Janay inhaled quickly and rage flashed in her eyes. "To hand, to hand!" She tried to jerk free of Tienan's hold but he held tight.

Her dirks struggled wildly and wrenched themselves out of the wall, but they didn't go to her hands.

"To hand, to hand!" she demanded. "We kill the hell-demon vampire!"

"Janay—" Tienan pinned her with his and Zad's combined gazes. "Tell Fox and Poke to point to the darkunskyve, the dark qi, in this room."

She stilled and frowned. "What did you just say?"

"I know what Poke and Fox can do against tormantratas. When you threw your dirks at Granger, why didn't your dirks go after him when he moved aside? Why did they impact the wall?"

Reality took a better foothold in her eyes. At least he hoped the blinking indicated she was closer to functioning rationally.

"Janay, remember checking me and Zad for dark qi? If Granger has partaken of the darkness, you have my word I will help you kill him."

"Promise?"

"Upon my veeded soul." He said the words clearly enough that she would know he meant it.

Sergeant Cholyn's voice rang out with absolute command. "Poke, Fox, show me the dark qi in this room."

The blades quickly circled the room to Boots, who had picked up the katana. Tienan silently blessed his partner for grabbing that blade and taking it out of Janay's reach.

The dirks sped for Granger, who took a step back, the look on his face one of uncertainty and a readiness to shift into vampire mode in the blink of an eye.

The dirks circled him three times, then sped for a turn around Tienan.

They abruptly came to hover, tips pointed at Janay's hip.

Granger let out a sigh of relief.

Boots muttered, "Blessed be the pure."

Janay swore so vehemently that Tienan's ears felt singed.

Yet, a cold numbness settled in his chest where his heart beat. There was no darkunskyve in Granger? How could that be? He'd been so sure Granger was tainted.

Boots came forward and gave Tienan's a look that said *I told you so*. She stopped at Janay's side. "Glad we have that settled. Now, do pay attention, Janay."

Janay met Boots' gaze.

"A few hours ago, I got a chance to see your military file. I understand what you went through in the Valley of Rathe and at the Blanoxx Military Hospital."

Janay hissed out, "And you think I'm insane?"

"No, just a little confused right now. Look, Janay, take a minute to calm down, and let's exchange some information because, if you won't behave, I'll have Tienan put you in cuffs so there's no chance you grab a weapon and slit Granger's throat."

"He's a hell-demon vampire!"

"He's a valuable asset to the Guardians of Occult Law. Correct me if I'm wrong, but didn't your dirks just verify he has no dark qi? Janay. Please—let's talk."

Janay eyed Granger. "I dig the demon graves."

Tienan quickly replied. "You are not the executioner."

"No, I am not the executioner." She heaved a sigh. "All right, I give my word to hear what you have to say, but I'm not guaranteeing anything when it comes to that hell-demon."

"That's good enough for me." Boots nodded to Tienan and he

released Janay's hands.

Janay, favoring her bad hip, headed for the fireplace.

Tienan strode past her. Once at the hearth, he triggered the starter which ignited the fire. It was a pity that the fire wasn't going to warm up the tense, chilly atmosphere between Janay and Granger.

Withdrawing his hand from the sensor, he noticed how badly his hand quivered. He'd just tackled a vampire and faced down a lunatic-minded Janay. No wonder his nerves were shot.

Tienan went to the liquor cabinet, poured, and drank two fingers worth of his best whiskey. Then he poured a snifter of brandy, which he took to Janay, who sat in the wingback chair before the fire.

She refused the drink.

Boots, returning from putting the katana away, took the snifter, chugged down the drink, and set the glass on the mantel.

Waving his now steady hand past the fireplace sensor, Tienan triggered the seat-drawers to come out from either side of the fireplace. He took the seat opposite Janay.

Boots took the one opposite Granger, who had seated himself in the other wingback chair.

Janay's eyes mirrored the fire, but her stare remained focused inward, on atrocities Tienan figured he could never adequately imagine. "Janay?"

Softly she recited, "In the Valley of Rathe, a daughter of Xenobia created Qtalq, the Eater of Souls. In the Valley of Rathe, against all odds, the peacekeepers fought the beasts. In the Valley of Rathe, the dead lost their souls. In the Valley of Rathe, the fallen lost their souls. In the Valley of Rathe — " She took in a breath, held it for a second, then sighed out, *"The survivors were shattered souls."*

She looked at him with vacant eyes. "Second Lieutenant Jedadiah H'nor wrote that. Jed's schizophrenic. The GOOLs came. They said we were all hallucinating, insisted we'd lost touch with reality."

"Janay, look at me." Boots' voice was gentle, imploring, not commanding.

Janay obeyed and said, "Too many died that day. A brigade of peacekeepers. Three legions of angels. Twenty-two thousand . . . Did you know we went up against a hundred thousand karsks in the Valley of Rathe? I lost my guardian angel to Qtalq."

She chuckled softly like the insane do. "But there was compensation for losing a guardian angel in the Valley of Rathe.

We survivors got to see qi. Pure qi of the angelics." She glared at Granger, her voice hardening. "And the dark qi of the darkons and hell-spawned demons." She touched her hip. "Karsks—ugly, armor-plated, scorpion-tailed creatures created of dark qi by a Zantharian witch to gut and rip bodies apart."

Tienan leaned forward and laid a hand over hers, willing her to dispel the memories. Zad whispered a thought-provoking idea. "Janay, if you lost your guardian angel, why didn't you get a replacement so you were spared, for the lack of a better term, the darkunskyve sight?"

"Don't know. Never thought to ask."

"But your compensation is also to wield the dirks?"

"No. They, the Infanatas, choose the souls they serve. Adrada created the blades. Red Oak commands them in Adrada's stead. That's why we have to see the general, to get Red Oak to make sense of Poke's and Fox's looniness."

"If you ask me," Boots said, one hand shoving a wayward strand of her hair into her topknot, "I think your dirks make perfect sense. They know you are one of us."

Janay half bellowed, half screamed, "I'm not a witch. I'm not veeded. I'm not Zantharian!"

"Ah," Boots said, "but you possess the blood of the Black Sword of Power."

Tienan sat back, shocked. Granger sat up straighter. Janay's brows flicked upward before she frowned.

Boots spoke in a gentle tone. "Remember the vial of blood I took from you, Janay?"

She nodded. "Neejera needed to find out whether the nanobots were still functioning, calcifying my hip bones."

"The good news is that the nanobots are, and Neejera wants to see you about adding a few more bots to the repertoire, but never mind that. What amazed Neejera was your DNA. You carry Iassian genetic markers, in particular the gene which allows a psychic connection to veed energy."

Janay shook her head. "No way."

"I triple checked the data myself." Boots turned to Tienan. "I know what you're going to say, partner, that Iassians have gray-streaked hair, even the part-bloods. But Neejera says the hair follicles for the streak Janay should have had were destroyed, likely when Janay was very young, say two or three years old. About the time those white hairs would have become noticeable. Neejera told me the colonists on Chytano, Janay's homeworld, equate streaked hair with demon worship." She looked at Janay. "Ever wonder about that upside-down V at the back of your neck?"

"No."

"That's where your hereditary Iassian streak was."

"And this makes me equivalent to you?"

"In a way. Definitely it makes you a daughter of Rom of the Black Sword of Death."

"Never heard of her or her sword."

Tienan offered Janay a reassuring smile and a pat on the hand. "Remember our discussion about the colors of demons and veeds?"

"You said there were only six colors for veeds."

"Those six colors are predicated on the colors of the Six Swords of Power. Our Zantharian veeds were begotten by the power of five of the swords, but the Iassian veeds were begotten only by the black sword."

"I still don't understand how this sword and genetic revelation makes me one of you."

Boots came over to Janay and squatted beside her chair. "My dear, Guardians of Occult Law are a special, covert branch of law enforcement. We seek Zantharians, and others, who turn to the dark side of their veed power. We bring to justice those who use dark magic and dark science to relish in sadism, or to kill in order to enhance themselves or their veed's power. We are demon hunters like you, and like you, we are diggers of demon graves."

Janay shook her head in disbelief. "I saw Granger feeding at Blanoxx. Doesn't that make his GOOLness an oxymoron?"

Granger leaned across the arm of his chair toward Janay. "It was a case of the means justifying the end. I had obtained the artifact, the *Fourth Book of Xenobia*. That book contains incantations and spells, scientific formulas and equations, everything dealing with using the darkunskyve to enhance veeds to give them tremendous power. It's even said that book can turn a host into a god."

He sat back and stared into the fire. "That night at Blanoxx, as I was about to leave the building, I heard shuffling noises coming my way. I ducked into an empty room and watched spike-headed gargoyles lumbering two-by-two, veering off, vanishing through doors, into rooms where soldiers began reliving the nightmare of battle." Granger's voice softened. "A white-haired angel, one with black wings, paused to pat one of the beasts on its spiny head before sending it into your cell. To this day, I doubt I'll ever forget that angel's grinning face or his icy eyes."

Janay blinked, her lips minutely quivered. "Did that angel have a snakeskin band across his forehead?"

"Now that you mention it, yes, he did. A narrow one that shimmered like mother-of-pearl. Why do you ask?"

"That was no angel. That was a Darkon Archangel." Janay looked at Tienan. "I saw a darkon like that the night I found Rowen. I was taking the alleys to the Chapel of J'Hi Baldama when I heard him coming. He met three tormantratas before the witch joined them. I hid. Watched."

"By the powers." Boots rose and demanded, "Janay, what did the witch look like? Could you identify her if you saw her again?"

"Not really, but, well, she did have red bangs down to her eyes." Janay fluttered her hands. "Her hands flew like pigeons in the park when she talked to the darkon." Janay put her hands on the armrests of her chair and settled back. "I was too far away to hear what was said. Next thing I know, the darkon flies off toward the bay, the tormantratas flew off — " She looked out, not focusing on anything in particular, as if sorting her thoughts. "I wonder if those tormantratas were part of the ones who were at Wolcott House when I brought Rowen home."

Boots entreated. "Can you remember anything more?"

The room became deathly quiet.

Tienan wondered if Granger and Boots were as impatient as he was to get more information from Janay, but he was loath to make any noise that would distract her.

"After the darkon and demons left," Janay said, "the witch put her hand out." She extended her left arm and demonstrated. "I saw a ruby light flash on her finger. Next thing I know this oval of glittery light appears, enlarges, she steps into it, and, poof, she's gone. The oval vanishes. I waited a bit, then went on my way and discovered Rowen."

Granger muttered, "Ruby is the color of a third power witch." He stared thoughtfully at the fire. "Third power doesn't have the ability to siddirel unless such a low-born veed is enhanced by ingesting the energy of other veeds."

Boots shook her head, the motion sent the wispy tendrils of hair fluttering against her cheek. She didn't sweep the hair back. "Damn the dark qi, it looks like we've got a third power witch killing to feed her veed and make herself a goddess. But how can that be?"

Granger's face paled. "What if she's using a spell from the *Fourth Book of Xenobia?*"

"People," Tienan said, "that book is locked away in the vault at headquarters."

Granger nodded. "Right, and only a handful of people have access to the vault."

"What if the witch has a copy?" The second the words were out of his mouth, Tienan knew he was grasping at short straws.

Granger shook his head. "Not likely. The enchantments and chemicals on the pages prevent the book from being copied by any of our modern scanner technology. And don't forget, everything in the book is written in Vidarian and Ancient Zantharian. The vampires I took the book from rued the day they killed the witch who had that book. None of them could read it. Even today, not many people can translate its archaic language."

Tienan whispered, "Confound the powers!" Everyone looked at him. "What if someone at Guardian command, who can decipher that book, made a copy and sold it?"

"Looks like we might have a felon, or worse, at HQ." Boots headed for the lift. "I'm going to contact the commander." She halted and eyed each in turn. "It goes without saying that what we've discussed is between us."

Janay nodded.

Tienan nodded.

Granger issued an, "Absolutely."

Boots entered the lift and the doors closed.

"I think," Granger said, "I better patrol the grounds." He left by the back door.

Tienan eyed the fire, pondering the revelations of the hour.

"Tienan, I know this may sound dumb, but what could be the connection between the redheaded hag of a vampire that was here last night and the red-haired witch with the bangs that I saw?"

❦ Chapter Sixteen

I have no tactics; I make Emptiness and Fullness my Tactics. — The Samurai Creed

Janay, warmed by a long soak in Tienan's sunken bathtub, donned a cream-colored nightshirt and pants set, then padded barefoot out of Tienan's bedroom. She headed for the guestroom and her footlocker to fetch a hairband to hold back her damp curls. Nearing the open door of the guestroom, she heard Boots' voice and paused.

"You can't succumb to a blood-haze," Boots said, "and forget what your duty is."

"I know my duty, Valenteena."

That was Granger, speaking without anger.

Should she interrupt and get her hairband? What if they were in bed? Together? Naked?

Janay tiptoed over to the wall and up to the doorjamb. She peeked into the room.

Granger stood, his back to the bedpost, holding Boots in his arms. He peered down into her upturned face and, smiling, pulled the band off her topknot. "I want my woman, not Guardian McMurdy."

Her hair toppled down and about her face. "Granger, quit messing my hair. I love you, and you love me. You only need a pint, and I have that much to spare. It's as simple as that." She brought her left hand up toward his mouth. "Sip, don't guzzle."

He took her wrist and kissed the exposed flesh. A blood-lusting glee brightened his eyes, his fangs appeared, and he sank them into her wrist.

Appalled, her stomach queasy, Janay backed away. With silent steps, she returned to the lounge and the liquor cabinet. From the first bottle her hand touched, she poured a jigger into a squat glass and added two splashes of soda, then chugged the drink down. The liquid left a trail of fire across her tongue, down her throat, and bombed in her stomach. She gripped the glass tightly until heat sped through her blood. She slipped the glass into the cleaner unit and went to the fireplace where she stood, watching the flames consuming one small log which lay half-burned among the dying red embers.

Hearing footsteps, she found Granger approaching.

His gaze ran from her mop of curls to her bare feet and his lips bowed in a smile of pure male appreciation. "I thought you were going to bed?"

How did she explain her presence here? "I was just pondering some things."

On eyebrow quirked upward. "Like my demise?"

With absolute certainty, she said, "It's on my to-do list but not right away. I can't afford to get mauled in the process of killing you, after all, I'm needed for Tal's birthing. But then, well . . ."

The panel door opened and Rowen stepped into the room carrying a large black plate.

"Hi." He looked at Janay then Granger and back to Janay. "What's up?" He continued walking toward the kitchen.

Granger spoke to Rowen's back. "I was assuring Janay that I would thoroughly check the trees for tormantratas. Now, if you'll excuse me, I must patrol." He bowed to Janay and left.

Hearing the clatter of plates, Janay moseyed over to Rowen, who had now sprinkled anchovies on top of the food on his plate.

He didn't look up from his culinary creation. "Want some?

"What exactly are you eating?"

"A thick-crust pizza topped with ground liver and onions topped with a few sardines. Oh, and lots of anchovies."

She almost retched. "I'll pass."

"Suit yourself." He put the empty anchovy container in the recycler, picked up his plate and a tall glass of milk, and returned to his room.

Janay dragged a handful of curls back from her forehead. She needed a headband. Moments later, she entered the guestroom and found Boots twisting her hair into a topknot, the ends springing out every which way.

Vivid recollections of Granger's fangs gorging blood from

Boots' wrist surfaced. Janay tamped them down. She knelt at her footlocker and rummaged for her hairband stash and soon donned a white one.

Boots swore.

Janay looked up.

Boots sat on the bed scratching her wrist through her uniform sleeve. The scratching seemed manic.

Curious, Janay went to Boots and knocked aside the clawing hand. Before Boots could react, Janay grabbed the wrist and slid the sleeve back to mid elbow. Where Granger's two fangs had slit into Boots' wrist, the area was surrounded by a dark red rash.

Boots pulled her hand free and scrutinized the rash. "A gredle rash? No, no, a gredle rash prickles. This looks more like a spider bite. All ragged around the edges. Only I've never had one so dark." A tight frown drew down her eyebrows and she sniffed the rash. "Roasted acorns?"

Roasted acorns . . . A second later, Janay made the connection — the rat bite.

Other memories flashed of Otto and his herbal concoctions. Medicinal brews he'd taught her to blend to ease his pain and one had been a red concoction with a faint acorn scent. What had he called it? "*Bloodwood.*"

"What?" Boots seemed more confused.

"Bloodwood. It's a poisonous concoction that smells like roasted acorns."

"Poison? How? Why? By the powers, Granger drank from me. *I've poisoned him!*"

Boots started to rise, but Janay put her hands on Boots' shoulders and stopped her. "I really doubt you're capable of poisoning Granger. *Think!* When he bit you, his saliva would have surrounded the fang pricks and transferred the poison to your skin."

Color vanished from Boots' face. For a moment, Janay wondered if Boots would faint.

Boots whispered out, "How can you be so sure?"

Technically she never wanted to really know what herbs Otto had obtained, personally used, and which, in his last months, she'd blended to mute his headaches. Better to go with a truth that would not be questioned. Janay cleared her throat. "When I was nine, maybe ten, I found a dead rat. I wanted to check it out up close and personal. I was, back then, a curious child. Well, the rat wasn't quite dead. It bit me. Unfortunately, that rat had eaten a mash containing a homemade poison containing a small amount of bloodwood. The rat's saliva transferred the poison to me. I got the same kind of dark, ragged-edged rash like yours. It itched like hell."

"So what do I do to stop the itching, make it go away?"

"I don't know."

"What do you mean you don't know?"

"Minn, a neighbor and herbalist, was summoned. She applied a poultice. It smelled of blueberries and rose hips. It neutralized the bloodwood and stopped the itching. I was fine in an hour. After that, well, I spent a lot of time with Minn, fascinated by the herbs she grew and blended. Turned out I had a nose that recognized the scents of various medicinal plants. I know most of their names, but I was never keen on becoming a pharmacist, or a herbalist."

Boots began to rub her rash. Realizing what she was doing, she quit and swiped her witch's ring across the nightstand's sensor. "Tienan, I need you, now, in the lounge." She headed out of the room.

Janay followed her.

A quarter of an hour later, Janay sat in the wingback chair before the fireplace. Boots sat in the other chair, and Tienan sat on a cherry blossom trunk he'd pulled up beside Boots.

Janay watched Tienan hold the edge of a glass vial in the thumb-groove of Boots' hand. The open end of the vial pointed to her wrist-rash.

Zad's aura flared to shield Tienan's flesh.

Boots hummed a mantra that sounded like OMMMM and stared at the rash. Soon seed beads of red liquid began to rise and glide over her skin, into the vial.

After consulting with Neejera, Boots felt confident she could use her p'si power, her telekinetic ability, to isolate and pull out the bloodwood poison.

Tienan agreed to help Boots by holding the vial and Boots' hand, thus leaving Boots to fully concentrate on pulling the bloodwood molecules out.

The mantra note stopped and Boots' eyes glossed with tears of relief. "Blessed be the powers."

Tienan grinned at his partner. "I'll definitely second that." He then lifted the vial where a large drop of red shimmered at the bottom. He screwed on the vial's cap.

Granger entered through the back door.

Boots shot out of her chair and stood before him. "You lying son of a bitch!"

Granger halted, surprise warring with confusion.

Fury rouged Boots' cheeks and fired her words. "You swore to me you were only drinking the blood rations headquarters provided and not succumbing to your hunger for human blood!"

Baffled even more, Granger's dark brows almost crimped together. "What are you talking about?"

Boots went and grabbed the vial from Tienan, who stood beside the chair she'd just vacated. She held the vial up for Granger to see. "I just extracted this from my wrist where you sipped my blood." She waggled the vial, causing the contents to slosh and coat the glass a translucent red. "This contains bloodwood poison. Who did you drain?"

"I swear to you, Valenteena, I have consumed no human blood — except for the half-pint you offered me."

"Then explain how this poison got into you!"

Feeling things might get out of hand, Janay spoke loud enough to get everyone's attention, but she did not leave her spot next to the fireplace. "You know, the better question is, *why isn't Granger dead?*"

Boots pivoted and faced Janay, the color draining from her face. "What did you say?"

"Bloodwood eventually kills. That's what I remember from the lecture Minn gave me about it. I also recall that it has a citric acid taste. It's tart, but it can be camouflaged by tart or tangy fruits — and rats love fruit. Not that I'm implying Granger is a rat, per se."

Granger didn't seem to take offense. What he took was the vial from Boots and squinted at the contents. "I drink blood. Animal blood from pigs, cows, sheep. None of it has ever tasted acidic. Is there any other way to ingest bloodwood?"

Janay searched her memories and drew up a few tidbits. "The bark of a bloodwood vine looks like any wild grape vine. The raw sap is lethal to the touch, requires a HAZMAT suit, gloves . . . The distilled sap smells like roasted acorns and is a dark red, the color of blood."

Tienan came over to her. "Would bloodwood grow in the woods around here?"

She thought a moment. "I think it prefers swamp or peat bogs. Not sure. It has been a long time, Tienan."

"Boots," Granger said, "I have not been anywhere near a

swamp or a peat bog. I've been in the city for a year. All around the city, not the suburbs. The only thing I've been hunting for are members of the Circle of Draqoolq. If Rowen's vampire-witch belongs to it, perhaps she—" He eyed Tienan. "What if the Circle discovered I'm a GOOL and wants me dead?"

Boots took the vial from him. "There are better ways for a vampire to kill a vampire and do it efficiently and quickly. Poison is still a woman's prerogative when it comes to killing, so what female have you ticked off lately?"

"None. I swear to you Valenteena. I've not bedded any woman since I met you." He toned down his exasperation. "My blood comes from headquarters. What you should ask is *how would someone get the poison into me?*" The color suddenly drained from his face. "Janay, how long have I got to live?"

"Beats me. If you were human, we likely wouldn't be having this conversation. As a vampire?" She shrugged.

"I wonder . . . " Tienan didn't look at anyone in particular. "How many people have access to Granger's blood supply? And, which one of them hates him and wants him dead?"

Boots scowled. "Other than you?"

Tienan ignored her sarcastic tone. "Said person could also be someone blackmailed or bribed into poisoning Granger."

"But why?" Boots raked both her hands through her hair as if to rake away her frustration.

Granger shook his head sadly and stepped to the nearest wingback chair. He settled into the cushions, eyes mirroring the bewilderment of a doomed man.

Boots went to him and placed a reassuring hand on his shoulder.

He looked up at her, eyes pleading for understanding.

"We need facts," Boots said to him. "I want very much to believe you drank only the blood you were given." She glanced at her traumatized wrist. "And what I gave you."

"Upon my honor, Valenteena, it is truth. My veed will tell you."

Out of him rose a scrawny, black lizard veed, its legs proportionally three times longer than what seemed right for its body. Its stubby bat wings remained tucked along its sides, and it perched on the top edge of the chair back.

"Magestrella Janay, I am Enz," the veed said with a lisp. "What My Lord Granger says is truth. I have not permitted him to drink anything but his allotment. Do you know if bloodwood increase one's appetite?"

"Can't say," Janay replied. "Why? Has Granger been hungrier than usual?"

"He has recently had bouts where, like tonight when you attacked him, rage heightens the blood-hunger and that threatens to overwhelm him. I have noted that the episodes are becoming more frequent. Such hungers can easily become full blown blood-haze killing. That is to be avoided."

Granger nodded. "I've been a vampire for a hundred and ten years, and in all that time, I've had only one blood-haze. I killed eight vampires and a dozen of their followers." He wiped a hand over his mouth. His thumb and index fingers seemed to pause over the fangs beneath his lips, as if remembering.

He lowered his hand to the armrest. "At that time, I was enraged because they were going to drain the blood from three pregnant women, tear them open, and devour the blood of their wailing babies."

Janay's imagination provided her with snippets of that bloody imagery and acid churned her stomach. "Demon is as demon does," came out as barely a whisper.

Seeing Boots glare at her, Janay said, "At least there are no pregnant women here."

"Just one is pregnant." Tienan moved toward Granger. "My brother. Rowen." Tienan clamped a hand on the vampire's arm and bent, eye-to-eye with Granger. "You touch Rowen and I'll—"

Enz morphed into a ball of dark energy and leapt into Granger's mind.

"Back off!" Boots pulled Tienan's arm away from Granger. "I said, back off."

Tienan backed until he stood beside Janay, all the while glaring at Granger, who remained seated.

For a second, Janay wondered what lay at the bottom of the animosity between Granger and Tienan.

"Now," Boots said with authority, "this is what we are going to do. Since the only blood Granger swears he's getting is at headquarters, we are going to test that blood and see if it's tainted. We are going to do this without alerting anyone. *Is that clear?*"

"Valenteena," Granger said, "why keep it a secret?"

"Because we need to be sure before we make any accusations." The love she had for Granger flickered in her eyes and gentled her voice. "What if you are being set up? What if your bouts of hunger are the result of the bloodwood and your target isn't Tienan, or

Rowen, but someone else? Like the upper echelon commanders at headquarters? Or Australe government officials? This is an election year. Politics being politics, can you imagine the ramifications of such a killing spree on our colony?"

Granger nodded. "You're right, and we're going to need Neejera's help, and a believable excuse to see her."

"Have no fear, the peacekeeper is here." Janay enjoyed her own little rhyme for all of three seconds because everyone scowled at her.

Obviously levity was not appreciated. "Look," she said solemnly, "I have the perfect excuse for seeing Neejera—Rowen. He's eating some unusual things—like a liver, sardine, and anchovy pizza."

"That's not unusual," Tienan said. "Mother craved the concoction the last trimester she carried Rowen."

"By the looks on Granger's and Boots' faces, they, like me, think Rowen's snack is disgusting."

Tienan turned to Boots. "I agree with Janay. Rowen is a good excuse to see Neejera and take her into our confidence."

After lunch the next afternoon, Janay sat under the brilliant sun, in the center of the pentagram, combing Zad's nappy black mane. The lion-veed's eyes were closed in contentment, and he purred. Cobalt blue energy twinkled when Janay pulled the shorter strands of hair up, making tiny curls and setting them flush with his skin in a neat row. She glanced at the house.

Tienan stood behind the kitchen's screen door.

She whispered to Zad, "Your master is studying us again."

"I know," Zad replied. "I sense him being close. Do you think him jealous of the attention you lavish on me?"

She chuckled. "Tienan doesn't strike me as the jealous type."

Zad opened his eyes, and something reflected deep within those dark orbs. "I love you, Janay."

She paused in making a curl and smiled with sincerity. "I know you do. I see it in your eyes, Zad. It's the love of a best friend for a best friend, but the question is, does the second soul love me as well?"

"Equally."

"And how do you figure that?"

"He's said as much."

"He talks to you?"

"Not in words I understand. In the dreaming time, when I sleep with you, beside you, I have heard his voice. He has an accent and sometimes he lapses into speaking a very strange language."

"Ah, so, not a twin's soul, but a reincarnated soul." Was it Otto's?

"A reincarnated soul? I do not know. Do you think that possible?"

She shrugged. "If you believe in reincarnation and karma, why not?"

She made two more curls before Zad spoke again. "Janay, the second soul seems frustrated about something. I am sure it has to do with Tienan and you." Zad butted his head to her chest.

"Ah, Zad . . ." She hugged him.

Tienan shouted from the kitchen doorway, "They're back!"

Zad morphed into his ball of energy and sped into Tienan.

By the time she got up, stretched, and made it into the house, Boots entered through the side door, her arms loaded with a large garment bag and several smaller shopping bags.

"Clothes for the princess." Boots dropped the bags onto the nearest chair.

Tienan gaped at Boots. "You went shopping?"

"You've forgotten what today is, haven't you?"

He had the blank-faced look of a man caught being forgetful.

"Solstice High Tea. In three hours?"

Tienan groaned, whispered an expletive, and said, "I forgot."

Boots grinned. "Aren't you glad I'm your partner and reminded you?"

He nodded.

Granger came in, ignored everyone, said nothing, and went through the holograph into the lift.

"Don't worry about him," Boots said. "He's having a hard time dealing with being poisoned. Com'on, I'll fill you in."

Tienan followed her and Janay followed him. When the study was secured for privacy, Boots said to Tienan, "Janay was right. Granger has been poisoned by *Poltenticium D'amore*, the Blood of Death, also known by six other names including bloodwood, which seems to be the least popular." She scowled at Tienan. "You should be pleased. There is no cure."

Tienan didn't look pleased. His tone seemed to demand assurance. "Granger is going to die?"

"If he were Zantharian, or human, yes. But he's veeded and he's a vampire. Neejera's investigating options. By the way, Granger's blood supply is tainted. *All of it.*"

"All of it?" Janay said, noting the surprise in her own voice.

"Every bag," Boots replied, not looking at Janay but Tienan. "The interesting thing is, the bags are labeled for his use and only his use. Each is tagged for a day of the week so he can't get more than one bag. Neejera said each contained ever-increasing amounts of the poison. With every passing day, he's been getting more and more poison. Based on the progression of the dosing, Neejera figures he's been poisoned over the past month. Which coincides with the change from pig's blood to lamalt blood. Neejera says the lamalt blood neutralizes the poison's natural acidity."

"So," Tienan said, "how many people had access or handled the blood?"

"Seventeen—and that includes six at headquarters. When Neejera went to Commander Dag, the commander agreed to look into the situation."

"Did you tell the commander our suspicions about the book?"

She nodded. "When I mentioned the *Fourth Book of Xenobia,* Dag almost had a heart attack. Ready for this? The book is missing. As in stolen. But, here's the thing. There is a book in the vault. Not a copy, but something that on the outside is a virtual duplicate of the *Fourth Book* but with enough blank pages to equal the weight of the real book."

Tienan's voice held disbelief. "Granger delivered a fake?"

"He did not! That was verified by vids and a dozen people. And for the record, Tienan, only three people at headquarters, besides the commander, knew about the theft. The conclusion is that someone working at headquarters stole the book. No clue who or how."

"So we're dealing with a very clever person or persons."

Boots heaved a sigh and her face became a neutral mask. "I've got more bad news. Dominic LeCarr went missing last night."

"Another boy dead?"

"No body yet. He's just missing. Seems he and his father had another row. Dominic went storming out of the house yesterday afternoon."

Tienan muttered, "Shades of Rowen . . ."

"And before you ask, yes, Dominic was tailed."

"But?"

"Late in the afternoon, he went into a gambling club. One of those rabbit warrens. Anyway, he vanished. They found his black hover car parked on East York, not far from Warehouse Row Boulevard. Plainclothesmen are canvassing the area."

"Another boy." He shook his head sadly and only for a moment. "What are our orders?"

She chuckled. "Tienan, you idiot. You and Janay are going to your grandmother's high tea and, if you don't get going, you'll be late. Granger and I will watch Rowen. He'll be fine."

❦ Chapter Seventeen

I have no talent; I make Ready Wit my Talent. — The
Samurai Creed

Janay rode the lift up to the main floor of Wolcott House
feeling decidedly uncomfortable in the organza jacket-dress Boots
had purchased for her.

The dress may have been a simple, sleeveless A-line, and the
cascading front of the jacket draped beautifully to mid-thigh, but
the fabric sparkled with seed beads and floral embroidery that
reeked of the elaborate dresses Grandmother Cholyn had made
her wear.

The swish of the dress brought back memories of sitting with
grownups who smiled condescendingly as if she were her
grandmother's lap dog, saying, "Such an adorable child. So well
mannered."

The lift doors opened to the kitchen.

Janay stepped out, spotted Tienan, and froze, her breath
trapped in her lungs.

All in black, Tienan looked the epitome of a powerful warlock,
regal king of cavernous realms.

Neatly pulled back and braided, his dark brown hair glistened
with brilliant mahogany highlights. His left earlobe bore a large
diamond stud in a square, black onyx setting.

Her gaze shifted to the cabochon pin that was centered at the
base of the mock turtleneck collar of his long-sleeved, slinky knit
shirt. The pin was a larger replica of his warlock ring. The gold
nyd rune shimmered with a glassy shine.

He also wore a black, knee-length tabard, the edges bound

with threads of twisted gold and silver.

Yet it was the expression on his face as he gazed at her that touched her most — pure male pleasure and admiration.

Boots' words echoed in Janay's mind — *Your outfit should not only wow Tienan but knock the heels off Silence's shoes.*

Squaring her shoulders, Janay walked toward him.

With each step, Tienan's smile blossomed like a miniature rose.

When she stopped in front of him, he took her right hand and kissed the back of it, sending a frisson of awareness of his sensual masculinity skittering through her.

"You look lovely, Janay." The tone of his voice and the sincerity of his words swelled her heart with joy.

Only she must be careful and not reveal her true feelings for him. "Thanks. You look handsome in black, but a tabard in this day and age?"

"It's traditional Zantharian costume. Required for high coven functions like the solstice tea."

Catching the side door opening, she found Neejera entering with a large carryall. The healer planted her cane for balance and set the carryall down. She looked from Janay to Tienan. "Off to a ball?"

Tienan faced her. "No, to my coven's annual T'mishaar."

"High tea? My, my, how quickly the seasons do pass."

Behind her, Janay sensed the lift open. Granger and Boots exited and headed for Neejera.

"Do you have news?" Granger's voice carried a tremor of hope.

Neejera leaned onto her cane. "Not the good news you'd like to hear." She pointed to the carryall. "Boots, in the front pocket are a couple of relay gizmos the commander wants installed. As to you, Granger, *no more snacking on Boots.*" She pointed to the carryall. "That's loaded with fresh pig's blood for when you need to squelch an urge. See that it gets refrigerated."

As he went to get the satchel, Neejera said, "Until the felon is caught, the commander insists we keep up the appearance that you're feeding as usual. So, even though we've traded the tainted blood for fresh, from now on I will test every bag before you indulge. And do be aware that other measures are being taken to limit access to all the blood at headquarters."

Granger brows pinched into a pensive frown. "That will arouse a lot of suspicion."

Neejera shook her head. "It's being done in the name of efficiency so no one should suspect a thing." She took a few steps toward Tienan and lowered her voice. "I contacted a botanist friend. The only bloodwood she knew of was at the GYC Starvision's science-research biodome. There might also be a chance the National Botanical Heritage Society has a vine. She'll check and get back to me."

Tienan nodded.

"By the way," Neejera said, "it is illegal to import or export the vine, or its tubers, not that such things hinder the truly clever and dedicated."

Tienan glanced at the clock. "Janay and I have to go. It's not fashionable to be late, unless, Neejera, you have something else to report?"

"Only that the Le Carr boy is still missing."

Tienan whispered in Janay's ear, "Welcome, to the covenstead."

With trepidation trampling her nerves, Janay entered Ozieron Hall, a sprawling glass and sandstone, multi-storied edifice. Going into the Valley of Rathe seemed preferable to facing a convention-sized hall of warlocks and witches — and Her Grace, Silence Tomosukovia.

Too late now to be the coward.

Tienan flashed his invitation, a five-by-nine centimeter black card embossed with a gold border, to the door sensors. The story and a half polished-wood doors, with their hammered black iron hinges, opened soundlessly.

As the doors parted, strains from violins and string instruments came from some distance away in the building along with the low buzz of conversations.

Janay beheld the massive, carved, walnut-dark beams of the foyer's archways. Some of her trepidation eased at seeing the massive sprays of live flowers in vivid reds, yellows, and blues that dotted among platter-sized, white Gerberis-like daisies. Walking through the strong fragrance given off by the flowers had Janay recalling Grandmother Cholyn's cloying perfume, Gardenia, and almost triggering a dry retch.

Approaching another set of black doors like those at the entrance, the doors automatically opened and cool fresh air surrounded Janay.

She tried not to gawk at the silver-veined marble floors, the black marble columns towering up to the vaulted ceiling's ornate plaster rococo and gilt beam work. All of it glittered in the light of huge, multi-tiered, silver and crystal chandeliers.

In almost a whisper, Janay said, "It looks like a cathedral."

"Wait until you enter the ballroom." Tienan took her hand and placed it on his arm. He flashed his invitation, and the next set of doors opened.

Elaborately carved and molded reliefs of trees, flowers, and fruits edged marble wainscoting and veined black marble columns where the Tree of Life relief had pride of place on the domed nave.

"Never mind the cathedral," Janay whispered, "this is a sultan's palace."

"Byzantine elegance appeals to our veeds' love of refined elegance, the formality of pomp and circumstance." He patted her hand and held it down for a moment on his arm, as if he were afraid she would bolt. "Smile, we are about to be presented." Tienan handed the major-domo their invitation.

The major-domo, dressed in darkest brown attire and a plain black tabard, wore a ruby cabochon pin at his collar. He swiped the invitation into his datapad and nodded once. "Please proceed." Over the loudspeakers came his sonorous voice. "Lord De'Argossi. Magestrella Cholyn."

Six paces later, Janay looked down the flight of the grand staircase at the nearly filled hall below. The majority of men wore black or dark brown, but all sported tabards. Every witch stood bedecked in finery, making for a rainbow assortment of exquisite dresses and designer pantsuits. Diamonds and other gemstones flashed from necklaces and earrings, embroidery, barrettes and tiaras.

Janay swallowed down the feeling she was about to stand in front of a firing squad.

Tienan gently tugged her forward.

She set her foot on the first step of the staircase and force-marched herself down each step. Nearing the bottom, a hush settled over the crowd.

Heads turned.

Too many eyes stared at her.

She wanted to retreat, but she drew strength from Tienan's

hand, which was once again resting over her own. She expelled a breath, quelling her unease. She could do this.

At the head of the receiving line, Tienan met his grandmother's gaze with the hardness of pride-hammered steel. He made the official introductions, but Janay's attention slid to the woman on the other side of Silence—Margo Riboji.

As usual, Margo's silver-gray hair was swept up in a French twist and her left-parted bangs cascaded over her ear in precise waves. The embroidery on her charcoal-gray pantsuit was festooned with sapphires that matched her blue eyes, but the sweeping V of the jacket's lapels reminded Janay of crossed swords.

Margo was the quintessential image of the legendary Australe Amazon Queen, the first Margo to set foot on the planet.

Yet, what gladdened Janay more was the man standing behind Margo. General Salkim stood elegantly poised in his dark-gray dress Zhayoda uniform with its black and blood-red piping trim and gold-edged epaulettes. General Salkim gave her a curt nod.

"Margo," Silence said. "Allow me to introduce—"

"Sergeant Cholyn! Janay! How good to see you again." Margo's smile was of welcome but the look in her blue eyes was of profound relief.

"Hello, Margo." Janay greeted her warmly. "Fancy meeting you here."

"It's an election year. Have to do my duty to my brother and the party. I am so very glad to meet a fellow citizen. Will you be at my table serving tea?"

What? Janay gave Silence the look that usually damned a new recruit. With an evenly controlled voice, Janay said, "Lady Tomosukovia, Your Grace, I wasn't aware I would be required to serve tea."

Hours after the solstice tea festivities ended, Annelisa headed for the warehouse. The night had deepened with a frosty chill, and she castigated herself for not donning a jacket instead of the black sweater she wore. Entering the warm warehouse, she strode past the plants, but slowed when she saw Sweets at the altar, dressed in her working apron-robe, grouping various items together at one corner of the altar.

"Hi," Annelisa said.

Sweets replied in a bland tone, "You're early."

"Only by thirty minutes or so."

"And how was the solstice tea?" Sweets crossed the room to the worktable wall and pulled out a task chair. "Come. Sit and tell me all about it."

From her ball state of energy floating in Annelisa's mind's eye, Ahl said, *She wanted to talk? Actually wanted to know about the tea?*

Why did the wisps of Ahl's blue and gold energy swirl with increasing intensity? Was she afraid? Of what?

Please my good lady, Ahl said, *do not hesitate. Sweets will notice. Do as Sweets demands.*

Yes, of course. Annelisa sat in the chair offered her and caught sight of mud splatter along the cuff of her brown slacks. "Oh trond! They're ruined."

"What are?"

"My brand new slacks. Look." She pointed to the mud.

"Serves you right," Sweets said. "You shouldn't have worn them when the weather is frightful."

"It's not the rain. It's having to walk through filthy alleyways. I hate parking on Warehouse Row."

"Once again, I remind you, Annelisa, that we cannot afford to have vehicles drawing attention to this warehouse after dark." She pulled over a task chair and seated herself. "Now, tell me, did Tienan take his whore to the tea?"

"He did, and she looked fabulous. The two of them made a handsome couple. And get this, Janay served tea."

"Oh, how wonderful! I take it Janay made a fool of herself in front of Coven Ozieron?"

"No, she most certainly did not. Her Grace was even adamant that Janay was a guest to be served, but Margo Riboji talked Janay into serving. Did you know Janay served formal teas for her general?"

"No, I didn't. How did Silence react to that?"

Annelisa laughed. "The look on Her Grace's face was price-less! Her Grace was actually speechless when Margo told her Janay served high tea to the emperor himself, then insisted Janay be at her table. Lady Bohem saved the day by switching places with Janay to please Margo."

Sweets slumped with disappointment. "No faux pas?"

"Not on Janay's part. Not on Tienan's. And, sadly, not on Her Grace's." She sighed forlornly. "It's a dreadful thing to have to admit, but Janay's good manners had the Hautonne embracing her. She and Tienan will likely be invited everywhere."

"But? I hear a but."

"When we got back to Wolcott Manor, Her Grace was uncommonly depressed."

"Why?"

"Because—" Annelisa let a slow grin push into her cheeks. "Her Grace thinks Tienan is in love with his familiaris."

Sweets clutched her hands, her face radiating joy. "In love? Are you sure?"

Annelisa shook her head. "I couldn't tell, but Her Grace says Tienan did a good job of hiding his feelings. She said when he thought no one was looking, she saw it in his eyes. I'd say a grandmother would know such things, wouldn't you?"

"Not necessarily. Silence's own fears may have had her jumping to that conclusion."

Annelisa recalled Tienan sitting beside Janay. "One thing was obvious to me, and everyone. Tienan is possessive and protective of Janay. Like when Lord Mynert said he would be happy to have Janay when Tienan was done with her. I thought Tienan was going to punch him in the face."

"But he didn't, did he?"

Annelisa shook her head. "No. Janay up and told Lord Mynert if he, or anyone, ever makes such a proposal, they'll either be eunuchs or dead because she knew twenty ways to geld or kill a man in under ten seconds."

A grin crinkled Sweets' cheeks and brightened her eyes. "What was Tienan's reaction to that?"

"I think it was pride."

"And Silence's?"

Recalling Silence's face made her laugh. "She was horrified."

"Do you think Janay loves Tienan?"

Annelisa shook her head. "Most of the time I got the feeling I was in the presence of Sergeant Cholyn, the soldier, not a woman who was any man's mistress."

"Is Her Grace scheming to separate to the two and end her son's budding romance?"

"I don't know. She tried to rationalize, convince herself it might be better to let nature take its course and let Tienan tire of his mistress, like her lady mother often did. Then she goes to the manor's sorcery, lights three prayer candles, and chants for Tienan to come to his senses."

"Then why, Annelisa, are you frowning?"

"Because it puzzles me that Her Grace insisted I add Tienan and Janay to the invitation list for the Sahhar Ball. I'm to hand deliver those invitations."

"It's said the ball makes or breaks relationships."

A creaking noise drew Annelisa's attention to the slowly opening door of the ceremonial cupboard. "What are you brewing? Or maybe I shouldn't ask."

"I was bored waiting. I wanted to try a quick spell. Would you like to help?"

"I should be tending Janay's bloodwood vine."

"Why?"

"It's not growing normally. It's a quarter of the size of any other vine Celinae's planted. I don't want Celinae to blame me for something that's not my fault. I thought as long as I was reporting on the tea, I'd mix up a more potent fertilizer for it and give it a dose."

Sweets patted Annelisa's knee.

She'd never patted her nor smiled with such a brilliant flash of white teeth.

"Annelisa, dear, that vine is very important to us so you go take care of it. I can do the spell by myself."

She wasn't going to argue. "Okay."

By the time Annelisa fed the plant and cleaned up, she found Sweets on the backside of the altar, the side facing the fireplace. From the shimmer of Sweets' skin and the blank look in her eyes, she was in a veed aura trance, softly whispering the spell she read from the *Fourth Book of Xenobia*. Fae, her veed, rose in her ghostliness.

Somehow the hawk-snake form seemed larger. To be expected considering all the veed energies it had ingested.

Annelisa almost sighed with disappointment. Her Ahl hadn't grown in size from the feedings. Instead, her veed had grown in wisdom, which translated into a remarkable memory and enhanced analytical abilities.

Then again, where Ahl had gained more coloring, more gold and amber in her fan-tail, there didn't look to be a color change in Fae. White wings. White hawk face. Black-edged beak. Even the lower extremities, the serpent's body, remained cobalt blue, the scales edged in amber and gold. Still no legs. Sweets had hoped for legs, four of them. Four legs would make Fae a Behringgreat, not a Behringlesser. Still, even in this trance state, Fae had a look of cruel elegance about her, just like her host.

Sweets slowly raised and lowered her left hand over a golden tazza.

Annelisa studied the goblet. A band of Vidarian runes were engraved around the squat rim and base. Sweets could read and write old Vidarian and Ancient Zantharian, but when Celinae had asked what the runes and words meant, Sweets merely said they were designs, a pretty pattern.

Sweets touched the goblet rim and it glimmered with Fae's aura. Glitter-like sparkles swirled into a ghostly blueness following her fingertips and spread like a whirlpool along the edge of the cup and over the bowl.

It probably would be a very bad idea to break Sweets' concentration. Annelisa almost tiptoed to the end of the workbench. She sat on a task chair, relieved the chair didn't squeak under her weight.

The whirlpool on the tazza vanished. Fae's aura receded from the cup. The *Fourth Book of Xenobia* shut itself with a loud clap of its cover and brought Sweets out of her trance.

As soon as Fae vanished inside her host, Sweets bent forward and studied the goblet's contents. "Annelisa! It worked. Come see."

Curious, Annelisa went and peered into the bowl.

A teal liquid pooled in the center among pale, shriveled leaves.

Detecting the smell of cooked grass, she almost gagged. "What is that stuff?"

"The liquid is pure ofirium. The leaves are Black Thistle Grass."

"I thought the thistle's flowers were the poisonous part."

"They are, but when you distill the leaves, you get ofirium."

"I assume it's toxic?"

"Absolutely."

"What kind of poison is it?"

"The lethal kind." She chuckled. "Okay, one eighth of a teaspoon causes a mild heart attack. A full teaspoon stops the heart. *Permanently.* The beauty of this poison is how quickly it breaks down in the body. When an autopsy is done, it's undetectable."

"Who's the intended victim?"

Looking at the smile edging Sweets' lips, goose bumps

erupted over Annelisa's arms along with the thought that she was the intended victim.

"Goodness, Annelisa, you've gone pale. Oh, you're thinking . . . No, no, this is not for you."

Annelisa exhaled a sigh of relief.

"It's for Celinae."

Annelisa suddenly couldn't breathe.

Sweets' sweet smile was all politeness, but her voice held a dagger's sharpness. "You must not tell her or *I will kill you*."

"You can't afford to kill either of us." Had she just said that?

I voiced the words for you, Ahl said and the colored swirls sped faster in her white ball of energy, as if readying to morph into her noncorporeal self to defend Annelisa's body from attack.

Sweets' head went up, stretching her long neck so she looked indignant. Her voice became harsh. "You do realize Celinae is likely to turn on the both of us, don't you? She will kill us and devour our veeds' energy."

Both hate me and are plotting my demise!

My lady, Ahl said, *do not shout at me. It's best to figure out what Sweets is up to. Cajole her, get her to reveal her intentions.*

I'm sorry. You're right. Annelisa sent her gaze to the floor, cloaking herself in a submissive, nonthreatening posture which always worked with people. "The thought crossed my mind."

"Oh, good!" Animosity vanished from Sweets. "Then we can be allies, can't we? You and I working together when the time comes to save ourselves from Celinae?"

"How are we to do that?" She looked up but maintained a submissive attitude. "I'm no match for her."

Sweets' face beamed with the smirk of a cat holding down a mouse it had just captured and had no intent of killing right away. "Tell me, have you ever wondered why Celinae insists you bring the blood-wine and the ruby glasses to the altar after our veeds feast on a veed?"

"No."

"Annelisa! It's because she doesn't trust me. She's paranoid I'll slip one of my poisons into her glass."

Same conclusion we drew, my lady, Ahl said.

Annelisa didn't reply to her veed. "You want me to put poison in her glass? That's impossible."

"Of course it is. She insists you put the goblets face down on the coasters and you bring the unopened bottle to the altar so there can be no additives, right?"

Annelisa nodded, bewildered as to what Sweets intended.

"Now, on the night when we partake of our last victim's blood, which must go into the special wine, you will have a little trip, a little skid, nothing which will break the wine bottle or the glasses. Just jiggle things about a bit, cause a moment's panic that the wine might tumble off the tray and break, ruining everything."

"But I don't understand. Why go to such trouble?"

"To distract her, silly. To make her rush to you and grab the bottle. Which will allow me to put this poison in her vial, the one containing the fresh blood of our victim. She will never realize her vial's been tampered with, now will she? Then, as we are accustomed to doing, we synchronize our movements and add our vials to the wine in our glasses, make our toast, say our enchantments, and down the mix before it curdles."

"Ingenious plan." And it truly was.

"Then you will assist me? It's for your own good, you know. I will have just enough time to poison her vial, so you can rest assured yours won't be tainted."

That was not much reassurance. "And then what? Am I next? I'm no match for you, Sweets."

"I know, and you must also know I need an ally. There are more spells in the *Fourth Book* that I want to use and most of them require a helper, an apprentice."

In awe, Annelisa said, "You want me to be your apprentice?"

Sweets took Annelisa's hands in her own. "Oh, yes, dear Annelisa. We are friends, aren't we?"

Better agree, Ahl said. *Don't let on you're smart enough to see through her lies.*

Annelisa nodded, and smiled appropriately for effect.

"Now help me. I'll need ice to cool the ofirium, so be a good friend and fetch some ice from the freezer."

When Annelisa opened the door to the walk-in freezer, she abruptly halted at the sight of the corpse with its Mohawk-spiked hair dulled by frost. She backed out and half yelled, "Sweets! Dominic's body's in the freezer."

"Yes, I know."

"Why didn't Celinae dispose of him in the bay?"

"Weather, my dear girl. Weather. The rains last night. Choppy water. Small craft warnings. She had to work today, so that leaves tonight to do the deed."

A quiver of panic seized Annelisa. "She's coming back tonight?"

"At midnight, or whenever Shelzat's done with her."

"Done with her? What are you talking about?"

Sweets paused in staring at the contents of the poison-filled goblet. "It's so obvious."

"What's so obvious?"

She looked at Annelisa. "Haven't you realized? I guess not. Celinae is in love with Shelzat. Been in love with him since she was sixteen and succumbed to the dark qi. They're likely indulging in sex with leather, chains, whips, or whatever appeals to them." She looked back into the goblet. "I never understood why she likes brutality with her orgasms. Of course, my sex with him is a lusting delight. Desire burns in me from the inside out, sets me on fire." A glaze of remembrance dilated her eyes and bowed her lips into a sensual smile. "Flames licking, licking, licking. Drawing, blazing hotter and hotter, embers tingling in the aftermath . . ."

Annelisa's mind reeled. Celinae was in love with one of Satanus's most powerful, depraved archangels. She enjoyed brutal sex, and Sweets enjoyed Shelzat too?

Did Celinae know about Sweets and Shelzat?

Lost in the revulsion of such revelations, Annelisa went to get the ice. She stepped over Dominic's corpse, ignored his dead-eye stare and the scrap of cocoon carcass twisted and seared to his naked chest.

❦ Chapter Eighteen

I have no friends; I make my Mind
my Friend. — The Samurai Creed

After returning to Wolcott House from the solstice tea, Janay changed into casual clothes. She sat in the lounge, on the bearskin in front of the fireplace and watched the wood crackle and burn.

Images burned brightly in her mind of the tea, and of Tienan, the epitome of a gentleman, of his impeccable manners, of his fluid movements practiced and ingrained so they seemed effortless, yet regal. Then again, he was Zantharian Hautonne aristocracy and he was in his element.

And how the women whispered and covertly studied him! Young or old, many women flirted with him, some blatantly, others shamelessly. Yet, none held his attention nor his interest. Why?

Because he'd been attentive to her, only her.

For a few hours, he made her feel important. Special. Even desirable.

She'd drawn on the quiet strength of his voice filling her in on who was who and what was what. And then there were those little gentle squeezes of her hand, squeezes of approval, encouragement, support.

Zad bounded into the room straight for her, skidding on the polished parquet floor and stopping at the edge of the bearskin. "You were magnificent!" His exuberance sparkled in his dark eyes.

"If a lion could smile, you'd be grinning." Janay rapidly

rubbed her fingers through the hair between his ears and uncoiled a dozen nappy curls.

Footfalls announced Tienan's approach.

Zad's ears flicked back, then he swung his attention to Tienan. "My lord, don't you think Janay handled Grandmother magnificently?"

"Yes." Tienan seated himself in the chair to Janay's left and gazed at the fire. "I also have to admit I have never seen Grandmother so courteous."

"She was courteous to everyone, my lord." Zad cocked his head at Tienan. "Why do you smile so?"

"Just remembering Grandmother's face when she found out Janay served high tea to the emperor."

Janay chuckled. "Yeah, that was priceless."

Tienan eased back in his chair, arms and hands relaxing on the armrests. "Janay, who taught you to serve tea?"

Her merriment vanished. "Grandmother Cholyn."

"I take it you and your grandmother don't get along?"

"She was a stickler for protocol. I got stuck with her for summer visits. The visits were a legal compromise so I could get the guardians I wanted." Janay watched a blue flame flicker and dance.

One memory flickered and danced to life. The memory of sitting across the wide fruitwood table in Grandmother Cholyn's pristine penthouse, wall-to-wall whiteness dotted with golds and royal blues so at odds with the black suits of advocates of the law who were finalizing the legal documents that set Janay free to be her own person.

Janay shook her head to dispel the images. "It was always the same when I went to Grandmother Cholyn's." She mimicked her grandmother's dour voice. "Remember you are a lady of quality. Sit up straight. Do not fidget. Do not look bored. A lady must have unquestionable sensibilities. A lady must embrace an appreciation of art, music, dance, wine, and gourmet food."

"That bad?" Tienan's voice teased.

"I'll bet you never had to endure lessons on deportment."

"I had a tutor and a valet who were well versed in how a De'Argossi should behave, along with a veed that embraced ritualistic deportment."

Zad leapt onto the other wingback chair. He circled, then folded his legs, tucking himself so he fit within the seat's width. "Veeds, my good lord," Zad said with a majestic lift of his chin, "have a fondness for elegance, ritual, and the finest things in life. I did not and do not embrace ritualistic deportment."

Janay scoffed. "I bet neither of you were dressed up and shown off like a purebred freak of a prize dog."

Tienan sat bolt upright. "Are you insinuating I was showing you off at the tea like a prize pet?"

"No, no. You weren't. Sorry, I don't know why I said that." She pulled her legs up, wrapped her arms about them, and rested her forehead against her knees.

Tienan left his chair and sat beside her on the bearskin. "Janay?"

She didn't raise her head. "I hated the way the men undressed me with their eyes tonight."

"I wasn't happy about that myself, but you handled yourself rather expertly, especially with Lord Mynert."

"Would you really have slugged him?"

"He would," Zad replied. "Tienan ordered a keen for the power to do so. I am glad such action was not required for I fear the blow would have been a killing one. Yet, it is understandable, Janay, dearest magestrella, for my good lord Tienan truly wished to protect you."

She lifted her head and scowled at Tienan. "Protect me? I remind you that I can protect myself."

"I know. You've proved that on several occasions." Looking again at the fire, some of the tension went out of him and his shoulders rounded.

She gazed at the fire. Yeah, she could protect herself, her body, but could she protect her heart? Skom! She wanted Tienan's love. Double skom! She was never going to get it.

And just sitting so close to the man like this, feeling his body heat, smelling his body odor mingling with the wood smoke, and the bedeviling nudges of her own desires that would never be satisfied was maddening torture. She had to get away. "Gotta go. I promised to fill Rowen in on the tea. I'll likely play kumdak with him so he can win some of his money back."

She was babbling.

She rose and exited as ladylike as she could.

Tienan studied the flames consuming the wood until the log became embers.

Zad lay with his chin on his paws and his claw tips peeped out over the edge of the chair cushion. "My lord, do you not think Janay is superior to any witch of our acquaintance?"

"Yes."

"Then why not court her?"

"Don't be foolish, Zad. Janay hated being dressed up and paraded among the Hautonne tonight. If it weren't for Rowen and the familiaris' contract, she wouldn't be in this house. Our worlds are galaxies apart. *We do not suit.*"

The comlink intoned an incoming call and Tienan answered it. Minutes later, he interrupted the kumdak game. "Janay, your general's aide called. We have an appointment at Jian-Qun tomorrow afternoon. The general's arranged for a military shuttlecraft to take us to the base, but we'll have to be at the spaceport at 0600 hours tomorrow."

Jian-Qun Military Base and Murad Sector Fleet Headquarters, north of the Imperial City of Bhutar

It had been a long trip into the wilderness to the base. Tienan was stiff from the ride but relieved to finally walk through General Artan Tarfooga's door.

The general, a stocky man, greeted Janay with a bear hug and a bear of a growl of laughter.

Watching the two, it struck Tienan that the general had an usually pale complexion, one sun and a hard military life hadn't tanned. Yet the general had gray edging his sandy-brown mustache, which rode over his steel-wool beard. Gray also edged the general's temples and thinning crew cut.

Tarfooga let Janay go and turned his electrifying blue eyes on Tienan.

The instant and full measure those eyes took had Tienan feeling like he'd been transported to medieval times and faced a towering crusader-knight and liege-lord.

"And who, sir, might you be?" The general's scruffy voice was not gruff.

Tienan extended his hand. "Tienan De'Argossi, sir." The general shook his hand briefly, but firmly.

"Sir," Janay said, "Tienan is a Guardian of the Law and, sad to say, a Zantharian warlock and a GOOL."

The general's delight vanished.

Poke and Fox suddenly whizzed out of Janay's boots. They entwined figure eights around the general, then Janay, before dashing to Tienan and circling him at chest height. All the while, Janay recapped the dirks' odd behavior for the general.

Tarfooga studied the dirks and concern began to darken his eyes.

"And lastly," Janay said, "the rascals insist I'll die if I don't sleep with Tienan."

One of the general's brows rose along with half a smile that twitched his mustache. "Sleeping with the devil, are you?"

"I put a substantial barrier between us."

The general grinned. "Well, let's have Red Oak see if he can make sense of your dirks' behavior."

Tienan followed Janay, who followed the general, into a room where a crescent-shaped desk and computer terminal stood at an angle, dividing the space in half.

A daybed and table cum nightstand occupied the area near a narrow window, its shutters keeping the afternoon sun at bay. At the opposite corner, the general stopped before a meter-tall by meter-and-a-half long, slope-sided, two-tiered chest topped with a rectangular cap piece. The chest's parquet-wood surface glistened like polished stone.

The overall design made Tienan think of two coffins stacked one on top of the other. Although the upper one was smaller than the bottom one, both were decorated with glyphs, hieroglyphics, and runes. Only why such wide-spaced, age-blackened metal drawer pulls when there appeared to be no drawers? Maybe the pulls were for toting the thing around?

My good lord, Zad said, *there are no latches, no hinges. No keyholes. I wonder how it opens?*

The general glanced at Tienan. "Impressive, isn't it?"

Tienan nodded.

"Centuries ago, this was to become a sarcophagus. It was made from pieces of rare woods by the T'zule." The general ran his fingers appreciatively along the front edge of the top piece. "Seems the original owner died in a temple fire and burned to ash, which the wind swept away. Now this chest houses The Blessed Blades."

Janay's dirks went to the top of the chest. Dancing a *pax de deux*, their tips traced the vine motif of the hammered, black metal centerpiece. Reaching the opposite end of the motif, the two pirouetted, backed toward the wall, and stilled.

With the groaning sounds of a millstone put into motion, sections of the top chest began to lift and fold back, showing a creamy-white, velvet interior.

From inside the depths of the chest, drawers cascaded and fanned out. Every drawer held a few art-nouveau designed daggers, knives, and dirks — lots of dirks — yet, three fourths of the depressions were empty.

From the very center rose a trellis of gold vining displaying a knight's broadsword in its scabbard. A giant, blood ruby in the shape of a teardrop graced the top of the hilt. An oak tree relief in silver and gold embellished the scabbard.

To the left of the broadsword rose a silver vine. By the shape of the bejeweled scabbard it held, a scimitar was missing.

To the right of the broadsword rose a brass vine with a katana sheathed in an ebony scabbard. The katana's hilt had a black, diamond-patterned, full-beaded shagreen leather grip.

Janay's dirks sped to the broadsword and slipped their tips five centimeters into the top junction of the blade and its crossbar.

An almost imperceptible humming ensued.

Tienan, my lord, Zad said, *that is a very odd harmonic. I do not like it. The katana . . . By the blessed swords! It's moving.*

The gleaming blade of the katana cleared its scabbard. The tip rose and pointed at Tienan a moment before the sword shot forward.

Zad! Protect.

Zad's aura engulfed Tienan a second before the katana's tip pierced the veed's shield — and him.

As the blade plunged into his body, the rushing in Tienan's ears became as loud as storm-surged ocean waves bashing rocky cliffs.

When the katana's tsuba hit and stopped the blade, Tienan felt engulfed by the freezing cold certainty of death.

Zad roared like a wounded animal.

All went black.

Tienan had no idea how long before the floating sensation eased or the blackness gave way to brilliant white light, but a sense of peace filled him.

From far away came, "He's going to be so pissed."

That was a feminine voice. Janay's voice? Yes.

A soft gruff laugh. "Everyone is initially."

That had to be . . . yes, General Tarfooga's voice.

My lord, Zad said. *We are fine. Please wake.*

Bits and pieces fell into place of the parquet chest opening, the katana rising. Renewed panic sliced into his heart. *The sword. Zad – *

It did not kill us. It did not harm us in any way. Please, Tienan, wake up. The general and Janay are worried. You have been unconscious too long. I am worried.

I'm okay?

Yes, you are, my good lord.

Tienan focused on his steady heartbeat.

If his heart beat, then he couldn't be dead, could he? He breathed in, filling his lungs with all the air they could hold.

No pain.

He exhaled.

Janay's worry-urgent voice pleaded, "Tienan? You're okay. Com'on, open your eyes."

On opening his eyes, he had to blink to focus. His direct line of sight was a pebbly-textured acoustic ceiling tile. He turned his head and found Janay sitting beside him. "Where am I?"

"On General Tarfooga's daybed."

"Hello, son." The general came into view and stood behind Janay. "We need you to do something for us. Say, *Sugi, to hand.*"

"Why?"

The shifting of the general's feet equaled a don't-argue-with me stance. "Son, I can't reveal the reason until after you say *Sugi, to hand.*"

"Sugi, to hand."

Nothing happened. Well, nothing except momentary surprise twitching the general's mustache and eyebrows.

Janay swore softly under her breath. "Tienan, let Zad out. We need to look at him."

Had he heard her right? She knew outsiders were never to know about veeds. Why would Janay betray that knowledge? "What did you say?"

"Take it easy. I told the General about Zad because he saw Zad's aura. Not that it mattered. The general counts half a dozen GOOLs as friends and they all have veeds. Now, let Zad out."

"No."

In her eyes flared the immutable determination that he'd seen on the night she'd brought Rowen home.

"Damn you and your oaths, Tienan!" Janay reached down and grabbed a square hand mirror off the floor. "Take a look at your chest. Your heart!"

He had no shirt? "What happened to my shirt?"

"Casualty of the katana," the General said. "My aid delivered a replacement shirt, but you can put that on later, after we sort things out."

"Sort things out? What things?"

Janay shoved the mirror at him. "Look! Look at your heart."

He took the mirror and soon focused it on the Templar-cross scar. His mind seemed to go blank, then he felt woozy, but managed a hoarse, "What did you do to me?"

"We did nothing," Janay replied. "You've been pierced by an executioner's sword, only your scar isn't right."

"Damn right it isn't right." He yelled at the general, "Remove it. NOW."

"Easy, son. No can do. You've been chosen, though it eludes me precisely why a warlock should merit the power to wield a Blessed Katana."

"We're getting off track." Janay took the mirror from Tienan and set it aside. "Look, Zad was in aura mode when the blade went through you."

"He saved my life!"

Janay shook her head. "His lion's heart was pierced. We need to find out if he bears the same scar as you."

My lord, Zad said, *the katana cut through my heart, but I cannot see if I bear a scar because of my nappy mane.* He reared up to show Tienan his chest.

I can't tell anything, Zad. You're miniature sized.

I have to know, my lord. I have to know!

Was that panic in Zad's voice? He never panicked.

All right, come out so I can look at you.

Zad left him and morphed into his corporeal form on the opposite side of the daybed from where Janay sat. Under Zad's weight, the mattress squished out air. Zad stepped back so Tienan could look at his chest.

Seeing the scar, Tienan closed his eyes, praying it wouldn't be there when he opened his eyes again. When he looked, the scar was there.

"It's there, isn't it?" Janay demanded. "Is it blank like yours?"

"Yes, it's there, and no, it's not blank. It has an image of the katana centered on it."

Both Janay and the general stared at him for a moment.

"Zad," the general said, "say *Sugi, to hand.*"

Zad looked at Tienan.

"Go ahead. Do it."

The instant Zad spoke the words, the katana appeared and slipped its hilt under Zad's right paw.

The general muttered something that sounded like profanity.

Tienan elbowed himself up. "Someone explain what's going on."

A bleep sounded and the general said, "Sergeant, I can't stay any longer. You're on your own. Explain things to him."

"Yes, sir."

When the door closed behind the general, Janay reset her headband.

Tienan had the feeling she was putting her thoughts in order more than her hair.

"Janay, did you bring me here knowing this would happen?"

"I did not. Red Oak told the general my dirks recognized a soul worthy of a Blessed Blade. Fox and Poke figured if they created enough havoc, I'd go see the general and take you with me. My dirks truly thought you merited one of their cousins. They had no idea Zad was worthy of the katana."

"Zad was worthy?"

"Yeah. Remember the Templar's cross over my heart?"

He nodded.

"It has a miniature of Poke and Fox below the cross which indicates I am the chosen warrior and they serve me."

His scar didn't have the sword—Zad's did. A sensation like being sucked down a black hole had Tienan lying back down. "What does it mean when I have the cross but no sword?"

"That you're not the executioner, that you cannot summon Sugi. By the way, the katana's name is Sugi. If it's any consolation, Sugi is female. Her name means Cedar in Japanese, which, according to Red Oak, a cedar tree is the symbol of moral rectitude." She scoffed. "Yeah right, you and moral rectitude."

Her stern gaze rankled.

"Rectitude," she said, "basically means correctness of judgment."

"Are you saying Zad has correct judgment, and I don't?"

She shrugged.

"You do realize Zad has paws? What is Zad supposed to do with a weapon he can't hold?"

"Not sure. Maybe Zad and you meld, become one, and then you let him use the sword. I've seen you two melded."

Fear and anger sent Tienan's heart thudding against his ribs.

"Melded yes, but I retain control of my veed. I've never swung a sword. If you think for one minute I will turn my body over for Zad's exclusive use, you have gone to the dark side!"

Janay crossed her arms over her chest, scowling like formidable Sergeant Cholyn. "You are so not worthy."

"What are you saying?"

"The Blessed Blades are intelligent entities, beings called Infanatas. Their purpose is to serve the warriors with pure and noble hearts, those who fight for justice, and those who protect those who cannot protect themselves. Obviously, you, as a Guardian of the Law and a GOOL, fall into the latter two categories, but you come up short in the pure and noble heart department."

"Pure and noble went by the wayside with knights and samurai."

"For your information, the Blessed Blades were created by Adrada, the Archangel of Departing Souls. The very epitome of a warrior-knight-samurai. Every blade serves as faithfully as does that great angel."

"I didn't ask to be picked. Why would your general do this to me?"

"Skom, you can be such a blockhead. The general has nothing to do with picking you. Now, pay attention. There is no exterior latches on the chest. The only way it opens is from the inside—from Red Oak opening it, usually to receive a returning blade or for one of the blades to come out to bond."

Anger kindled in the recesses of Tienan's mind. "You're saying Zad is noble hearted, worthy, and I'm not?"

"It's complicated. Remember when you removed the veed spittle from me and I told you I heard another song?"

He nodded, his anger banking, unsure what she was getting at. "I presumed it belonged to a dead twin-in-utero. But I can't prove it."

"Well, I think Sugi choosing you confirms my suspicions that the second string-song doesn't belong to a deceased twin of yours."

Zad laid down and put his head on Tienan's chest. "My good lord, that song belongs to Kiyoshi, the soul of a reincarnated samurai."

The room spun. Tienan blinked and his focus steadied. He managed to whisper out, "How do you know that?"

"When you blacked out, my lord, I conversed with Adrada, the archangel. You were in limbo or suspended animation—I know not which — but it does not matter. I was terrified, and Adrada calmed my fears. He introduced me to the soul of Kiyoshi, the samurai, the soul given to me."

His veed had a reincarnated soul? One of a samurai? No, not possible. Anger thundered out of Tienan. "All these years and you kept that a secret!"

"No, my lord, I did not! Please, I beg you to listen. I did not know we possessed such a soul until Janay revealed the second string song. Only after Adrada came to me today did I know it to be my soul."

Janay's brow furled into a curmudgeon of a frown. Then she nodded slowly. "You certainly have to appreciate it."

He didn't appreciate anything right now, especially the insanity of Zad having a soul and being the summoner of a katana. "What's there to appreciate?"

Janay smiled. "The irony of it. Zad is your soul, but Zad possesses a reincarnated soul. You have, in essence, two souls. You cannot wield Sugi, the katana, unless Zad melds with you and takes over your body."

"How many times must I tell you that every Zantharian who has ever given over to their veed has turned to the darkunskyve. Look at Granger. Look at what he's become!"

"Boots told me Granger believed he could do more good working undercover as a vampire than as a human. He has done good. I also remind you that when you asked if he contained dark qi, my blades didn't find any."

"His veed is evolving into a more powerful entity, likely able to camouflage its darkunskyve. If he hasn't already, well, eventually he'll succumb, and I hope to have the honor of beheading him myself."

"Revenge is a double-edged sword, Tienan, and maybe your lust for revenge is what makes you unsuitable to wield Sugi."

"I'm never wielding that katana."

She looked at Zad. "You better tell Sugi *home* so she's safely out of sight until you and Tienan have need of her."

Zad nodded. He eyed the sword and lifted his paw. "Sugi, home."

The katana vanished.

Tienan hardened his voice. "Zad."

Zad blinked, but he did not utter a protest as the chains and shackles went on him, along with a muzzle. Tienan commanded, "Return to me, *ensphere*."

The veed morphed into a ball of energy and entered Tienan's head.

Janay's face flushed with anger. "How dare you! You — you — unfeeling bastard! How dare you shackle Zad. You — " Her jaw stopped in mid-word, as if some thought connection disengaged her voice. Her anger vanished. "How scared and insecure you are. Not a man but a mouse."

"You don't understand."

"Oh, I do." Her voice was low, hard as stone. "You're a control freak and a bigot."

"Janay — "

"ENOUGH!" She got up and went to the desk. She tossed him a peacekeeper-issue camo-shirt. "Get dressed. I have to say goodbye to the general. Then we leave. A shuttle's waiting to take us back to Bhutar." She strode out of the room.

In his mind's eye, inside the clear bubble that was the Sphere of Discipline, Zad lay as motionless as a sphinx, front paws extended, head high. In addition to his shackles, he now wore the black Collar of Obedience around his neck. A heavy, black chain anchored that collar to the base of the sphere.

A memory flitted in Tienan's mind of his father and grandfather walking him through how to chain Zad, how to create and place Zad in the sphere. Zad had to be punished because Tienan had let Zad talk him into stealing a brand new hoverbike for a joy ride at breakneck speeds.

Tienan sent his hand to his left thigh. He rubbed the area where the thin, jagged scar was a reminder of going over a cliff in that bike. Zad had almost killed him . . .

As Zad laid down, his chains rattled.

Another time came to mind.

Tienan at eighteen. Zad and he had been furious because Penelope Roh had bragged about having sex with him. He'd never bedded her.

Zad was all for raping her to show her what happens to liars.

He'd considered it. Dreamt and plotted how to do it.

Tienan's mother's image suddenly flitted to life. Her beguiling smile came with her soft-spoken words that echoed, *A wise man is slow to anger.*

He wasn't angry. He was outraged.

Tienan got up and put on the camo-shirt.

All the while, Janay's words went round and round in his mind. *Scared. Insecure. A mouse not a man. Control freak. Bigot.*

❦ Chapter Nineteen

I have no enemy; I make Incautiousness
my Enemy. — The Samurai Creed

Feeling exhausted, eyes closed, half dozing, Janay lay in the hammock behind the pergola wearing a newly purchased blouse and striped shorts that felt as comfortable as her old fatigues.

Since getting back from Jian-Qun, her dirks had no reason to insist she sleep with Tienan, so she'd slept in the guestroom. Only she tossed and turned, longing for the reassurance of Zad's purring, longing more for the nearness of Tienan's body, his arms about her. How could she long for a man who was so wrong for her and who was so cruel to Zad?

Skom, even if she did doze off, dreams skittered her awake. Erotic dreams of being naked with Tienan, of him laughing that she was his whore not his wife.

Most troubling were the dreams of a faceless Japanese female. That woman stole a samurai's wakinzashi from under a bed cushion, then, weeping, she ran into a forest. Janay had woken with the feeling that the woman had killed herself because the man she loved didn't love her back. The idea of having little to live for felt too close to the truth of her own life.

Hearing Zad purr, Janay looked at the lion in the center of the Pentagram. She hated the black collar around his neck. At least when Tienan permitted the veed to reenergize, the shackles came off.

She finger tapped, HOW LONG B 4 YOU HAVE 2 GO BACK 2 T?

A black claw covertly protruded from the front paw nearest her and tapped softly, NOW. LOOK DOOR.

She glanced over and found Tienan standing at the kitchen doorway, sipping from a white mug.

MUST GO. Zad morphed into a ball of energy and whizzed into Tienan.

She met Tienan's stoic gaze.

He backed a step and closed the screen door.

It was a good thing she'd taught Zad the code for talking to the Blessed Blades because it had become Zad's only way to have a conversation with her.

Tienan had ordered Zad not to speak to Janay because he figured she would fill Zad's head with nonsense about using Sugi. At first, Janay figured it was out of spite, but now, well, now she figured it was out of his illogical fear of being taken over by Zad-the-monster.

Zad was no monster.

She closed her eyes. The sun-warmed wind caressed her cheeks and carried away her disgust. Birds chirped . . . Bees buzzed . . .

"Janay?"

Rowen's voice woke Janay, and she came upright fast enough that the hammock swung wildly. She countered the movements.

Rowen staggered to the nearby wicker chair. Seating himself caused the cushions to squelch under his weight. His rotund belly pushed the limits of the navy sweatsuit he wore. His face looked puffy, so did his hands and ankles. Definitely the last stages of pregnancy were taking their toll on the boy.

She glanced over to the Pentagram, where the lines glistened in the sun.

Not many more days before she would have to endure the reunification rite. Once that was over, she would leave Wolcott House, and not look back. She couldn't afford to look back on what might have been.

Rowen's voice pleaded, "Janay, it's been over a week since you and Tienan returned from the base and the tension between my brother and you is downright unbearable. Lover's quarrels shouldn't last this long."

"It's not a lover's quarrel. We're having a difference of opinion, and your brother is being a pigheaded ass."

He grinned. "Not the usual blockhead?"

"That too."

"Is this difference of opinion about you being his familiaris? Or him selling his samurai collection?"

Tienan was selling his collection? She swung her bare legs over the side of the hammock. "Why is he selling the collection?"

"Beats me. Boots and I thought you would know."

"I don't. Oh, I get it. You want me to find out why he's selling the collection and report back to you?"

His grin dazzled. "How else?"

"Right. Go prop your feet up and let me to the dirty work."

She ignored his laughter and padded, barefoot, across sun-heated pavers and into the house. She took the lift to the lounge.

There she found Tienan, datapad in hand, sitting on one of the lacquered chests before the display of the five katanas.

"Is it true, you're selling your samurai collection?"

He didn't turn around. "Yes. Everything goes."

"Why?"

"To forgo a catastrophe."

"Skom, Tienan! Do you hate your veed so much?"

He swung around. His cheeks flamed and anger simmered in his voice. "Zad and I are brothers. For your information, I'm trying to avoid tempting Zad. This collection is a constant reminder of that blasted katana that's chosen him. If Zad ever kills anyone — ANYONE — by Zantharian law, *my life is forfeit.*"

"That's ridiculous. Zad can't wield the sword until you two meld and you refuse to do that. Selling all this — " She widened her arms to encompass the room's collection. " —It's like cutting off your nose to spite your face."

A hurricane-force of fury darkened his cheeks and gray eyes. "I'm trying to protect myself and others."

A ping resounded, followed by Rowen's, "Hey, Tienan, Boots has arrived. She needs to talk to you and Janay. In the study. Immediately."

Tienan set his datapad on the chest and headed for the lift. "On my way."

She followed.

From her seat in the chair in front of Tienan's desk, Boots asked Tienan to set the room's security shielding in place. As soon as it engaged and, with no trace of his lingering anger with Janay evident, he said, "I take it you've got bad news?"

"Afraid so. Dominic LeCarr's body was found around dawn this morning, or rather was netted this morning. A fishing trawler found him among their catch." Boots drew back a wayward strand of her hair and tucked it into her unkempt topknot. "Coroner figures the boy died the night he went missing. Autopsy says his body had been frozen, then dumped in the bay. Likely after the storm, after the small boat advisory had been lifted."

Tienan settled his buttocks on the edge of his desk. "Cause of death?"

"Same as the other boys. Overdose of varnum. A strip of veed cocoon seared on the chest, throat slit, but this time the two puncture wounds were evident. Not vampire fangs. The wounds match the ones Rowen had on his neck after he escaped the witches."

"In other words, the witches are trying to make it look like vampires killed the boys?"

"That's the current theory."

He wiped a hand down his jaw. "It doesn't make sense. If the same vampire-witch who visited Rowen is involved, why isn't she drinking the victims to death?"

From her spot with her back to a bookcase, Janay said, "Maybe it's the varnum in the blood."

"I thought of that," Boots replied. "Neejera says varnum would have no effect on a vampire."

Tienan muttered. "Nothing makes much sense."

"Agreed." The way Boots paused and took in a breath through her mouth, made Janay curious and, yet, she dreaded what Boots was about to say.

Boots tucked another wayward strand back into her topknot. "There's more bad news. We've reached a dead-end on the bloodwood tuber. Neejera heard back from her botanist friend. GYC Starvision had a bloodwood vine, but it died of old age. According to the company's records, the vine was incinerated. Vids showed three people witnessing it."

"What about the vine at the botanical heritage place?"

"They only have three roots, all in a cryogenic tank. They were kind enough to run a scan on the tubers. All three are there, frozen. Of course, there's the outside chance a plant, or a tuber, was smuggled onto the planet."

"Is there any good news?"

"Sort of. Last night Granger attended a Betwixton Moon celebration and met a sexy *redheaded witch with long straight bangs*." Boots looked at Janay. "The redhead's hands punctuated her sentences, that is, when they weren't rummaging over Granger's body, or so he says."

Tienan demanded, "What's her name?"

"She wouldn't tell Granger, thought it was fun to keep him guessing. Come to find out she didn't give her name to anyone at the party, let alone a clue to where she lives."

"Did Granger follow her when she left?"

"He did. She went down to the docks, got into a speedboat, went straight out into the bay, and vanished into the night. When we checked on the boat—"

"It was stolen?"

Boots nodded. "No prints. Nothing. But get this, the woman bragged she would soon bind with a powerful vampire and be his consort."

"Will Granger see her again?"

"She promised to take him to the Circle of Draqoolq celebration come the eve of the new moon. She has his contact number and, no, she never gave him hers."

"Or so he says."

Boots folded her arms across her chest and scowled. "I really resent your attitude, Tienan."

He gave her a one-shoulder shrug. "So, did Granger discover anything else about the red-haired witch?"

Boots shook her head slowly. "She wore elbow-length gloves, which she never took off, leaving no fingerprints." Boots half smiled. "Ah, but Granger flattered the little wench into revealing her gloves and dress were custom-made. The gloves had tiny white rosebuds embroidered on the cuffs. I found out the gloves were designer originals purchased by Silence Tomosukovia for last year's Sahhar Ball."

Tienan's jaw dropped, then closed with a snap.

Boot ignored his reaction. "According to Lady Tomosukovia's personal assistant, the gloves and a bundle of other clothing went to a downtown boutique specializing in the resale of designer and custom-made goods. Unfortunately, the boutique had no record of the glove's sale. Which may only mean it was a cash purchase."

"In other words," Tienan said, as if thinking out loud, "we have a young witch who likes designer fashions and consorts with vampires. She likes boats, which could mean she was the one who dumped LeCarr's body in the bay."

"Who knows? All we can do is wait and see if the redhead contacts Granger."

Janay sighed. Waiting was going to be so boring, especially in a house where no one was really speaking to anyone.

The Warehouse

Annelisa knelt before the planter that held Janay's spindly bloodwood vine. The stalk was barely large enough to provide fibers for the netting necessary to hold Janay's qi dirks. The fertilizer treatments had promoted growth but something was still not right with the vine.

She rocked back, sitting, resting her muddied, gloved hands on her cobbler's apron. The source had to be Janay's blood. But what? Sweets had said there was nothing out of the ordinary in the medical reports and tests she saw. At least Sweets was going to look at the reports again.

The crackling of a duvara opening caught Annelisa's attention, and she scrambled to her feet. Just outside the Druid's Circle at the top of the Pentagram, a siddirelling portal widened and out stepped Celinae.

Annelisa timed her steps to reach Celinae when the portal vanished. "Hi."

"Hi, yourself." Celinae's voice sounded pleasant for a change, but Annelisa waited for her to remove her cloak and hang it on the peg nearest the front door.

As Celinae patted down her straight bangs, her gaze went to the streaks of mud on Annelisa's apron.

"I was tending Janay's vine. I can't figure out what's wrong with it."

"I have my suspicions."

"You do? Like what?"

"Like Sweets did something to Janay's blood, or the tuber, or the potting mix to foil its growth."

"Why would she do that?"

"To rid herself of us!"

Good grief, what brought on that paranoid conclusion?

"Annelisa, dear, haven't you figured it out? Sweets intends to kill us and devour our veeds' power."

"Impossible."

"Not if she uses the *Trinitas D'eth Spell.*"

"The what?"

"Trinitas D'eth. It's a spell in the *Fourth Book of Xenobia.*"

Celinae smiled with malevolent glee. "*My little friend,* I know this because my veed can now read Ancient Zantharian."

Annelisa cringed, but she wasn't sure whether she cringed from being called Celinae's little friend or because Celinae's veed could now translate old Zantharian, which meant Celinae, and Sweets, had access to all the secrets of the *Fourth Book of Xenobia.*

Despite her mounting fears, Annelisa had to know. "What kind of spell is the *trinitas?*"

"It makes it possible for one of the members of a blood-bonded trinity, such as ours, to immobilize the other two—then kill them and devour their veeds."

Terror stuck in Annelisa's throat.

Calm down, take hold of yourself, my lady, Ahl said from her swirling ball of energy in Annelisa's mind's eye. *Remember, Sweets intends to kill Celinae. You are now privileged to know Celinae fears Sweets and has a way to kill her. We must turn this situation to our advantage.*

Yes, you're right — and so wise. Breathlessly, Annelisa said, "Is there a way to stop Sweets from using the spell? I—I don't want to die."

"I am so glad to hear that. We need to be allies, you and I, in order to stop Sweets and turn the spell on her."

Being allies with Celinae felt like offering one's hand to a cobra to sink fangs into. "I don't understand."

"It's simple. Quite simple." Celinae hugged herself and spun around, laughing, her face upturned to the rafters. "So simple the simpleminded can do it!" Abruptly she halted. From under the cowl neckline of her blouse, she pulled a dark copper chain that brought up an oval disk of hand-hammered, darkened copper with two ornate Fleur-de-lis, one marking the top and one the bottom. She placed her hand so the rune of her witch's ring's was underneath the bottom fleur. She muttered ancient words and removed her hand.

The disk began to play a tune.

"The sound reminds me of an antique music box." Annelisa continued to listen, trying to identify the tune. Then she noticed Celinae's eyes danced with interest, and something else.

A tingling vibrated its way from Annelisa's hands to the crown of her head, and she realized she couldn't move. "What's happening?"

The tingling skittered down her legs. She was paralyzed. Fear sank its fangs into her.

In fascinated horror, Annelisa watched Ahl morph into her noncorporeal goose form, rise, and exit, without one word of command to do so.

The music stopped.

Ahl honked and, with a flutter of her goose wings, transformed into her ball of energy, fleeing into Annelisa.

Celinae clapped her hands and laughed triumphantly. "It works!"

Outraged by what just happened, Annelisa bellowed, "You didn't know that thing would work so you tested it on me!"

"I had to know. It worked perfectly."

"And now you're going to use it on Sweets and me?"

"Just Sweets. I need you, Annelisa. Many of the spells in the *Fourth Book* require two veeded witches. You'll be my partner. Yes, my partner. We shall maximize our veeds full potentials." She tucked the pendant under her shirt.

Annelisa felt stunned until she realized nothing mattered but enhancing Ahl's power.

My lady, Ahl whispered, *Celinae will not permit me to become an equal to her veed nor you equal to her.*

I realize that, but we shall have the advantage. We know what she plans to do. Somehow we must find something to block the sound of that music.

It is not the music, my lady. It is the pulsing of the higher frequency which interferes with our body song, paralyzes you, and forces me to obey. But for some reason, Celinae is not affected.

Shelzat is our ally. I bet he knows how to prevent us succumbing to the tune.

I do not trust him. He likes games of intrigue and manipulation. What if he gave that pendant to Celinae?

She almost shuddered at that thought.

"Annelisa?" Celinae entreated.

"What?"

"Were you chatting with your veed?" A slight creasing wrinkled her brow.

It was not good to have Celinae curious and probe. Best say something to divert her. "Yes. I was. Ahl was upset about finding herself outside me and not knowing how she got there. I had to calm her."

The wrinkles vanished. "What does your veed think of us being partners?"

"Ahl's in favor of it, as I am." Oh, how convincingly she lied.

Celinae's grin equaled the size of a noon-day sun. "Wonderful! And you promise to be careful what you say and do so as not to make Sweets suspicious?"

"Yes. Positively. Certainly."

Celinae looked at the clock on the wall over the main doors. "Two hours to midnight and we are here as Sweets ordered, but where is Sweets?"

Annelisa went to the workbench, sent her gardening gloves to the recycle bin, and triggered the screen to check the perimeter security cameras. "She's coming down the alley behind the building. Ought to be here in a couple minutes."

"Good." Celinae walked around the Druid Circle's blood-red bricks.

By the time Annelisa had hung up her apron, Sweets came through the back entrance. When she spotted Celinae, anger tinged her cheeks. "You idiot!"

Celinae spun around and faced Sweets. "What did Annelisa do this time?"

"Not her — you. You idiot!"

Celinae took a defensive stance, hands on hips, and growled back, "I am not an idiot."

"Then explain how Dominic's body ended up at the morgue this morning?"

"What?" The fight went out of Celinae. She slipped her hands off her hips, resting them at her sides. "How?"

"Thanks to your ineptness, this morning some fishing trawler caught Dominic's body in their net."

"You can't blame me. *I followed your plan.*"

Sweets glared at Celinae who glared at Sweets.

Annelisa stepped toward the two, stopping on the Druid line. No need to get too close. "Sweets, was there any way to know a fishing vessel would be in the area?"

Sweets frowned. "No. I don't think so."

Celinae smiled smugly. "Then how can you blame me?"

"You're right." With effort but no sincerity, she added, "My apologies."

Celinae stance didn't change. "Is that why you called this meeting, to tell us Dominic has been found?"

Sweets removed her cloak and hung it on the end peg before facing Celinae.

With knuckles on her hips, Celinae demanded, "Well? Aren't you going to answer me?"

"Yes, I called you both here for more than a report on Dominic. Be assured that although the Guardians have Dominic's corpse, they remain clueless." Her voice held satisfaction. "Thanks to your ruse in Rowen's bedroom, Celinae, the Guardians have tasked Granger with finding the ancient vampire-witch." Her voice went hard. "However, we have bigger problems."

She squared her shoulders. Her voice twanged with tension. "New measures have gone into effect regarding all the blood stored at headquarters. They've installed refrigerated lockers in the infirmary next to Neejera's office. Granger's blood supply was sent there this afternoon. All of it. I can't get access to it anymore."

Celinae huffed. "You worry for nothing. Granger needs only a few more doses before the craving for human blood will be so strong he can't stop himself from killing."

"I know that! Don't you realize that with him patrolling Wolcott House grounds in case the old hag-witch returns, if the blood lust hits, he could kill Rowen? Then where will we be?"

"Not to worry," Celinae said. "I've seen to it that Granger will be occupied elsewhere." With an upward tilt of her jaw, she patted down her bangs, as if she were patting herself on the back. She eyed Annelisa. "I met Granger last night at a Betwixton celebration. I flirted, intrigued, and seduced him just like I've seen Annelisa do. I even wafted a little bloodwood-seed cologne under his nose."

Sweets gasped. "Have you lost your mind? We're counting on the perfume to send him into an immediate bloodlust. By the darkness, what if he has identified you?"

"Don't be melodramatic. *I used cologne not perfume.* The cologne barely made him sexually aware of me as a woman. As to him identifying me? Nonsense."

"I wouldn't be so sure of that," Annelisa said softly.

Both women glared at her.

"I got a call late this afternoon from Boots. The gloves you wore last night, Celinae, they were ones Her Grace wore to last year's Sahhar Ball."

"You gave them to me." Her voice lowered, hardened, and she demanded, "What did you tell Boots?"

"That Her Grace gave the gloves and a bundle of other clothes to her favorite boutique for resale."

Celinae chuckled. "Since that place never had the gloves, no one can trace them to me."

Sweets threw up her hands. "Trond! You two are idiots. What

happens when the store says they never had the gloves on inventory?"

"Actually," Annelisa said, "I picked that boutique because they keep lousy records so Her Grace would never know I sold some of her things and pocketed the cash. Besides, I doubt anyone at the store can remember any of the gloves they sell. After all, they get dozens and dozens after every ball."

Sweets shook her head as if to say, *why me?* She stopped and stared at the center of the Pentagram. The way she suddenly went still meant she was conversing with her veed.

Moments later, Sweets looked first to Annelisa then to Celinae. "We have come far but we are not as powerful as we'd like, and each time we kill for a veed, our risk of being discovered increases, agreed?"

Annelisa nodded, so did Celinae.

Sweets began to walk the Druid's circle. "I would like to propose something extraordinary, something wildly wicked, something no one at Guardian Headquarters will expect."

"And what would that be?" Celinae's eyes danced with curiosity.

"On the night we take Rowen's veed, we take Tienan's as well, sap the power from Janay's dirks, and bring Silence Tomosukovia to her knees."

Celinae tapped a finger to her lips and muttered, "All in one night? In one fell swoop?" She shook her head. "No, that's dangerous. Risky. Way too risky. I say we stick to the original plan. One veed at a time."

Anger flushed Sweets' cheeks. Her words came hard and crisp. "Our original plan did not include Janay's interference. Our original plan did not include Rowen surviving. Our plan did not include Dominic's body being found so quickly!"

For a long moment, long enough for the fiery redness to leave Sweets' cheeks, no one spoke.

In her heart, Annelisa knew Sweets had the right of it. They had to do something extraordinary to gain the power to overcome veeded GOOLs.

Celinae suddenly grinned, her eyes sparkling. In a soft voice, she said, "I agree with you Sweets and would suggest we go a step further. What if we snare Granger, and after we partake of the veeds, we send Granger into a killing spree? He'll be so demented by our bloodwood potions that everyone will believe he killed the De'Argossi brothers, the Cholyn woman, and Her Grace."

Sweets seemed dumbfounded, then she, too, smiled. "I like that. Yes. Let's do it!"

Annelisa felt queasy. They might overcome Her Grace, two men, and a soldier, but could they control a maniac vampire?

❦ Chapter Twenty

I have no armor; I make Benevolence my Armor. — *The Samurai Creed*

Wolcott Manor

Annelisa stood before the door to Her Grace's office and took two fortifying breaths. Tonight was the eve of the new moon, and she was about to play her part in Sweets' Grand Slam Plan.

Annelisa entered, finding Her Grace sitting at her French Provincial desk doing correspondence at her computer station. Her Grace didn't look up. "Yes?"

"It's about the ball, Your Grace."

She still didn't look up. "Please tell me the florist has not called again."

"No. It's about the RSVPs. Yesterday was the deadline. I checked the mail a few minutes ago, but there was no acceptance from your grandson or his familiaris." Which was the truth. Funny how the truth suited a lie.

Her Grace's hands stilled. She raised her head, and wistfully said, "I was hoping Tienan's woman would come. I so wanted to get a better idea of what attracted him to her."

Annelisa put on a show of biting her lip and shifting her weight from foot to foot, giving the illusion of unease.

"What troubles you, Annelisa?"

"Oh, Your Grace, I know I shouldn't have without checking

with you first, but I called Rowen and asked if the RSVPs had been sent back. He checked. They were still on Tienan's desk. Rowen said I should come over for supper and maybe between us we could convince Tienan and Janay to go to the ball."

Rowen had sounded eager for the two to go to the ball, and there was a hint all was not well between Tienan and Janay, which she needed to determine so it didn't interfere with Sweets' and Celinae's plans.

"What a marvelous idea, Annelisa. I trust you said you would go, didn't you?"

"Yes, but if that's not all right with you . . ."

"Nonsense. I'm pleased you took the initiative." She pursed her lips in thought. "Tell you what, come back with Janay's acceptance for the ball in hand and I will give you a drail an hour raise."

Three drails an hour would be better, but it was a moot point. "Oh, Your Grace, you are so generous."

"Yes, I am, am I not? Now, don't keep Rowen waiting."

Almost to the door, Annelisa paused to compose herself before she looked over her shoulder at Her Grace. "Don't forget Lady Bohem's sending a car to pick you up at 1900 hours."

In reality, Sweets would be driving that car and abducting Her Grace.

Wolcott House

When Boots entered Tienan's study, he glanced up from the estate quarterly spreadsheet on his holographic screen.

Instead of coming to the side of his desk like she usually did, Boots began pacing the width of the fireplace where a small fire took the evening damp out of the room. "Granger's leaving."

Tienan turned his holo-screen off. "Is Granger's leave-taking temporary or permanent?"

"Don't be facetious, Tienan. He got a call from the redheaded witch. He's to meet her at sunset."

Out of the corner of his eye, he could see through the window that the sun had already touched the horizon. "Then I trust he's hurrying so he won't be late."

"He is, and I'm worried."

"He's a vampire. Not much can harm him, certainly not a young and inexperienced witch."

"I know, I know. But what if he encounters the old hag, the vampire-witch, one of the Circle of Draqoolq's members?" Boots swung around and came to the desk, setting both hands on the polished surface. "Tienan, my gut says this is an ominous night. It's the eve of a new moon. Granger is going to Fiely Park—"

Now he knew what bothered her. "It was, what, eight years ago to the day that your husband died there?"

She nodded as if she fought to keep those memories at bay.

"Boots, your husband was killed in a shootout with escaped felons. They were Australes. Mortal humans, not Zantharians. *Not vampires.*"

She pounded her palms on the desktop. "How can you dismiss the night of a new moon? Bloodwood vine poison is still in Granger's system and, if there are vampires feeding, you know what Neejera said, Granger could succumb to a bloodlust and kill until dawn to sate it."

"Granger is aware of that. He knows the odds."

"Yes, but—*I don't know what I'll do if he gives in to the bloodlust.*" She stood and tightly wrapped her arms about her, as if to keep her fears contained. Her voice dropped to a deathly quiet level. "I love him, Tienan. He's agreed that we troth at the Sahhar Ball. I don't want to lose another man . . ."

Shockwaves rippled through him. Boots and Granger trothing? "I see."

Her temper flared anew. "I doubt you see anything!"

"Why are you angry with me?"

"Because you've hardly spoken to Janay, or any of us, for days. You keep your veed collared. You're more arrogantly sullen than ever I've seen you. By the blessed powers, it's making Janay withdrawn and morose."

"Chalk it up to the peculiarities of her temperament."

"Is that how you see it? Peculiarities of temperament? If anyone has peculiarities, it's you."

He strove to keep his temper in check. "I realize you're upset but there's no need to take your frustrations out on me."

"Are you blind? Rowen's remarked on the changes in you and Janay. We're both concerned Janay no longer feels welcome at Wolcott House. Technically, once Tal is restored to Rowen, she's no longer needed, and we think that preys on her mind."

"She signed a contract to be my familiaris for six months.

She'll uphold the bargain as a matter of honor."

"At least she has personal honor."

He clenched his teeth. He would not allow her to bait him into saying something he would regret. "You go too far, Boots."

"Not far enough. Someone has to speak. A woman can only endure so much, and I fear Janay is at the end of her endurance."

Now he truly didn't understand. "Meaning?"

"It might not take much to push her over the edge into such a depression that she commits suicide."

Suicide? That was a chilling thought. "Don't be ridiculous. You're so wrapped up in your own emotions about Granger that you've lost sight of what being a GOOL is."

She stood tall, spine ramrod straight, hands fisted at her sides. Her voice carried the power of thunder. "A GOOL doesn't seek revenge."

That salvo hit home. "I only want justice for my mother, not revenge."

"Same difference." Anger flared her nostrils.

He continued to stare at her, willing her to calm down, be rational.

A bleep sounded from the security system.

Saved by a distraction! Tienan passed his ring over the comlink access. "Display."

The picture above the fireplace morphed to show a white town car approaching the house.

Boots swore softly. "I forgot to tell you, Rowen invited Annelisa to supper." She headed for the door.

When the door closed, he leaned back into his chair.

Why was everyone angry with him?

He was only doing the right thing by keeping Zad under control. Doing the right thing by seeking justice for his mother. Doing the right thing by helping Janay for saving Rowen.

The knelling of the bells of the Chapel of J'Hi Baldama summoning vespers broke into the silence of the room.

Janay quit the assault game on the screen in the game room. She felt as restless as when her squad had packed into the shuttles for the incursion into the Valley of Rathe.

Now why was she visiting that old memory?

Possibly because of Boots' agitation over Granger going to see the redheaded witch and fearing for his safety. After all, hadn't Boots been adamant that the worst elements of the darkunskyve come out on the eve of a new moon?

Women in love worried too much.

She entered the lounge and walked to her favorite spot — the katana display. Only this time her eyes focused on *The Samurai Creed* framed above them. Her gaze alighted on the line *I have no strategy; I make the Right to Kill and the Right to Restore Life my Strategy.*

I make the right to kill . . .

She had the right to kill as a peacekeeper, a citizen of the Empire, and as The Digger of Demon Graves.

The right to restore life . . .

She, a female capable of childbearing, was needed for the reunification rite so Rowen could have his life and his veed back.

No strategy . . .

Unintentionally, she'd become a familiaris, the companion of a Zantharian warlock, a man she was pretending she didn't love but did.

And then there was Zad.

Poor Zad whose plight tugged at her heartstrings. Tienan was jealous of his own veed, a noble veed judged worthy to summon an executioner's katana.

No strategy.

Skom! Things happen. Bad things happen to good people. All intangibles.

Life made no sense.

And just why was she having such a neurotic, one-sided conversation with herself?

Her gaze drifted to the adjacent case. On a red velvet cushion under protective glass, rested an aged-to-dilapidation wakinzashi, a samurai's short sword, his *honor blade*.

If dishonor came to a samurai, he committed seppuku, ritual suicide, with his wakinzashi. Below the blade was the naginata, the favorite dagger-weapon of a samurai's wife and warrior monks.

She heaved a futile sigh and eyed the oldest of the katanas.

From behind her came Tienan's voice. "If you like the katanas so much, I'll gift them to you."

She half turned. "I have no use for them except to admire the craftsmanship."

She had no words to convince him to change his mind about Zad. She also sensed the tension in him, that he likely didn't want to go another round about Zad and Sugi.

She went over to the lacquered cupboard, putting a comfort zone between her and Tienan. She passed her ring over the locking mechanism and opened the doors.

Looking at her ramrod stiff spine, Tienan knew Boots had been right. There was too much dissension between Janay and him. The resulting stress wasn't good for Janay's health, his, or Rowen's. He had to find a way to compromise with her, be on better terms again. But how?

Gazing at the samurai armor, she said, "So, what brings you down here?"

He lied and kept his voice neutral. "I was looking for Annelisa and Rowen. They weren't upstairs."

"They adjourned to his suite to play kumdak. They invited me, but I bowed out. You know, two's company, three's a crowd."

"Did you remind him about taking a chance Annelisa would see he's pregnant?"

Janay chuckled. "Blockhead, she figured it out for herself when she brought over the invitations to the ball."

"What?"

"Not to worry. Annelisa hasn't told your grandmother about *the bulge.*"

Confound the powers, there was nothing he could do now, was there? No. *So, change the subject.* "Is Boots in the guestroom?"

"No. She's in The Sorcery making a tisane to sooth her worries over Granger. Does she have a sixth sense about danger?"

"No, she only has telekinetic p'si. Why?"

"Love is a strong bond. It often creates a link between the beloved so that one knows the other is in trouble or danger. Love is stronger than death."

"So is honor."

"And what's that supposed to mean?"

Here was his opportunity to talk things out. "Boots thinks once we reunite Tal with Rowen, you'll end the familiaris contract with me."

"And what's to prevent you from ending it instead of me?"

"My honor."

She chuckled derisively. "Ah, the pseudo-samurai speaks. Honor, reverence, ritual." She faced him. "*A code of dignity that goes to the silent depths of a powerful mind, and a more powerful will that does not fear death, either their own or the killing of another."*

She made no sense.

"Who are you quoting?"

"General Tarfooga, Peacekeeper Extraordinaire, a blessed Templar Knight Executioner, Wielder of Red Oak."

"You're the samurai, Janay, not I." The truth of his own words stunned him.

She sighed. "Yeah, in more ways than even I realized." Her gaze flitted to various cabinets of artifacts, then bore into him like one of her dirks. "You know what, Tienan, I think what really stands in your way of being the samurai of your dreams, and youth, is that you have never faced your own death nor the inevitability of the death of others."

"There are fears worse than death, Janay — *like insanity.*" Why did that sound like an accusation and a low blow?

"Ah, so you think me mentally unbalanced? Well, technically I never was insane. I was drugged insane and tormented by real demons no one saw. There's a difference."

"I did not mean to — "

She held up a hand to silence him. "Don't bother with the apology." Anger shimmered in her dark eyes. "What you're doing to Zad is wrong!"

"It's necessary. The risks are too great."

She shook her head in disbelief. "You are the most obtuse idiot I have ever met!" She stormed away, activating the door to open and striding outside.

"Go ahead, run away!"

Damn the powers. What a cheap shot.

No, damn him. He was supposed to make her understand, not make her angrier, not send her away. Tienan looked inward, to the Sphere of Discipline where Zad sat shackled, chained, collared, and muzzled.

Zad shook his head sadly and lay down.

Damned by his own veed.

As Tienan sighed, his gaze alighted on *The Samurai Creed,* which he knew by heart but couldn't read from where he stood.

A line whispered to him, *I have no divine power; I make honesty my Divine Power.*

When had he lost his Divine Power? Lost being honest with himself?

He glanced about the room's artifacts and reproductions. If he were being honest, he didn't want to part with his samurai collection. Being honest, he didn't want to part with Janay. Being honest — *he was terrified of Zad's Behringgreat power, that it was too much for a mortal man to handle.*

Shaken by such a revelation, Tienan went to the liquor cabinet and took out a water glass, filled it with whiskey and ice, and took a long swig. Glass in hand, he went and stood in front of the samurai armor.

Janay's words echoed, *A code of dignity that goes to the silent depths of a powerful mind, and a more powerful will . . .*

Samurai did not fear dying or killing. Death was death. He'd almost died once . . .

He touched the scar on his leg. Plunging off the cliff had horrified him, made him aware of his mortality. Was he afraid of dying, or more afraid of becoming Zad's puppet?

Janay's words whispered, *Love is stronger than death.*

He chugged down the rest of the liquor in the glass and refilled it from the bottle.

Was love more frightening than death?

❦ Chapter Twenty One

I have no castle; I make Immovable Mind
my Castle. — The Samurai Creed

Annelisa took another look through the panel viewport into the lounge and returned to Rowen. Her favorite pink skirt whisper-swished with each hurried stride and her breasts jiggled, straining the neckline tie that gathered her peasant-style blouse. She passed Rowen, who sat in his chair at the table littered with kumdak chips and cards. Winning fifty drails from him had been a satisfying bonus for what was to happen in the next hour.

Rowen's gaze followed her.

He was paralyzed, unable to speak or move, but aware of what was going on around him. And terrified. Just the way he was supposed to be.

All her worrying about actually injecting Rowen had been for nothing. She focused on the deep red nail polish of her fake nails, then turned her hand to momentarily study and marvel at the middle finger where the tiny needle resided. Feeling satisfied and elated, she lowered her hand, went to Rowen's corner desk, and placed a call.

Sweets appeared on the comlink's surface screen. Her blond hair was French braided from the forehead back.

Annelisa spoke softly. "Rowen is ours, and you won't believe it, but Tienan is in the lounge. He's drunk. Dead drunk! Should I give him the hypo now, or wait?"

"How much liquor has he had?"

"More than a third of a bottle of whiskey."

"That won't affect the tranquilizer. Put him out as soon as you can. Where's Boots?"

"Guestroom. She made herself an extra-strength tisane to calm her nerves. I think it was too strong. When I saw her half an hour ago, she was all smiles and kinda serene-like. I doubt she can offer much resistance."

"Good." Sweets eyed something to the right. "Looks like Celinae's ETA is less than five minutes. Granger is ours. Everything is going according to plan."

"Not quite."

"What do you mean?"

"Janay and Tienan had a row. Janay went for a sulk. When I asked Boots where she was, Boots said off the grid, meaning she's out of the range of the house's security systems."

"She's bound to return. I'll tell Celinae. Now, stick to the plan!" The call disconnected.

Annelisa pulled the miniature hyposprayer from her skirt pocket, and set the dose for Tienan.

Only after Janay had cried herself out in the center of the Labyrinth of Meditation behind the Chapel of J'Hi Baldama did she head back to Wolcott House.

The tears had flowed because Tienan was unreasonably bullheaded. He thought her insane. Only, he was the madman. Hadn't Adrada said a veed was a warlock's soul and his conscience? Tienan was so afraid Zad would go to the dark side of the qi that he had stepped over the line. He was the one with the darkness in his heart. He was the one torturing Zad. Tienan was incapable of seeing anything but duty to his family, duty to his brother, duty to his job.

She trudged up the sidewalk, passing under street lights that barely penetrated the dark canopy of daoka leaves shadowing the walk. She sent her gaze far ahead, to the greyhound sitting on the gate post to Wolcott House and the open gates.

She stopped. *Why were the gates open?* Tienan kept them closed and locked all the time.

Foreboding seeped like cold swamp ooze over her flesh. She glanced about, listening.

Night chirpings. Echo of a barking dog. Shuttlecraft high above heading to or from the spaceport.

With silent footfalls and sticking to the darkest shadows, she arrived at a tree near the gate. She hoisted herself up into the tree until she could see over the wall.

Tienan's van stood under the portico, its back doors open. The light inside the van revealed Rowen lying on the floor on his back, his belly bulging against his dark green kaftan.

Like thick fog, fear swirled about Janay's heart, chilling her.

Was Rowen alive or dead?

The side door of the house opened and Granger, dressed in black, face snarled and vampire fangs glistening white, came out carrying Tienan in a fireman's lift.

Janay's heart lurched. *Oh, dear J'Hi, no!*

Annelisa came out of the house and followed Granger, her hand motions ordering him where to put Tienan.

This couldn't be happening.

Maybe she was hallucinating, or maybe there were tormantratas about.

She closed her eyes, took a calming breath, and opened her eyes. She scanned the trees and shadows for tormantratas.

Nothing.

Then she glimpsed something silvery.

The source? A wide band of narrow silver rectangles encircling Annelisa's neck. Not a necklace. So what was it and why was she wearing it?

Granger dumped Tienan in the van, on the opposite side from his brother. Tienan's hands had been restrained. From the look of it, by his own Guardian-issue cuffs.

Hearing the hum of a vehicle approaching, Janay spotted a black limousine speed up the hill.

The vehicle braked and turned into the drive to Wolcott House. With a flash of brake lights, the vehicle stopped at an angle behind the van.

Annelisa jogged to the passenger door, her skirt swishing about her legs.

She summoned Granger, who came, opened the back door she pointed to, and reached into the car. He lifted out a woman dressed in a pale green pantsuit. The woman had short, platinum-gray hair. As Granger manhandled her, the woman flopped about like a rag doll. Granger soon deposited the woman between Tienan and Rowen.

Annelisa took out white Guardian-issue cuffs from her skirt pocket and cuffed the woman.

Janay's heart pounded. What were Annelisa and Granger doing?

Annelisa stepped back, and Granger closed the van doors.

Brake lights flashed on the limo as it was turned around.

At the house, the side door opened and light framed a petite redhead with straight bangs.

The redheaded witch!

Terror slammed into Janay with the force of a tank.

The woman stepped onto the portico and stopped. Like Annelisa, the redhead wore something metallic around her neck, under the open collar of her blouse.

Annelisa got into the van and soon had the vehicle turned and heading down the driveway, following the limousine.

The redhead summoned Granger into the house.

Just as that door closed, the front door to the house opened inward. Boots, bound hands and feet, and with a blue patch-gag over her mouth, inchwormed across the hardwood floor toward the doorway.

Shocked, Janay nearly lost her perch.

Boots was using her telekinetic ability to escape.

The redheaded witch ran through the foyer to Boots and grabbed Boots' unruly topknot.

Boots' muffled yelp of pain whispered into the night.

The redhead yelled behind her, "Granger, come here!"

The moment Granger appeared, the witch gave commands, her hands twittering and pointing at Boots and the door.

Granger dragged Boots into the house, then closed the door.

Headlights flashed into the branches below Janay. She froze tight to the tree limb.

The van and limousine turned out of the driveway and drove down the hill.

Janay watched the van's running lights until they went around the bend and out of sight.

Whispering in her thoughts came Boots' voice saying that the worst elements of the darkunskyve came out on the eve of a dark moon.

Well, they were certainly out tonight.

But why kidnap Rowen and Tienan? Who was the gray-haired woman? Why leave Boots behind? There had been room for Boots in the van.

And skom, what relationship did Annelisa have with the redheaded witch? Who was driving the limousine?

Questions without answers.

A shudder of dread sent gooseflesh over Janay's arms as another thought assailed her. If Rowen and Tienan weren't back by midnight, and the reunification rite wasn't done, Rowen and his veed would die.

She had to get help, summon the Guardians.

A shadowy silhouette moved away from the corner of Tienan's study window. A second later, the light in the room went out.

A lookout.

Were the redhead and Granger expecting someone to return? Like her? If they were, then going into Wolcott House would be walking into a trap. All she had were her dirks. She had never gone up against a veeded person, or a witch, or a vampire.

Skom, but Tienan had the right of it. Granger had gone to the dark side and now served a witch.

She went to tap the com on her left wrist and realized that she'd gotten so mad at Tienan that she'd left the house without it. Skom!

Did she dare risk being seen going back down the hill to summon help?

Think, woman, think! What was the quickest way to alert the Guardians? The house alarms? No, wait. *The failsafe.* The silent alarm Tienan had installed in his study. But how to trigger it?

Ah, yes. A little distraction and a flanking maneuver.

After summoning and giving Fox and Poke instructions, Janay left the tree. She strode up to the open gate, paused, put her head down, hunched her shoulders, and continued toward the front door, which was closest to Tienan's office. With every step, fear stalked her footfalls.

General Tarfooga's words when they faced the karsks whispered. *Embrace the fear — it will keep your senses sharp.*

At the door, she passed her ring before the sensor.

The door opened inward.

As she stepped into the empty foyer, Fox whizzed out of her boot and into Tienan's study to set off the silent alarm.

Janay listened but heard no one moving about.

Where was the enemy?

"Yo! I'm back." She closed the front door, making as much noise as she could to draw the fiends out. When she turned around, she felt Fox nudge her ankle just before slipping into its sheath.

Janay stepped forward. "Hey, where is everyone!"

The redheaded witch with the bangs stepped out from the kitchen proper and into view. She wore the black cloak Janay had seen her wear in front of the Chapel of J'Hi Baldama that first time. Only this time, something bulged beneath the witch's cape. Something she held in her left hand.

Janay strove for a surprised who-are-you greeting. "Hello."

"Good evening, Janay. We meet at last." Never turning her head, the redhead put her right arm out the side slit of her cloak and crooked her finger, signaling someone. "Don't be alarmed, Janay." She put her hand back under her cloak.

Granger came into view, his strong arms wrapped about Boots' waist, pinning her back tightly to his chest, stretching taunt her sleeveless, Guardian-blue undershirt. That shirt's deep U neckline exposed her throat, where her jugular vein pulsed her terror.

Granger snarled, his face contorted into the vampire he was, his fangs deadly long.

Boots struggled to get free of Granger, but being cuffed and gagged, her efforts proved fruitless.

Granger sniffed, as if to enjoy the fear-induced sweat beaded at Boots' temple, then he lowered his fangs for her neck.

"Ah, ah, ah, Granger, not yet. Be patient." To Janay the witch said, "If you don't do exactly as I say, I assure you I will allow Granger to drain the life out of Boots."

The demented sheen in Granger's eyes was nothing compared to the fear that rattled about Janay's rib cage. Could she stall long enough for the Guardians to get here? What was taking them so long?

Tearing her gaze away from Granger to bore into the redhead's chestnut-brown eyes, Janay grabbed the mien of unflappable Sergeant Cholyn and held on with all the courage she could muster. "Who are you and what do you want?"

"I'm Celinae and what I want are your daggers in exchange for Boots' life."

"Haven't got any daggers."

"Oh, forgive me, I believe you call them dirks."

This witch wanted Fox and Poke? "Slight problem. The dirks are bonded to me. They won't let anyone touch them. They're useless to you."

"Don't insult my intelligence and don't presume you can summon and throw one blade at me and one at Granger. They may hit their targets, but they will not kill us." Certainty rang in her voice.

"Sorry, I'm inclined to test that theory for myself."

Celinae chuckled. "Ever the soldier. Come, come, Janay, think of the consequences. Boots' will die. You don't really want her blood on your hands, do you? Of course not. Just give me the dirks." From between the center flaps of her cloak, she shoved out a loosely woven, dark brown bag with a rope closure. Another loop of rope dangled from her other hand. "Call your dirks. Order them into this bag, and I'll let Boots go."

She had to stall, buy time. "What's to prevent you from killing Boots, then feeding me to Granger?"

Celinae held up her witch's ring, took a step back, and, in a grand gesture, passed the ring under Granger's nose.

Instantly, his vampire face became his regular face. He momentarily swayed, but his grip remained tight around Boots, whose eyes pleaded for Janay to run, to save herself.

Janay had never left a comrade behind, and she wasn't about to now. Besides, the bag didn't look all that strong. Poke and Fox could cut their way out.

Maybe not.

"What's the bag made of?"

Celinae chuckled. "Just a silly old vine."

"And you think it'll hold my dirks?"

"It's been, shall we say, reinforced with them in mind. Now, enough stalling." Without looking directly at Granger, she put her ring hand out and touched her cabochon to the back of his hand.

With a snarl of hunger, Granger became his vampire self. He lowered his head and sank his fangs into Boots' jugular.

The whites of Boots' eyes shown and she shrieked, the cry trapped in her throat.

Panic blasted through Janay like a barrage of rodgun fire. "All right, you win! Call him off!"

"Summon the dirks. Quickly now."

"Poke, Fox."

The blades shot out of her boots and into her hands.

Celinae waved her ring under Granger's nose, but it took him a few seconds to respond and stop drinking from Boots. Reluctantly, he lifted his head. It took another long moment before the vampire yielded to the man.

Blood trickled from the puncture wounds on Boots' neck. Tears slipped down her cheeks.

"Come, come, Janay. Put the dirks in the bag or I will force Granger to drink Boots dry."

Force Granger? "I didn't think anyone could make a vampire do their bidding."

Celinae raised her nose in an arrogant display of pride that reflected in her voice. "If you have the right potions, and know how to use them to effect, it's easily done." Her smile blossomed as did the vileness which deepened in her darkening eyes. Glaring back at Janay was the haughty gleam of the woman's veed.

Janay conceded defeat. She was no match for veed power. Nor were her dirks. And where in J'Hi's great universe were the Guardians?

"Janay. I grow impatient." Celinae raised her ring hand.

Janay stepped forward.

Celinae held the bag open.

The instant Janay dropped the dirks into the bag, the witch pulled the drawstring rope and fastened it off with a bow knot. "Now, Janay, I must tie you up. Give me your hands."

Granger growled low in his throat. His eyes mirrored hopelessness and helplessness.

How soon before Celinae ordered Granger to kill her? For surely the witch would.

May death be kind and quick.

Janay put her hands out.

Celinae bound her wrists with the rope.

Janay eyed the twine on her wrists. Praise the lord J'hi, this witch didn't know a peacekeeper was trained to fight with hands tied in front of them.

"Sit down," Celinae ordered. "You might as well be comfortable while you pass out."

"Pass out? From what?"

Celinae's grin went tormantrata wide. She pushed the rope cord back from Janay's right wrist and exposed a red spot. She held up one of her long, painted black, pointed fingernails, showing off a small needle located beneath the nail. "You didn't even feel me inject you."

Janay's heart raced, making her aware of the taste of cloves. Skom! Esquivalum. With her body becoming more and more lethargic, Janay backed. Her knees hit the sofa, and she plunked down.

Celinae passed her ring beneath Granger's nose. The vampire fangs appeared, and he sank those fangs into Boots' neck.

Boots closed her eyes.

She didn't scream.

❧ Chapter Twenty Two

I have no sword; I make No Mind my Sword. — *The Samurai Creed*

 Tienan stood on a periwinkle sea surrounded by billowing white fog so brilliant it eclipsed sunshine.

Lord Tienan. Come. Follow the breath of the wind.

The timbre of that voice speaking inside his head was deeper than Zad's.

Tienan looked about, but saw no one.

"Who's talking inside my head?"

Follow the wind.

A breeze buffeted Tienan, bringing with it the smell of hyacinths. He turned a full circle, seeing only swirling winter-whiteness. Looking down at himself, he found he wore his guardian uniform. The long-sleeved midnight blue turtleneck's cuffs clung tightly about his wrists. His matching pants skimmed his standard-issue half boots that had been polished to a brilliant, gleaming shine.

The wind nudged him forward.

He walked on.

A nudge left, toward a dark spot ahead.

Soon he made out the profile of a stout Japanese man wearing a gray and black kimono. The man stood with hands folded one over the other at waist height. His long raven black hair was drawn back into a thin, tight braid that jutted out from the crown of his head. He had clean-shaven cheeks and a black mustache, the ends dangling to mid-chest and ending in tiny circles.

Dark, oriental eyes — eyes that had seen much and knew much

of life and death — studied Tienan.

The wind stilled.

Tienan halted a meter from the man. "Are you an angel, God, or a samurai?"

He bowed. "I am Kiyoshi. I am samurai. I am soul of your soul."

Soul of his soul? Why did that sound familiar? Why couldn't he remember how he got here? "Where are we?"

"On a lower dimensional plain of enlightenment."

"What am I doing here?"

"Speaking to me."

"I know that, but why am I here?"

"You might call it karma."

Laughter tugged at Tienan's lips. "As in Destiny? Fate? The Powers? Or the Will of God?"

"I am Kiyoshi, a samurai soul."

"Okay, so, why are you here?"

"Because you stand in the way of my attaining nirvana. I have been allowed to make myself known to you and to offer wisdom so that you and I may survive an ordeal."

"What ordeal?"

"On a grand scale, it is the ages-old one where the darkunskyve attempts to douse the living light, where good and evil collide and struggle for supremacy. On a smaller scale, it is the one that has brought you to me."

Memories refused to sort into any kind of sense. "I can't seem to recall . . ."

"Too much saki embalms the senses."

"Saki? I don't drink saki. What are you talking about?"

"You, Lord Tienan, drank yourself into a stupor." He pointed to his left, to a dark, swirling vortex forming. In the glassy center, Tienan found an image of himself slumped in the wingback chair before the fireplace at Wolcott House. In his hand, a glass of DeLupian whiskey, nearly empty. "Okay, I get it. I'm drunk. This is an alcoholic hallucination."

Kiyoshi voice vibrated with a low, ominous reprimand. "No. You are having an out-of-body experience." He snapped his fingers. The image vanished and so did the vortex.

"I'm confused. I don't understand."

"Precisely. I am here to help you understand. We must deal with transgressions."

"Transgressions? Are they anything like sins?" Now why had

he drawn that conclusion? Guilt. Over what?

"Sins? Ahh, yes. In the interest of clarity, Lord Tienan, let us call them sins. My first sin was duty to my shogun. That also is your sin."

Tienan didn't like the sound of that. "I don't have a shogun."

"My second sin was obtaining revenge. Your sin may be revenge."

He definitely didn't like the sound of that. *Wait a minute.* "Revenge may be my sin? It isn't yet?"

"Not yet, but you desire revenge. As is your desire, so becomes your deed. Now, my third sin — for which I genuinely regret my choice — has also become your greatest sin."

What a sobering thought. "I still don't understand."

Kiyoshi stroked one side of his long mustache before speaking. "In my life, I believed being a samurai was everything, that love could not exist harmoniously with being a warrior. Lust could be dealt with, but love? Ahh, love." His voice softened. "What is love, Lord Tienan?"

He recalled what Janay had said and quoted her. "Love is stronger than death."

Kiyoshi nodded like an ancient sage. "Ahh, yes, it is that. Love is also a light which illuminates the darkest corners of a man's soul. Love is the song which sings to a hardened warrior's heart. Love is a kiss which binds a man and a woman for an hour, a day, a lifetime — an eternity."

What was he talking about? "Just get to the point."

Kiyoshi stroked his mustache again, and wound the end around his finger. "A young woman, her name was Lotus Blossom, came into my shogun's court one spring. She was beautiful. I was ashamed that I, a true samurai, a warrior feared in the shoganate, could be brought to my knees by a slip of a woman with dark eyes and a flashing smile."

The image appeared in Tienan's mind of Janay's flashing dark eyes, her impish smile, her riot of dark, curly hair. But Janay hadn't brought him to his knees. No woman had.

"My duty, Lord Tienan, was to the shogun, so I hardened my heart. The night I made love to Lotus Blossom, she told me she loved me. She said she would gladly be my wife but that she could never be my, or any man's, concubine. Her words angered me. I only wanted her as a courtesan. When she refused to remain in my bed, her defiance flamed my outrage. Those flames overtook my good judgment."

The desolate look in Kiyoshi's eyes told Tienan that, in his fury, the samurai had struck Lotus Blossom.

"Anger, Lord Tienan, it cleaves like a katana. The woman who loves you is now part of your life. Why do you not partake of her comfort and pleasure?"

Woman? Comfort? Pleasure? An image flared in Tienan's mind. "Are we talking about Boots?"

Kiyoshi laughed heartily, and briefly. "Wrong woman."

Another image flared. "Janay?"

Kiyoshi sobered and nodded. "As a soldier, she has proven she is obedient, strong, self-controlled, loyal. Such traits are much sought after in a samurai's wife."

"Such traits can drive a man crazy, and I am not a samurai. I don't need that kind of wife."

"You are the katana."

"What?"

A long moment of silence passed. Regret shimmered in Kiyoshi's eyes. "Lotus Blossom believed I did not love her."

They were back on that subject, were they?

"Lord Tienan, I defiled Lotus Blossom and continued to defile her until she ran away, back to her family. They refused to let me see or speak to her. During the first snow of winter, Lotus Blossom committed *jigai* — suicide — with my wakinzashi. She had taken the short sword the night she left me."

The sadness in the sigh he let out seemed to deflate him and weaken his voice. "After her family told me of her death, my heart broke. I wept and drank too much saki. One night, I admitted my love for her, and my remorse, to the heavens."

He cleared his throat and stood samurai proud again. "Because of my arrogance, I had destroyed the one thing in my life which was sacred — a woman's love for me. I assure you, Lord Tienan, if you, too, succumb to pride and revenge, you will lose what truly matters."

"Were you punished for Lotus Blossom's death?"

"In a thousand ways unseen. To silence my guilt and anguish, I led battles against hordes. Always, I survived."

"In other words, you attempted to kill yourself without resorting to *seppuku* — suicide — right?"

He nodded.

"Then how did you die, if I might ask?"

"My heart stilled in battle."

"You had a heart attack?"

"Burst a vessel. When the Great Shogun Adrada came for my soul, I truly believed I was going to the cold depths of nothingness—I believe you call it Sh'olv. I deserved such a fate."

"Well, you're here, so that obviously didn't happen."

"Truly spoken, Lord Tienan, and to sate your curiosity, I spent centuries in what you call purgatory before going to the Hall of Redemption. You see, there remained a place in my heart that remained dark, bleak, cold. Then the Great Angel Shogun, Adrada, summoned me with an offer of salvation."

"How good of him."

Kiyoshi quirked one brow up, accentuating his reprimanding glare.

Tienan regretted sounding flippant, and remained silent.

"As I was saying, to attain salvation, I had to return to the living and become an executioner of demonic fiends. I thought that if forgiveness was attainable, and a samurai was a samurai, why not? So I told the Great Shogun Adrada, *Give me my daisho and set me before the darkons.*"

Daisho? Daisho . . . That was the name for the combination of the two swords, the katana and the companion sword, the wakinzashi. "I take it getting the swords wasn't easy?"

He shook his head. "First, I had to be reborn, reincarnated, into a new body." He snorted.

In Tienan's mind, a memory began to coalesce only to vanish before he could grasp it.

"It was not a human body, Lord Tienan. It was your veed's."

The image of the blessed katana, Sugi, held under Zad's paw formed in his mind's eye.

"Ah, I see you now recall. Good." Kiyoshi nodded slowly. "Yes, because Zad was fascinated by all things samurai, he had embraced the Code, he understood the creed of the samurai. But you?" Kiyoshi threw up his hands. "You look at all things samurai but do not touch. Collect, but do not use!" He stopped his rant as if enlightened. "Which only proves what the Great Shogun Adrada meant when he said the katana would have a mind of its own." Kiyoshi's riveting gaze held Tienan silent. "Adrada also told me that you, the katana, would have a heritage of magic and power. Imagine my astonishment to discover that your magic, your power and your true soul, was your veed."

"And you've remained dormant since my conception?"

"No. I was reincarnated in the last minute of the hour before Zad emerged from his cocoon as an adult."

Other memories flared to life, and he blurted out, "You've been interfering with my having sex with women, haven't you!"

"I interceded because those women were wrong for you."

Blue-white anger flamed inside Tienan. "You have no right to presume what woman I should or should not bed."

"Soul beckons to soul, Lord Tienan. Soul draws to soul. The best of wives, as any samurai knows, must be a woman without deceit, a woman of wisdom, and a woman with a depth of courage. A complicated woman, to be sure, but one who is not influenced by money or social status."

"That's a woman that's too good to be true."

"Open the eyes of your heart."

"Meaning?"

"Do you not recall the Great Shogun Adrada telling you after you performed the reunification rite for your brother that your prayer had been answered? Your prayer for a worthy woman to wife?"

Recollection of the event flashed in Tienan's mind and sent his thoughts reeling. *Janay was the answer to that prayer?* By powers — "Why reveal this to me now?"

"I was forbidden to reveal myself to you or Zad until the wakinzashi wept."

Why did the old man have to talk in riddles? "Are you referring to the blood wicking off a blade?"

Kiyoshi shook his head. "I refer to Janay's tears."

"Janay? Janay is the wakinzashi? Why was she crying?"

"Over the revelations of her heart."

"When?"

"The day after your brother was attacked in your home and you, to save her, thought to rape her."

A band of iron squeezed around Tienan's heart. "It was a ruse to get her adrenaline going."

He nodded once. "Ahh, but she wept again, Lord Tienan. Tonight. On holy ground. She wept because she believes you will never love her as she loves you."

Janay loved him?

His heart seemed to pause, then beat again, swelling so fast it broke the iron band that had been around it.

"Know this, Lord Tienan, a samurai is not whole without his daisho."

"More riddles. You're confusing me. If I'm your katana and Janay is your wakinzashi, how can Janay and I be your daisho, particularly when the real katana, which is Sugi, belongs to Zad, who is my veed and my soul?"

"The door to wisdom is difficult to open."

"Trond! Make sense."

"I will admit that the concept of the swords troubles me, but remember that Zad possesses correct judgment."

"And I don't?"

"Sugi's name means Cedar, which is the symbol of moral rectitude which means correct judgment."

"Yes, yes, I know. Janay told me. What's your point?"

"That veed beckons to veed. Veed draws to veed."

The man made no sense. "Are you saying Sugi is a veed?"

"Sugi is qi. Pure, blessed, qi." Kiyoshi curled the tip of his mustache around his index finger. "The situation has become most critical and complex. The task formidable, but you, Lord Tienan, are as clever and as resourceful as I was in life. Your veed is good and powerful. Janay is a trained warrior, agile and quick. She possess two powerful dirks. Heed the wisdom of this old warrior. Yield your heart to Janay and become worthy of wielding the sacred katana."

"Sugi prefers Zad."

"Ahh, yes, and rightly so." Kiyoshi cracked a smile that twitched his whiskers. "Women can be fickle." He cast a glance at the billowing whiteness above, which now roiled with dove gray. "Time is fleeting. You must wake soon. Know that I am here for you and Zad." Kiyoshi bowed. His voice warned, "A scar you bear is a forever reminder of the lies built upon your lie. Fear and lies destroy the spirit. Resist both, reconcile both, and power is yours."

His next words came in earnest. "Do not, Lord Tienan, remain blind to love, friendship, and family for they are what is truly important. *As your deed is, so is your destiny!*"

The cloud around Tienan gave way to darkness.

As Tienan descended through the ever-blackening cloud, he pondered Kiyoshi's words.

The scar on his leg throbbed, bringing remembrances of the truth of that day Zad and he had gone over the cliff.

He'd lied about that day.

He'd built lies upon that lie . . .

❦ Chapter Twenty Three

When you sacrifice your life, you must
make full use of your weaponry.
—Miyamoto Musashi, **A Book of Five Rings**

Pleased to be on time and on schedule with Tienan, Rowen, and Her Grace trussed up in the van, Annelisa followed Sweets' black limousine.

Soon they were at the back of a small mansion where Sweets parked the limo in the garage.

It had been Celinae, who worked for Protectors Incorporated, who knew the owners would be out of town for a month and gotten all the security codes, including ones for the limo.

Celinae had even procured the knockout gas Sweets used so effectively on Her Grace.

The garage door closed.

Sweets, wearing a brown chauffeur's jumpsuit, opened the van's passenger door and got in.

As Annelisa drove the van away, toward the warehouse district, she glimpsed Sweets pulling off her facial mask and wig. She tossed them behind her seat, then released the clip so her blond braid dangled.

It wasn't long before Annelisa parked the van in their warehouse and got out.

The clatter and squeak of the closing loading dock door sent a shiver down her spine.

"Why so jumpy?" Sweets' tone was one of reprimand.

"The noise."

"We quit worrying about that last week, remember?"

Annelisa nodded.

A week ago, Shelzat had seen to it that the security for this section of warehouses had become the responsibility of Protectors Incorporated. Celinae had then reprogrammed the neighboring patrol-bots to ignore noise coming from this building.

Sweets' wristcom pinged.

Annelisa waited for Sweets to study her incoming message. Another ping issued, signaling the disconnect.

Sweets looked at her. "Celinae is on her way. She has Janay and Granger."

Tienan rose out of his alcohol-and-tranquilizer induced fog, recalling Annelisa taking the whiskey glass from his hand, shoving his sleeve up, and hypo-injecting something in the vein on his forearm.

He had tried to sit up but couldn't move, or speak. Twenty minutes later, he watched Annelisa open the lounge door and let Granger in.

Behind Granger came a redheaded witch.

Annelisa ecstatically told the redhead all had gone as planned. Annelisa called the redhead Celinae.

With hands aflutter, her words low, too soft for him to hear, Celinae addressed Granger. Celinae then followed Granger.

Moments later, over the lounge's comlink, came the witch's, "Boots is subdued. Get Rowen ready."

Like a demon specter, panic reached into Tienan's chest, crushing the breath out of him. He was helpless, drunk, drugged, incapable of stopping the trio.

In his mind, Tienan heard the sound of jangling chains. He focused inward, on the glassy sphere where Zad, tail tip twitching, paced frantically and dragged his chain to and fro when he made his turns.

Tienan reached deep into himself and willed away the chains, the muzzle, the shackles. They vanished as did the sphere. *Zad?*

Zad stopped in mid-pace. A firestorm of tension, fear, and anxiety reflected in the silvery shards of the veed's dark eyes. *Tienan, my good lord, is that you?*

Yes, it's me. I'm sorry, please forgive me.

Forgive you, my lord? I do not understand. Your mind was empty for so long. Silent. So silent that I feared you were brain dead from the drug Annelisa injected into you.

Memories whirled and flashed. His own words replayed, *I make honesty my Devine Power . . .*

Honesty. Yes, honesty. No more lies.

My brain may have been briefly pickled from the alcohol, but no, the drug didn't harm me. My mind was silent because I had an out-of-body experience. I met Kiyoshi, the samurai, the soul of my soul.

Zad eyes went wide. He abruptly sat down. *Forgive me for saying so, my lord, but perhaps you have been hallucinating from the combination of the drug and the alcohol.*

I'm fine, Zad. I think I attained a sort of enlightenment.

Zad tilted his head right, then left, and hesitantly said, *Enlightenment? How so, my lord?*

I had time to sort things out. To face some hard truths. The first truth is that I have blamed you for the joyride we took so many years ago. I lied and told my parents stealing the bike was your idea, and that I was powerless to stop you from taking us over the cliff. I then lied and deceived myself all these years because the truth is, I wanted to kill myself that day. I was jealous of Rowen, my baby brother. I hated the attention my parents lavished on him. I felt ignored, left out, abandoned, unloved.

Zad nodded. *Going over the cliff certainly succeeded in gaining your parents' attention.*

Only because they feared I would become a juvenile delinquent. No child in the history of the De'Argossi family was ever a juvenile delinquent. Or possessed by their own veed.

True, my lord. So true.

Zad, listen, I will also admit that you're wiser than I'm ever likely to be. Tienan heard the knot of guilt and remorse chocking his words. *I apologize for the humiliations I've subjected you to, not only since you got Sugi but for everything over all the years.*

Oh, my lord . . . Tiny gold tears welled at the corners of Zad's eyes. His voice quivered with sincerity and joy. *You are forgiven.*

The knot about Tienan's heart and mind loosened even more.

I want to thank you, too, Zad, for being a true friend despite my not being the friend I should have been to you.

A rainbow of colors sparked from beneath Zad's nappy black mane. *You do not know how I have longed for you to face these truths. Oh, my good lord, I am so happy that I fear I shall succumb to weeping.* A golden tear slipped from his left eye.

Tienan felt the warmth of his own tears at the corners of his eyes. *What say we let the past go and begin anew?*

Yes, my good lord, yes! The past is the past.

The last strands of the knot within him released. Tienan smiled. *Thank you, Zad. Now, can you do anything about my paralysis? We have to save Rowen.*

Janay came out of the stupor of being tranquilized and listened, sorting out voices, the clang of metals, metallic ringing, jinglings.

How long had she been unconscious?

She opened her eyelids enough to see she sat slumped against a wall. Her wrists had been shackled with semi-rigid, plasti-cuffs bearing the imprint of *Australe Militia Surplus.*

She had used such shackle-cuffs on terrorist and detainees, and now they were being used on her? Such irony . . .

From the look of things, the cuff chains ran upward, above her head, likely to rings on the wall.

She opened her eyes more, taking in the view of an old warehouse, one with a giant pentagram inlaid in the cement floor with a blood-red brick Druid's Circle.

Two small oval tables, one with a black velvet covering, stood near a black oval altar.

Beyond the altar, a lattice wall of vines. The huge, deep green leaves of one vine trellised over an archway, shading an aisle.

Slowly she tilted her head to the right.

Rowen lay on a heavy, sheet-metal slab in front of a wide fireplace. Militia shackles bound his wrists and ankles. The wrist shackles were fastened to rings on either side of his head but his ankle shackles were linked to a single ring at the base of the slab.

A rectangle of shiny blue gagged his mouth. When he turned his face to his right, she followed his line of sight.

Seeing Tienan, her heart raced, then steadied.

Like Rowen, Tienan lay gagged and shackled, only antigrav boxes were attached to Tienan's metal slab.

The rattling and whisperings to her left sent the hair prickling along Janay's nape.

Four meters away stood a cage capable of holding an armored

personnel carrier. The cage was divided into two cells.

In the cell closest to her, Granger sat on the grate floor, his back to the bars. His eyes held that vacant, drug-induced stare she'd seen too many times at Blanoxx.

Question was — was he currently drugged or in a lull between kills?

He'd killed Boots.

He'd been ordered to kill her by Celinae.

Damn that witch's soul.

In the adjacent cell, Janay spotted the back of the gray-haired woman in the pale green pantsuit.

Slowly, as if in extreme pain, the woman gripped the bars with her hands, pulling herself up to stand.

No easy task since she was handcuffed and swayed as if drugged.

Beyond the cage, greenery. A jungle of plants, all in rows, all in containers on gravel drainage.

At the end row, catercorner from the caged woman, came three slender women — the redheaded Celinae, the dark-haired Annelisa, and a blonde with French braided hair, the long pigtail draping over her back. Each wore silver-slatted neck collars.

The blonde looked vaguely familiar, but Janay couldn't place her.

The blonde stepped closer to the caged woman, her grin one of malevolent glee. "Finally, you're awake."

Whether from shock or surprise, the woman's knees buckled. She grabbed the bars, steadying herself.

Self-satisfaction purred from the blonde's smile. "Turn around."

The woman seemed to draw on her dignity and obeyed.

Silence Tomosukovia?

Janay took a harder look.

It was Her Grace!

When Silence spotted her grandsons, she shrieked, the sound muffled by her blue gag. She staggered across the cage and clung to the bars. Face ghostly pale, she stared at Tienan, then Rowen, then Rowen's swollen belly.

The blonde laughed. "Oh, what a joy it is to see your face, hear your anguish!"

Celinae chuckled softly, her face glowing with the glee of a cat that had devoured half a dozen mice and a bowl of cream. "That it is, Sweets, that it is."

So the blonde's name was Sweets. The name wasn't familiar, but that face? Yes, she'd seen the woman before. Where?

Out of Silence's head rose the noncorporeal, ghostly head of Liss, Silence's demon-ugly dragryphon veed. Instead of completely shielding her host in her golden aura, Liss's noncorporeal head rode high enough that she could demand, "What is the meaning of this? If this is a kidnapping, I assure you no one will pay you ransom."

"Legally speaking," Sweets replied, "I suppose this is a kidnapping, but it's so much more. It's payback. We're going to see you and your malicious host pay dearly for what you've done to my parents and me."

"What are you talking about? Who are you?" Liss spoke with all of Silence's unflinching authority.

Sweets circled the cage until she was directly in front of Silence. "I am Ioni Trevina Adesko, daughter of Uberto Phelix Eugenus Adesko, Tenth House Hautonne. And I am second assistant to the senior advocate at Guardian headquarters.

Memories assailed Janay of arriving in the back of Tienan's van at Guardian headquarters, of Neejera bidding Ioni Adesko to fetch maleet juice . . .

The gold aura darkened around Liss's head and she demanded, "What is it you accuse me and my host of doing?"

Celinae scoffed. "Such selective amnesia." She pivoted about. "Typical of Her Grace, isn't it, Annelisa?"

Annelisa nodded.

Celinae walked to the sleek, black altar where a clear glass bowl sat upside-down over a model of what looked to be a section of Bhutar's spaceport city.

Silence turned, slumping a shoulder against the bars for support. She eyed the small bundle of red twigs Annelisa held in one hand and then the black Bowie knife she held in her other hand. Liss spoke. "Annelisa?"

"What am I doing here, you wonder?" Annelisa said. "I'm helping a couple of friends right injustices."

"How could you be in league with them?" Liss demanded.

A sardonic smile floated about Annelisa's lips. "Tonight you pay for killing Sweets' mother and father."

Silence's and Liss's gaze swung back to Sweets. Liss spoke, her voice shaky, "We killed no one."

Two spots of red anger darkened Sweets' cheekbones. "So easy for you to sweep your crimes away and forget about them, isn't it?

Well, tonight you shall remember — and suffer."

Desperation sent Liss's voice octaves higher. "You'll never get away with this!"

The three witches laughed, Sweets the loudest.

Celinae began to lay out daggers and knives on the table with the black velvet covering. "We have time, Sweets, for you to jog Her Grace's deplorable memory."

Sweets jutted her chin up, giving it an imperious tilt. "My mother was Krysta Roshona Madison Casat, a dancer. A very fine and famous dancer. When my father bonded with her, he brought her into society, but you, and your friends of the Inner Circle, branded her a gold-digging whore. *My mother was never a whore!*"

The expression on Silence's face said she frantically searched for memories. Her ah-ha moment sent her eyes wide open.

Liss spoke. "Your father was sixty-four, and your mother eighteen at the time of the bonding."

"True, but you and your society friends made my mother *persona non gratta* because he lavished his money on things for her comfort and enjoyment. She never asked him for such luxuries. She loved him. Only she couldn't go anywhere without being stared at and ridiculed with gossip and the lies you spread. *You made her life hell.*"

"Your father was a lewd drunk. That's why he was not welcome to the coven's events."

"Wrong. He became a drunk thanks to your ostracizing my mother, the woman he loved, from the social whirl of the colony. *You drove him to drink* and that drink drove him into depression and anger."

Liss muttered, "We remember. Uberto murdered his wife in a drunken rage and then committed suicide." The veed's gaze hardened. "My host is not to blame."

Sweets' face flushed rage red. "Will you never take responsibility for your actions? Tell me, who made the motion at Coven Ozieron's Inner Circle meeting to have my father and mother's privileges at the covenstead revoked?"

Remembrance drained color from Silence's cheeks.

"Who wrote the official decree?"

Silence looked about to faint.

Hate glittered in Sweets' eyes. "Ah, Silence is silent, is she?"

"Wait." Liss spoke. "Who told you about your mother and father? You had to be four or five years old at the time of your parents' death."

"Five. My grandparents raised me. They loved me. They loved my father. They were proud of their only son."

"Yes, we remember," Liss replied. "He could do no wrong in their eyes. As we recall, they thought you a little princess, one who could do no wrong."

"They told me what you did, showed me the documents. *They never lied to me!*"

Celinae, now wearing a blood-red robe, came over and handed Sweets a red robe. "I believe it's my turn to dig the blade into the hag's heart."

Liss blurted out indignantly, "Silence is not a hag!"

Sweets chuckled, then donned the robe, and went to the altar.

"I am Celinae Yvonne Sykes." Loathing sharpened Celinae's words. "I'm a bastard because of you. My mother may have been young and foolish, but she was in love with my father, *Francesco Salvatore Louis Martinez Sykes.*"

Liss said nothing. Silence's face remained pale.

Celinae patted her straight bangs with both hands. "You may recall Francesco was twin to Hugo'mattan Sykes, first born, heir to the Sykes' fortunes. You will recall my father acknowledged me because he signed my birth into the covenstead registry."

"Francesco was seventeen," Liss replied. "Legally underage for a bonding."

She nodded. "True, but his parents refused to sign the papers which would have allowed a special bonding ceremony." Her voice rose with increasing anger. "They expected him to wed a woman higher in the ranks of the Hautonne. They accused my mother of seducing my father and getting herself pregnant to extort money from them. They forced her to sign legal documents so she and I could never, ever, claim or inherit any of the Sykes' fortunes. When my mother died, she was penniless. I was raised in eight different foster homes."

She took a deep breath of victory. "Tonight, Silence, you will die after you watch your own sons die." She spun on her heels, sending her robe hem twirling, and strode for the altar.

Tears glistened in Silence's eyes, and anguish shuddered through her.

Annelisa came over to Silence.

"*Et tu, Brute?*" Liss said.

Though her voice was businesslike, Annelisa's smile was one of gratification. "Even I have a few words."

"You hate us?"

"Hate? No. Dislike is more the word. Sweets and Celinae warned me about you, but until I actually worked for you, I didn't believe how badly you could disrupt and destroy others' lives. I'm appalled by the way you use your social status and wealth to manipulate people. I abhor the way you snoop into people's lives, then blackmail them to behave as you think they should. Who are you to judge who is or is not fit to marry whom?"

Liss stammered out, "We have only the best interests of our friends in our hearts."

"Friends? Best interests? No, no. You have only your personal interests at heart. You are a selfish miser and you take the people who work for you for granted." She squared her shoulders and stood taller. "All that ends tonight, *Your Grace*, and I say that with absolute disgust because you possess no true grace. We three are dedicated to delivering retribution for ourselves and all the people and families you've wrecked."

"What," Liss ventured, "do you plan to do with us, and Silence's grandsons?"

Annelisa turned, facing the other two witches at the altar who were lighting a circle of short, fat black candles around the upside-down bowl. "Sweets. Celinae."

The two met her gaze.

"Silence wants to know what we're going to do to her and her grandsons. May I tell her?"

"No, Annelisa, let me." Sweets handed her lighter to Celinae.

Annelisa went to the altar with her bundle of twigs and began setting them in a pattern on top of the glass bowl.

When she faced Silence, Sweets' voice preened. "Since I masterminded this evening's festivities, and I am the one most offended by your actions, it is I who will tell you what will take place tonight." She cleared her throat. "First, we summon our benefactor, Shelzat, the Darkon Archangel, The Obtainer of Souls."

Silence trembled, as did Liss.

"Then we place a Dome of Gloom over this warehouse so we are not disturbed by people, veeds, or angelic forces. The dome will last until sunlight dissipates it. I tell you this so you understand that escape is impossible. Next, we make Melg of Reddam, an acid to apply to Tienan's bare feet. Although he may think he can endure the pain of the acid amputating his feet, in the end, he will release his veed. Our veeds will then devour his veed."

Janay fought the burn of horror in her chest that she would be forced to watch and listen to Tienan suffer and die.

Silence screamed her protests, but the gag muffled them.

Sweets raised her chin higher. "Next, we cut Rowen's veed out of his belly, kill it, and devour the power."

Liss squawked. "*His veed is in his belly?*"

Janay spoke her thought. "Their first attempt to get Rowen's veed met with less than satisfactory results."

Sweets spun around. "Well, well, well. You are awake. How splendid. And yes, the results of our initial removal of Rowen's veed had, let us say, unplanned results."

Keeping her back to the wall, Janay pushed with her feet until she stood. If the bitch came within grabbing range, there was enough slack in the chain to strangle her.

Sweets grinned. "Command code three one."

Instantly the slack left Janay's shackle chains. Her wrists were drawn away from her sides at an angle and her feet pulled apart, but only enough so she could remain standing.

"Now where was I? Ah, yes." Sweets once more faced Silence. "Once we have devoured Rowen's veed, we turn Granger loose. He's a vampire. You, Lady Tomosukovia, will die just like your daughter Estephanie did."

Tienan growled his rage.

Sweets looked over her shoulder and laughed at him. "Oh, poor, Tienan. All along you have blamed Granger for your mother's death but he didn't kill her. *I did.*"

Tienan's eyes nearly bugged out of his face before pure rage and veed rage flamed in his eyes.

"I needed your mother's Xenobia blood for a charm that became the key to opening the *Fourth Book of Xenobia.*"

Sweets wagged an accusing finger at Silence. "How naughty of you. You kept secret the fact that Tienan's mother was one of Xenobia's daughters, just three generations removed."

She turned and chuckled at Tienan. "All these years, Lord De'Argossi, I've laughed at your desire for revenge, knowing you would never guess who killed your mother." Sweets placed a hand on her hip, puffed out her chest, and self-satisfaction oozed from her. "I was fifteen when I learned how to control vampires with bloodwood vine. Did you know, Estephanie was my first test subject? Back then, I commanded a very virile, young, handsome vamp by the name of Gideon. So fitting a name for my avenger."

Unease skittered down Janay's spine. Did another vampire lurk somewhere in the building? "So, what happened to Gideon?"

Sweets met Janay's gaze. "Gideon died of the bloodwood poison, just like Granger will."

"In other words, Gideon could identify you. He was a liability."

"Exactly. It's the same with Granger. As it was back then, it shall be tomorrow. The idiot Guardians will blame everything on Granger's bloodlust killing spree. No one will be the wiser for what takes place here tonight."

"Excuse me," Janay said, "but where do I fit in with this little scheme of things?"

"It is not a little scheme. It is A Grand Plan. As for your part? Your dirks are our dessert."

"I don't follow."

"Your dirks are qi energy, veed energy. The *Fourth Book of Xenobia* has shown us a way to devour their essence. Once we consume Rowen's and Tienan's veeds, plus Silence's, your dirks, and, lastly, Granger's veed, we three witches will be so powerful that we'll be able to command the elements, including time travel." Joy flashed in her eyes and gaiety bubbled out with her words. "We will be able to accumulate great wealth. We will live in the manner our birthrights should have allowed us to live."

Skom, skom, skom! This was deep shit.

Janay swallowed down her fear. "You're saying I'm fodder for Granger?"

All three witches laughed.

The merry sound skittered three waves of terror down Janay's spine.

When the laughter died down, Sweets said, "No, Granger isn't to have you."

A sizzling noise near the center of the pentagram rose into a black whirlwind that morphed into a darkon archangel, the one she'd seen the night she found Rowen.

Janay cringed and pinned her back tight to the wall.

The devil's own was here? And this darkon was dressed in black leather with a black snakeskin breast sash. He'd come with a weapon, a black sword hung from his wide belt.

Before he stepped toward Sweets, he drew back his wings so the tips did not skim the pentagram.

Sweets grinned. "Excellent timing, dearest Shelzat."

"And how is that, my pretty?"

"Janay just asked what part she played in tonight's activities." She giggled. "Janay thinks she's fodder for Granger, but I assured her she was not."

He grinned with demon cunning and ice-sharded eyes. "What were you going to tell her?"

Cold fingers of dread gripped Janay, and she labored to breathe.

Sweets looked coyly at Janay from under her long lashes. "Magestrella Cholyn, you are our gift to Shelzat. He has long been desiring to pay you back for dismembering his tormantratas. I'm sure he has a few, *very personal*, amusements planned for himself." Her lips bowed into a wide and malevolent smile. "At your expense, of course."

Janay's knees threatened to buckle.

❦ Chapter Twenty Four

The Fourth Oath — Get beyond love and grief:
exist for the good of man.
— Miyamoto Musashi, **A Book of Five Rings**

Fighting back the imagined horrors that Shelzat intended for her, Janay watched the darkon make a full turn, obviously checking who was where and what was what.

When he smiled at Sweets, she nodded with pride and said, "Just one last thing to do." Swiftly she put her hand in her robe pocket and brought out a blue rectangle that she slapped over Janay's mouth. "Can't have you summoning any angels to disturb us, now can we?" She hurried to the altar.

Shelzat clapped his hands twice and four of the ugliest, mud-brown, spike-headed tormantratas Janay had ever seen appeared. They squatted, a pair to his right and a pair to his left. He stepped closer to her but the tormantratas remained where they were, covertly looking around, waiting for his command.

The witches began to chant.

Shelzat leaned close to Janay.

She inhaled the nauseating odor of brimstone and lust wafting from him.

He reached a hand up to her face. Slowly, he stroked his ice-white fingernail, filed to a claw-sharp point, along her jaw line. His cold breath fanned her cheek. He whispered into her ear. "These four tormantratas are the sires and dams of half the tormantratas you maimed and had Tarfooga kill at Blanoxx. They will enjoy hearing you scream, like their offspring screamed." He chuckled softly in his throat.

Janay tasted bile and fought not to throw up and drown in her own puke.

Shelzat drew back slowly, eyes glittering with delight. His voice whispered like a lover's. "These four will tear the flesh from your bones, and do it ever so slowly so you scream and scream and scream . . ."

Remembered screams from karsks tearing apart her comrades in the Valley of Rathe roared in her mind. She again felt their terror and her own of that day.

Shelzat's muted chuckle held triumph. He backed away, turned, and momentarily glanced down at Tienan before striding for the altar. He stopped half a step from the Druid's line.

At the altar, the witches held hands, forming a circle. Their black-polished nails glowed with veed power, their chant synchronized into one voice, one droning melody. The red twigs over the glass dome ignited, the smoke rising to swirl above the witches' heads. On the altar, the black candles flickered brightly.

Looking at the candle flames quelled and burned back the memories of Rathe and Shelzat's words. Janay eyed the tormantratas who now faced the altar.

She was trapped. She was chained. She was as good as dead.

So were Tienan and Rowen, Silence and Granger. They were all as good as dead at the hands of the darkon and his witches three.

Janay's focus drifted to Tienan, who had raised his head. In the moment when her gaze met his, she saw hope, and something else shimmering brightly in his dove-gray irises that wasn't veed power.

His forefinger tapped dirk code against his thumb. B 4 I DIE KNOW I LOVE U.

Her heart raced. He loved her?

She leaned back, knocking her head against the wall. Dear J'Hi, there was nothing like a death-moment confession.

Or was it Zad who'd sent the message for himself?

Skom, she loved Tienan, but how could she be sure his love was genuine, the everlasting kind?

She tapped out, IF WE LIVE WILL U MARRY ME?

Tienan's eyes went wide. Joy crinkled his cheeks into what smile his gag allowed. His fingers rapidly tapped, YES YES YES YES YES YES.

For a moment, time stood still.

Tienan loved her enough to marry her!

The radiant warmth of love flared in her heart into a sparkling array of joy. Being the wife of a GOOL would not be easy. Adapting to Zantharian society, the pits. Yet, it was something to look forward to—a love worth living for. *A love worth fighting to the death for.*

She rapidly scanned the warehouse.

On the workbench near the coat rack, she spotted the sisal bag that held Poke and Fox. Both dirks' flower-faces were pressed against the sisal, watching her intently.

Janay used her forefinger against her thumb to tap the code R Y S— report your situation.

Poke rose so its blade tip could tap silently against one of the cross-strands of the bag. BLOODWOOD. CANNOT CUT.

Skom.

Wait, the fibers were like hemp that could be made into rope or woven. The bag had to be hand woven. How well was it made? She tapped out, UNDO KNOTS. STRETCH HOLES. B QUICK.

Rattling of shackles drew Janay's attention to Rowen, whose face contorted with pain. Then his expression relaxed.

Dearest J'Hi, was he going into labor? He wasn't due to birth Tal until midnight, which was hours away, wasn't it?

Janay met Tienan's worried gaze. His index and thumb moved, signaling, SUGI READY. WHAT IS PLAN?

Plan? He expected her to have a plan?

Oh, right, he lay tied up on the floor. He couldn't see much.

She panned her gaze right to left. Ideas flickered faster than laser fire in the dark of night on a skirmish line. She analyzed and sought what could be used as weapons, protection, or defenses.

Shelzat was the most dangerous. He had his archangel's sword. Was Sugi powerful enough to disable that sword?

Only Shelzat had been wielding his sword for millennium and Tienan didn't know squat about using a katana. Zad did, but in theory, not in actual combat.

As to her dirks, if she got them, could she disable Shelzat and give Tienan and Zad an opening to deliver a killing blow?

She could try.

Then there were the tormantratas. She could maim them, which would effectively neutralize them for a time.

As to the three witches? Which witch was the most powerful, the most dangerous? Annelisa seemed the least dangerous, but you never knew. Those quiet ones were often the deadliest.

Skom, too many questions, not enough answers.

She eyed her dirks. They had latched onto one of the bag's drawstrings. By taking turns winding the cord about themselves, they were pulling the slack out of the bow loop.

Janay laughed to herself. Leave it to a woman to tie a bowknot that could be undone.

Fox suddenly stood, hilt braced against the top of the bag, tip on the workbench's surface.

Poke strained to make one last turn of cord.

Suddenly the knot gave way.

Poke did a reverse spin, untangling herself from the coils.

Both blades pushed apart the gathered top and stilled.

Janay nodded and both blades tipped a bow to her.

With her fingers, she gave the dirks their orders.

A glance at Tienan repositioning his hands was acknowledgment that he'd understood. He flashed as wide a smile to her as his gag permitted. That smile radiant with his love.

Her heart swelled, and tears of joy threatened to blur her vision.

She blinked the tears back.

The chanting stopped.

At the altar, Celinae and Sweets, one on each side of the rectangular base that held the glass-domed model, carefully moved the unit off the altar to the table that had no cloth covering.

Inside the glass dome, ominous gray smoke billowed.

Celinae and Sweets went to Tienan, removed his shoes and socks, then engaged the antigrav motors on his slab. As soon as Annelisa removed the candles and dumped them into a wall recycler, the three hoisted Tienan onto the altar.

Annelisa went to the cupboard and came back with a quart-sized black cauldron riding on top of a scruffy, leather-bound book. At the workbench, Celinae triggered a button and a single burner cook top slid into view. She took the cauldron and placed it on the unit, turning the flame up until it was a pale blue.

About to take the book from Annelisa, Sweets glanced at Silence. Brutally swearing, Sweets headed for the cage, leaving Annelisa to set the book on the black velvet table.

Sweets flashed her ring across the cage door's access and Silence's door opened.

Silence huddled in the corner against the back bars, forehead on her knees. Liss was not visible.

In two strides, Sweets grabbed Silence by the jacket lapels and jerked her to her feet. She slammed Silence's back against the unforgiving metal bars.

Tears cascaded anew down Silence's already wet cheeks.

Liss's head came out as before, but this time she stabbed her beak into Sweets' veed-protected hands. When the beak hit, sparklers of energy flickered. Liss squawked in pain and pulled her beak back.

"Don't try that again," Sweets said to Liss. "If you do, my veed will burn off your beak!" She shook Silence. "What's the matter, Your Grace, don't you want to see your grandson's feet burned off?"

Silence shook her head rapidly and sobbed.

"Too bad. I want you to look. I want you to watch every moment of his pain." Sweets hauled Silence to the other side of the cage and slammed Silence, chest first, into the bars. She undid Silence's handcuffs and re-cuffed her hands so they were outside the cage, above the crossbar so Silence couldn't turn or drop to her knees.

"If I see you hide your eyes or close your eyes, I will stab Tienan with my stiletto." She removed the stiletto from the sheath at the back of her neck. "Do you understand?"

Silence nodded, tears and sobs flowing anew.

Sweets left the cage, locked the door, and strode for the workbench. En route, she sheathed her dagger.

Shelzat came toward Janay. He snapped his fingers. The four tormantratas followed, a pair on each side of him.

He ripped the gag off her mouth, tossing it away, toward the plants. The gag left a sensation like the crackling of static electricity on her lips.

"Now, Sergeant Cholyn, you have to appreciate that this building is protected by a Dome of Gloom, a very unique force field. None of your angel friends can enter or exit."

Janay mustered all the bravado she could tap into. "Which also means you and yours cannot exit."

He quirked one fine-feathered blond eyebrow up, but she caught the fleeting humor in his eyes.

Instinct warned Janay he had an escape route.

No, wait. What if he wanted her to think there was a way out? What if he wanted to give her false hope? Demons were devious. Darkons devilishly so.

Shelzat's smile slowly grew wider, sending a salvo of fear through Janay that imploded in her gut.

"Ah, sweet, Janay," Shelzat said, his voice mesmerizingly low. "So young, so beautiful." Shelzat's form blurred before her eyes.

Suddenly she was seventeen again, out on the town with friends the night her path crossed that of her father, who she hadn't seen in six years. A second later, Janay was inside the hotel, leading her father to a darkened, private corner beside tapestry curtains. She did a ladylike turn on her high heels, proud that she didn't wobble, and was about to say, 'Look, Father, see how much I've grown up.' Instead, she stared up, into the confidently cocky, dark brown eyes of her father.

He leaned forward, his warmth scented with expensive cologne, and his charismatic voice whispered, "Room 4528. I pay exceedingly well for my pleasures."

The shock of those words brought home the shame of what he thought, and she blurted out, "Fathers don't seduce their daughters." As she took in her next gulping breath, her inner voice screamed, *Idiot! Your father is the pervert your mother said he was!* On the exhale, she banked her anger and embarrassment, managing, "I'm Janay. *Your daughter.*"

He drew back, his expression neutral. His gaze searched her face. Realization paled his cheeks before rage flashed in his eyes. "You are no better than your whoring mother!"

Just as the slap of those words had cleared her vision back then, those words now reasserted reality and who actually stood before her—Shelzat.

She took in a breath through her nostrils, clearing away the folly of her youth. She summoned her sergeant-hard voice. "My father had no idea who I was and nothing ever happened between us. *You are a disgusting hellkite!*"

He grinned with sadistic glee. "Your father likes them young, nubile."

She couldn't deny that nor would she give Shelzat the satisfaction of a reply.

"You, Janay, like a mature man's touch." He cupped her breast.

She fought not to cringe and managed a jeering, "It's only a body. You can never have my soul."

He laughed. "But you flinched, Janay. *You flinched.* I will take delight in hearing you scream until dawn."

She gulped in air and fought to stop the quivering of her guts, her knees, her heart.

Chuckling, Shelzat stepped away and headed for the tormantratas.

Catching movement at the corner of her eye, she focused on Tienan and instantly knew Shelzat had allowed him—and all of them—to witness her youthful indiscretion.

Damn the darkon.

She locked her gaze on Shelzat's back, an open spot between his folded wings. She had the urge to summon Poke and Fox and drive their blades deep into the darkon's back. Only, other lives were at stake. She had to wait for the right moment, the right opportunity because there might be only one chance to pull off a miracle.

Shelzat stopped and spoke in the soft timbre of gargling words to the four attentive tormantratas.

She shifted her gaze to the backs of the three witches huddled around the burner and the book.

No one was looking this way? She checked Tienan, who winked at her.

It was now or never. Janay mouthed, "To hand, to hand."

The dirks whizzed out of the bag straight for Tienan, parting trajectories so each blade went under his wrist shackles and sliced the plastic. The blades kept going, crossed each other over his belly and aimed for his ankle shackles, easily slitting them.

Swooping upward, they headed for Janay.

Tienan blessed the powers and felt Zad's aura envelop him. Once his hands were free, he ripped the gag from his mouth and slipped off he altar.

Inside his mind, he heard Zad's, *Sugi, to hand! *

The katana appeared, blade gleaming, and the black diamond-patterned hilt smacked into Tienan's right hand.

Shelzat's "No!" thundered through the warehouse, half deafening Tienan.

The three witches turned, their veeds encasing them with protective auras.

Shelzat's wings collapsed tightly back. He drew his sword and stepped into the path of Janay's dirks. He sliced his black sword left to right. The blade smacked one dirk so it arced upwards, but regained a course for Janay. As the sword picked up continuing momentum of its swoop to the right, the blade slammed the other dirk, smashing it toward the hearth. The tip hit a hand's width from Rowen's head, then flipped end over end and into the fire pit.

Shelzat growled the language of the tormantratas.

The four beasts headed for Janay, claws extended.

The flying dirk, still on course, slit through Janay's left wrist shackle, did a back flip, and stopped with its hilt in her palm. She gripped the blade and yelled at the four oncoming tormantratas, "I am The Grave Digger. I dig demon graves. I will dig yours deeper than deep!"

Two of the tormantratas slowed, hesitated, then hung back.

The leaders kept coming and leapt.

Heart in his throat, Tienan headed for Janay.

She ducked the tormantrata and slashed her ankle shackles apart.

One of the tormantratas' hind talons caught a cluster of Janay's curls, searing her hair.

The tormantrata scrambled up the wall, turned and came down, snarling.

Janay cut her other hand free. "Poke! To hand!"

The second oncoming tormantrata reared onto its hand legs, its front claws extended, heading for Janay's chest.

Zad, full meld. Use me. Save, Janay!

The power unleashed by his veed came with the soft drone of that power and, behind it, lower, the twang of another harmonic — Kiyoshi?

Tienan found himself on his feet, lunging forward. In a flash of katana steel, he decapitated the rearing tormantrata. The demon's body fell sideways. The head rolled away. Both deflated into a sticky brown slime that ignited and burned to nothingness.

The demon on the wall went for Janay's throat, but Janay pushed away from the wall.

The claws raked air.

She raced between the two other demons, slicing her dirks into their guts. She ran for the aisles of plants with the tormantrata on the wall leaping across the wall until it leapt for her, and missed, smashing into plants and pots.

Zad pivoted Tienan and sent Sugi up in a hard swing that collided with Shelzat's blade.

Sword rang against sword.

Out of the corner of his eye, Tienan glimpsed the three witches grabbing the ceremonial knives off the small table. Sweets was in the lead with a blade that resembled a short sword.

Hyper-aware, he sensed she was going to plunge the blade into his back, and yet he was not afraid. Somehow he understood Zad and Kiyoshi knew what to do.

Shelzat's next blow pounded down, and the shock hammered both Tienan's shoulders. Then, in a blink of his eyes, his hands sent Sugi down and back, the blade going under his arm, behind him into Sweets' gut. Just as swiftly, Zad twisted the blade free of her body and whipped Sugi forward to block Shelzat's slashing blade meant to cleave his head in two.

When Annelisa saw Tienan ram his sword into Sweets, she felt her heart stop.

She focused on Sweets, who stood still, head bowed, looking down at the blood gushing from her abdomen.

"Impossible," Sweets whispered through her paling lips.

Annelisa backed two steps. How could a sword cut through a veed-shield? Whatever kind of sword Tienan had, it was deadly.

As deadly as Shelzat's?

Sweets dropped to her knees, then fell face forward in death. Fae, her veed, wriggled out of her.

Celinae halted beside Sweets' body. Celinae's peacock of a veed rose out of her. The veed sank spurs into Fae's serpent tail, then plunged her beak into Fae's neck and began ingesting the veed's energy.

Seeing Janay dodge a tormantrata and trip, smacking her knee and hip against a meter-tall ceramic planter, and that Shelzat had maneuvered Tienan against the cage, Annelisa ordered, *Ahl! Go. Get your share.*

Her veed flew out of her and plunged her beak into the other side of Fae's neck.

The two veeds quickly consumed Fae, then backed away from each other. Morphing into their balls of energy, they returned to their hosts.

Once inside Annelisa, Ahl whispered, *Buy me time to convert Fae's energy.*

Yes, of course. It wouldn't take more than a minute for the energy conversion because, during the triad ritc, the three veeds individual harmonic string-song had been retuned into one subatomic melody that they shared. Thus they held a common synergy, working as one to more easily devour other veeds and convert that veed energy to their own harmonic string-song.

A sword rang against metal bars and Annelisa eyed the cage. Somehow Tienan had cut the cuffs holding his grandmother and Silence scurried away. Only Shelzat went to thrust his sword through the bars to kill her.

Tienan plowed a fist into Shelzat's jaw, which sent the darkon reeling sideways a pace, his wings flaring to counterbalance and keep him on his feet.

Tienan attacked for the kill, but the darkon moved, his blade deflecting Tienan's blow. The darkon's sword skittered along Sugi with a razoring hiss of metal against metal.

The two tormantratas, with gut wounds quickly closing, galumphed toward Janay who emerged, hobbling from between plants. She saw the two coming for her and headed toward the back door.

Annelisa? Ahl said, *Where is Celinae*

Annelisa looked about.

Celinae stood at Granger's cage door. She unlocked the door with a pass of her witch's ring and sent the door opening so fast it banged on the bars and bounced back, drifting to close.

Granger stood motionless, human-faced, under the stupefying power of the bloodwood seed mist Celinae had given him after he'd placed Silence in her cage and the men on their slabs.

The motion of Celinae's hand over her ring meant she had opened the outer band of the ring. She aimed her ring for Granger's face to give him a strong whiff of pure bloodwood oil.

Yes, that's what they needed. Granger-the-vampire would kill Tienan and stop this nonsense.

Granger's hand shot out and gripped Celinae's ring hand. His vampire face contorted with rage and his fangs glistened for blood. In the blink of Annelisa's eyes, he yanked Celinae forward, grabbed her jaw and jerked her head aside. He plunged his fangs toward her neck.

Annelisa backed and rammed into the freezer door. Her hands involuntarily went to her throat, where the silver-slatted collar rode easily on her neck. Would the collar stop his vampire fangs as Sweets said it would?

When Granger's fangs hit Celinae's collar, he yowled.

With a bellow of fury, he tore the collar from her neck along with the oval copper disk she wore.

As he flung the metals aside, Celinae gutted him in the groin with her dagger.

He froze for a moment, letting her go.

She abandoned the dagger and sprinted for the cage door.

She wasn't fast enough.

Granger grabbed a handful of her red hair, snatching her back.

She screamed.

With a growling roar, he snapped her neck and tossed her to the grate floor.

The cage door shut, clicking and locking him in.

Shelzat bellowed his rage.

The fight between Shelzat and Tienan had moved to the altar where both men circled.

Shelzat's head rose a fraction to see something behind Tienan.

Janay.

As if in slow motion, Annelisa watched Janay slide under the arch of the bloodwood mother-vine, arm extended so the dirk in her right hand sliced into a fat offshoot.

Oh, no, no no! Terror whipped Annelisa's mind and soul.

The old vine shuddered, leaves aquiver.

The offshoot twisted and soon small pods at its tip burst apart.

Janay grabbed the vine's cut end.

Time seemed to crawl as the twist came whirling down.

Janay aimed the vine at the tormantratas, bathing them in bloody sap that ignited their flesh.

The tormantratas shrieked, and the flames quickly killed and consumed them.

Pop. Crackle. Sizzle.

Annelisa turned her attention to the sounds.

Spray from the offshoot that had not landed on the tormantratas had splashed onto many of the vines and bushes. Stems exploded, others rapidly wilted. Two bushes belched fire and sent up a hazy cloud of celery-green smoke that hung in place, then wended toward the back wall of the building.

Terrified as she was, Annelisa knew she needed help—Shelzat's help. She spotted the darkon and Tienan. Both had momentarily stopped fighting. Both watched the tormantratas die.

Eyes glazed with fury, Shelzat looked at her. His lips mimed, "NOW!"

Now? By the dark powers   She must fulfill her pledge to Shelzat and save the book? For the love of Satanus, the alternative didn't bear thinking! She ran to the table where the *Fourth Book of Xenobia* had been left.

About to lay her dagger down, she eyed the miniature of the Dome of Gloom and recalled what Shelzat had once told her. *Ahl, heat the dagger!*

Ahl sent veed power through Annelisa's hand to the blade she held. As soon as the tip became molten red, she aimed the tip and pushed it through the dome where the secret door was located.

The smoke in the dome burned away from the heat, revealing the doorway.

She shoved the blade into the model's base where it would stay upright, keeping the shield at bay until the blade cooled, giving her a few minutes to escape. She grabbed the book, then checked to see where everyone was.

Silence had her back to the cage door, a look of horror on her face, staring at Granger who remained standing, the dagger from his gut in hand, his wound closing. His other hand held onto a crossbar along the divider of the two cage sections. As he steadied himself, he stared at Silence, his vampire face drooling for blood.

Silence whimpered.

With Tienan in pursuit, their swords clanging with each step, Shelzat retreated, angling toward Rowen.

Janay, breathing hard and favoring her right leg, circled the cage to get to Shelzat and help Tienan defeat the archangel.

Bless Shelzat! He was leading everyone away from her. The path to the door was clear!

She dashed around the altar and into the row of dwarf trees that had not been sprayed by bloodwood. At the back of the row, she turned right and saw the green cloud hovering between her and the door. She sucked in a deep breath, then ran through the cloud.

The chilling gas tingled on her exposed skin and hands, but she made it through. Her lungs burned by the time she stepped into the night and gulped fresh air. She ran toward the street.

Glancing back, she saw the ghostly aurora of the Dome of Gloom's shielding reseal itself.

No one was coming after her.

She slowed to a jog.

All she had to do now was get to her cousin, Alreatha, who Shelzat said possessed the blood of Xenobia. Together, she and her cousin would perform spells from the book and become powerful witches.

Inside the warehouse, Janay spotted Annelisa racing through the dwarf trees with a book clutched to her chest and run through the green cloud of gas.

The idiot. She was as good as dead. When latchcan and spikestake burned, they created one lethal green gas. And just where was the panicked woman going? The place was covered with the Dome of Gloom. Or maybe not. Damn the lying darkon. *There had been a way out!*

Granger lunged at his cage door, startling Janay. The door shuddered with the impact of the enraged vampire and rattled, but it did not yield.

Janay scooted away. Jogging for Tienan, pain reminded her that her rebuilt hip shouldn't be put to such abuse.

Shelzat slugged Tienan in the jaw, sending him sprawling back onto the floor. Shelzat sped for the altar. Tienan rolled over, onto his knees, to his feet, and went after the darkon, raising Sugi for a killing blow.

Shelzat's wings suddenly snapped open. He transformed into a black whirlwind that vanished down into the center of the pentagram.

Janay reached Tienan. Being out of breath, she mimicked him, resting the palms of her hands on her knees.

"Hey, you two," Granger said loudly. "Tienan. Janay."

She looked at Granger and found his face normal.

"I'm all right," Granger said. "Let me out."

Tienan went to stand up, but Janay said between gasps for air, "He killed Boots. Saw him do it."

Granger yelled, "I did not kill Boots."

Tienan's gaze went from Granger to her and back again, his expression unreadable.

"Before I blacked out," Janay managed between breaths. "I saw his fangs sink into Boots neck. She went down for the count."

"You're staying put," Tienan rasped out to Granger. Several breaths later, he said, "Janay, free my grandmother. I'll tend to Rowen."

Janay hobbled to the cage and, with Poke's help, unlocked the door. Silence seemed to have aged twenty centuries. The moment Janay pulled the gag off, Silence whispered, "Thank you."

Using Sugi, Tienan slit the shackles apart, freeing Rowen. The sword vanished, and Zad's aura faded. Tienan's face blanched. "Rowen's gone into labor!"

Janay glanced at the clock over the front doors. Ten minutes to midnight. Skom. *"Tienan! The time."* She pointed to the clock.

Using her jacket sleeve, Silence wiped away her tears, then demanded, "What's going on?"

"Long story," Tienan replied. "Janay and I were supposed to do a reunification rite for Rowen at midnight and under the dark of a new moon, otherwise Tal and Rowen die."

"By the powers, no." New tears welled in Silence's eyes. "Can't we do something?"

"We're sort of trapped in here with a Dome of Gloom in place," Janay said, her breathing almost normal. "The back door is surrounded by a green gas that will kill us. There's no way we can make it to Wolcott House and the pentagram there."

Tienan heard his brother mutter, "Reunification . . . Pentagram . . ."

My lord, Zad said, **all pentagrams channel power. This one seethes with magnetic energy, which is — **

Liss's specialty!

"Grandmother," Tienan ordered, "remove that altar from the pentagram."

"What? Why?"

"Pentagram. Reunification rite. *Planet core energy.*"

The instant realization of what he meant dawned. Her eyes went wide and she nearly gasped. Pivoting, she headed for the altar, found the controls that unlocked the base, and shoved the unit aside, toward the plants.

Tienan, with Zad augmenting his strength, maneuvered Rowen's slab near the pentagram's center, and Rowen scooted onto the pentagram. Tienan sent the slab skittering toward the altar.

Janay frowned, looking confused. "I thought we needed the energy from the moon so Zad could convert it into veed power. Have you forgotten we're inside a building?"

As a contraction hit, Rowen gritted his teeth. "It's okay. You gave it your best shot."

"Nonsense." Silence's commanding demeanor armored her voice. "Rowen you are going to live." She gave Tienan a tepid smile. "Liss informs me this pentagram is over a natural magnetic field. Liss will have no trouble drawing whatever energy Zad needs."

Tienan caught Janay's questioning look and scowl before she said, "That ugly bitch-veed of hers can really do that?"

Silence's chin came up a fraction. Her words came out laced with certainty. "I am an Eighth Power Witch. My veed can summon quantum amounts of magnetic energy. Now, stop wasting time. Do what you must. Let us get this rite underway and save Rowen."

Tienan stepped over to his grandmother and whispered to her.

Silence glanced at Rowen. "Naked?"

Rowan groaned. "Gawd, my own grandmother seeing me naked?"

"Boy," Silence said, "I changed your diapers."

Tienan held up his hand, palm open, the gesture staying Rowen's rebuttal, and said sternly, "We have no choice."

Silence turned her attention to Janay for a moment before addressing Tienan. "The idea of seeing my grandsons *au naturel* is repugnant, but not as abhorrent as having to witness that *jossierj* coupling with you."

Tienan gave her a wrathful scowl. "Rowen's life depends on us."

Hearing the disparaging tone Silence had used, Janay wasn't keen on being naked in front of the old woman, or Rowen, nor nude on a pentagram, all her scars to behold, but Tienan was right. This was no time for modesty. As she took off her boots, Janay said loudly, "Listen, you two, we're trapped. It's not like you can put your heads under a blanket and do the rite."

In her confident, matriarchal voice, Silence said, "Maybe I can."

What did she mean by that? Janay looked up and found Silence heading, with purposeful strides, to a cupboard. She flung the door open, pulled out, then donned a ceremonial black robe with silver trim along the front edges and hood. She returned to the pentagram, walking around the Druid's Circle, head bowed in concentration. She stopped at the southern point, turned, and faced Rowen's back.

She kicked off her shoes, sending them behind her, then

planted her heels together at the point and spread her toes apart so the big toes were directly on the lines. "I am standing on the point of the main magnetic flow. The stream is plentiful, quite powerful." She flipped the robe's hood up, pulling it down so it completely hid her face. "Rowen, I have covered my face and have commanded Liss to blind me, make me deaf, cease all my sensory perceptions so I will not witness nor retain memories of what transpires during your rite. *What happens here will be your secret.*"

"Thank you — " Whatever else Rowen intended to say was lost to a contraction, and a barely audible, "Hurry."

"Tienan," Silence commanded, "begin the rite." She extended her arms like a priest about to give a blessing. Her hands began to glow with her veed's aura. Like a ripple of heat rising from a sun-scorched tarmac, magnetic power rose up into her hands, gathering into a pink-tinged bubbling whirlpool, the center condensing, darkening ominously.

Janay gave orders to her dirks, and they quickly undressed Rowen, then helped her remove the last of her garments.

Panting in the aftermath of a contraction, Rowen pulled his knees up, as best he could with a round belly, fingertips resting on his kneecaps. He closed his eyes. "Hurry. Please hurry."

Janay took her place at Rowen's back, sinking her dirks, foot and head. "Tienan?"

"I'm here," he said from behind her, and lowered himself, straddling her, mounting her as he had at the first rite, only this time, her skin was warm, silken smooth, not sweat-sheened and hot.

She made no sound nor did she tense when his chest and stomach settled onto her back. Lowering his hips, he slipped his hot penis into her cool wetness. She was wetter than wet . . . This was his woman. The woman he loved. A woman like no other.

His penis swelled. The tightness both pleasure and torment. Yet, being inside her felt right, oh so right! He cupped her breasts. Both were firm handfuls, the teats hardening.

This was a flesh to flesh joining. A heart-to-heart joining. A soul mate to soul mate joining.

Tienan whispered in her ear, the love he felt etched into each word. "I love you, Janay. We can do this."

She whispered, "I love you, Tienan."

My good lord, Zad said, *Liss is beaming the magnetic power to me. Brace for an oscillating aura that will intensify.*

I'm ready. Tienan pecked a kiss to Janay's cheek and felt her smile push her cheek back. He settled his chin on her collar bone. With his next inhale came a heady whiff of her peachy scent followed by the tingling of Zad's aura engulfing him.

Janay's jaw trembled with anxiety. "Am I going to get fried again?"

"No. This is magnetic power."

She minutely jerked. "As in prickles like electricity?"

"Yes," Tienan whispered. "It shouldn't become too intense."

She hunched and almost squeaked, "Yeah, right!"

"Relax, Janay, relax."

Liss sharply ordered, "Start your mantra!" A second later, Silence's soft-spoken chant droned and seemed to echo about the pentagram.

Tienan started the chant, the one they'd said at the first rite, *"Esiojer en eth . . ."*

Janay joined in.

Another voice, an older one, underscored Zad's voice before Zad flared his aura.

Quicksilver heavy, quicksilver cool, the energy tingled and flowed into Tienan, then down Janay's arms. The dirks glowed and soon flared lines of light which exploded into a brilliant colored array that became diamond bright.

A line of light halved Rowen's stomach from ribs to groin. Tal, sporting his male genitals, stepped out, roared with delight, shook himself, and then morphed into a ball of energy. Rowen's belly seam closed, sealing as if it had never parted, the skin shrinking as if never stretched.

When the energy withdrew and Zad backed off his aura, Tienan quit his chant and said quietly, "Janay, hang onto your dirks until I get off you. No repeat —"

"Of the first tumble we took," she finished for him.

Tienan pecked a pride-filled kiss onto Janay's cheek, and as quickly as he could, got to his feet.

Janay let go of the dirks and sat back, gasping for breath. She stared at her trembling hands.

"Janay? Are you all right?"

"Fine. I was concentrating so hard holding onto the dirks, I forgot to breathe." Her gaze shifted to the center of the pentagram. "Hey. Where's Rowen?"

"I'm here." Rowen replied. He stood in front of the cupboard, struggling to get a robe over his nakedness. The robe hem barely went to his knobby knees.

Liss's voice commanded, "Enough chatter. Tienan, Janay. Dress so I may release Her Grace."

Once clothed, Tienan took a moment to look at Rowen. Joy filled him. His brother was whole again, and Tal was a male veed.

Turning, Tienan found his grandmother still stood on point, her veed's aura shimmering about her. Still deaf, dumb, and blind. Yet, it wouldn't be long before Liss withdrew.

As to Janay? She sat on the edge of a planter. After locking the last catch on her boot, she put her foot down. She began finger combing the riot of her hair into a semblance of order.

His woman looked none the worse for all the magnetic energy she had channeled. All was well.

And now he had a personal task. "Janay, I'm holding you to the wedding."

"What wedding?" Silence demanded.

He braced himself and met his grandmother's light brown eyes that seemed frost-pale. He would leave nothing to chance nor to her meddling. In a don't-challenge-me tone, he said, "Grandmother, Janay asked me to be her husband *and I accepted.* We are to be bonded as soon as possible."

"Nonsense. We will discuss this later. At home." She drew herself up, shoulders squared, the Dowan Matriarch. "Right now you boys must fetch that glass-encased model of this warehouse. Put it in the center of the pentagram so I can break the dome-spell."

Tienan ordered Zad to augment his muscles and, moments later, he and Rowen set the dome-model in place. Tienan strode over to Janay.

Rowen went to Silence's side, briefly touching her forearm to gain her attention. "Have you ever done this before?"

"My father would often set a dome in place to insure his gardens would not be disturbed. Trouble was, I liked walking in the gardens. However, undoing the protective spell was time-consuming and power draining. But I was young back then. This is now." Liss's darkly golden aura coated Silence with a shimmering glow. "Rowen, best you go stand with your brother."

Liss spread her noncorporeal gryphon wings and power surged up from the floor like shooting stars, all heading for a point near the ceiling, then arched downward, plunging one spark after another, bombarding and chipping away at the glass dome until, minutes later, the dome shattered and vanished. Another moment passed before Liss retreated into her host. Silence looked exhausted, but pleased.

The front doors burst open and in came Boots, rodgun in hand, half a dozen members of the local Guardian SWAT team in her wake.

"By the powers—" Tienan muttered.

From Janay came, "Boots? You're alive?"

Boots grinned. "Of course I am."

Janay's jaw worked up and down a couple times before she stammered out, "I saw Granger kill you." She sucked in a fortifying breath. "And just how did you know we were here?"

"Granger faked killing me. So glad to know you believed I was dead." Boots turned her attention to Tienan. "As to finding you, partner, I talked Neejera into implanting a homing device into Granger but not reporting it. After all, we had someone at HQ tainting Granger's blood and if he went berserk—"

"Boots!" Granger yelled. "Get me out of here."

Spotting Granger, she jogged to his cage.

Tienan took Janay's hand in his and drew her around so she stood in front of him. He wrapped his arms around her. "I truly do love you." He kissed her with all the love of a man redeemed and reborn.

🍂 Epilogue

Then sings my soul to sun and sky
as I walk the day,
Then sings my soul to moon and starry sky
as I walk the night,
Always unto Him, always to Him,
sings my soul, sings my soul.

— "Soul Song" by Brother Oktokar "Otto" Ptarmiga, Brother-Priest of the Chapel of J'Hi Chymara

Dawn had broken the night sky, but the sun had not yet risen. At Wolcott House, Tienan lay on his bed, feeling warm under the black coverlet. He was also naked after soaking his muscle-sore body in the hot tub. Wielding the katana had proved how out of shape he was.

After entwining his stiff fingers together and setting them to rest on top of the covers over his chest, he glanced at the bathroom door.

Janay was taking a shower. He could hear the water pelting her and quickly imagined her body, rivulets cascading down her silken flesh.

As much as he wanted to join her, he could hardly move.

With effort, he raised his left hand and focused on the shiny gold band circling his ring finger. By the blessed powers, he was legally married to Janay.

Memories wafted of being inside the Guardian van with Janay, Rowen, and his grandmother. The three were being driven home, to Wolcott House. Then, suddenly, emphatically, Janay had ordered the driver to, "Pull in here!"

Through the van's side window, Tienan glimpsed the Chapel of J'Hi Baldama. He'd sent a questioning gaze to Janay, who said, "We're getting married. Here and now." Not an order. Not a request. Just a simple statement of fact.

He'd been shocked. And delighted.

Rowen had grinned.

Silence's face had gone fury-red.

He did not want his grandmother interfering, so he scooted forward enough to grasp the side of the seat in front of him where his grandmother sat. He whispered into her ear, "*As your deed is, so is your destiny.*"

Her cheek paled, confirming she'd gotten his message and remembered the hatred of the three witches she'd just survived. Yet what surprised him was that she didn't offer any further protest. As a matter of fact, she insisted on witnessing the ceremony. Rowen, too, had witnessed it.

More memories flared — Janay rousting the priest. The ivory interior walls of the chapel with its dark wood pews. The unadorned, vaulted sanctuary where a mahogany wood altar stood.

He hadn't known that J'Hian brother-priests could perform a legal marriage ceremony nor that the drawer of their altars held wedding bands for impromptu marriage services.

Tienan again eyed his gold wedding band. He was well and truly wed. Which made him feel happy. Even ecstatic.

He loved Janay to the very depths of his being and she loved him. That thought humbled him. Invigorated him.

Trond, but love was bedeviling.

Janay entered the bedroom, damp from her shower, her curls coiled like springs. She wore his toweling robe, the hem trailing along the floor. Her saucy smile rouged her cheeks and joy glistened in her earth-brown eyes. "What are you grinning about?"

"My good fortune," Tienan replied. "Actually, it's our good fortune. Zad ordered the dirks out. He left, locking the door so we can partake of a nap, and *undisturbed private time.*"

"We're alone?"

"*All alone.*" The house was empty. Rowen decided to stay with Silence, saying there were too many traumatic memories at Wolcott House for him to deal with right now. As to Boots and Granger, they remained at the warehouse. The two had volunteered to file reports at headquarters so he and Janay could go home to recover.

"So, dear husband," Janay said, "I have you all to myself, do I?"

He nodded, feeling as though his grin shoved his cheeks all the way back to his ears.

Janay slipped under the covers. "You know I am about to share this big old bed of yours for a lifetime." She squirmed toward him and snuggled close, placing her left hand next to his. Her gold wedding band gleamed. "They look good on our fingers, so why the frown? Are you having second thoughts about us marrying in haste?"

"Absolutely not. I was just thinking how odd it was to be married in a church."

"Where else would you get married?"

"The usual procedure is to troth and live together for a year. If a child is born during that year, the couple becomes legally married, husband and wife."

"The only purpose of a union is to produce kids? Your society is weird."

He chuckled. "No, not so weird. I'll explain it some other time." But the idea of procreation stirred him, and his penis. He gave her a lopsided grin.

"And just what are you thinking about, dear husband?"

He blurted out in a whisper, "Sex." Bright red spots dotted his cheekbones. "I didn't mean that quite the way it sounded."

She giggled. "Ah, how a man's mind turns to that when he has a woman in his bed."

"Not just any woman, *my wife*." His gaze focused on her cleavage, which was exposed between her robe's lapels.

"Tienan?"

He heaved a forlorn sigh. "Janay, every muscle I have is sore. I don't want to disappoint you."

Disappoint her? Not likely. "I realize how much you must hurt, but it's no problem." She set a saucy smile in place. "Like they say, *where there's a will, there's a way.* Question is, are you willing?"

He opened his arms, the movements stiff. "Ah, Janay, good wife . . ."

She went into his arms, regretting the barrier of her robe between them.

His voice was hoarse with need. "Kiss me, Janay."

She set her lips to his. The fire of that kiss ignited a fluttering in her womb and warmth poured forth. She loved this man with all her heart, all her being. She pushed back, breaking the kiss.

Tienan's eyes were glossed with a desire she knew matched her own.

"Now, husband, despite you being as incapacitated as you are, we can consummate this marriage of ours, that is, if you'll just lay back *and let me do us in.*" She backed a little ways, untied her robe, and let it fall off her shoulders. She flipped the coverlet down, exposing his body and the dark hair on his chest that tapered to a fluffy mound covering his groin.

She felt her breasts surge to fullness, the puckering of her nipples, and more warmth radiate between her legs. Although she watched Tienan, pleased with his smile and his gaze transfixed on her breasts, out of the corner of her eye, she caught his penis springing rigid and rising up through his dark mound of hair.

"Ah, so that's the way of it, is it?" Her voice held the husky timbre of her need. She fought a budding grin and slipped her bare leg over his, then hesitated, looking into his passion-darkened gray eyes, wanting to be sure he was up for intercourse.

"Wife, soldier mine," he said softly, "lock and load."

In the lounge in front of the fireplace, Zad stretched on the bearskin and yawned. As he brought his tail back to rest against his flank, he felt the two dirks resettle themselves in his tail's dreadlocks. It seemed an odd place for them to be, but at least he could keep an eye on them so they left Tienan and Janay alone to rest quietly.

Two meters away, the ghost of Kiyoshi, eyes closed, sat on the floor in a lotus position. The samurai's shoulders were rounded, as if he were downcast, disheartened. But why?

Suddenly Adrada alighted near the back door and walked across the parquet floor toward Kiyoshi. Adrada smiled at Kiyoshi like a father to a son. "Do not look so distressed, great samurai."

Kiyoshi eyed the angel with profound melancholy. "I have failed to accomplish the task set for me. The book changed hands."

"True, but there will be a few more instances when the cosmic connections allow an opportunity to retrieve the book from the dark ones."

Kiyoshi nodded, but he did not seem happier.

Adrada's golden feathers brightened and many half purple feathers turned golden. "Rejoice, Kiyoshi. You softened Tienan's hardened heart. You gave Janay purpose in life, a reason to dance in many new days."

"I merely sought to bring lovers together."

"You did more than that. Because of what you have said and done, I am free to tell you that Tienan is the son of your heart, Zad is the son of your soul, and *Janay is the daughter of your blood.*"

Shock sent Kiyoshi's brows upward then slamming down, crinkling them so they almost met as one. His lips moved, but he uttered nothing. Anger flushed his cheeks. "I sired no children!"

"Lotus Blossom did not commit *jigai*. She died in childbirth. She was afraid to tell you she was pregnant with your child. She knew you would cast her off, so she ran away. Her parents took her in. They felt it just punishment for you to never know she bore you a son." His voice gentled. "One suitable day, ask Janay to show you her family tree. It makes for fascinating reading."

Kiyoshi's smile was one of dawning realization and joy. "Lotus Blossom gave me a son?" He sobered.

"What troubles you now, good samurai?"

"If you are telling me this, reason tells me that I have achieved nirvana. My soul is free to enter the eternal, celestial light."

Adrada chuckled. "Yes and no. Yes, you have achieved nirvana but no, you cannot go yet. I must ask you to remain part of Tienan's life. He is now worthy to wield the katana, worthy to fight and execute demons. However, he needs training. Much training. No one can train him better nor look after the training of his sons and daughters than you."

Kiyoshi struggled to his feet. With jubilant tears plummeting down his cheeks, and a great smile parting his mustache, he bowed. "It is, Great Shogun, my honor to serve."

 THE END

Thank you for reading Karma & Mayhem.

Please consider giving a review
either where you purchased this book or
leave a comment/review at the
Karma & Mayhem blog

http://karmaandmayhem.blogspot.com

AFTERWARD

The Samurai Creed

A poem-song by an anonymous fourteenth century samurai.(This is only one of many versions on the Internet.)

I have no parents; I make the Heavens and the Earth my parents.

I have no home; I make the Tan Tien my home.

I have no divine power; I make honesty my Divine Power.

I have no means; I make Docility my means.

I have no magic power; I make personality my Magic Power.

I have neither life nor death; I make A Um my Life and Death.

I have no body; I make Stoicism my Body.

I have no eyes; I make The Flash of Lightning my eyes.

I have no ears; I make Sensibility my Ears.

I have no limbs; I make Promptitude my Limbs.

I have no laws; I make Self-Protection my Laws.

I have no strategy; I make the Right to Kill and the Right to Restore Life my Strategy.

I have no designs; I make Seizing the Opportunity by the Forelock my Designs.

I have no miracles; I make Righteous Laws my Miracle.

I have no principles; I make Adaptability to all circumstances my Principle.

I have no tactics; I make Emptiness and Fullness my Tactics.

I have no talent; I make Ready Wit my Talent.

I have no friends; I make my Mind my Friend.

I have no enemy; I make Incautiousness my Enemy.

I have no armor; I make Benevolence my Armor.

I have no castle; I make Immovable Mind my Castle.

I have no sword; I make No Mind my Sword.

❧ ❧ ❧

Recipes

The first year *Karma and Mayhem* was launched coincided with Halloween. For the launch, I consulted with a chef who helped me create a real recipe for the *bloody red wine of ages* in the text (originally known as Chokeberry Shalamiz).

Each year thereafter for the anniversary of the publication, I devised a new recipe with the same "bloody" theme. The various recipes follow.

In 2016, *Karma and Mayhem*'s copyright reverted back to me and so with this 2017 re-release and update as *Karma & Mayhem*, I shortened the name in the text to *choberimiz* and renamed the recipes.

Enjoy the drink and the other "blood-red" goodies of *Karma & Mayhem*.

Catherine E. McLean

~~~~~~

Choberimiz

© 2012 as Chokeberry Shalamiz, Revised 2017
by Catherine E. McLean *** www.CatherineEmclean.com

Single Serving — A non-alcoholic beverage
A "bloody" good drink for Halloween!

Into a 4 cup glass measuring cup add:
- 1/4 tsp minced ginger
- 1/4 cup 100% tart cherry juice
- 1/4 cup 100% pomegranate juice
- 1/4 cup DARK cream soda
- ½ cup ginger ale

Blend and then add: 1/4 tsp from an individual Natural Cherry-Pomegranate Crystal Light drink packet. There will be a very red-bloody foam as you stir this in. (Kids will love that!)
Pour half the mix over ice in a tall glass. Makes 2 servings. For sweeter taste, add more cream soda. Keep refrigerated if not used immediately.

✳ ✳ ✳

Karma & Mayhem **Choberimiz Punch**

© 2013-2017 Catherine E. McLean

Into a punch bowl combine in this order:

64 oz. 100% Tart Cherry or Wild Cherry Juice (no sugar added)
64 oz. 100% Pomegranate Juice (no sugar added)
1 tablespoon minced ginger
24 oz. Cream Soda (the darker the color the better)
16 oz. RC Cola
1 tablespoon fruit punch drink mix (or 1 packet that makes 2 qts.)
Lightly stir to mix in the minced ginger
Chill and serve
Optional: serve with crushed ice

Karma & Mayhem **Red Velvet Bar Cookies**

© 2015-2017 - Catherine E. McLean *** www.CatherineEmclean.com

INTO A MIXING BOWL, COMBINE:

1 RED VELVET CAKE MIX
1 stick of butter (½ cup) MELTED
1 egg
1/3 cup of 100% pomegranate juice

Spread onto the bottom of a GREASED 9X13 baking pan

TOP evenly with one 12 oz. Bag of Mariani's New England Crunch which contains cranberries, cinnamon apples, and honey-roasted almonds (this dried fruit is available at most Walmarts).

SPRINKLE ON 1 tablespoon granulated sugar

MELT AND DRIZZLE OVER ALL with 1 stick of butter (½ cup)

BAKE at 350°F for 30–35 minutes
Cool
Cut into bars and serve. – May be topped with Cream Cheese Frosting, Cool-Whip, or Whipped Cream.

* * *

Karma & Mayhem Coberimiz Cookies

© 2014-2017 Catherine E. McLean *** www.CatherineEmclean.com

Makes approx. 5 dozen, cake-like cookies
Preheat oven to 400°F   —   Lightly grease cookie sheets

Prepare in advance:
  1 cup dried CHERRIES* (coarsely chopped)
  1 cup dried POMEGRANATE berries, coarsely chopped (try Ocean
    Spray's juice-infused cranberries found in the dried fruits section
    of most grocery stores)
Mix berries together and place in a small microwave-safe bowl Add ½
cup of water. Microwave on high for 1.5 minutes (90 second) until very
hot but not boiling). Let set a few minutes, until liquid is absorbed, then
refrigerate to cool. Do not place hot liquid-and-berries into the cookie
dough!

In a LARGE cake-accommodating mixing bowl, cream together:
                1 cup butter (softened)
                1-1/2 cups granulated sugar
                1/4 teaspoon salt
                1 teaspoon ALMOND extract
                ½ teaspoon ORANGE extract
Mix in: 2 large eggs, then mix in:
    1 cup white raisins (coarsely chopped)
    1 cup peppermint bits - the kind used for cookie baking, not the
    hard candy type
    1 cup pecans (coarsely chopped)

Sift together and then mix into the batter:
    3 cups all-purpose flour
    1 teaspoon baking soda
    2 teaspoons Cream of Tarter

ADD the COOLED and saturated-plump pomegranates and cherries.

Drop dough onto cookie sheet to form rounds with slightly flattened
tops (no ragged edges nor high peaks). Bake 10–12 minutes in a 400°F
oven. Cookie tops should be light to golden-brown. Allow cookies to
cool a few minutes before removing onto cooling sheets.

❉ ❉ ❉

About the Author

Catherine E. McLean

Besides Catherine being an author, writing instructor, and workshop speaker, she is a wife and mother. She has ridden and exhibited Morgan Sport Horses. She's an avid clothing and costume designer, an award-winning amateur photographer, a retired 4-H leader, a member of the Society for Creative Anachronism, and a Red Hatter who loves bling.

She lives on a farm nestled in the foothills of the Allegheny Mountains of Western Pennsylvania. In the quiet of the countryside, she writes tales of phantasy realms and stardust (fantasy, futuristic, and paranormal stories) where a reader can escape to other worlds, other realms, for adventure and romance.

Her short stories have been published in hard copy and online anthologies and magazines. Her books include:

Karma & Mayhem
Hearts Akilter (novella)
Jewels of the Sky
Adrada to Zool (short story anthology)
Revision is a Process — How to take the Frustration out of Self-Editing (nonfiction for writers)

Connect with Catherine

http://www.CatherineEmclean.com
Email: Catherine@CatherineEmclean.com

Catherine gives one-on-one writing workshops as well as online courses, and in-person workshops. Current topics can be found at her Writers Cheat Sheets website:

http://www.WritersCheatSheets.com

Her blog for writers is – http://writerscheatsheets.blogspot.com

In the Works . . .

Be sure to connect with Catherine
for advanced notice of the progress and
release of the sequel that's Rowen's story —

Karma & Chaos

http://www.catherineemclean.com/connect-with-catherine-form.html

---

**Like lighthearted
short stories?**

Get Adrada To Zool

You can also read a
free short story by
Catherine E. McLean at —

http://www.catherineemclean.com/free-story—just-desserts.html

http://www.CatherineEmclean.com

love, vengeance, attempted murder, and a bomb...
No reason to panic.

Hearts Akilter

Catherine E. McLean

Love, vengeance, attempted murder, and a bomb . . .
No reason to Panic

When a medical robot insists he's having a heart attack, Marlee Evans, a pragmatic maintenance technician, has every reason to panic. There's a bomb inside him. Since Marlee can't risk the bomber discovering she's found the device, her only option is to kidnap Deacon Black, an unflappable bomb expert, and secretly convince him to disarm it.

Things go slightly awry when Deacon sets a trap for someone who is trying to kill him and, inadvertently, captures Marlee instead. Instantly intrigued by her refreshingly forthright and gutsy attitude, he's smitten. Unfortunately for Deacon, Marlee recently hardened her heart and swore off men, especially handsome ones with boy-next-door grins. But as Marlee and Deacon attempt to identify and prevent the bomber from detonating the device, they discover that love may be the most explosive force of all.

http://www.CatherineEmclean.com

Jewels of the Sky

Survival or extinction? Mercy or miracle?
One woman's choice.

Catherine E. McLean

Survival or extinction?
Mercy or miracle?
One woman's choice.

Being a direct descendant of the captain who massacred the Mayans, Darq is a Wysotti woman and a duty-oriented, pragmatic interstellar fighter pilot. She doesn't believe in miracles or forgiveness, or that J'Hi-inti (god) would ever rescind the death curse on her people for what happened to the Mayans. Only J'Hi-inti hears one compelling plea for reconciliation and decides to let chaos rule—and test Darq. After all, she's a wild card like her nefarious ancestor. What will she do when she faces the ruthless alien fleet commander who spearheads the blitzkrieg that is to finally destroy her homeworld, and who she once witnessed murder her cadet comrades? Blinded by hate and survivor guilt, all that stands between survival and extinction, heaven or hell, for Darq and her people is mercy— or a miracle.

http://www.CatherineEmclean.com

FOR WRITERS

https://www.amazon.com/dp/0988587440

Shortcuts, Secrets, Tips, and
Practical Advice on Writing Fiction

ALSO OFFERING —
One-on-One, Step-by-Step Fiction Writing Courses

http://www.writerscheatsheets.com
Blog **—** http://writerscheatsheets.blogspot.com

www.ingramcontent.com/pod-product-compliance
Lightning Source LLC
Chambersburg PA
CBHW071308200626
46813CB00015B/641